The Blind Man's House

BOOKS BY
HUGH WALPOLE

HUGH WALPOLE

The Blind Man's House

Doubleday, Doran and Company, Inc.

GARDEN CITY   *1941*   NEW YORK

PRINTED AT THE *Country Life Press*, GARDEN CITY, N. Y., U. S. A.

For

JOSEPHINE *and* ALAN BOTT

with love

Forsooth, brothers, fellowship is heaven, and lack
of fellowship is hell; fellowship is life, and lack of
fellowship is death, and the deeds that ye do upon the
earth, it is for fellowship's sake that ye do them, and
the life that is in it, that shall live on for ever and
ever, and each one of you part of it, while many a
man's life upon the earth from the earth shall wane.
Therefore, I bid you not dwell in hell but in heaven,
or while ye must, upon earth, which is a part of
heaven, and forsooth no foul part.

Willam Moore's: THE DREAM OF JOHN BALL

Contents

ix

PART I

The Hawthorn Window

CHAPTER I

*Pelynt Cross—Passing Sizyn Church—At the Rectory
—Inside Garth House—At the Rectory*

SHE WAS FRIGHTENED. The fear was as sudden and, in one sense,
as unexpected as an unheralded sharp stab in the breast. And yet
not unexpected, because it had been hovering near her, almost
out of her consciousness but not quite, for many weeks.

They were at the Cross-roads. Pelynt Cross. She knew where
they were, for Julius had told her and in her hands was a map.
The Cross-roads. Pelynt Cross. You can smell the sea here,
Julius said. She sniffed through the open window. Yes, she could
smell it. On a clear day you could catch a glimpse of the sea
from the Cross, which stood naked and bare on the edge of the
Moor. But today you could not see far because of the summer
honey haze which veiled the world in trembling heat.

The car had stopped for a moment while Curtis hesitated.
Then he saw the finger—'Garth in Roselands 1½ M.–Rafiel
10 M.' To the left of them ran Pelynt Moor for miles and miles.
The light enwrapped it and struck at fragments of quartz, at
rough white stones. It seemed to shake with voluptuous pleasure

3

at being thus enwrapped. The air through the window smelt of honey and gorse.

The car went on. She had taken off her hat, and the short curls of her dark hair moved in the breeze. She had thrown back her coat, and her body drank in the heat. She loved, she *loved* the sun! She looked quickly across to Julius and then quickly back again. Was he asleep? Who could tell? His eyes were closed, but that meant nothing at all. She had been married to him for six months, and yet about a matter like that she could not be certain. His big body sprawled against the corner of the car. He too had taken off his hat, and his hair, so fair a yellow that in certain lights it seemed white, moved a little against his forehead.

His face, which she loved so dearly, was composed and calm. Why had she been frightened? Was it because she was coming to a new place? No. She was never frightened of a new place. She loved new places and new people because she always conquered them with her charm. She did not pride herself on her charm. She had no conceit. But she was pleased, as anyone would be, with its effects.

Was it because her new home was his *old* home that she was frightened? No. Anything that was his was hers. He gave her everything freely, abundantly, completely. She would never feel a stranger where he was.

Was it because of herself that she was frightened? She sat up very straight and looked out of the window, shaking her little head as though she would have the sun penetrate and enrich the curls.

Well, what about herself? For six months she had made Julius so happy that he told her he was 'mad' with happiness. She had behaved well. She had lost her temper only twice, once with that silly old Mrs. Gayner, the housekeeper whom Julius adored so. Only once had she broken something and then it was only a glass—old it was, but you could always find another like it. She had forgotten engagements scarcely at all and had shown im-

patience with tiresome visitors very seldom. She could not help
it if she showed her feelings clearly. That was her character.
After all, she loved people twice as often as she hated them. She
had tried in every way to make herself a good wife and she had
succeeded.

Was she frightened because he was fifteen years older than
she? The husband ought to be older than the wife. When Julius
was sixty she would be forty-five, an old, old woman.

Was she frightened because he had been married before? Oh,
these were ancient questions! She had asked them before and
found happy answers to all of them. Wasn't Julius the kindest,
noblest, most loving, most tender, most unselfish of men? Didn't
she look up to him and admire him dreadfully, and didn't she, in
spite of that admiration, find him a friend and a companion?
Was he ever a bore? No. Never, never! Never a bore. But . . .

Yes, now they were coming down the hill, and that lovely
wood, sparkling like a dark fire, must be the Well. Julius had
told her about the Well. It was the most famous wood in all
Glebeshire for primroses. They left the wood and climbed the
hill, and now the salt wind from the sea really met them, fresh
and taut and vigorous in spite of the blazing heat of the summer
afternoon. Into endless distance now stretched the Moor. You
could hear the telegraph wires singing.

No. Julius was never a bore, but . . .

She heard him move, push out his great chest as though he
would drink in the sea air, put his hand to his hair. His blue
eyes were wide open. He smiled.

She knew why she was frightened.

On the left of them now was the square, sturdy, solitary little
church, Sizyn Church, that contained the wonderful window,
the 'Hawthorn Window' that people came from miles to see.
Julius had told her that when he was a child at Garth in Roselands it was almost the first thing that his mother had taken
him to see. He described the window to her: the masses of

hawthorn blossom, the two priests, the patient donkey with the silver bells, the inscription to the dead Prior of the Franciscans. (She had said 'Abbot' and Julius had corrected her. The Franciscans had Priors.)

This window had been placed in the church in the early years of Elizabeth. There had been a Trenchard in Garth House even then. That Tudor house had been burned down in the eighteenth century. She was thinking of all these things, trying to arrange them in her disorderly mind, when, with a consciousness of that guilt for something neglected that was always with her, she remembered how she had promised Julius to tell him when they were passing Sizyn Church.

It was already out of sight, but he wouldn't know that, so she tugged at his sleeve.

'The Church, Julius! The Hawthorn Church! We're just passing it! You told me to tell you.'

He turned upon her his sightless blue eyes.

'We *have* passed it, darling! We are going downhill again. Did you see it, take a good look at it?'

She was beginning to be aware, ever more and more, of her uncertainty as to the sharpness of his senses. His sense of touch, his sense of smell, his sense of hearing. These were all so far stronger than her own that always when she was with him she felt as though her hands were muffled, her nose blocked, her ears dimmed. Should he ever use these senses against her . . .

As it was now he put out his big strong hand and caught her little one. She thought that she had fallen in love with him partly because of his hands. Large though they were they were most beautifully shaped. They were a man's hands. You could feel the bones, strong and supple beneath the smooth fine skin. His nails were especially beautiful. From the very beginning she had thought it remarkable that a blind man should have such beautiful nails, so perfect in colour and shape and yet a man's nails, beautiful by nature and not by artifice.

And now as his hand held hers and his wide, staring blue

eyes gazed at her, through her, beyond her, as he drew her towards him, closer and closer until her cheek and ear rested against his side and she heard his heart claiming her with its steady possessive beat, she murmured, 'Oliphant!'

Oliphant was Julius' valet, that small, active, devoted, aloof man who, as yet, knew so much more about Julius than she did. He was seated, very straight, beside Curtis the chauffeur.

Julius laughed.

'Oliphant is part of myself—like my waistcoat buttons.' He bent down and kissed her warm sun-drenched cheek.

'Did you see the Church? Do you remember what I told you —about the window and everything?'

'Of course I remember.'

His strong hand moved about her body. Because his blindness strengthened incredibly his sense of touch she felt an especial significance when he touched her. His hand now pressed her breast through her coat, and that pressure was so strong, so certain, that she was divided, as all women of character are when a man possesses them, between joyous resignation and irritated rebellion.

They were going down the hill and very soon they would be in Garth. She *would* not ride into their own village for all the villagers to see her for the first time, lying publicly in his embrace.

'Garth in Roselands! Garth in Roselands!' he was murmuring into her ear. 'Isn't it the loveliest of names? Haven't I repeated it to myself over and over again all these years I've been away.'

She gave an impatient push and separated herself from him.

'I can't be driven into Garth for the first time in my life lying in your arms. I'm sure people are watching from every window!'

He laughed. He was so happy, and she adored him to be happy. So, at this moment, as they rode down the hill and then passed the alms-houses into Garth, she adored him *because* he was happy. She was to remember this at a later time. Nevertheless he held her hand tightly.

'It is too fine an afternoon for them to be bothering. All the same the Rectory drawing-room windows look on to the village green, so there *may* be . . .' He stared through the window as though he could see. 'When I was a boy at Catsholt there used to be Trenchards at the House. There were Trenchards there for centuries. It seems a shame that now it should be *us*. But we never knew the Trenchards. He was a fine man—quite famous in his day—wrote books about the English Poets. But she was a bit of a Tartar, I believe, and had some sort of row with my father. . . . Ah, now, now! Soon we will be turning up the drive! In a minute we will be there! Hold my hand tight. I am so excited that I can scarcely breathe!'

Before the car turned from the green towards the drive beyond the little street it was held for a moment by a big dray. While it was so held the ladies in the Rectory drawing-room had a fine free look and made the very most of it.

There were four of them: Miss Vergil, Mrs. Lamplough, Miss Phyllis Lock, and Mrs. Ironing. They were gathered there for the Ladies' Sewing Meeting. Now so very often, in English novels and plays, have the Sewing Meetings of English country towns and villages been made a mock, a sport, a derision, that there shall be no derision here. To tell the truth, on this especial afternoon very little sewing had been done, and that was partly because Mrs. Brennan, the Rector's wife, was absent in London. It was also because, for the last hour, these ladies had been expecting the arrival of Mr. Julius Cromwell and his wife, and had been eagerly on the lookout for it. It was an event of great, even supreme importance in the village of Garth in Roselands, and lest that should seem an old-fashioned sentence that might have come straight from the pages of one of Mrs. Gaskell's delightful fragrant novels, let it be said at once that not telegraphs, telephones, wireless telegraphy, motor-cars, or aeroplanes have made the very slightest difference to the excited interest that ladies of an English village feel concerning their neighbours.

Although Mr. and Mrs. Cromwell arrived in a motor-car it

was exactly, in so far as excitement obtained, as though they had arrived a hundred and fifty years earlier in a barouche, except that they were, physically, less visible.

Of the four ladies Miss Vergil was the eldest and most cynical, Miss Phyllis Lock the youngest and gayest. Miss Vergil had short cropped hair, wore a hat like a gamekeeper's, a short brown jacket, a waistcoat with brass buttons, and a short rough skirt. Her legs were strong and shapeless, and in her hat there was fastened a bright green and crimson fly such as fishermen use.

Miss Phyllis Lock was auburn-haired, inclining to the plump, and dressed in so flimsy a dress that even in these days it was not quite respectable. But then Miss Lock did not care at all about being respectable. She lived with her old mother at the end of the village, drove her own car, went frequently into Polchester for parties, and was supposed to 'send men mad.' She appeared to be of a type only too frequent both in novels and real life. She was not, however, quite what she appeared.

Mrs. Lamplough looked an old dear. She was short and plump, very like Queen Victoria in appearance, and wore bonnets and shawls. She had a soft, purring voice and was always leading people into corners for confidences.

Mrs. Ironing was the stupid member of the party. She might be said to be passing through life without understanding anything about it at all. She was a widow with a comfortable income which was managed for her by her brother, Fred Ironing, who lived on her most cheerfully and was considered by everyone to be a good, jolly fellow, and remarkably patient. He said that he had known his sister so long that he had never expected her to be anything but what she was, and that she was a lot deeper than people gave her credit for. Gladys Ironing was a tall, thin woman with a face like an enquiring sheep's.

These ladies were good ladies and only one of the four had any malice in her. They were in the position of many English ladies during this period of history between 1920 and 1940. Because investments were continually going down and because they were unfit (owing to their excellent English education) for any useful job in the world, they collected in little groups in London or provincial towns or villages and made life as interesting as possible by taking in one another's social washing.

It is true that, in this present instance, both Mrs. Lamplough and Mrs. Ironing had ample means, but Mrs. Lamplough was not imaginatively generous and Mrs. Ironing was not imaginatively clever, so they stayed where they were and found it good. Miss Vergil had barely enough to pay her bills but paid them all the same—she had an English gentleman's sense of honour. Miss Lock and her mother were moderately comfortable. These ladies, then, formed a kind of guard of honour to Mrs. Brennan, a superb woman whom they were lucky to find in a simple little village like Garth. Having found her they treated her like a queen, as indeed she deserved to be treated.

And now the four ladies looked out of the broad windows of the Rectory, saw the Cromwell car held for a moment by the dray, saw within the car the dark curly hair of Mrs. Cromwell, the light-golden head of Mr. Cromwell, the fine chauffeur and the neat little man beside him.

'You'd never think he was blind!' Phyllis Lock said as they turned away from the window.

Celia Cromwell saw the house in front of her like a ship sailing through golden mist. Everything was light—even the thick, dark rhododendrons were penetrated with light, the lawn shone like glass and the giant oak at the end of it was illuminated, every leaf a thin gold plate and the great trunk dark with splendour. Excitement always rose in her very swiftly. She passed from mood to mood like a child. Now, as she stepped from the car, she thought like a child: 'Oh, I *will* be good! I will make them all love me! I'll never lose my temper, I'll be wise and quiet and so very happy!'

She moved forward to help Julius, but Oliphant, as always, was in front of her. Julius stood for a moment breathing in the air which was scented with hay, carnations, roses, and a salt tang of the sea. His hand groped for hers. She caught it. He bent down and kissed her lightly on the cheek.

'Welcome home, my darling,' he said, and they went into the house together.

The hall was long and, even on this summer's day, dark. There was a large oak chest opposite the door and beside it a staircase with a lovely black twisted balustrade. Mrs. Gayner, the house-keeper, stood there. She was a little, plump woman some sixty years of age, incredibly neat, her grey hair sleek and charming, a gold brooch fastened on to her black dress. She had been with Julius for ten years.

'How are you, Mrs. Gayner?' Celia said. Mrs. Gayner had come ahead of them to see that everything was right, to engage the maids.

'Very well, thank you, ma'am.'

'That's good. Isn't it a lovely day?'

'It is indeed, ma'am. I hope you had a pleasant journey.'

'Lovely! What good luck that I should see everything for the first time in such lovely weather!'

'Yes, ma'am.'

'Is everything all right?'

'Quite all right, ma'am. I've got two maids and the cook is from Polchester. She's a nice woman and a good cook—at least, she promises to be.'

'That's grand.'

But she noticed that Mrs. Gayner's eyes looked beyond her towards her husband. That had irritated her before. It irritated her now. It was natural that Mrs. Gayner, Curtis, Oliphant, who had all been with her husband for a long time, served him, loved him, should consider him always, but was not she someone too?

'Is that Mrs. Gayner?' Julius' voice was full of happiness and joy.

'Yes, sir.'

He stretched out his hand and caught Mrs. Gayner's plump one.

'Everything all right?'

'Oh yes, sir. Very satisfactory indeed.'

He turned to his wife, who was close to him, put his arm around her waist and began slowly to mount the stairs.

'I was only in this house once. I came with my mother one time. I was about ten. Yet I remember it all. Is that oak chest still there? They told me a story that someone was caught in it once and couldn't get out. One of those stories. It's Italian. I told them to buy some of the old things that had belonged to the Trenchards, but for the most part you'll find everything you had at Bramgrove, darling. And of course you can arrange things just as you please. The drawing-room, now. It's here on the left. Everything *ought* to be just as it was at Bramgrove. Only of course the room isn't quite the same shape.'

They stood in the drawing-room. It was flooded with sunlight. Celia gave a little cry, for the view from the windows was enchanting. Beyond the old stone wall that bordered the garden, fields ran down the hill to a straggling wood, then slightly up again to a level horizon, and above this was a line of sea, now one stroke of trembling gold. In the fields were old trees, set deep into the soil, and under their cool soft shadow cows were lying. The windows were open and the sea breeze blew, very delicately, the fawn-coloured curtains.

All the Bramgrove things were here: the water-colours that her father had collected—Wilson and Cotman and David Cox, the sofa chairs with their pale primrose chintz, the piano, the oil-painting of Julius as a young soldier just before he went to the war where he was blinded.

She raised herself a little, caught Julius around the neck and kissed him again and again.

'Oh, Julius, we're going to be happy here! I know we are. It's a lovely house! I'll do everything—everything!'

She was crying. He felt the salt on her cheek as he kissed it.

Afterwards they went together to their bedroom. There was nothing that she loved better than this leading him through strange places. She felt now his utter dependence upon her. He leant against her, holding her tightly to him. His blue eyes stared without winking and he moved, step after step, rather as a walker on a tight-rope does. She felt then that his whole body belonged to her. It was as though she, little though she was, surrounded his great girth and breadth. He was naked in her hands and she could do what she would with him. And all that she wanted to do was to love him!

They stood in the bedroom enwrapped in one another's arms, the sunlight bathing them.

There was a knock on the door. It was Curtis in his chauffeur's uniform, looking so smart, so official, so impersonal that Celia turned away. Curtis was all right, but just then she didn't want to see him. And of course there was already something important that Julius must go and settle. They had not been in the house five minutes. It was always so.

'Come down as soon as you've washed, darling, and we'll have tea in the garden. Under the oak.'

He put his hand through Curtis' arm and they went away.

She had told him that she wanted their bedroom to be exactly as it was at Bramgrove. Yes. Perfect. The twin beds, the long mirror, his dressing-room to the left, the same glorious view as the drawing-room's (this was better, far, far better than Bramgrove), two pictures by Russell Flint of people bathing, their own bathroom to the right, everything fresh, cool, fragrant.

She looked at herself in the glass. Very small she was, but her figure, for her size, was perfect. She looked like a boy in girl's clothes, perhaps—but no, her colouring, her small breasts, her beautiful arms and hands could never belong to a boy. She raised her arms above her head, breathing with happiness and pleasure. She began to dance about the room, moving most gracefully in the sunlight, and the room reflected her in her pale dress, with her dark hair, her big excited eyes.

'This *will* do! This *will* do! The loveliest place I've ever known.'

There was again a knock on the door. The maid came in, a pretty, tall girl with brown hair.

'I've come, ma'am, to unpack.'

'Oh yes—but never mind just now. I'm going down to tea. You can unpack then.'

'Yes, ma'am.'

'What's your name?'

'Violet.'

'Violet. That's a nice name. Where do you come from?'

'Oh, I was born in London, ma'am. But five years ago I went to service with Mrs. Ironing—Mrs. Ironing of Cumberleigh, ma'am.'

'Oh yes. And Mrs. Gayner stole you from her?'

'Oh no, ma'am. There were reasons—I had left——'

'I see. I'm sure we will be friends.'

Celia smiled and Violet smiled too. They *were* friends already. Violet departed.

Celia looked out of the window and saw tea being laid under the oak tree.

When she was ready to go she knelt down beside the bed and prayed. She didn't know whether she believed in prayers, but they gave you a comfortable feeling as though someone very strong put his arm around you and told you you need not fear.

Why had she been afraid in the car? She had forgotten why. How foolish! There was indeed no reason for any fear.

She rushed down the stairs, crying out: 'Julius! Julius!'

The light had mellowed across the village green, sinking deeply into every blade of grass, then soaking the soil like wine. The sky above Mr. Boss the butcher, Mrs. Irwin, post-mistress, Teak, stationer and bookseller, and the Methodist Chapel, was of a blue so magnificently self-satisfied that only one small ragged cloud, urchin and homeless, dared to cock at it a streaming finger.

The four ladies were gathered about the table.

Mrs. Ironing smiled brightly about her. It was one of her irritating traits that she should be so bright as well as so stupid, for this lent weight to the theory, very prevalent during these years in England, that if you had any brains you must be a cynic. To think well of life meant simply that you were Shakespeare's Idiot's Tale signifying nothing—as indeed Mrs. Ironing did.

She said now, with a kind of gurgle because she was biting her thread:

'I expect there are compensations in being blind.'

'Oh yes, Gladys dear,' Miss Vergil in her deep, booming voice replied. 'Just as it is the best luck in the world to have no roof to your mouth, and there's *nothing* so lucky as being born with one leg shorter than the other!'

'Oh, do you think so?' said Mrs. Ironing happily. 'I should regard it as most unfortunate to have no roof——'

'Hell!' Miss Vergil cried, abruptly rising. 'I can't stand this any longer. To be blind! My God! And to come back to the very place you were in as a boy when you could see.'

'At any rate,' Mrs. Lamplough murmured, purring like a little kettle, 'he's got a young wife—years younger than himself— to lead him about. I hear from someone who lived quite near their place in Wiltshire that she's very undependable.'

'What do you mean, Alice?' Miss Vergil said sharply. 'Undependable?'

'Oh, I don't mean anything except that she's *very* young for her years and loses her temper in public and then apologizes in public too, which is so very embarrassing. Then she's fifteen years younger than her husband, which is quite a lot. They say she likes young men's company, and that, after all, is quite natural.'

'Certainly,' said Gladys Ironing. 'I like young men much better than old ones, just as Fred likes young girls——'

This was interrupted by hearty laughter from everybody, and Gladys opened her mouth and stared and rubbed her nose and said:

'Well, I really don't know what I've said . . .'

Ten minutes later May Vergil and Phyllis Lock were alone in the room. They moved towards the door.

'I meant what I said,' May Vergil said. 'To be blind—in this weather. To be married to someone years younger— Isn't life awful, Phil? Intolerable! Oh no, of course you don't find it so. There are always men around, aren't there? Men! What a lot! However, I won't start that again.' She put her hand for a moment on Phyllis' sleeve, then quickly removed it.

'Did you see her?' Phyllis Lock asked. 'In the car, I mean. Wasn't she lovely? With that dark curly head? Isn't it funny to think he's never *seen* her? Held her in his arms and all that, but never *seen* her? He can't really know what she's like, however often he's told. And she's so lovely—with a head like a Greek statue.'

The village green enjoyed a space and time of absolute peace and tranquillity. Two seagulls, after circling the roofs and screaming their eager, scornful content, settled down upon the sun-warmed grass, and moved, raising at a moment their blood-stained beaks to heaven, deliberately—arrogant owners of this lovely world.

CHAPTER II

At the Rectory

THE REVEREND FRANK BRENNAN, Rector of the parish of Garth in Roselands in the county of Glebeshire, was quite possibly the handsomest clergyman in the whole of England, and quite certainly the laziest.

His hair was thick on his head, and snow-white although he was but sixty years of age. He had the face of an aesthetic poet of the Eighteen-Nineties, a figure supple and erect, and a voice, as Phyllis Lock said, filled with 'organ notes.' His charm too was beautiful, and although he never did anything for any man, woman, or child in the village, save when nature, by bringing to birth or urging to matrimony or slaying in due time, forced him, he was everywhere popular because he never interfered with anyone or anything, was shocked by nothing and nobody, and laughed so infectiously when he had forgotten the name of a farmer with whom he had had tea only the day before.

He conducted as few of the church services as possible and left a great deal to his red-haired kindly curate, Mr. Townley. Strange it was that he had not even any hobbies. He liked a novel in front of the fire, a drive in the little family Austin, food, drink, and a pretty woman, although his morals were irreproachable. What spirit slumbered inside his slumbering form no one knew. He wore shabby old clothes, but his linen was always shining and his person as clean as a new penny. He was seldom seen without a pipe in his mouth and he would look at you, his hands deep in his pockets, his brown eyes half closed and a little smile hovering about his handsome lips.

Now, oddly enough, his wife, Daisy Brennan, was also a beauty. Phyllis called her once 'a Juno in the cornfield,' and although this meant really nothing at all, everyone liked and repeated it. She was a tall, big, full-breasted woman with masses of corn-coloured hair which was piled, in old-fashioned style, on the top of her head and braided above her temples. She wore clothes in bright gay colours that fitted her closely so that her bosom, her thighs were handsomely defined. She walked with her head up gloriously, and only Mrs. Irwin, the post-mistress, who hated her, made the rude comment: 'Pantomime Queen, that's what I call her. You know, one of them big girls in tights walks down a lot of steps at the end and calls herself Canada.'

This magnificent pair had three children: Dorothy, Gilbert, and Simon. Dorothy was aged seventeen, Gilbert fourteen, Simon eight. Gilbert was at school at Polchester but was at present home for the holidays. These children were very unsophisticated and unmodern. They had all been born in the Garth Rectory, and, until Gilbert had gone to boarding-school, none of them had been away from there except to the Glebeshire seaside on expeditions.

They had mingled with the village children quite happily. They had known a number of governesses, and the best of these had been Miss Fritch, who had led them carefully first through *Stumps, Rags and Tatters, Alice in Wonderland,* then *The Cuckoo Clock, Mrs. Overtheway's Remembrances, Engel the Fearless,* then *The Daisy Chain* and *The Dove in the Eagle's Nest,* then *Micah Clarke, Lamb's Tales, The Wind in the Willows,* and *The Talisman,* then *David Copperfield, Pride and Prejudice, The Oxford Book of English Verse, The Path to Rome, The Cock-House at Fellsgarth,* and *Don Quixote;* after which nothing else mattered.

Unhappily Miss Fritch departed after a quarrel with Mrs. Brennan, a mysterious quarrel because only Mrs. Brennan gave any account of it, and from this it was clear that Miss Fritch had been quite impossible.

No governess succeeded Miss Fritch. Gilbert went to school and Mrs. Brennan taught Dorothy and Dorothy taught Simon. At least, that was the idea.

The three children adored their father, who never denied them anything; they thought their mother wonderful.

They had, however, none of the experiences of good modern children. They had never been given handsome toys, nor been taken to the theatre, nor learned of the troubles and perplexities of the mature from the lips of the mature. Dorothy was tall and slim with a face as honest as a human face can be. Gilbert was slim, pale, and inclined to take things seriously, while Simon was short and thick and led a very intense life of his own.

Two years at school seemed to have made very little difference to Gilbert, for whom Garth was still the centre of his world, his father the most wonderful person *in* the world, his mother the loveliest, Dorothy the best companion. He led, it seemed, a rather solitary life at school, although he was quite happy there.

Mr. Brennan looked at his children with surprise, whenever he saw them. He was delighted to discover that he had such charming children, and this discovery was fresh every new day. Mrs. Brennan was, as Phyllis again recorded, 'the mother *facile princeps*.' To see her move with her children along the village street was a sight never to be forgotten.

Three days after the arrival of the Cromwells the children had just finished tea, and Lucy, the maid of all possible and impossible work, was clearing away the tea, which she did with a great deal of banging and clashing as though she were a Salvation Army girl and the china were timbrels. At the same time she steamed through her nose as though her inside were a kettle. But she was a good girl and a warm-hearted.

When Lucy was gone Gilbert suddenly said:

'I want something frightfully.'

Dorothy, who was gulping down *Chicot the Jester* as though he were a life-restorer, and turning one ear to Simon who was telling a story both to her and himself, said, rather impatiently, 'What do you want?' She knew that in five minutes' time they must go down to the drawing-room to spend half an hour with their mother, and she wanted to reach the end of her chapter.

Gilbert, standing straight in front of her, his eyes fixed anxiously on her face, told her. He expressed his desires so very seldom and they were intense within him when they *did* appear. He spoke slowly, choosing his words.

'Well, you see, there's an awfully decent chap·called Paynter. I like him better than anyone else at school—in fact I like him awfully. His people have taken a house for the summer just outside Rafiel—on the cliff—and he wants me to go on Tuesday and spend the day with them. And I can take a bus. It's quite all right, but Tuesday's the only day. They go back to Polchester on Thursday. His father's a Canon there. He wants me to go for the whole day.'

'Which day did you say?' asked Dorothy. At the same moment she snatched a line or two of *Chicot*, and said 'Yes, dear' to Simon, who, seated on the floor like a Buddha, was half chanting: 'Which he *couldn't* do because there was a river right across, a great big river with rocks and stones and serpents and dozens of croc——'

She cleared her brain.

'*Which* day did you say, Gillie?'

'Tuesday.'

'But that's the day Mother said she might take us into Polchester.'

'I know—that's the awful part.'

They looked at one another. She had forgotten *Chicot* and Simon. Here was a real trouble. Gilbert so very seldom said that he wanted anything; when he did it was serious. They were devoted. Gilbert, in spite of his time at school, still thought that Dorothy could settle every difficulty, that she was the wisest, most far-seeing person in the world. At school he would say: 'Oh, but you should see my sister. She's marvellous!' and said it so convincingly that no one ever thought of teasing him about it.

Dorothy on her side was aware that Gilbert was more sensitive than the others, felt things more severely and for a longer time. Her feeling over him was, although she did not know it, partly maternal. She *hated* that any misfortune should happen to Gilbert. Simon did not seem to need her care in the same way.

'You see,' Gilbert went on, 'it isn't as though Mother could go *only* on that day. She said she had several days to choose from. And it's the *only* day for the Paynters.'

'Yes, but——,' Dorothy looked anxious. Why did they both know that as soon as their mother heard that *that* was the day the Paynters wanted, *that* would be the day that she wanted too?

'The only thing, Mother may think that the *best* day for Polchester. Thursday's early closing, I know, and that only leaves Wednesday and Friday.'

'That's two days, isn't it?' Gilbert's voice had in it a new note that she thought she had never heard before. 'You see, I like Paynter better than anyone I've ever known, except the family of course. He plays in the Second Fifteen and will be in the First next year, I shouldn't wonder, and I didn't think he was keen on me at all, although I was awfully keen on him. So when I got the letter this morning I was awfully pleased, as anybody would be, and if I don't go he'll think I'm being snooty or something, and besides I do want to go most awfully.'

He ended with a deep breath. His eyes were pleading into Dorothy's face.

Simon suddenly said from the floor:

'Dorothy and me saw the blind man this morning.'

She raised her head and looked at the schoolroom window that a thin weeping rain was misting. It had been clear but not sunny this morning when, coming out of the stationer's with Simon, she had seen Mr. Cromwell and his wife walking across the green. He had his arm in hers. He walked, his head very erect, staring straight in front of him and talking all the time. He had a most pleasant smile. She had told Simon that he couldn't see.

'Why can't he see?' Simon asked her.

'He was hit with a bullet in the War.'

'He can't see the teeniest, teeniest thing?'

'Nothing at all.'

'Not the teeniest?'

'No. Nothing.'

At the same moment she had seen the postman going to the Rectory gate. He must have had the letter for Gilbert.

It seemed to her now as though that had been a dramatic moment—the blind man and the letter for Gilbert.

'I'm going to ask Mother.'

'Yes, of course.'

'If I tell her it's the only day——'

'Don't make her feel we don't *want* to go with her to Polchester.'

'No. Of course not.'

They looked at one another. He was changed. His mouth was set and his eyes angry.

'I'm going to ask at once, now, as soon as we go down.'

'Yes. We'd better go down. It's time.'

Simon got up from the floor. He enjoyed going down to the drawing-room. He enjoyed practically everything except cold fat, barking dogs, and women who kissed him.

'Here. Let me brush your hair.'

He had a lot of light brown hair that would, unless he was care-ful, fall over his forehead into his eyes. One of his most character-istic gestures was tossing his hair back from his eyes. Then he was like a little pony stamping.

He slept in a room with Gilbert, and into that they now went. He stood grinning while Dorothy brushed his hair. He looked so pleasant, so independent and sturdy in his blue smock, that Doro-thy would have kissed him had she not known how greatly he dis-liked it.

He rushed down the stairs crying out: 'Mum—Mum—Mum.'

However, when they reached the drawing-room only their father was there. He stood in front of the fireplace, which was defended by a very hideous screen of green elephants walking up to pink pagodas. As usual Simon rushed up to him and hugged him round the thighs, and as usual Mr. Brennan looked at his offspring as though he had never seen them before.

'Well, well, how are you all?'

'Quite well, thank you,' Gilbert answered gravely, and then went straight on without waiting a moment: 'Father, there's a boy called Paynter at school and his people have asked me to spend next Tuesday at Rafiel with them. Do you think I can?"

'Why, of course, certainly, do you good.'

'The only thing is, Father,' Dorothy said, 'Mother said she'd take us into Polchester next Tuesday to see about Gillie's new suit.'

'Your mother can take you another day.'

'Oh, Father, do you think she can?'

It was as though little fires had suddenly been lit in Gilbert's eyes.

'Certainly. Of course.'

He was so handsome and knew this so well that he had a trick, picked up long ago and now quite unconscious, of turning his head first to one side and then to the other as though to test which profile were the finer. He did this now.

'Where's Mother?' Dorothy asked.

'She's been out to tea with Mrs. Lamplough. Should be back any moment.'

He stretched himself and yawned.

'I must be off to work. Work, work, work—nothing but work!' He grinned at Simon. 'Your old father is a slave—a slave to duty. Aren't you sorry for him?'

But Simon was considering something else.

'I saw a man who was blind this morning. He couldn't see anything, not the teeniest thing.' Then he tried to do what he was always trying to do, turn a somersault. But, as usual, he failed. When, rather confused by the upside-downness of the drawing-room, he looked about him, his father was gone.

Gilbert was greatly excited.

'Did you hear what Father said? He said that of course she would.'

Dorothy shook her head.

'Father often says things without thinking. And then he forgets that he's said them.'

'All the same, he's quite right. It can't matter to Mother which day it is.'

Daisy Brennan came in. She was wearing a pale blue dress with a white rose pinned at her waist. She looked lovely and was a little cross. However, she took them all with her to the sofa, threw her hat on the floor, stretched her length, gathering them all about her.

'Oh, you darlings! You darlings! I ought to have told you I'd be out. You've had your tea? Yes. That's right. Oh dear, how tired I am and what a day! We were to have had tea in the garden and of course it rained, so there we were all crowded into the drawing-room and such a noise—my head's simply splitting. What do you say, Simon, pet? You saw a blind man with Dorothy? Oh, you mean you were *with* Dorothy when you saw a blind man. Oh, of course, poor Mr. Cromwell. And now tell me what you've all been doing, because I've *such* a headache I shall go straight up to my room and lie down. Yes, Gillie, tell me everything. What do you say? You had a letter? When? This morning? Who are they? Paynter? Never heard of them.'

Gilbert stood in front of her as though he were reciting a lesson.

'Paynter's father's a Canon at the Cathedral. He's awfully decent, so's Mrs. Paynter. They've taken a house at Rafiel for the summer—on the cliff. You know, over the harbour. Above the Warren. Well, they want me to go on Tuesday for the whole day. There's the nine o'clock bus and one comes back at six. Can I, Mother? Can I?'

'Rafiel? All day? I know you'll get into some awful trouble—fall into the sea and be drowned.'

'Of course I won't, Mother. I've been going to Rafiel all my life.'

'Heavens, child! You say that as though you were a hundred. *What's* the name of these people?'

'Paynter.'

Dorothy knew from his breathing that he was growing more desperate with every moment.

'But *I* don't know them. They could easily have called if they're only at Rafiel.'

'They *will* call. I'll ask Mrs. Paynter.'

'But she ought to have called without being asked. What day do you say it is?'

'Tuesday.'

'On Tuesday! That settles it. We're going into Polchester that day. You've got to have your suit fitted.'

There was a short pause. Gilbert was heaving up his determination.

'But, Mother, there's Wednesday and Friday——'

'Wednesday won't do. I forget why. Friday's too late in the week. No, it's got to be Tuesday. You can go to those people some other time—only I *would* prefer that she should call on me first.'

'Father says I can go.'

('Oh,' thought Dorothy, 'that's a mistake!')

'Your father! What's *he* got to do with it?'

'He said you might go another day.'

'Oh, he did, did he? Well, I've explained to you why I can't.'

'No, Mother, you haven't. I *want* to go. I want to go most awfully.'

At this his mother sat up, patting at her golden braids with her large strong hand.

'My *dear* Gillie! You want to go, do you? More than you want to come with your mother. That isn't very kind.'

'No. It's not that. Of course I want to come with you.'

'It always *used* to be the greatest treat coming into Polchester with me. You'd look forward to it for weeks. But now going to Rafiel to have a day with some strange people is more important to you than being with your mother. Well, I suppose every mother must expect that. That's what school does.'

'No. It isn't. But——'

'Every mother must expect to lose her son. She is everything to him while he needs her, but the moment he can fend for himself the mother's set aside——'

Dorothy could not endure this.

'Gillie isn't saying he doesn't want to go to Polchester, Mother. He does want to go—as much as ever he did. Only he thought we might go to Polchester another day——'

'Thank you, Dorothy. I don't want you to explain Gillie to me. I understand him perfectly well.'

Gilbert, white of face, holding his small thin body rigidly

together, moistening his lower lip with his tongue, began again.

'Paynter is a form higher than me. I didn't know he'd ever ask me in the holidays. If I refuse now he'll think me snooty.'

'Snooty! What a disgusting word!'

'Well, he will. And it will make all the difference next term, because I like him most awfully.'

'So I perceive,' said Mrs. Brennan coldly. 'You like him much better than your mother.'

'I don't,' said Gilbert between his gritted teeth. Then he burst out: 'Oh, Mother, let me go! It isn't I don't want to go to Polchester. Of course I do, just as I always did. But we can go on Friday. If you let me go to Rafiel on Tuesday I'll be ever so good. You see, it means *everything*, because if Paynter's my friend next term I can get on ever so fast with maths and geography, and next term's Rugger, and I'm not much good, that's *quite* certain, but Paynter's most awfully good and he'll show me a lot of things.'

He paused, breathless, his eyes shining with hope. His mother looked at him with tenderness.

'My dear Gillie, you've hurt me not a little. When you're older you'll understand. You are all I have, you and Dorothy and Simon. It's quite natural that you should want to leave me for perfect strangers. Quite natural. But it hurts me all the same. You shall go into Rafiel on Tuesday and you shall have the suit fitted later. I'm sorry. It isn't kind. . . . '

Her lower lip quivered.

Gilbert looked at her

'I didn't want to hurt you.'

'No, I'm sure you didn't.' She waited. Everyone, even Simon, expected that he would say that he did *not* wish to go to Rafiel.

'It's just the same as it always was about Polchester,' he said.

'I'm glad to hear it.'

Mother and son looked at one another. Then Gilbert turned and, with his head down, like an animal butting, ran from the room.

Mrs. Brennan sighed and lay back against the cushions.

'Do you know these people, Dorothy?'

'No, Mother, I don't.'

'How very odd of Gilbert! He's never been like that before!'

'I don't think he's ever wanted anything so much before.'

'No. That's what I said. It's the beginning of the end. My headache's frightful. Go up to my room, darling, and get those cachets. Two with a glass of water.'

Dorothy went and found Gilbert sitting on his bed, stony-eyed and speechless.

Downstairs Mrs. Brennan and her youngest-born enjoyed one another's company. For they had a good deal in common. It was quite impossible to hurt Simon's feelings. He went his own way and always got what he wanted.

'Thank you, darling,' Mrs. Brennan said, took her cachets and leaned back against the cushions, closing her eyes. But her repose was not for long.

The door most unexpectedly opened and in came Mr. Brennan. With him a lady. The lady was short but not stout, grey hair under her hat, brown eyes, very quietly dressed. All this Daisy Brennan, who was no fool, at once took in. She rose from the sofa. Simon rose from the floor. Dorothy stayed where she was.

'My dear,' Frank Brennan said, 'I have brought someone in for a moment whom I want you to know. This is Mrs. Mark.'

Mrs. Brennan, entirely bewildered, stepped forward. The little lady smiled and they shook hands.

Brennan went on: 'That will mean nothing to you, but it *will* mean something when I tell you that Mrs. Mark's maiden name was Trenchard and that she was born in Garth House and lived there most of her time until she was married. She knows every turn and twist of *this* house, by the way.'

They had sat down by now, Mrs. Brennan and Mrs. Mark side by side on the sofa.

'I really ought to apologize——' Mrs. Mark began. She had a soft gentle voice.

'Oh, but I'm delighted.'

'The fact is I've never come back to Garth all these years! More than thirty years. I haven't dared. I was so happy here, but my husband didn't like it. So, until his death, I stayed away. He died three years ago and since then I've been trying to pluck up my courage and face my memories. And now I've taken Copley's Cottage at the end of the village for a month or two.'

'How very charming!' Mrs. Brennan murmured. 'We shall be neighbours. You must find a lot of changes.'

'I don't know yet. I've only been here three days. But I don't think I shall—not externally, at any rate.' She smiled and looked across at Dorothy, for the first time, with a friendly glance.

'I was born in the House. We all were. And now I'm the only one left. My father and mother died long ago. I'm sixty, you know! My sister Millie died five years ago, and my brother Henry was killed in a motor accident. You probably read about it at the time. He was quite famous as a dramatist.'

'Why, of course. Henry Trenchard. How sad that was!'

'Yes. Very. He ought never to have driven himself. He was so very absent-minded. Dear Henry!'

She paused for a moment, her eyes misted a little.

'And so you see why I've dreaded coming back. I'm not quite alone in the world. I have a son who's an astronomer. Isn't that an odd thing to be? But he's married now and so—well, here I am!'

Her confidences were so quiet and so simple that no one felt it at all strange that she should tell them these things.

'And so you knew this house quite well?'

'Oh, very well—as well as our own. The clergyman at that time—just before I married—was called Smart. He used to race through the services, especially in the summer when he wanted to be gardening.' She laughed. 'I remember him so very well. And Mrs. Smart was a big, stout woman who wore the most outrageous hats. But before that, when we were children, there was a clergyman called Penny and he had ever so many children.

That was when we were here so often. We used to play Hide-and-Seek all over this house, and Henry would be lost and we'd find him at last somewhere in a corner reading a book.'

'What a nice lady,' Dorothy thought. 'I never knew anyone more natural.' Simon, after he had taken one look at her and summed her up to his satisfaction, continued his own life on the carpet, now and then making a little hissing noise, and Mrs. Brennan said: 'Hush, Simon!'

'It *will* be interesting for you, noticing all the changes,' Frank Brennan said. 'You know that some new people have taken the House.'

'Yes,' said Mrs. Mark. 'They arrived, I believe, the same day as I did.'

'He was blinded, poor man, in the War,' Mrs. Brennan said. 'This is his second wife and she's years younger. He's got plenty of money, I believe.'

'I hope I shall meet them.. I do want to see the House again.'

'Of course you will. Won't you have some tea?'

'No, thank you. I must be going.' She rose. 'Your husband found me in the church and. insisted on bringing me in.'

'I'm so glad.'

But there was to be yet one more interruption.

The window that led to the lawn opened. They all turned.

A young man stood there. He was dressed in rather dirty flannels, he was as brown as a chestnut, his hair stood up above his ears, he was very good-looking. He looked at them with an amused and rather cheeky greeting. 'Hullo!' he said, and was gone the moment after, leaving the window open behind him.

'Good heavens!' Brennan cried. 'That was Jim Burke!'

'He's back again!' Daisy Brennan said.

'How like him!' said Brennan. He went to the window and called: 'Jim! Jim!'

But there was not a sign of him in the warm misty rain.

Brennan said to Mrs. Mark: 'Now isn't that like him? He's a young man called Burke. He used to help Fred Ironing— Oh, but you don't know, of course. A wild young fellow. We all liked him. He's been away two years. I wonder what he's back for.'

He closed the window. Mrs. Mark made her farewells.

CHAPTER III

Garth House: Mrs. Gayner's Room

DEAR ALICE,

I should have answered your letter ever so long back but the fact is I've been so terribly busy that I've hardly known whether I'm on my head or my heels. Well, Alice, you know I always tell you everything and what's a loving sister for if you don't, but the fact is I'm writing this very letter in a bit of a tremble and the reason is that only a quarter of an hour ago Mrs. Cromwell's been in here and lost her temper in a shocking fashion. Of course I never said a word as where would I be by now if I hadn't learned to control my temper, besides which I can't help liking her. She's only a child when all is said and done. Besides as you well know I'd do any mortal thing for him and well he knows it. Besides, Alice, he loves her something terrible and so does she but she doesn't understand him one little bit nor what it is to be blind, although she wants *to understand if you get me.*

Mind you she's a grown woman and she's no right to get in the states she does. I don't think she's happy and that's the cause of a lot of it. When you're unhappy about something you just want to fly out at someone, at least that's how it used to take me until I'd had such a lot of unhappiness that I saw flying out about anything was just a waste of time. But she comes in just now and asks me why the letters haven't gone to the post. That's not my business as she well knows but Curtis the chauffeur's, but not wanting to put the blame on Curtis, I say I'll see to it and then she's in a rage and says she doesn't know why it is but every-

thing's been sixes and sevens ever since we've come to this house and I say we've only been here a fortnight and then she *says that I'm getting careless so then I just smile and say I'm doing as I've always done and she flings out of the room banging the door just like a naughty child.*

You know what it is, Alice, she's jealous poor thing. Jealous of me and Curtis and especially of Oliphant—anyone her husband has a kind word for. I think she's frightened of his blindness, not realizing it at first but thinking she'd have all the more power with him because he was *blind and now finding that he seems to get away from her where she can't get after him.*

You and I know what jealousy is don't we, Alice, and yet if I could have Henry back with all his unfaithful ways I would and gladly just to feel the roughness of his cheek and lay my hand on his shirt where his heart beats because it's that much more lonely here, Alice, than it was at Bramgrove and it's an old house with dark passages and I can't help thinking half the time—well, you know who I'm always thinking of. All the same we've settled in well enough seeing that they've been here only a fortnight and the cook and the girls get along finely together. Mrs. Cromwell's very good with them I must say and goes into the kitchen just like one of them. She's not a snob that I must say and yet they mind what she tells them. The housemaid Violet simply worships the ground she treads on.

I know what you're asking all the time, Alice—how's he getting along? Well I've never seen him so happy, never, and it does your heart good to hear him humming to himself and laughing and kissing her when he thinks there isn't anyone there. It ought *to be all right when two people are as much in love with one another as those two are but she's restless all the same, jealous one minute and flirting with someone the next. She doesn't mean any harm you know but there's something in him she's frightened of and not at ease with, and there's a sort of relief and ease comes over her when she's found someone her own age who isn't blind and can see just what* she *sees.*

We've had a lot of people calling, the Rector and his wife. They're a handsome pair if you like with three nice children but she's stuck on herself and her fine appearance if you want my opinion.

Then there's a Mrs. Mark staying in the village who was a Miss Trenchard and was born in this house and her family lived here for hundreds of years. She's quiet and a proper lady.

There are some old maids of course as there are in every village but it's not bad as villages go and they leave me to myself which is a blessing. I have only one trouble as you know, Alice, and a grievous trouble it is but not one word have I had although I've written three times to the address he gave and I really don't know what to think. If it weren't for God's goodness I don't know where I'd be I'm sure but I leave it all in His hands as He bid us do. Write soon and tell me how that Mrs. Nutting works out. Don't let her have her way too much but she seems a good soul from what you tell me.

Your loving sister

ELIZABETH GAYNER

Lizzie Gayner finished her letter with a sigh and sighed again as she licked it, fastened it up. Alice Fisher, housekeeper to old Mrs. Nutting in St. John's Wood, London, was her only sister. Funny that they should both be widows and both be housekeepers. But then it had run like that all their lives long. Alice was five years younger. They had been always devoted—'never a cross word.' They knew everything about one another. Alice knew Lizzie's one great secret and Lizzie knew about the week Alice had spent with the Commercial Traveller at Bournemouth. Alice's William had been alive, in his second year of his illness it was, and Alice had gone off just because of that. She had been nursing William so arduously that she had to do something, and the Commercial Traveller, who had been after her for months, was what she had done.

She had liked him, too, and told Lizzie that she could gather

him up in her arms 'like a bit of laundry.' She had never seen
him again, or so Lizzie understood. Anyway, he was married and
his wife didn't die as Alice's William had done. Lizzie had felt no
moral shock at Alice's adventure. She had been glad for her to
have her bit of fun.

For herself, if it were not for one constant gnawing anxiety
she would be a happy and contented woman. She had had now,
for ten years, a perfect place and a perfect master. The coming
of this second wife, Mrs. Cromwell, could not make any difference at all. She, Lizzie Gayner, and her beloved master, Julius
Cromwell, had by now a relationship that no person on this
blessed globe could break. Besides, Lizzie Gayner would make
a friend of this Mrs. Cromwell before all was over. You see!

Mrs. Gayner turned in her chair and surveyed her room. It
was nine o'clock in the evening and she debated as to whether
she would listen to the News or not. No. She would not. There
was nothing but trouble these days with those Germans stirring
everybody up. You'd have thought they'd had enough in the
last war, but it seems they hadn't.

She sighed again, but this time it was a sigh of satisfaction, for,
really and truly, her room did look nice. It was as bright and
shining as the silver slip of new moon outside the window in the
sparkling star-scattered heavens.

First she looked at the cat, Peter, on the hearthrug. Those
rude men Curtis and Oliphant called it Goering because of its
great size. When she had it as the smallest black cat in the world
it was operated on for the world's future happiness if not for its
own, and that was why it was the size it was. It was a great black
barrel as it lay there with its paws folded under it and its head
cradled in its own fur. Lizzie Gayner loved it in spite of its size.

What she liked about her room was the cleanliness. Also the
colour. Also the cosiness. In fact it was the loveliest, most perfect
room in the world, and Lizzie really thought this because she had
seen so many grand rooms but never a one to her own taste as
this one.

On the cream-coloured walls were views of Windsor Castle, a photograph of the King and Queen and the two Princesses, and an especial picture of the Duchess of Kent, whom Lizzie considered simply the loveliest woman in the world. There was a round table covered with a crochet mat in red and blue, and on the crochet mat a vase of iridescent yellow, and in the vase pink and white roses. There was a coal-scuttle of shining brass, a small sideboard on which were two empty silver vases, a silver christening mug, and a silver cake-plate. On another small table were her Bible and prayer-book and a photograph in a green plush frame of herself and her Henry on their wedding day. He was a big stout man with a great buttonhole, a great grin, and a bowler hat several sizes too small for him. There was a small cane bookcase containing her books: the poems of Longfellow, the poems of Tennyson, a book of General Knowledge, *What Can the Answer Be?*, *The Channings* and *Lord Oakburn's Daughters* by Mrs. Henry Wood, two stories by Dorothy Sayers, *Missionary Work in India,* and a number of Penguins. On the mantelpiece were a clock in solid oak, two pink vases, and a photograph of her sister Alice. There was a door to the left leading to her bedroom. The window looked on to the drive, the rhododendrons, the little wood on the left of the house, and the stables where in these days the two cars were kept.

Yes, it was a perfect room and any widow would be glad and lucky to end her days in it.

She got up and went to the table. Now was her time for reading. There were two new Penguins that she had bought for herself on the journey down and had not had time as yet for reading.

There was a knock on the door. She opened it, and there before her was Julius Cromwell. She took him by the hand and led him to the best chair. He sank down into it, crossing his big legs, folding his hands after straightening his black tie. He looked, she thought, splendid in his evening clothes—a proper gentleman if there ever was one.

'That's right, Lizzie. Thank you. I haven't been in here before.'

'No, sir.'

'I thought I'd come in here for a little talk.'

'Yes, sir. I'm very pleased, sir, I'm sure, sir. Won't you smoke your pipe?'

'Yes, I will.' He filled it. 'Tell me just how the room is. I can find my way alone all over the house now.'

'Well, sir, there's the round table in the middle. The chair you're in is to the left of it. There's a little table behind you to the right. The chair I'm in is to your right. There's nothing else in the room to be a bother, sir.'

'That's splendid. Have you everything you want in here?'

'Yes, sir. Thank you, sir.'

'Fine. Everything as it was in the other house?'

'Yes, sir. Thank you, sir.'

'Grand. How have you been getting on?'

'Very well, I think, sir. The new maids seem quite all right. I hope the cooking's satisfactory.'

'Very good indeed.'

He paused. He seemed to be staring at her with his blue eyes as though he saw straight into her very soul. She remembered how, years ago, this intense gaze had frightened her. How much did he see? How much did he really know?

'Do you know one odd thing, Lizzie? Every new house I live in I seem to be able to see further than in the last one. Oh, not really, of course! But we've been in three now, haven't we? You came to us first in Eastwood, didn't you? I remember that first day so well. I got Elinor to describe you. "She's short and round and very tidy and has a *good* face!" That's what she said.'

They both laughed.

'Very complimentary of Mrs. Cromwell, I'm sure,' said Lizzie.

'Yes. You liked her, didn't you? Always. You never had a row.'

'Not a single one, sir.'

'And when she was ill you were wonderful. She always said that you made all the difference.'

'I'm very glad of that, sir.'

'Yes. And she still seems to be with me. I'm not a spiritualist, you know, but when you're blind you live in another world. It's easier to imagine that someone's not really dead. Isn't it queer to think that I never saw her? What do you remember now best about her—physically, I mean?'

'Well, sir, she was tall and carried herself beautifully. But what I remember best was her face—the calmness and goodness of it. She was a saint if there ever was one!'

'Yes, she was. She was never angry, never impatient, never in a hurry. And in all that suffering at the end she never complained once. And yet she wasn't a prig. She had a great sense of humour. I never felt dependent on her and yet I knew everything was all right if she was there.'

He paused again, puffing at his pipe. Lizzie Gayner sat upright, sometimes smoothing her black silk dress with her hand.

'You know, Lizzie, the odd thing is the blindness doesn't get any easier with the passing of time.'

'I'm sorry to hear that, sir.'

'Oh, of course the earlier difficulties are gone. I don't rebel and curse and swear as I once did. I've resigned myself. But the calm I ought to find. It doesn't come.'

'It will, sir, God helping you.'

'I don't know whether He helps or not. I don't want to shock you, Lizzie, because I know how much He means to you, but I'm not sure that He's there at all. The world I live in is made up of scent and sound and touch. I hear so many things that people with sight don't hear, and my mind seems to go deeper, deeper into things, until I reach a place where there is only my body. You know how I love music, and when the gramophone is playing, or the wireless, even in the grandest things it seems to stop at the sound. I say "That's beautiful," and that's all. Whereas, before the War, when I could see, music carried me on further and further. . . . Now it stops with the sound.'

'I think, sir,' Lizzie said, 'that's because you don't want to be cheated. You were always a great one for honesty.'

'That's very clever of you, Lizzie. But it's partly because I
don't want anything to carry me too far. When I sit staring into
myself I dare not go—dare not go to where I may find that
everything's a cheat. When you can see, you know what's real.
When you can't, reality and unreality mix.' He pulled himself up.
'But now I'm getting dismal and I'm most awfully happy just
now. Only I like talking to you. I always did. There wasn't
anyone I could talk to in the same way, even Elinor.'

'I'm very glad and honoured, too.'

'Yes, it's because everything with you is so straight and simple.
You believe in God and trust Him. You do your job and your
duty. And that's all. You haven't a complication in your life, have
you?'

How far could he see? What did he mean by that question?
She didn't answer him and he went on.

'We're such wonderful friends. I can tell you anything and
know you'll be wise about it.' He sat up, he caught his knee
with one hand.

'Lizzie, I'm so terribly, so fearfully in love!'

'Yes, sir. I know you are, sir.'

He seemed now to be engaged in some terrible struggle with
himself. She watched his face, yearning to help him, striving
with all that she had in her to help him.

'There are things I suppose a man should always keep to himself. Englishmen especially think it wrong. But we've been close
friends for ten years, haven't we?'

'Yes, sir. I'm proud to say we have.'

'You know me so well. You're the only human being alive now
who knew both Elinor and myself as we were truly together.'

'Yes, sir.'

'You know how devoted we were, what a grand, fine human
being she was, so much finer than myself. You know how lost
I was after she went. You comforted me as no one else did.'

'I did my best, sir.'

'And so, Lizzie, you can understand better than anyone else

what it means when I say that I never knew what love really was before I met my present wife. I don't know what it is now. I'm making new discoveries every day. And—listen to this, Lizzie, mark it, put it deep in your mind—if ever I have regretted being blind, if ever I have agonized over it, and cursed it, and regretted it, I'm cursing and regretting it now. I told you just now that the cursing part of it was over long ago. Well, it's all come back. I love her so terribly, Lizzie, and I can't see her, I can't tell where she goes to, I don't know what she's doing. She may be making faces at me for all I know!'

'She loves you, sir, quite as much as you love her. I'm sure of it.'

'Then listen to this. Two nights ago I woke up. Our beds are so close that I can reach out with my hand and make sure that she's there. I reached out my hand and she wasn't there. I heard her laughing somewhere in the room. She said, "You were snoring, so I woke you up." I asked her to come back but she wouldn't. She said, "I'm going—I'm going—I'm gone." Then I got out of bed to find her, but of course I couldn't. She turned on the light—I could feel it against my eyes—but she wouldn't let me find her. Then I barked my shin against a chair and at once she was in my arms, crying. Crying, Lizzie! swearing that she loved me, that she loved me so terribly but I didn't love her and liked Oliphant better—nonsense, nonsense—and I had to take her in my arms and console her and she went to sleep. . . . '

He was shaking from head to foot, trembling. His blind eyes were closed.

'I know how it is, sir,' Mrs. Gayner said. 'You haven't been married long enough. They always say the first year is difficult for anybody, getting to know one another and fitting in. I know my Henry used to be queer as queer the first year or two, wanting to do the strangest things. I used to be angry with him, but years later I wished him back again as he was at first. When people are new to one another they're like Columbus discovering America—don't know whether it's poisoned arrows or ropes of pearls they'll be finding. . . . Then she's only a child, if I may say so. She's never been married before and you have. She's ready to try any trick to be sure of you. It's not being sure of you, sir, makes her temperamental.'

'Do you think I'm too old for her, Lizzie?'

'Why, no, sir. What's fifteen years when all's said and done?'

'She lost her temper with you this very evening, didn't she?'

'She *was* in a bit of an upset.'

'She came and told me. She said: "Julius, I've been misbehaving," just like a child. She was very sorry.'

'Oh, that was nothing, sir. She'll get to know me in time. We'll be great friends before the year's out.'

'Do you think she's frightened of my blindness? What I mean is, that she mayn't have realized it at first. And now she does. What it's like being married to a blind man. Elinor was patient and just made to look after people. But Celia is impatient. More impatient than anyone I've ever known. And she can't hide anything. She says things that hurt me, but I won't let her see that they do. She can do what she likes to *me*. It's the way she hurts herself that matters.'

Mrs. Gayner said gently:

'You must be patient, sir, like your first lady was. I used to think when I saw you together that each of you was getting something of the other. People do when they're always together and fond of one another. You know, sir, when I came first to you I'd think that you liked to be made a fuss of. People with your misfortune always attract the sympathy of others. It's natural enough they should, although I'd think myself to be totally deaf would be as sad a trial, but deaf people don't get half the sympathy. And because they don't they are often grumpy and won't say a word to you. While people with your misfortune, sir, are charming and sweet-natured just because everyone wants to help them and be good to them.

'And I used to think, if you'll forgive me, sir, that when I first knew you you looked out for that sympathy and indulged yourself with it. You were young about your misfortune, sir, if I may put it that way. But your wife showed you a better thing. You came to think of yourself less and less and of her more and more. Isn't it the other way with you now? Aren't you thinking too much of her, and so finding yourself impatient? Give her time, sir. Let her grow. She's not been married before. You have. You're older and wiser and can study her more wisely than she can study herself.'

He got up and she rose too and began to lead him towards the door.

'Bless you, Lizzie. You're right as usual. Only I'm not wise enough. That's the trouble. When you're in love it isn't so easy!'

He sighed and stood still.

'By the way, I've taken on someone else. A young gentleman called Burke.'

'Yes, sir.'

'He was with the Ironings. He went away and now he's come back again. Ironing says he's a marvel about the house, in the garden, everywhere. A bit wild, but I liked his voice. He came to see me and told me all about himself. He wants little more than his keep. He'll help Cotterill in the garden and do odd jobs generally. He's the son of a clergyman, Ironing says. He knows shorthand, can type, and, Ironing says, is sober and honest. But he can't stick anywhere for long. He'll disappear one day without a word to anyone. Be decent to him. I know you will. I liked his voice. The timbre of it . . . "

'Yes, sir.'

He said good-night and for an instant put his arm round her.

When she was alone again she sat there thinking, her hands tightly pressed together. With one solitary exception she loved him more than any single human being on earth. She loved him as though he were her son although in truth he was her master and she was his housekeeper.

But she loved him also in another way—she loved him as though she were his defender, his protector. When Elinor Cromwell had died this suddenly had come to her—that now he was alone in the world. He had a brother and a sister, but both were married, with families of their own. He had no children and no friends of a close intimacy. His blindness marked him off from normal men. So she took him as her charge without his knowing it. When he told her that he was going to marry again she had known, for a little, a wounding, hurting jealousy. But only for a little. Her love for him was big enough to want his happiness beyond all else. He was a strong, lusty, physical being and she was wise about men. Men need women. She could not give him more than her secret protection. She was sorry at first when she knew that his second wife was little more than a girl, and even now, tonight, when she felt his passion, saw him tremble with it, there was a stab of jealousy again. She was sixty years of age but was she never to give any man love ever any more? No. Of course not. That was over for her, but the memory of it, the thoughts of it, were not over.

So she took up her Bible and read in the Revelation of St. John the Divine, which always led her into grander, more brilliant worlds, worlds where her own small weaknesses and desires were lost. She finished a chapter and moved towards the door of her bedroom. Time for bed. She pulled the curtain back and saw the silver sickle moon caught in a tall tree above the little wood and stars dancing between white moonlit clouds.

And even then her evening was not yet over, for once again there was a knock on the door. Startled she said, 'Come in,' and standing there was Mrs. Cromwell.

'Oh!' she cried, but the girl didn't move, only, in a small frightened voice, almost whispered:

'I've come to apologize!'

'Oh, please, ma'am. Come in. Sit down, please.'

'No, I won't stay. I'm on my way to bed. But I thought that I must apologize. I was angry about something that wasn't your business at all.'

'Oh, it doesn't matter, ma'am . . . please.'

'But it does matter.' She moved a step or two into the room.

'Mrs. Gayner, I want you to help me. . . .' She began to finger the things on the table, looking down on them. 'You're a very old friend of my husband's. I want to help *him*. I want to do everything for him I can—and you must tell me if I make mistakes.'

'Oh no, ma'am,' Mrs. Gayner said. 'I couldn't do that. It's not my place to interfere in anything except the running of the house.' Her voice was, in spite of herself, a little hard.

Mrs. Cromwell broke in.

'I'm very young and inexperienced. I know I am. All of us who have grown up since the War are stupid about other people. It's been our own fault. We are selfish and conceited. We have our good points, too. We're tough and we're honest, and we don't whine or bewail our fate or anything Victorian like that. But we're *not* good about other people and we're so honest that we show our feelings all the time.

'I want you to help me with a little advice when you see me going wrong. Will you? I'll take anything you give me. Will you? Please?'

She held out her hand. She looked entirely charming, her eyes smiling, her wide, unlined forehead open and honest.

Mrs. Gayner took her hand. 'Indeed, ma'am, I will do anything—anything.'

'Thank you so much. Good night.'

CHAPTER IV

By Sizyn Church

By SIZYN CHURCH there is a very old wall. It runs straight across the Moor until it reaches another wall, a very modern one which Frank Partridge of Sizyn Farm helped to make with his own strong hands. But the wall by the Church is very, very old, thirteenth-century they say, although nobody really knows. Some who have been up very early in the morning and have passed that way as evening light is fading, say that they have seen a donkey close to the wall, cropping at the grass—a ghost donkey, of course. It is said that you can walk right through it. The donkey, they say, belonged to the Franciscan who designed the famous Hawthorn Window early in Queen Elizabeth's reign —so early that there were still Franciscans to be found wandering the country.

In any case that part of the Moor is a haunted place, for behind Sizyn Farm is the oak tree where the young lady hanged herself in Monmouth's time because she was going to have a baby. And there are the Crazy Stones, eight of them, in a half-circle, on the projecting spike of the Moor above the wood known as the Well, and nobody knows how old *they* are! And at the very Cross-roads themselves, on the Garth in Roselands–Rafiel road, they say that the highwayman of Charles II's time, whose treasure is still supposed to be hidden somewhere on the Moor, was buried with a stake through his heart. Across this Moor the English marched to defend their country against the Spaniards, to fight for Cromwell, to die for Monmouth, to challenge the French in 1812—yes, and many, many marched before those days. We can see them, horde upon horde of naked men and women driven like cattle, the hide-whips of the Danes whistling in the air above them. And before them again, the men with bowed hairy backs and monkey-faces, and before them again the giant horny beast with the long neck and the tiny head rising sluggishly from the sea which lapped with its crystal wave the very edge of the Moor where the Church now stands.

Through it all the Moor unchanged, the tough little grasses blowing, the sea-birds screaming against the sun even as they are today.

For it is a fine day and everyone is thankful—Mr. and Mrs. Cromwell, Mrs. Brennan and her children, Dorothy, Gilbert, and

Simon, Mr. and Mrs. Lamplough, Miss Vergil, Mrs. Ironing and Fred Ironing her brother, Miss Phyllis Lock, her old mother, Oliphant, Curtis, and Jim Burke—all, all are thankful that it is a fine day.

For what is a picnic when it rains, or, worse than that, when the sea-mist comes up, as on the Glebeshire coast it does so often, and veils the world in water? Dangerous thing, Jim Burke warned Oliphant and Curtis, to have a picnic on the Moor late in August. Weather can change there in the twinkling of a firefly—seen fifty weathers up there, Jim Burke had, all of one afternoon. Queer place the Moor. Many a picnic had been ruined by it. The Moor doesn't like ginger-beer bottles, silver chocolate paper, orange peel, ladies' lipstick. Upon which crazy statement Oliphant, who had no imagination but only knew his duty, and Curtis, whose mind was entirely mechanical, stared at him as though Jim Burke were mad.

Whereupon Jim Burke, straddling his lively body on his restless legs and sticking his thumbs into his trouser-pockets, saw fit to say:

'That's all blighters like you can think of. All right, Dick Oliphant, I've known you just a fortnight, haven't I? What's the matter with that? I think you champion but limited. Why shouldn't you be limited? Much happier that way. But you ask your master you're so sure of whether he's sure of himself— whether since he was blinded he hasn't been more and more uncertain about the past, the present, and the future. What's the past, the present, the future? Just words. And haven't I seen a little short man in a brown habit going into Sizyn Church carrying the box he's going to make Mass out of? But if I haven't, I haven't. But do you, Dick Oliphant, know the Moor as I know it? Have you watched it all times of day in all weathers as I have? Alone, mind you. Alone. That's what you've got to be. And that's what your master, Dick Oliphant, is the only one in the whole of this blessed place to be save myself. We're alike in that, him and I.'

The cars drove up the hill and stopped near the Church. It was a day of a pale lighted sky, warm in sunshine, the faint odorous chill of approaching autumn in the shadow. The line of sea stretched milk-white against the blue-white sky.

Out they all tumbled: Julius and Celia from one car, Mrs. Brennan, Dorothy, Gilbert, and Simon from another, Mr. and Mrs. Lamplough with Miss Vergil from a third, Mrs. Ironing, her brother Fred, and Mrs. Mark from a fourth, Phyllis Lock and her old mother from a fifth. After them came Oliphant, Curtis, and Jim Burke bearing baskets.

There was a great female chattering as of birds released from cages into the sunlight.

'Where is it to be?' 'There's a lovely spot to the right of the Church—there, where those stones are!' 'How charming of you, Mr. Cromwell, giving us this party. I do love a picnic above all things.'

The children ran ahead.

Julius Cromwell was led slowly forward by Oliphant.

'Now don't take your coat off, Alice. This time of the year it's most treacherous.'

Little Mrs. Lamplough, who had no intention of taking her coat off and knew exactly always what she intended to do, murmured to Phyllis: 'I do think it was very strange of Mr. Cromwell to engage that Burke boy. Everyone knows the things he did when he was with the Ironings. To be with someone who's *blind* must always have been his dearest wish.'

'He's very good-looking,' Phyllis said, with a sigh.

Mrs. Brennan was advancing, a splendid ship in full sail.

'It was so very good of you, Mrs. Cromwell, to invite us all— such a lot of us, but I'm sure you'll find the children no trouble. My husband, poor man, had to stay behind and write his sermon. This afternoon was his only chance.'

'I always think,' Celia said, 'that clergymen and doctors are the most unselfish and overworked people in the world.'

She didn't mean a word of it—she had been told that Mr.

Brennan always *read* his sermons, choosing them from some clever *other* clergyman's clever book, so that she wondered that Mrs. Brennan should bother with so obvious a lie. Still it was no business of hers, nor did she care in the least. She was amazingly happy. Mrs. Brennan could tell as many lies as she liked.

They found a perfect site, almost under the Church wall and yet in the sunshine.

'I think,' said Celia, 'that we'll have lunch at once. It's almost one, and I know I'm fearfully hungry.'

'Oh yes! Oh yes!' everyone cried, all except Gabriel Lamplough, who began to wander away with a vague independence.

Celia thought that he was a very odd-looking man, so tall and thin, with a broken nose and eyes fierce and haughty.

They were all conscious of Julius. A blind man made an unexpected difference. There he was, his big body planted against the wall, his long legs stuck out, his blue eyes staring into space, his hands folded, saying nothing, but a queer secret little smile on his lips. Mrs. Mark was seated beside him.

'Did you come up here often when you were a boy?' she said.

'We came very seldom. My mother for some reason disliked the Moor. She forbade us to come here alone even when we were quite old.'

Julius turned his face toward her.

'I was always coming here. Catsholt was no distance. I loved this Church. You know the old story about the window?'

'No. I've forgotten . . . '

'It's in one of Baring-Gould's books. When the Franciscan was sitting in the Church painting his design for the window a young gentleman came riding by. His name was Herries. He stopped and ate with the Franciscan, and then they found that the Monk's beloved donkey had been stolen. They knew who had stolen it and I'm afraid it was an ancestor of yours, Mrs. Mark. He was the big man of the place and lived at the House. One of his soldiers had stolen it, so young Mr. Herries, who was a bashful kind of boy, bravely went and faced the grand people at the

House and demanded the donkey back. But your ancestor said
it wasn't the Monk's donkey. Young Herries had been told that
the donkey had her initials cut under her belly. The Monk had
told him. And with that knowledge young Herries was able to
prove that it was the Monk's donkey and bring it back to the
Monk. And they say, if you're up *very* early in the morning,
you can see the donkey waiting patiently for her master.'

'That's a very pretty story.'

'Yes, isn't it? Now tell me—is the House dreadfully changed?
Have we ruined it?'

'Oh no, it's ever so much more beautiful than when we were
there, although of course I don't like it nearly so much. In our
day it was filled with odds and ends, old things that were of no
use, but that nobody could bear to destroy.'

'It must have been an exciting moment the first time you saw
it again.'

'Yes.' Her voice dropped. 'I stood in the door out of which
my husband and I eloped. It was a wild stormy evening, but I
remember there was one brilliant star shining between the clouds.
Just before I left I met my brother Henry on the stairs, and he,
thinking I was just going to the village, said: "You'll be late for
dinner," which was an awful crime in those days. I said, "No,
I won't. I shall hurry." I wanted to kiss him but didn't, and I ran
out. I eloped because Philip and my mother didn't agree. They
were both domineering people.'

'It seems to be,' he said, 'a house in which things happen.'

'Yes, I think it is.' She added quietly, 'I do hope, Mr. Cromwell,
you'll be very happy there. Mrs. Cromwell is so charming. I like
her already so very much.'

'Thank you. She likes you, too. You can be a good friend to
her, Mrs. Mark, if you will. She's younger than her age in some
ways. I want our marriage to be simply perfect!' He laughed.
'I suppose no marriage is that. But perhaps we'll be the exception.'

Mrs. Mark said: 'Mine was as near perfection, I think, as you

could have. Philip grew finer and finer as he grew older, and
we were companions in everything.'

'Yes,' Julius said. 'That's just it. You see, Mrs. Mark, I'm blind
and fifteen years older than my wife. Do you think we can be
companions in everything?'

'Yes—if you are both patient and both unselfish. Trouble often
comes, I think, from trying to make someone you love the same
as yourself. It's the differences between you that give life to the
companionship. But I don't know. I'm only a looker-on now and,
as a looker-on, I find I can't help anyone much. The world's so
strange and young people want things to be right in such a
hurry.'

The food was spread. Oliphant came over and touched his
master on the shoulder and said: 'Luncheon is ready, sir!' Celia
stood, waving her hand. 'Come on, everybody! Time for food!'

Even old Mr. Lamplough, standing like a stork against the
pale horizon, heard her. He turned back slowly towards them.

Very possibly the last rich picnic in Great Britain. The
Ichthyosaurus raises its scaly head above the slime, the naked
Pict dances on his splay-toed feet, young Mr. Herries shifts his
hand to his jewelled dagger and turns for a last look before he
rides away, the psalm of the marching Ironsides comes faintly on
the sea-breeze—and Phyllis Lock cries out: 'Oh! Galantine of
chicken! I love galantine! Have some, May!' and Miss Vergil
answers deeply: 'Doing very well, thank you, Phyllis.' Oliphant,
Curtis, Jim Burke move about offering champagne, hock, cider-
cup, ginger-beer. 'How pleasant,' the ladies think, 'to have a
wealthy man living in Garth again! There are so many things
he will be able to do.'

But, as the meal proceeds, they all feel a little queer—queer
not from the food and drink. Oh no! But they are being fed
by a blind man. Soon they will be accustomed to him, of course.
But will they? Won't he always be outside their world, reminding them of more worlds than their own, worlds more dangerous,
worlds leading to other worlds? . . .

Phyllis Lock couldn't take her eyes off him and yet didn't wish to be seen looking at him. May Vergil's eyes were always on *her*, and May could be so very sarcastic and beastly! Moreover, she must think of her old mother, who, sunk into her old furs, her hat a little askew, her bony brown fingers clutching at the food, looked more like a monkey than many monkeys look.

Phyllis, the young child of her middle years, hissed at her: 'Do sit up straight, Ma, for heaven's sake do. Here! What is it you want? A piece of that pie? You'll never be able to eat it with those bad teeth of yours! There's Mr. Lamplough speaking to you. . . . Shake yourself together, for pity's sake.'

And to cover her daughterly embarrassment she began brightly: 'I was reading the other day about a picnic in a novel—just like this it was—sitting near the sea. Only they all began to quarrel. Such a funny novel—it had the Devil in it. Yes, really, I mean it. The Devil in modern clothes, and there was a man with a Punch and Judy. No. I don't remember its name, nor who it was by. I never remember the name of a book nor who it's by. I read so many.'

It was at this moment that Mrs. Brennan felt that she was being left out of it, and this feeling led, in the end, to unfortunate consequences. On so slender threads do human fortunes hang! Had Phyllis Lock attended, at that moment, to Daisy Brennan instead of to her old mother, the lives of several persons might have been different.

For Daisy Brennan was accustomed to worship. She was not getting it. Why? Because little Mrs. Cromwell, in her dark hat with the red feather, was dominating the scene. True, it was her party, but need May Vergil and Phyllis Lock and the Lamploughs and Fred Ironing all behave as though they had never seen a pretty woman in their lives before?

As a matter of record Daisy Brennan did not care at all for that childish, girlish figure, that excited laugh, that obvious courting of anybody's favour! Cheap! That was what Celia Cromwell

was! No dignity! No sense of a married woman's proper behaviour!

How preposterous if now, just because she had money and
laughed and chattered like a schoolgirl, Mrs. Cromwell were to
take the lead in a district that had belonged for years to Mrs.
Brennan! And, most unexpectedly, Daisy Brennan felt a hot
suspicion of tears behind her eyelids when she thought of the
shabby Rectory, and the trouble to meet the bills, and the ex-
pense of Gilbert at school—yes, and of Gilbert's very peculiar
behaviour, for he had spent the day with those people at Rafiel
and had never apologized but had rather shown a sulkiness. . . .
Nor was her husband of the least use when she complained,
but only laughed and shrugged his shoulders.

So she was angry and looked about her and saw that no one
was paying her any attention, and from that moment she began
to dislike Celia Cromwell very much indeed.

The Brennan children had eaten their fill. Simon, who was a
realist, had eaten more than his fill, but he had a stomach that
was his true friend, accommodating and adventurous like himself.

He was now absorbed by the food, not because he was greedy
but because he always flung himself wholeheartedly into anything
that at the moment he was doing. Short and sturdy, with his
bullet-shaped head, large clear brown eyes, in his cricket-shirt
and grey flannel shorts, sitting back on his haunches, staring, he
was like some friendly self-possessed animal who had found the
picnic by chance and was seeing human beings' food for the
first time. His eyes took in everything: the big crusted pies, the
egg-stuffed veal and ham, the pale marble-coloured galantine,
the new crisp-crusted bread, the brilliantly yellow pats of butter
with roses stamped on them, the sandwiches with sticks that had
names on little flags—Foie gras, Chicken, Tongue, Smoked Salmon
—the fresh curling lettuce with brilliant red stabs of beetroot
against its green, the two giant trifles with red cherries and
streaks of jam, the cutglass bowl with the fresh fruit—melon,

pineapple, peach, oranges, apples, floating in a sea of golden liquor—the round, wide-eyed box of preserved fruit, and, best of all, perhaps, a great cake with icing in the shape of a fortress with two red and blue soldiers—real wooden ones.

He stared and stared; then, as always, when he was absorbed, talked to himself aloud—and also to Dorothy.

'I wouldn't mind being sick if I could have everything once.' He was leaning right forward now, his chubby hands pressing on to his bare knees. 'Because perhaps never'—here there was a deep sigh—'never and never and never will it all be at one place again— will it, Dorothy?—not the *same* place. And no person could eat it all but he'd be sorry afterwards, wouldn't he?' Then, in a husky whisper, 'Won't they cut the cake? Do you think we'll all go away and they *haven't* cut the cake?'

'Hush, Simon, you mustn't be so greedy.'

He felt, as he so often felt, a deep disappointment in his strange and unpredictable elders. Living a life of his own that was altogether wise and completely satisfying, he could never understand the omissions, both in deed and thought, of grown-up people. They seemed to have *no* sense at all! For instance, they all sat round looking so silly and talking such nonsense and *not* apparently even wanting to try all those wonderful things. What did it matter if they *were* sick (he was so thoroughly accustomed to that grown-up monition: 'No, Simon! Not another piece. You'll be sick if you do!')? They would forget the sickness and have wonderful things to remember!

'It isn't greedy about the cake,' he said to Dorothy, but not turning his head away from the glorious sight. 'I just want to try!' Then he added disgustedly: 'What do they bring everything for if no one *eats* anything!'

At that moment Celia Cromwell jumped up, waved a knife and cried: 'Who's going to cut the cake?' He could scarcely believe his ears when she went on: 'You're the youngest, Simon! You must cut it! We'll do it together!'

Jim Burke brought her the cake. Simon knelt on the grass be-

side her and she guided his hand. She smelt of violets. He cut
down into the cake with ferocity. He would show them! It was
an enormous piece and was divided on a plate. Then he murmured, so that no one else could hear:

'Can I have a little soldier?'

He had been told again and again never to ask for anything,
but when he wanted something he got it. 'Of course,' she said
quite practically. She gave him the soldier and, miraculously,
did not kiss him. From that moment he was her devoted slave.

'You mustn't let him bother you, dear Mrs. Cromwell.'

'Oh, he doesn't a bit.'

'Only a little piece for Simon. . . . No, darling, not that bit.
It's too rich. You'll be sick.'

She began to explain the children, whom she had gathered
around her, to Mrs. Mark.

'What I should do without my Dorothy I simply *don't* know!
She's the little mother in the house. Yes, Gilbert goes to school
in Polchester. You like school, don't you, Gilbert?'

'Yes, Mother.'

'He isn't very distinguished for anything *yet*—but he will be one
day, won't he, Gilbert?'

Gilbert said nothing.

'My Anthony,' Mrs. Mark said, 'was quite uncertain until he
went to Cambridge what he was going to do. We never dreamed
it would be astronomy.'

'Oh, I'm afraid Gilbert will never be clever enough for that.
Something much more ordinary.'

Dorothy, who hated it when grown-up people talked about
them over their heads, was really watching Jim Burke.

The three children adored Jim Burke. When he had been in
Garth before he had shown them every kind of thing. He had
been like an elder brother to them. She was so very glad that
he had come to Garth again. His immediate duties over, he was
sitting away by himself against the Church wall doing something

with a knife and a piece of wood. That was so very like him. He must always be at something. She watched his brown quick fingers moving. Every part of him was alive and the warm sun lit up his body with a kind of flame.

She heard her mother's voice. 'Yes, they're a nuisance sometimes, but who would be without them? No, Simon—*not* one of those fruits. Oh, you naughty boy! Well, only the one. No, please, Mrs. Cromwell, don't offer him another— *What* a wonderful spread! I'm sure I've eaten far too much.'

But now the meal was over and they must all do what they will: lie back against the wall with a handkerchief over his face like Mr. Lamplough, or sit smoking a great cigar and talking silly talk to Phyllis and Miss Vergil like Fred Ironing, or sit with a book like Mrs. Lamplough and watch, with bright restless eyes, over the book's innocent edge, or spread yourself out and sit, as on a throne, Queen of the Moor, waiting for humble people to come and talk to you, as Daisy Brennan does, or run off laughing with the three children, crying 'We'll explore, shall we?' as Celia Cromwell has done, or sit, motionless like a happy boy gazing at the sky for signs, like Julius, or crouch, whistling, making a pipe of Pan out of the clean white wood as Jim Burke is doing. . . .

'Well, what do you think of him, Fred?' said May Vergil, smoking a little cheroot and watching Phyllis Lock. Fred Ironing was a big fat jolly man who must either kill some animal or kiss some woman if life were to have any kind of flavour.

'Him? Who?' he asked. He was always rather short with May Vergil, because it was one of his creeds that if a woman wasn't a woman she'd better take strychnine at once. And he had no interest in Phyllis Lock, because he had discovered that her policy with men was to tease rather than satisfy. But Celia Cromwell! By golly, there was a neat little woman with lovely legs! *And* a blind husband! What more could you ask?

'Who? . . . Why, Julius Cromwell, of course.'

'Well, I think it's very decent of him to give us all such a grand meal!'

'Oh, that, of course! No—idiot! What sort of a man do you think he is? Is he a fool, or isn't he?'

'I suppose he's like the rest of us—sometimes a fool, sometimes not such a fool. For instance, he's a fool for one thing because he's taken Jim Burke to work for him. I could have told him a thing or two about Jim Burke, but he didn't ask me. All he asked me was whether he was industrious. Industrious! I should say!' Fred Ironing grinned.

'Oh, you mean he's always after girls!'

'*And* some! However, that's Cromwell's affair. Only he must be a simple, trusting kind of chap.'

'Phyllis thinks he's Sir Galahad and St. Christopher rolled into one. Look at her! She's staring round the corner of her nose at him now!' May Vergil coughed but not kindly. Then she rose on to her knees and said very affectionately: 'Come for a stroll, Phil, old girl. Do you good.'

They strolled off together while Fred looked after them with cynical good-temper.

Mrs. Lamplough, seated beside her husband still lying with a handkerchief over his face, whispered without moving her eyes from her book: 'Phyllis Lock has fallen in love with Mr. Cromwell already. May Vergil's furious.'

When Celia returned with the children she went to her husband, sat down beside him, and caught his hand.

'Happy?' she asked. 'Julius, those are the sweetest children, especially the small one.'

'I expect they are.' He put his arm around her and drew her close to him, not caring who was there.

'Darling, I want to go into the Church. Shall we?'

'I'd love to.'

'I'd been waiting for the right moment. I've been waiting ever since I came to Garth.' He raised himself up, he stretched his arms, breathing in the air. 'Salt and sun and the grass. I put my ear to the ground just now and I could hear a million animals marching.'

He gave her again his broad strong hand and she helped to lift him until he stood on his feet.

'Aren't I a weight? The last time I was in that Church I was eighteen years of age and I went in with a girl whom I thought I'd fallen in love with. I sat and looked at the window and knew that I didn't love the girl a bit. Perhaps I shall have another revelation now!'

'Oh, I hope not!' Celia's cry had in it a fear.

'The difference, my pet, is that now I can't see the window —or I still see it as it was that day all those years ago. And there have been wars and rumours of wars ever since. And yet the window is the same. I bet it's the same.'

'Of course it's the same, you silly. It's been the same for hundreds of years.'

'I'm the only one of all of you that sees it the same. Your eyes change every time you see it. But you!— Of course, I was forgetting. *You've* never seen it at all yet!'

Celia looked around her. She wanted passionately that they two should go alone into the Church.

It was so. Mrs. Brennan was seated with her back to them, queening it with Phyllis, Miss Vergil, and Mrs. Lamplough. The Brennan children were with Jim Burke. No one observed them. She took his arm and they slipped round the corner, pushed their way through the little door, and sat down on one of the old benches.

The sun was shining fiercely behind the Hawthorn Window. The fierce white of the hawthorn blossom, the brilliant green of the grass, the purple that coloured the name of the Prior to whom the window was dedicated, burned brilliantly as though the old glass were beaten into the air that was sun-flamed. The little Church wrapped them round with friendliness. They sat close together, hand in hand.

'The sun is shining behind the window,' Celia said. 'It makes the colours very brilliant.'

'It was the first coloured window I ever saw,' Julius said. 'As a little boy my mother brought me the first time here. I thought the figures of the monk and the donkey were alive.'

'They are alive now. The donkey has silver bells.'

'It can never be spoiled for me again. Whatever the weather, however dark or cold it is, when the rain is thundering on the roof or there is sea-mist everywhere, it makes no difference. It will always be brilliant and burning and alive.'

He pressed her hand. 'I love you so dearly, Celia. Whatever may happen, never forget that. Nothing can change it. If ever you are troubled think of this moment. Remember it always. Darling, remember it. Never let it go.'

'I will. I will. I will always remember it. I love you, Julius, so deeply that I'm afraid. I think perhaps I haven't the character to love anyone so much. It's as though love of this kind had come to the wrong person. I don't deserve it.'

'We none of us deserve it. It's a gift, maybe, more than either of us can carry. We mustn't be cheated by lesser things.' He laughed. 'I was going to say "blinded." '

'Be patient with me, Julius. When we were married six months ago I thought it was all going to be so easy. I would look after you and we would love one another and everything would be lovely. But of course it's not going to be like that. I'll tell you something. When we were driving in the car that first day, just as we were passing this place I was suddenly terrified. I wanted to get out of the car and run.'

'Why?'

'I don't know. I think I saw myself clearly for the first time. I've been so rottenly brought up. Father was always abroad, and Mother never bothered about training me in anything. She only wanted me to be happy so that I wouldn't be a nuisance. I had everything far too early. Boys made love to me before I was fifteen. I was bored with sex before I was eighteen, bored

with everything, really. Everyone said that religion was rot
and that all anyone cared for was to have a good time, and that
life was a take-in anyway, however good a time one had.
Until I fell in love with you I was a complete waster. And now
I'm beginning to see that I've got a job that I'm simply not up to.'

'Why?' he said, smiling at her. 'Am I so difficult?'

'No. Of course not. You're adorable. But you don't know what
someone like me is capable of. And when one day you *do* know
. . . I seem to be about half a dozen different people and some
of the half-dozen are really beastly. I've never been taught
restraint or self-sacrifice. I'm greedy and vain and selfish. I
ought never to have married you. It's a *damned* shame. . . .'

He laughed.

'I'm not much to shout about either. I've been blind for
twenty years and that's made me selfish and self-centred. I've
always had as much money as I wanted, which in *these* days is
a crime as bad as murder. I've always been waited on hand and
foot. I've liked all sorts of women, some pretty rotten ones.
I get very depressed sometimes and then I'm as cross as a bear.
There are days when I think I'd be much better dead, just
cumbering the ground. So you see, you'll have to put up with
a lot. . . .

'But the great thing is we love one another—*really* love one
another. I know lots of other people have thought the same
and it hasn't been true. But that's because they haven't been
able to stand enough. They've been beaten halfway through.
We won't be, will we?'

'No. Never. Nothing shall beat us.'

She stared at the window as though she were committing her
oath to the Prior, the Monk, and the Donkey.

She laid the palm of her hand against his cheek. 'If I loved
you less I wouldn't ever be frightened.'

The sun shone down hot on to the grass and the heads of
Jim Burke and the three children. The children were absorbed,

for Jim was cutting a head out of a piece of wood. There it was emerging as the fragments of white wood scattered through the air—the round head, the small ears, the wide blind eyes, the mouth smiling.

'He's blind like Mr. Cromwell,' Gilbert said. He could scarcely speak for excitement. This was what he wanted to do. Jim should show him.

'Can I have it afterwards?' Simon asked.

'Hush!' Dorothy said. 'You mustn't ask for things.'

'Why mustn't I?' Then he smiled mischievously. 'I've got this,' he said, showing the little red and blue soldier.

'Of course you can have it,' Jim Burke said. He was whistling. All his body, his bright eyes, his brown neck, his arms bare to the elbow, seemed to work with his hands.

Dorothy watched him and thought him wonderful. He could do anything and was always pleasant. He looked up for a moment at her and their eyes met.

'Now it's done! Now it's done!' Simon cried.

'No, it isn't. Wait a minute. I knew a man once could carve animals out of stone—rabbits and dogs and horses. He made a bird once. It was a yellowhammer and you could see it moving, against the gorse and such. It seemed to be all gold, but it wasn't really. There wasn't a spot of paint on it. Only he could make you fancy things, that man could!'

'Jim,' Gilbert asked again, almost below his breath, 'could you teach me to make things out of wood? I'd work and work——'

'Oh, I daresay. But you've got to have it in you.'

'I've got it in me! I've got it in me!' Simon cried out.

'That's just what I think you haven't. You want the things *after* they're done, not *before*. I know your sort.' Jim grinned. 'There. You can have it now! Yes. He's blind like Mr. Cromwell.'

Simon caught at it as though he were afraid lest someone should get it before him.

Jim took a long look at Dorothy.

'I'll do something for you much finer than that one day,' he said.

They were having tea.

Simon, although he had eaten so much at luncheon, could manage very easily scones with strawberry jam, saffron cake, and rock buns so new that they were still warm.

But there was a greater fascination for him than food. He could not take his eyes from Mr. Cromwell. That big man and yet not able to see anything! Did he feel like ordinary people? If you touched him was he just the same all over as everybody else?

Unknown almost to himself he crept nearer and nearer. No one noticed him. Everyone was talking, drinking tea, thinking 'This has been a nice day, this has!'

Simon had arrived. He put out his very grubby hand and laid it on Julius' knee.

Julius started. 'Hullo, who's that?'

'It's me,' Simon said.

Julius' big hand came down on Simon's little one.

'Well—what do *you* want?'

'A piece more of the sugar cake,' Simon said in a husky whisper, terrified of his mother, who was not far away. Julius' thigh was warm and strong and altogether reassuring. Julius put an arm around him.

'You're Simon?'

'Yes.'

'That's right. Enjoyed yourself?'

'Yes. Thank you.'

'Will you come and see me in my own home one day?'

'Yes, I will—if Mother lets me.'

'Why shouldn't she?'

'She says I'm not to bother.'

'Oh, you won't bother. I like little boys. How old are you?'

'Eight and twenty-six days.'

'It isn't too late for me to give you a birthday present.'

Simon was about to say: 'Look what Jim's given me.' But he suddenly remembered. Poor Mr. Cromwell couldn't see *anything!* A stray impulse of protectiveness commanded his heart. He felt exactly as he had felt a week ago when he had seen a small terrier at the farm that had broken its leg and lay, with helpless eyes, in a basket.

So, while he ate his cake, he clutched Julius' hand very hard.

Tea was over. They all prepared to go. Mrs. Ironing, of course, made the only tactless remark of the whole afternoon.

'Oh, Mr. Cromwell, I wish you could see! Then you'd know how happy we've all been!'

But Julius was delighted.

CHAPTER V

Garth House: In the Garden—In Julius' Study— In Mrs. Gayner's Room

CELIA CROMWELL found herself in the little wood to the left of the House and lost in it.

Now, at the end of the real summer, there was a thick pressure from the trees of leaves about to burgeon into amber, gold, saffron, a glorious transmutation before death. She had noticed it before—that hushed listening pressure of senses before the change—silent, heavy, ominous as with the passing of a human being. Death itself is light, almost careless. Preoccupation with death is sinister, as though it were against the law.

The little wood, weighted with darkness, was pierced with shafts and spears of light. How ridiculous to be lost in it when it was so very small and already she knew it so well! In the very centre of the little wood was a holly tree that seemed to be more alive than any tree should be. The leaves are so dark that they suggest steel, but the bark is white. The leaves are fiercely independent, caring neither for God nor man, but the bark is silk. The wood of the holly is so close-grained that in country-made furniture it has been inlaid to look like ebony, and in its natural state to imitate ivory.

This tree was shaped into a provocative hostility and, for a moment, Celia had the foolish fancy that it caught and enveloped her. She even looked at her hand to see whether the flesh were torn. Ever since she could remember she had suffered from a kind of claustrophobia, hating to be shut in, to be held by any one or anything unless she loved.

Now she shook off the imbecility. Was it to right or left? With her arms she brushed some branches aside and burst out on to the long, smooth, open lawn, green, sparkly, clear under the early afternoon sun like water.

She stood, without moving, the little trees behind her, gazing on that open view, with the fields that ran down to the hollow, the hill that ran up beyond, moving with rhythm like a sloping green wave of an endless ocean. She saw Jim Burke, with his back to her, bending down above a flower-bed that bordered the path in front of the house.

She moved across the lawn towards him and stood again watching the strong sturdy figure working with such easy pleasant naturalness.

'Well, Jim,' she said.

He started as though a bird had cried in his ear. The whole world had been so very still. He straightened up and turned to her.

'Planting some chrysanths.'

He wiped the back of his hand on his cheek. He was hot and his forehead shone with sweat.

'I might help you if it weren't so hot.'

'The last days of summer.' He always looked at her with an honest amused frankness. He always seemed to find something funny about her, and that she didn't like.

'I hope you find plenty to do,' she said.

His shirt was open and the hair on his chest was golden and damp.

'Plenty,' he said. 'But I like work.'

'And do you like being with us?'

He grinned. 'I always like where I am for the time being.'

'Do you never mean to settle down to anything?'

'No. Why should I? This isn't a world for settling down. The settling-down days are over. There'll be another war soon and then I'll have a real job to do.'

'Oh, I hope there won't be another war!'

'Of course there will. It's like turning the soil over before you plant the new seed. My father was a parson, you know, and he used to say: "Give us Peace in our time, O Lord." But I say: "Give us War, and War until human beings are made to realize the sort of world there ought to be. Shove it down our throats and then we'll realize!" '

She thought of the holly tree.

'That is very fierce of you. You speak as though you'd had a hard time.'

'I haven't. Not at all. I've enjoyed my life. It's been just what I wanted.'

She disliked his self-confidence.

'You're lucky. Very few of us can say that.'

'That's because most people do what they think they ought to do, not what they want to do.'

'If everyone always did just what they wanted, everyone would be miserable. You have to think of others.'

'Do you?' he said, looking at her and laughing. 'I mean—does everybody? Not as I see it. Everyone's for himself. It's only cowardice makes them think of others.'

'What an extraordinary idea! Don't you believe in the goodness of anyone then?'

'Oh, I like people! Everybody, almost. But that doesn't mean that I admire them—any more than I admire myself. Everyone's the same—look after number one.'

She was suddenly angry.

'Well, I don't agree with you. I know lots of unselfish people
—my husband, for instance.'

'Mr. Cromwell. He's different. I think the world of him.
There's nothing that I wouldn't do for him. That's how I feel
at present, anyway. I may change, of course, and when I do
I'll go somewhere else.'

'Did you like it at Mr. Ironing's?'

She was sure that it was wrong to gossip about her neighbours,
but curiosity drove her on.

'Fred Ironing!' he laughed. 'Oh, he's all right. You didn't
have to bother yourself with admiring *him*. We had some times
together, we had——'

'Where have you been in between?'

'Let me see.' He considered. 'I was steward on a liner for a
bit. Then I helped in a joint in New York. Then I trekked
out to Hollywood and did Extra work for a bit. I was valet
to a man in London. Then I helped with some fishing down at
Penzance.'

'What brought you back here?'

'I've never liked any place in the world as much as this. I used
to think of it over and over again in America. It's got everything,
this place has—the sea only a few miles away, and the Moor, and
the prettiest little church in England. I like the people here too
—Fred Ironing and old Mr. Lamplough and Corbin at "The
Three Crows" and the kids at the Rectory.'

'Weren't you surprised when my husband took you without
knowing anything about you?'

'No, I wasn't. He could tell I meant it when I said I would
do anything for him.' Then he added: 'There, that's enough
questions for one day, isn't it? I must be getting on with my
work. I promised Cotterill.' He turned his back to her and
went on with his gardening.

She laughed.

'Your manners aren't terribly good, are they?' She heard
him chuckle.

By tea-time she had decided that she would ask Julius to get rid of him. There was something she didn't at all like about him. Besides, he wasn't needed. They had already Cotterill the gardener, a gardener's boy, Curtis and Oliphant. Four males! Quite sufficient, surely. What with Mrs. Gayner and all these men about the house there seemed to be no place for her at all. If it came to that, Mrs. Gayner wasn't *really* needed. Julius adored her and was dreadfully under her influence. One day Mrs. Gayner should go—but not yet. She must work slowly and with caution there. It was not in her nature, however, to work slowly about anything. This business of Jim Burke's should be settled at once.

Between six and seven she went into the room that they called the Study, a foolish name perhaps, but it was Julius' own room where he had the gramophone, his Braille library, and his own writing-table.

When she came in music filled the room.

'What's that?' she asked, going over and sitting on the arm of his chair.

'Elgar's Second Symphony. Shut it off.'

'Not if you want it.'

'I don't want it if you're here.'

'You mean,' she said, laughing, 'I don't like good music.'

'You don't, as a matter of fact. But what I really mean is that when you're here I like to talk: I don't want any sound but your voice.'

She shut off the music, went back to him, kissed him and moved away.

'I'm not going to sit with you, because there's something I want to say.'

'Can't you say it just as well if we're together?'

'No. Because when you're holding my hand I'm weak. And now I want to be strong.'

'Go ahead then.'

'First—I hate Daisy Brennan.'

He turned on his side and stared about the room as though he were looking for her.

'How terrible! I don't like her very much myself.'

'She hates me, too. Mrs. Lamplough told me——'

He interrupted her almost harshly.

'Look here, Celia, you're not to listen to a word that woman says.'

'Oh, I know she's a cat——'

'I mean that seriously. We've come to live in a little village and villages are full of gossip. Some people aren't harmed by it, but you're so made that you take everything seriously. You must pay attention to *nothing!*'

'Why, how serious you are!'

'Yes. I get a sort of warning of things sometimes. Perhaps it's being as I am. I hear more than most people. Come here!'

She didn't move.

'Come here! Come here!'

His voice had a crying note in it, of unexpected urgency.

She ran across to him, threw herself on to him, kissed his eyes, his cheek, his mouth.

'I tease you. I shouldn't. It's the worst thing I do. But I want you to love me. I want you to! I want you to! I like to hear you cry out like that! I mustn't. I shall tease you once too often!'

After a little while she got up and stood out of his reach. 'No. What I said is true. I *can't* fight for myself when I'm touching you. I believe you have twice as much magnetism in your body as people who can see.'

'We need some compensation. Come back. Come back. I want you.'

'No . . .'

He stretched out his arms.

'No, Julius. . . . Look here, what do we need to keep Jim Burke for?'

At that name passion that had filled the room died suddenly

from it—just as a drum on an instant ceases to beat. In the new silence their words fell coldly.

'Jim Burke? Why—what's the matter with him?'

'I don't like him.'

'First Mrs. Brennan, now Jim Burke.'

'Oh, you *are* tiresome! What I mean is that we don't *need* Jim Burke.'

'Don't we?'

'We've got Cotterill and Johnny and Oliphant and Curtis. I know you want this place to look nice, but surely we don't need Jim Burke as well as all these other men.'

He leaned right over the fat leather arm of the chair, staring just a little to the right of her.

'Now—this interests me. What *have* you got against Jim Burke?'

'It isn't that I have anything against him. I simply don't see what you want him for.'

'I like him.'

'Oh, you can't like him already. You only met him a week or two ago. It isn't as though you could *see* him, and anyway you're not a woman. He's awfully good-looking, of course.'

'No, it's not his physical charms,' Julius said, grinning. 'I like him—that's all.'

'Why do you?' she said tempestuously. 'There's nothing to like about him. He's a gentleman by birth. What's he doing loafing around——'

'He doesn't loaf.'

'No, I must say he doesn't. Anyway he's a waster. In the last two years he's been every sort of thing from a tramp to gentleman's valet. He told me so.'

'Oh—so you've been having some talks with him?'

'I asked him a question or two. He has the most *dreadful* reputation, Julius. When he was with the Ironings no girl in the place was safe from him. He's said to be the father of at least half a dozen children in the village.'

'Said to be! Said to be!' Julius retorted. 'There you are! Gossip again! I know he's not a saint, but I don't want saints to work for me. They'd make me feel uncomfortable, not being a saint myself.'

How maddening and irritating he could be! Yes, and frightening! The change was coming that she knew so well, when he passed out of her reach—with his blind eyes he looked into a room where she was not.

'It was silly of me,' she said, 'to talk about his character. You're quite right. That has nothing to do with it. The point is you don't *need* him.'

'That's for me to say.'

'No, it isn't altogether. It's to do with me a little, too. You've got all these men about the place *and* Mrs. Gayner. *I'm* not wanted.'

She felt a sudden horrid little fear within herself lest he should suddenly say: 'No. You're not.'

'If it weren't for you,' he answered slowly, as though he were counting his words, 'we shouldn't be here at all. I wouldn't bother to have a house or servants. I'd have a room at my club and sometimes go to sea.'

'And you'd have Oliphant to look after you and be twice as happy as you are now.'

He nodded his head. 'No. Not *more* happy. A different kind of happiness.'

He was gone. He wasn't in the room at all. She was alone. He was always removed from her as soon as he began to see. He was seeing now.

'Then,' she cried, 'you can have your old ship and your room at the club and Oliphant! If you don't want me you needn't think——'

He was back in the room again.

'Come here. Come here,' he said softly. 'Don't be angry so often. Like a little child. . . . When I love you so . . . so very, very much.'

She came to him.

Exactly as eight-thirty struck from the grandfather's clock half-way up the stairs Violet brought in Mrs. Gayner's supper. Mrs. Gayner liked that her meals should be precisely punctual.

Just before Violet's entry Mrs. Gayner had drawn her curtains. The sky was dark but luminous, promise of the rising moon. Stars silver and virgin shone with a brilliant quiet. The little clustered wood lifted its ragged head against the waiting sky.

She saw that the ladder was still outside her window. Cotterill had been tending the creeper that covered her side of the house.

She gave the curtains a last loving tug and turned back to the table. There was her favourite supper: cold tongue and cold chicken, a salad, some Stilton, an apple, and a jug of beer. Violet stood waiting.

'Will that be everything, Mrs. Gayner?'

'No. As a matter of fact it will not.'

How pretty the girl was! With her dark hair and rose colouring, her large black eyes with the black eyelashes, her body held erect but lightly. The girl had breeding from somewhere. She had impertinence too. She stood there now, expecting a scolding, angry, her mouth curved with scorn.

'Oh yes—she thinks I'm an old dumpy woman whom men can't love any longer—so what's the use of me?'

She showed no temper, however, but said quietly:

'Violet, I have a job in this house just as everyone else has. And that job is to see that everything goes along quietly.'

'What have I been doing then?'

'You know well enough. You were impertinent to Mr. Curtis this morning when there was no call to be. It wasn't your place to tell him to be quicker about his work.'

'Mrs. Cromwell wanted the car and sent me to tell him so.'

'Did she tell you to be rude to him?'

'He doesn't bother with her. He only thinks of Mr. Cromwell.'

'That isn't true, but even though it were it's none of it your business.'

'It's my business to see that my mistress is properly served.'

Mrs. Gayner looked at her. She felt a kindly warmth—she was little more than a child and so very pretty! She sat down to her supper.

'Sit down for a moment, Violet. I don't mean to be angry. I know that Curtis is sometimes irritating. He's been with Mr. Cromwell so long and he doesn't like new faces. But with a girl as pretty as you he can't be unfriendly long.'

Violet had sat down, but on the very edge of her chair. Her face was clouded with sulkiness. She didn't speak.

'We've all got to get along together,' Mrs. Gayner went on. 'You haven't been here very long, have you?'

'No, I haven't.'

'It takes time to know people, and this house isn't quite like others, Mr. Cromwell being blind.'

'I tell you what it is, Mrs. Gayner, there's a lot too much made of Mr. Cromwell's blindness. Oh, I know it's an awful thing to be blind. I'm sorry for him all right. But there are plenty of other people blind. Look at all the St. Dunstan's men! Anyway, you'd think from the way Curtis and Oliphant go on—yes, and yourself too, Mrs. Gayner—you'd think no one had ever been blind before.'

'It isn't only that Mr. Cromwell is blind,' Mrs. Gayner said quietly. 'It is that we have become very attached to him. You will also when you've been here a little.'

'Oh, he's all right,' the girl said impatiently. 'I've nothing against him, but it's my mistress I'm thinking of. You all of you behave as though she were of no account at all.'

There was a little pause, then Mrs. Gayner said:

'I didn't ask you to stop, Violet, to discuss our mistress and master. That's not our business. All I want to say is that if you can't behave you'll have to go.'

Violet sprang to her feet.

'Oh, will I? And who's to have the saying of that? Am I at your beck and call or Mrs. Cromwell's? Mrs. Cromwell seems well enough satisfied with me, and that's good enough for *me*.'

She left the room, banging the door behind her.

Well, really! . . . Well, really!

Lizzie Gayner ate her supper, but without enjoyment. In all her time with Mr. Cromwell such a thing as this had never occurred. There had been troubles, of course, and girls had been impertinent, but unless they apologized they went. There had been little apology here.

And Mrs. Cromwell? Would she be behind this impertinence? The trouble came from the fact that Lizzie Gayner did not yet know Mrs. Cromwell. All that she knew about her was that she was young, spoilt, impetuous, with a real heart, kindly but probably ill-judging.

She realized that Violet had conceived for her mistress a passion and that Mrs. Cromwell was indulging the girl more than was wise. How Lizzie wished that she had never engaged the girl at all! She had hesitated between her and a plain-faced child from Rafiel. Something had warned her that Violet would be difficult. Things were not as easy in this house as she had hoped they would be. She did not like this Jim Burke who was under nobody's orders and was a gentleman really. She profoundly distrusted gentlemen who were servants. It was against nature.

She pushed her tray away from her and sat there thinking. She must proceed carefully. It would never do to complain of Violet to Mrs. Cromwell and then not be supported. This would need tact and knowledge of human nature.

She raised her hand to pull the standard lamp nearer to her so that she might see well to read, and fancied that she heard a tap on the window-pane. No, that it couldn't be. One of the tendrils of the creeper. . . . There was the knock again! Something told her that this was a human being.

She stood up, her hand at her breast. She was frightened. Then she shook her head. No, she was *not* frightened. She was in God's hands. So she went to the window, drew back the curtain and looked out. Because of the light in the room she could see very little, but someone was there, balancing on the top of the ladder. He was peering in with his nose against the pane.

She knew who it was.

'Oh God! God help me!'

She pulled the window open and drew him in. He jumped on to the floor.

'Gee, Mother,' he said, 'you do take a time!'

He was a thin man with high shoulders, large bony hands, a face that was ancient and babyish—a timeless face with light watery eyes, faint eyebrows, a large mobile mouth, and a small thin nose. He stood there, peering about him as though he had been living in a cellar. He was not a beauty and he was Lizzie Gayner's only son, Douglas. She had hold of his arm and the first thing she said was:

'Are the police after you?'

He looked at her with scorn.

'No, of course not.'

His suit, although too big for him, was not shabby, and he wore in his buttonhole a faded flower.

She held him off, looking at him. Then she kissed him.

'All right, Mother. Don't eat me.'

'Where have you been all this while?' she asked sternly.

'What while?'

'It's four months since I heard from you.'

'Well, I couldn't. I've been moving about!'

'Moving about!' she spoke scornfully. 'I'm sure you have. And now what a nice way to come and see your mother—through the window.'

'Well, how was I to know?' He spoke in a whine and you expected him to put up his arm and shield his face from a blow. Not that Lizzie Gayner had ever struck him. It was his general attitude to life, that he was one of the strikable.

'You're in a posh position here. You wouldn't want me coming in at the front door, would you?'

No, she wouldn't. She gave a quick look at the door. No one must, for the moment, know.

She had seated him by the table, herself close to him.

'He hasn't prosecuted you—Mr. Menzies, I mean?'

'He hasn't caught me.'

'He easily could. You aren't so difficult to find. They got the cigarette-case back and everything.'

'Of course they did—I was a mug.'

'Oh dear, whatever did you do it for? Such a nice place as you had, and Mr. Menzies so good to you.'

'That's what I complain of. If he was so good to me why couldn't he be a bit better? He wouldn't let me have the money when I asked him for it, so, I being in the mess I was, I had to take something, didn't I?'

'Where have you been all these four months?'

'Oh, moving about!' He suddenly grinned. It was the strangest smile, wicked, tragic, and forlorn. 'I've been on the Halls! I have really! Doing my song and dance. Listen, Mother!'

And of all things, he moved back and began a shuffling tap-toe kind of dance and at the same time, with a voice as hoarse as a frog's, sang something about 'Smile, Smile, and Happy Days are coming!'

She jumped up in alarm.

'Stop! Stop! Do you want them all to hear you?'

'Well, I was only showing you.'

He collapsed like a bagpipe and, all huddled up with his shoulders perched so high that it was almost a deformity, sat leaning over the table.

'Do you want something to eat?'

'I had a feed at the pub. I don't mind finishing the beer though.'

He poured it out into her glass and drank greedily.

'How did you know which my room was?'

'I saw you an hour ago looking out of it. I was standing in that there little wood.'

'And what do you mean to do now?'

'Stay here for a bit.'

'Oh no! You can't do that!'

'Not in the house, silly. In the village.'

In spite of her fears she was pleased. She loved him and he would be near her.

'You might get me a job. Oh, I don't mean to claim relationship. I don't want you to lose your job.'

'I shouldn't. Mr. Cromwell would understand. All the same, it's better that way.'

She was thinking of Mrs. Cromwell. If Mrs. Cromwell knew she had a thief for a son, who was, perhaps, at that very moment being sought for by the police, it would be awkward for everybody.

'What do you call yourself?'

'Henry Sharp. That's my stage name. Don't you forget it.'

'Where are you staying?'

'I'm at the "Three Crows." Got a bedroom that's cheap as things go. And that reminds me. Got any money?'

'Yes. A little.'

She went across to the little bureau, unlocked a drawer, and returned with three pounds.

'There!'

He had watched her every movement, his eyes as sharp as a pocket-knife, although they were watery.

'Thanks, Mother. And now, so-long! I'll be seeing you.'

He let her enfold him in her arms. She stroked his sleek watered hair. She held him away for a moment and looked at him anxiously.

'You want feeding up.'

'I'm all right. So-long.'

When the window was closed and there was silence in the room, she fell on her knees and began to pray.

CHAPTER VI

The Road to Rafiel

DOROTHY BRENNAN had never as yet known a close friend. Because she had never gone to school, and because there had never been, in her lifetime, large families either in or near Garth, she had never exchanged confidences with anyone of her own age. She read books and newspapers, listened to the wireless, and went once a year to a dance in Polchester.

A horrid girl, older than herself, Sylvia Bond, who stayed for a while with the Ironings, enlightened her as to the processes of conception and birth, and offered some pictorial anecdotes of the behaviour of men under stress when a beautiful young female chooses to tease them. None of this entered Dorothy's real world. She was not a silly girl: she was not more sentimental and romantic than any child of her age who has had no friends outside her own family. She was, for one thing, extremely busy. When the governess departed she had to be governess to Simon. All day long there were things to be done for her mother.

She adored her mother. It seemed to her, quite simply, that there could be no one else in the world so beautiful, so wise, so noble. That the ladies of Garth should make her their queen seemed to Dorothy inevitable. When they visited Polchester and people turned and looked, Dorothy thought it only the inevitable tribute, not realizing at all that people turned to look at the slim girl with the honest eyes and the nobly-carried head, quite as much as the magnificent woman, her mother.

Dorothy, up to this present time, never thought of herself at all. No one had ever expected her to think of herself. Her ideas were very simple. She believed in God and, although she admitted to herself the foolishness of it, still saw Him, a stout old man with a white beard, sitting on a cloud in the heavens. His eye was always upon her and He would have given her up long ago in despair had it not been for His son, Jesus Christ, who was her friend and watched over her.

She did not, in fact, feel very remorseful about her sins, because she had no time to think about them. So soon as she was in bed at night she was asleep, and she slept until the bell roused her in the morning. But as she never thought of herself, so she never thought herself either good or wicked.

It was her heart that was for ever engaged. Her immediate family—her father, her mother, Gilbert, and Simon—took up all her time, for if any one of them was unwell or unhappy she could not rest until everything was right again. After the family came various people in the village, the curate, and anyone who was nice to her. She believed, up to the present, everything that anyone said to her.

She was still very much of a baby in many things. She was easily hurt and tears would come into her eyes, and sometimes she would retire into her bedroom to cry. Any little pleasure excited her, and when they went to *The Pirates of Penzance* in Polchester she thought of it, in all its details, for weeks and weeks afterwards. She loved dearly to read books but had little time for that extravagance, and one of the very few things that she did not understand in her mother was that she thought reading 'time wasted.'

'Now, Dorothy! I *told* you to go to the post-office and there you are reading a silly book!'

Well, it *wasn't* a 'silly book.' It was *Vanity Fair*.

'I'm reading *Vanity Fair*, Mother. I simply love it.'

'Never mind what you're reading. I want you to go to the post-office.'

One of the principal characteristics of the Brennan household was that there was never any money. Dorothy took this quite naturally. She had never lived where there was any money. She did not know what it felt like to have any.

But she did know that the house and her clothes were with

every swallowing week a little shabbier. Her mother always looked magnificent, but her father was not as he should be, nor was Gilbert, whom she was ever having to patch up. He was greatly distressed about his clothes, and that made it the odder that he should take so little interest in the visit to Polchester to have his new suit fitted. He had been very quiet all that day and had not been excited even over the luncheon at the hotel in the Town Square.

She loved Gilbert and Simon so passionately that everything that happened to them happened to herself. Simon's independent and completely satisfactory personal life did not admit her, of course, but she did not wish that it should. All that she wanted was that he should be happy, and that he most certainly was.

But Gilbert was altogether another affair. Gilbert told her everything, and believed absolutely in her judgment. It was this belief in her judgment that sometimes frightened her. It made her so very responsible.

Now, quite suddenly, he had said to her: 'Dorothy, Mother doesn't *want* me to have a good time. She'd rather I didn't.'

At the moment she made no answer except to say: 'Don't be an ass, Gillie.' But that night she did not fall asleep at once, but lay, listening to the owl hoot and seeing the moonlight shadow with pale austerity the old red carpet. She slept always with her window open and the curtains undrawn.

What was the matter with Gillie? Ever since the day when he had been asked to Rafiel, the day when Mrs. Mark had paid her call and Jim Burke returned, something had been wrong between Gillie and his mother. For the first time in her memory Dorothy would not be sorry when the time came in a fortnight or so for Gillie to return to school.

Simon was to give trouble too. On a dim, smoky, purple-shadowed September afternoon, Mrs. Brennan appeared in the schoolroom and said:

'Where's Simon? I've been looking for him everywhere. I want to take him into the village.'

There was no Simon, and Dorothy, with a pang of apprehension, knew where he must be. There were times when she
was frightened of her mother. She was frightened now.

'Get him for me, Dorothy. I haven't much time.'

She said:

'He's not in the house.'

'Not in the house! What *do* you mean?'

'I know where he is. He's at the Cromwells'.'

'At the Cromwells'? . . . Was he asked, and if so, why wasn't
I told?'

'He wasn't asked. He just went. I'm sure that's where he is.'

'You're only sure? You don't know, then. I thought you were
looking after him this afternoon.'

'Yes, Mother. But Father wanted me to take a message to
Mr. Boss—and while I went Simon disappeared.'

'He may be dead—he may be anything! It's awful his going to
the Cromwells' when they don't want him. What were you
thinking of, Dorothy? You could have taken him across the
street with you. What's come to you, all of you? Gillie looks
at me as though he hates me, you lose your head, even Simon
wants to be with those Cromwells all the time!'

Mrs. Brennan came close to her daughter. Her face was white.
She was shaking.

They looked at one another and it was as though Dorothy
said: 'I love you. Don't be angry with me. There's nothing I
won't do for you. I, too, realize that something has happened.'

Mrs. Brennan looked out of the window, then turned and
left the room.

Dorothy felt an awful desolation. She had betrayed the trust
in her. She should have gone at once to the Cromwells' and
found Simon there. She ought to go now, but she did not, for
out of the window she saw Simon, his hand in that of old Wallace
the gardener, pointing excitedly to a bonfire beyond the lawn
that Wallace was making.

So Simon had not gone to the Cromwells'. Why had she not

tried to find him? Some anger in her mother's face had paralysed her, made her stupid.

She ran out of the room and found her mother, her hat still on, seated writing a letter. She flung her arms around her and kissed her.

'Mother, it's all right. Simon's out in the garden with Wallace. Shall I call him in?'

But her mother did not respond. Her lovely cheek was cold.

'Never mind, Dorothy. Never mind. But you ought to look after him better than that. Now run away, dear, I'm writing a letter.'

Dorothy went out and started walking down the road to Rafiel. One of those moments had come to her that come to all of us, when, without warning, the fancied walls of security are removed and life is revealed as a menacing enemy. Her mother did not care for her any more. Simon preferred the gardener. Gillie was in a dreadful state of rebellion. She did not know what to do, nor where to go. She was ice-bound by a dreadful loneliness. She could get at nobody: nobody could get at her.

Why had she said that Simon had gone to the Cromwells'? Why was she for ever thinking of the Cromwells? Why had her mother been so cold and unresponsive? Why was her mother angry with Gilbert? How could she bring the two of them together again?

She saw nothing as she walked. She knew that she was near to tears and was determined that she would not cry. She stopped for a moment and looked over the hedge to the faint early September sky, coloured around the sun with the burnished gold of the breast of a kingfisher. Everywhere else it was too brilliantly full of light to have colour. She looked at the sky, smelt the air, which seemed to her to have a cold blackberry freshness in it, and her unhappiness, her loneliness left her. Unhappiness belonged to the past, never the future.

She saw a cottage and someone picking flowers from the rose-bushes near the gate. The cottage was Copley's Cottage

and the lady picking flowers was Mrs. Mark. Dorothy did not
know whether she would pass on, and then Mrs. Mark saw her.
She straightened herself up and shaded her eyes against the burnished sky.

'Why, it's Dorothy Brennan.'

'Yes,' said Dorothy, smiling.

'Come in. Come in. And soon we'll have some tea.'

Dorothy came into the little garden and stood there rather
shyly. She did not know Mrs. Mark very well.

'Thank you. But I mustn't stay to tea. I've got to get back and
look after Simon.'

'Stay a minute or two anyway.' Mrs. Mark went into the
porch and produced two very faded deck-chairs. 'I think they'll
hold us. I found them here when I took over. It will be nice
to rest for five minutes. Aren't I lucky, looking on the road as
I do? I can pick up people like you as they go by.'

'Aren't the motors tiresome?'

'To be frank, I thought the motors would beat me. But they
don't. There are no corners just here and so they hoot scarcely
at all. And I've had the very worst of it, the real tourist time.
There'll be many less after September.' She leant forward. 'I'll
tell you a secret, Dorothy. No one else knows it. I rather like
to see people rushing about enjoying themselves.'

'I suppose when you were here as a child you were *very*
cut-off.'

'We were indeed. Going to the sea to Rafiel was a whole day's
expedition. We'd start off quite early in the morning, and Sleath
Hill was a terrible business. We went in every year to the Feast
in a waggonette, and how that waggonette creaked down the
hill; you could hear it miles away!'

'The Feast's all spoilt now. It's become all trippery.'

'Yes, and Rafiel's spoilt too, I expect. I dare not go there.
But as I remember going in to the Feast in March it used to
be so beautiful. In spite of the Methodist Chapel with 1870
stamped on it, there was the valley stream making little chuckling

noises. Then, before every house there was a garden filled at that time of the year with daffodils, primroses, hyacinths; there would be a forge full of fire, and then that sudden wonderful view of the sea! The bridge, the harbour, the houses rising one above the other on the rock. All so wild, and the Peak, guarding the little bay, the two streams tossing over the harbour ridges, and all the boats of the fishing fleet rocking as though to a dance-tune, and a flurry of gulls overhead. . . . No, no! I wouldn't dare go back. I don't believe I ever shall!'

'Yes, it's all spoilt,' Dorothy said mournfully, 'even I can see that! There's a great big garage in the middle of the village and "Ye Olde Tea Shoppes" everywhere, and "Bed and Breakfast" in every window. The motor-buses and cars are everywhere. Nobody minds, though—it doesn't matter if nobody minds, does it?'

'I don't know,' Mrs. Mark said. 'I never can be sure. It cuts both ways. Everyone can enjoy beautiful places now, but if too many people enjoy them they aren't beautiful places any more. So there you are!' She added: 'I must say, Garth isn't changed one scrap.'

'Oh, isn't it? I'm glad.'

'No. It's almost frightening. I walk about and find two lots of people with me all the time—the dead people and the living ones. The funny thing is that at present the dead people are very much more alive than the living ones. For I haven't got to know anyone here very well yet. Especially my sister Millie seems to be everywhere with me.'

'Did you love her very much?'

'Very much. She was delightful. I'll never forget the day she came back from Paris, where she had been living quite a long time. We were all waiting to receive her—it was in London—grandfather, our great-aunt in a white feather boa, father, mother, Henry, our two aunts, my dear Philip, and myself. That was before I had married Philip, of course. There she stood in the doorway, looking so lovely, the darling! I remember she was

wearing a smart black hat with a blue feather. I remember my
mother saying: "It must be nice to be home again, Millie dear."
That was so characteristic of all of us! We couldn't imagine but
that London and England, and especially our family, *must* be
nicer than any other country, town, or family in the world.
And when Mother said that, I caught a look in Millie's eyes
which showed me that she was cosmopolitan now, that she'd
never be the same again as she was before she went away! . . .
Oh dear, it is as though it were yesterday. . . . And then she
and I went up to her room alone together. And at once she
asked me about Philip, whom, of course, she'd never seen before.
"My dear, who's that nice-looking man?" That's what she
said! And I was so pleased that she called him nice-looking. Oh
dear, and I'm over sixty and they are all gone—all gone!' Her
eyes were dim. She blew her nose.

Dorothy was enchanted. No one had ever talked to her like
this before. Mrs. Mark spoke to her as though she were grown-up
and, better than that, as though she trusted her.

'I'm longing to grow up,' she said, 'really grow up. Of course
I'm proud of helping Mother, though. Were you proud of helping your mother?'

'No. I'm afraid I wasn't. Not after Philip appeared. You
wait, my dear, until suddenly somebody——'

'Oh, I shall never be married,' Dorothy said. 'I've got to look
after Gillie and Simon until they go to College, anyway, and
then there are so many things to do in the house. We haven't
very much money, you know. You mustn't tell anyone—although
I suppose everyone in the village is fully aware of the fact!'
Dorothy shook her head. 'Don't you think it's a shame that Father
should be paid so little when he works so hard? Anyway it's
a shame for Mother, and I know she felt it the other day when
we went to that lovely picnic. I'd never seen such lovely food
in my life before—nor had Gillie and Simon.'

'Yes, it *was* a nice picnic,' Mrs. Mark said.

Dorothy, now thoroughly happy, went on: 'Isn't it strange

what a difference Mr. Cromwell has made to everybody by just coming to live here?'

'What kind of a difference?'

'Everyone's changed. I don't know why. Simon, for instance, has gone simply mad about him. We can't keep him at home. He goes slipping off and just turns up at the Cromwells' house. Isn't it awful, when they haven't asked him or anything? I thought at first it was Jim Burke he was after. He's working there now. But it isn't. It's Mr. Cromwell. He's simply fascinated by him.' Her forehead was puckered. She sighed. 'The boys are a terrible responsibility.'

'Are they?'

'Yes, you see—Gillie's sweet but he believes everything I say, and I often say the wrong thing. And now——'

She paused.

'Oh, well, I don't know whether I ought to say anything. But I've been very worried and there isn't anybody——'

Katherine Mark laid her hand for a moment on Dorothy's knee.

'I'm such an old woman you can tell me anything. You don't know how many secrets I've had to keep in my time!'

'No, I expect you have,' Dorothy said, looking at her with intense admiration. 'It all began the day Simon saw Mr. Cromwell for the first time. He saw him walking in the village and when I told him he was blind he couldn't get over it. And at the same time'—Dorothy nodded her head at this as though it were terribly important—'I saw the postman going into our house and he had a letter from some people asking Gillie to spend the day with them at Rafiel. Gillie wanted to go most dreadfully, because they were the father and mother of his best friend, but Mother had arranged to take Gillie into Polchester that same day to have his new suit tried on. In the ordinary way Gillie would have gone with Mother, but this time he wouldn't change and Mother was awfully hurt.'

'Why was she hurt?' Katherine Mark asked.

'Well, of course she was! Gillie ought to have done what she wanted.'

'Couldn't she have changed her day for going into Polchester?'

'That's what she did do, but even then Gillie was sulky about it and wouldn't thank her or anything. And he hasn't been the same since. Mother's most awfully hurt. And I feel in a sort of way it's my fault.'

'No, of course it isn't your fault.'

'Well, I don't know. You see, Mother expects me to look after the boys. It's my job. I love Gillie more than anybody except Father and Mother and Simon, of course.'

'I see. Can't your father do anything about it?'

'No. Father's always so dreadfully busy.'

'I see.'

There was a little pause. Then Dorothy said:

'Mrs. Mark, what makes the real difference between people?'

'How do you mean?'

'It seems to me that, although people are all different from each other, of course, there's another difference. I can't explain.'

'I think the great difference is whether people are generous-hearted or not. I don't mean whether people just give money away or not, but whether their hearts are generous or mean. Whether they'll take risks and be generous in ideas, in love, in trust, in optimism, in not wanting to own the people they love, in defending their friends if they're attacked—ready to lose their souls, you know, unselfishly, and so gain them. Some people, although they seem very pleasant, are mean and greedy. They won't give away a thing. They won't have a generous view about anything. They want to assert their power. They want to be safe and rich. They're cautious about everything. I think that's the *real* difference in human beings. Of course some people are clever and some are stupid, some are well educated and some are not, some are beautiful and some are ugly, some are lucky and some unlucky. But none of that *really* matters. It's the generous-hearted who see God—now, just as it was thousands of

years ago.' She laughed. 'There, my dear, I've been preaching a
sermon, but you asked me, you know.'

'Thank you very much,' Dorothy said warmly. 'I'd never
thought of that.' She got up and looked gravely in front of her.
'I'm afraid *I'm* not very generous-hearted, but I shall try to be.
. . . Oh, damn! There's a ladder in my stocking!' She twisted
her head to see the back of her leg. 'And I shouldn't have said
"Damn," either.'

Mrs. Mark kissed her.

'I shouldn't worry about that. I'm so glad I caught you. Come
and see me whenever you like.'

'Oh yes, I will. . . . Thanks most awfully.'

She was rather shy, as she always was when she felt anything
deeply. When she was in the road she looked back and waved
her hand.

She had made a new friend. When she thought of her friends
she always began with Jim Burke. After that she was at a loss,
not because she had no other friends, but because·she liked everyone in general and no one in particular.

She thought everyone was 'awfully nice.' She smiled, and they
smiled. She said, 'Isn't the weather horrid?' or 'What a ripping
day!' and they said, grinning, 'Yes, dear,' or, if they were of the
village, 'Yes, miss' or 'Yes, Miss Dorothy.'

Walking along she discovered this curious fact—that she had
no friends. You couldn't call Miss Vergil one, or Mrs. Lamplough,
or Mr. Ironing, or Phyllis Lock, or Mrs. Boss the butcher's wife,
or Mr. Teak the stationer. She liked them as, until now, she had
liked everything and everybody. But now—what had happened
to her?

She stood looking about her, as though she were seeing a new
world. On the day of the picnic something . . . something . . .
She recalled things. She remembered Jim Burke saying he would
make her something really good one day. And she remembered
looking across the table-cloth while they were having tea and

noticing that Simon had his hand on Mr. Cromwell's knee. Her impulse had been to go quietly and take Simon away, but there had been something in Mr. Cromwell's expression, in his gazing, abstracted face, his yellow hair, his large, strong, casual body, that had caught her imagination. He *liked* Simon to be there, and he was moving, because of his blindness, in some wonderful country where none of those around him could follow him.

So she, at that moment when Jim Burke had looked at her, at *this* moment in the garden with Mrs. Mark, had begun to move into some new country. New forces were stirring in her—forces that made her feel radiantly happy, so that she could sing and dance down the road, and hug the first person who came along.

A gate from a field opened and shut with a click and, turning, she saw a man. Was he a man or a boy? A man. Wearing a rather shabby mackintosh that reached to his feet. He moved with an odd quick shuffle and she saw that his face was pale and sharp, with small restless eyes.

All these things she noticed because at once, without thought or reason, she hated him. So badly did she hate him that she looked and saw that she had yet quite a piece of country road to cover before the outskirts of the village began.

He shuffled along and spoke to her.

'Fine day, miss!'

'Yes,' she said, looking straight in front of her.

'I've been for a walk—over the fields and far away!' He half sang the last part of the sentence. He had a husky speaking voice, as though he were always a little breathless.

'I say, miss, you might tell me. I haven't been here long. Are you resident here?'

'Yes, I am.'

He dropped his voice confidentially. He was walking quite close to her.

'Why, to tell you the truth, miss, I know who you are. I won't try to deceive you. Why should I? You're the Rector's daughter —the Reverend Mr. Brennan. That's right, isn't it?'

'Yes, I am. If you don't mind, I'm in a hurry.'

'That's all right, miss, I quite understand. But you might tell me all the same if you know of any job round here.'

'No, I don't.'

'I'm very adaptable. I am really. I can sing *and* dance, I've been on the Halls. It's truth I'm telling you, and my turn was popular too. But it's wearing work. Always on the move. So I thought I'd settle here for a bit—quiet-like.'

He was so close to her that she thought for a horrible moment that he would put his hand on her arm. His teeth were bad and a faint breath came from him like the distant odour of bad cheese.

She was walking so fast that she was almost running, but he kept pace with her very easily, shuffling along and now and then giving a little skip.

'I could be a servant to a gentleman. Perhaps your reverend father could do with some assistance. Or I could write his letters for him. I'm handy at letters.' He drew in his breath with a little whistling sound. 'Your father would like me. I'm a wonder for stories and I'd always respect the cloth. Oh, I know what's what. I've been about the world a bit. One day, if you care for it, miss, I'll do my song and dance for you, same as I do on the Halls!'

How she hated him! He was to her like something out of a dream. In another moment he would touch her. He must not, he must not!

Someone passed them slowly on a bicycle. It was Jim Burke! She cried out: 'Jim! Jim!' He looked back, he got off his bicycle and came towards her, grinning. The strange man touched his hat, muttered something, and shuffled off to the other side of the road.

Jim reached her side.

'Hullo! What are *you* doing?'

She was breathless. She caught his arm, pressed it as though to thank him, then dropped it again.

'Oh, Jim, I'm so glad! . . . No, it's nothing. But that strange man spoke to me and I didn't like him!'

'Did he, by blazes!'

Jim Burke looked after him.

'No. He didn't do any harm. He only asked me if I knew of any job anywhere. He says he's staying in the village.'

'He won't be here long if he makes trouble. I'll see to that!'

She was perfectly happy again, walking along beside him.

'How are you, Jim? Do you like it at the Cromwells'?'

'Certainly I do. He's a grand man, he is truly.'

'And what's she like?'

'Oh, she's funny. A bit wild, I fancy. But I like her all right.'

'I'm very glad. That means you'll be staying here.'

'I'll be staying if *you* want me to!'

Dorothy laughed. 'Of course I do. We all want you to. We missed you like anything when you were away.'

'Did *you* miss me?'

'Of course I did.'

'That's fine. How's your father?'

'He's all right. There's *such* a lot to do in the village.'

'I bet there is. I'll be coming in to have a chat with him one day.'

They had reached the first houses. He got on to his bicycle, waved his hand, and rode ahead.

CHAPTER VII

Garth House: In Julius' Study

JULIUS CROMWELL'S JOURNAL

September 5.—I began a Journal once, I remember, in hospital when I was well enough to amuse myself. I had just learned that I would be blind as long as I lived. I wasn't unhappy. It seemed an exciting new experience and everybody was so kind to me. I was revelling in a new sense of touch. There was a nurse whose hands were miraculous. I daresay she was hideous. I never knew. But I remember touching the cool firm edge of her palm and the sensation was as exciting as though I had all her body in my arms. I remember thinking: 'I shan't go searching now for women who are beautiful and finding them but rarely. Any woman who is kind and has smooth skin and isn't too fat and soft . . .' I was very young. I was young enough to have said to Alfredson: 'I'm beginning to believe Beethoven has been over-praised,' just before I took that moment's look over the top and got the bullet that blinded me. I was awfully well that day. No indigestion. No constipation. Light in the eyes, the mouth, the heart, the bowels. . . . Light! My God. Light! For the very last time. Had I only known, I would have taken in every last detail of that hateful desert, the blue sky and the filthy soil. Every last grain of dust I would have taken in.

Now I'm writing melodrama. 'Take it quietly, my son,' is what the doctor said before he operated. I did and I will.

I have always wanted to write. That's why I keep this Journal. I've read almost nothing in the last twenty years. I hate being read to. Reading Braille is somehow for me not amusing. The writer in Braille has to be so damned swell. Shakespeare, Dickens, and a Braille anthology of poetry. But I have found that there are other things I enjoy more.

I kept up the other Journal for a long time. I was twenty years younger then. I stopped when I married. I used to tell Elinor everything, so why write? After her death I began again, and went on until I met Celia. Then I stopped. I was too happy to go on. Now I've begun again. Does that mean, then, that I'm unhappy? No. That something's wrong? Not quite. But nearly. It isn't working out as I expected. This house isn't. Celia isn't. I'm not.

What is happening?

Well, then, to begin with, I am in a way obsessed by my blindness. After twenty years I perhaps oughtn't to be. But, in a way,

I am obsessed more than I was twenty years ago, and I believe that that is true of everyone who is blind, whether they will admit it or no.

I have repeated *in a way* because *that* is the point.

What kind of a man was I before the War? Not a man, but a boy. Physically very strong and loving to excel at games, keeping myself fit for them, never having a woman, drinking very little, that ascetic corporeal life whose origins are Greek, whose business development is British.

But I felt, behind this, that I was some sort of an artist. I never mentioned this to anybody except when once, a boy of fourteen at Eton, in love with Headley, I told him. And how he laughed! He shamed me out of a lot of it, but not out of music. Young as I was I realized that neither he nor anyone else could touch that. And yet I refused to learn the piano. I think I had a sort of fore-knowledge that I'd only be a tenth-rate amateur and that that was a sort of insult to Beethoven and Bach. The same with writing. I remember that I got an alpha plus at Eton for an essay on 'Cromwell after Naseby.' For a little while I thought that I would be an historian or a novelist. No. There again, an insult to Shakespeare, Keats, and Cervantes.

Queerly enough, I never cared very much about reading. And then I had all my games—Squash, Tennis, Rugger—good fun while it lasted.

I didn't mind the War, did I? Honestly I liked the reality of it —the reality of friendship, comradeship, fear, boredom. I was planning what I would do after it. I knew that I would have plenty of money through my father's steel. Money made out of war. I planned to create a kind of perfect workman's Paradise. To give myself heart and soul to that, to bring up my sons to the true Utopian Socialism. And I would marry a woman who cared also for those things.

September 8.—The greatest division between men is, I think, whether they are conscious of their individuality or no. I'm sure that we'll be fighting for this same individuality sooner or later, so we may as well be aware of what it means.

If I were not blind I should scarcely have time to stop and think, and so it is, I suspect, with millions of people everywhere, but *being* blind there's almost nothing that I like so much. For blindness has placed me for twenty years altogether apart from other men. Only Elinor and Lizzie Gayner in my whole world have understood that they must come to me. I cannot go to them. This is not egotism or conceit. It is a law. It is as though I were in a cage. This Celia cannot understand.

But it is a cage that, for myself (and only myself), opens into a new world of light and infinity. I have for twenty years now been constantly tempted to explore this new mysterious world that my blindness has opened for me. I go a little way and then retrace my steps, *because the further I go the more deeply removed I am from those I love.* I have underlined this (a little crookedly I expect) because this is the cause of the trouble between Celia and me. We love one another, but she wants to possess me totally. My blindness eludes her. Both her heart and her pride are frightened. . . .

September 11.—There has been a stupid little scene. I suppose Celia and I are in the wrong. For some weeks now little Simon Brennan, aged eight, has taken it into his head to come over here. The fact is that ever since a day when I gave a picnic by Sizyn Church I have fascinated him.

It began with his surprise at my blindness. He did not conceive it possible that there could be anyone who could not see. Then I became fond of him. I always liked children, but after my blindness they became very dear to me, for the tactfulness, the thoughtfulness of children to me is astonishing. It is one of the things for which I am most grateful.

Simon has been like a kitten or a puppy tumbling over me. He turns up quite suddenly. I hear his voice at my knee. 'Hullo, Mr. Cromwell!' For some reason or other he always declares himself in a whisper as though we had some kind of mysterious

pact together. I say 'Hullo.' He then climbs on to my thigh with
my assistance and kisses me. I understand that in general he hates
to kiss or be kissed, but he kisses me enquiringly, with a kind of
lingering wonder as to whether I am really true flesh and blood.
Then I put him down and he begins on his own affairs, happy
and independent.

I hear him hissing or chuckling and he will suddenly say something like: 'Cheese is twopence today, Mr. Brown.' Once I
overheard him indignantly come out with 'You dirty bastard,' so
I chided him, asked him where he heard such things. Apparently
from Jim Burke. I asked him did he know what the word meant.
He said, of course he did, and that a bastard was a bird that lived
in hot countries and waited until you were dead to pick your
bones. 'A dirty bird! A dirty bird!' he went round the room
shouting as a kind of warlike challenge.

Celia and I, honestly, are already devoted to him. He has an
honest courageous independence beyond all praise. We'll have
one like him ourselves one day. We've done wrong, though, to
keep him, not to send him home. For myself, I supposed that he
came with the full approval of his parents. Not so, however.

Yesterday afternoon about three he arrived, kissed me and
went off with Jim Burke into the garden. Half an hour later
Celia had given me a hug, preparatory to going off to tea with
the Ironings, was making sure that I was all right, when—Mrs.
Brennan is announced.

She comes in full sail. I could tell at once from the little sounds
she made that she was indignant, and I couldn't help thinking of
the arrival of Mr. and Miss Murdstone in Betsey Trotwood's
cottage.

'Where's Simon?' she said at once, as though we had kidnapped
him. I did the wrong thing. I laughed.

She turned on me. 'It's all very well for you to laugh, Mr.
Cromwell, but it is really past a joke. The child is always disap-
pearing, without a word to any of us, and it's here that he comes.'

I was at once apologetic and conciliatory. I said that we had done very ill, but that in fact we thought that he came here with his parents' knowledge. He liked the house and the garden.

'Not at all,' she broke in. 'It's you that he likes, Mr. Cromwell. He's mad about you.' Everything might then have been well. She approves of me for some reason or other. But Celia burst in with something about our naturally supposing that Mrs. Brennan knew where he was. We should never imagine that so young a child would be allowed to wander off just as he pleased.

And that set Mrs. Brennan off. Mrs. Cromwell hadn't any children and therefore would naturally not understand the modern child. Then the two ladies were at it, icily polite, their voices packed with dynamite. In the middle of this, Simon innocently arrived with his cheerful sentence about 'the dirty bastard.' It was of no use my saying that he thought it was a bird. The damage was done. Mrs. Brennan dragged Simon away and Celia made herself sick with laughing.

The real pity is that we shan't have Simon any more. If he does arrive he must be sent at once home again.

September 13.—Sitting alone and thinking, I have a number of what seem to me marvellous convictions. For instance, that the Saint is the only human being that knows real happiness. That if only I can become unselfish enough, undetached enough, I will solve the mystery of living. It is there waiting for me. I know the key that will unlock it. I possess the key and yet I am too lazy or too preoccupied to apply it. That love of one's fellow man, of one's enemies, of the people that bore one, is essential if one is to learn anything about life at all.

I write these down and they are the oldest platitudes. All in the New Testament, put much better. And yet, as I sit here alone, and one of them hits me, I'm inclined to jump up and shout: 'By Jove—*that's* what it all means!' as one does under an anaesthetic. It's as though someone were for ever whispering in your ear: 'Come on. Stir your stumps. Start on your journey. *Why* don't you start?'

September 14.—Old Lamplough in to tea today. A rum old

bird, always speaking as though his mouth were full of cold potato. He told me today that his great private pleasure is Shake-
spearian research. He tells no one of it. He has volume after volume of notes but intends never to publish any of it. He delves in
the obscurer plays. None of your *Hamlets* for him. No. He has
been more than a year now over *The Two Gentlemen of Verona.*
He is at present delving into the psychology of Proteus! Hard
gemlike flame of austere scholarship for its own sake.

He told me he had been reading a recently published autobiography of a great scientist. A long book, some six hundred
pages, for many years eagerly expected by the world. But the
scientist says almost nothing of his discoveries, his adventures
with scandalized Puritans, his correspondence with other scien-
tists, his friendships with his fellow pioneers, but for five hundred
pages maunders on about his love for his second-rate, hysterical,
domineering wife, giving many silly love letters, praising her
madly but obviously finding much more comfort and happiness
with her successor! This is Lamplough's disgusted description.

How well, though, I can understand the fellow! Were Celia
dead and I a great man writing my autobiography it would be
filled with Celia. What achievement, what discovery, what
acquaintance with great men can compare for a single instant
with a great love? Now about Elinor there would be in my
autobiography very little. Yet how good she was, how happy we
were, how she guarded and protected me, how grateful I was
and am!

It was, I suppose, just because this wife of his was difficult and
unsatisfactory and hysterical that the scientist was obsessed by
her, never reaching the peace and security that he thought he
longed for.

So with Celia. She is *not* second-rate. She has something in her
of the finest and noblest. But I have perhaps done her the greatest injustice by marrying her. I am for ever haunted by this. Too
young she was to realize what marriage to a blind man must
mean. Only now, since we came to this house, is she beginning

to realize it. Most truly does she love *me* but *not* my blindness. That she *hates*. She is too young, too vital to be intimate with any impotence, any disfigurement. She loves me all the more because I am blind, but she cannot *cohabit* with my blindness. She loves to protect, to mother me, but *at the same time* she wants me to be free, to be a strong able man and *to be always with her in spirit*. I escape her when I am adventuring into the world that my blindness has made for me and *that only blind men can enter*.

She doesn't analyse any of this. She is too young to analyse. She only knows what she wants, what she feels. At present she is an egotist because of her youth. The only egotists who are disgusting are the mature egotists. Perhaps mature egotism, whatever achievements it leads to, is the real sin against the Holy Ghost.

Elinor understood my inevitable *apartness*. So does Lizzie Gayner. And I *think* the nice Mrs. Mark who once lived in this house. But that is because they have all deeply suffered. Celia has not *suffered* in any deep sense at all. She has only sometimes been frustrated or been made to wait. Everything has yet to happen to her, and it is through me that it will happen. Sometimes, when I am depressed, I think it may be ruin for us both if we are *both* not fine enough.

I am amused with myself for being as bad as Queen Victoria in underlining, and I daresay that my lines go right through the words, making it all null and void.

No matter. This Journal has a lock and key. *No eyes* will ever read these words. I cannot tell, looking back, what I have written. It clears my brain, though—the double brain, the seeing brain that is blind, the blind brain that is beginning to see new things.

September 18.—A morning of the most desperate depression yesterday. I was removed, far removed, from all human beings. I wanted none of them.

Celia as yet cannot leave me alone. If I am lost and bewildered and away from everyone, she thinks that it is with her that I am hurt. It must be with *her* that I am hurt!

And so last night I told her, having her in my arms, that she must realize, once and for all, that I am *maimed* for life, that when that bullet hit me it not only killed my sight but also did me some general damage—my soul, my mind, my body. Upon that she protested that it was not so, that it was exactly that morbid idea of myself that I must conquer. That I *brooded* and was too much alone thinking about myself. That she would take me out of myself, wouldn't allow me to brood, and so on. That I listened all by myself to that stupid music far too much. That I was far too self-centred, and that often she must say things twice over before I would answer her. She *hated* to see me sitting in my chair, not speaking, not smiling. If I allowed myself to brood it would grow on me. And so on. Oh God, and so on!

Very quietly, and I hope lovingly, I tried to show her that it was *not* brooding nor melancholy, but only love of following my own thoughts. That I had been blind for twenty years now and that naturally I lived often inside my own mind, but that my doing so did not mean that I loved her less or was angry or unhappy.

She made love to me then with a kind of ferocity, as though she was determined to make sure that I was really there. Did she, after all, make sure? Is skin and bone enough?

My depression yesterday morning was a return of the mood that I got sometimes in the trenches—that we all got—that the war was going on for ever—but really for ever as far as our personal lives were concerned—year after year, and year after year, and we, all of us, at last dead. Some few survivors perhaps advancing out of the trenches, half blinded, into the devastated open.

Jim Burke reads for an hour every morning bits out of the papers for me. He does it very well, with sense and humour. I can see very clearly that another world war is inevitable and that it will be more devastating than the last, simply because, for all of us, our resources will be fewer. After a year or two our civilization really will be smashed. And then what? And why so horrified? It has happened often enough before.

But what a fate! A blind man sitting in his chair as chaos creeps like a fog across the garden towards him. I thought of Celia, so lovely, so young—and perhaps our son. But beyond them this lovely world that I still see in retrospect, night skies scattered with stars, and the line of the foam on a marbled shore, and this first musty-cold scent of chrysanthemums.

I was in despair all morning. I sat there with my hands folded waiting for some kind of sound announcing destruction.

And then Celia rushed in and thrust a chrysanthemum under my nose and my hand closed about that wet, papery texture. . . . That other tug at my brain began to work. 'Follow me. Let yourself go. There's a solution to all this and the solution is in yourself. Be yourself enough and lose yourself in love of others, and chaos is meaningless. Chaos is the background. The movement is all with *you*, not with civilization. You *are* civilization, and your sons and your sons' sons.'

Celia at lunch said that she was wearing a fawn jacket with ruby buttons, and that she had put it on for me. She was right. I could *see* the buttons and the jacket open on either side of her neck, and her curls on her round hard boy's head, and the chrysanthemums, pale, she told me, almost the colour of wash-leather gloves, and my happiness sailed up like a fish from translucent depths, cleaving its path like a knife, and then feeling the sun between its fins.

I catch her hands: I feel her standing, her heart thumping. I know her eyes are on my face, serious, enquiring like a child's. I hold her close to me, her head against my beating heart. Our two selves meet then as scattered mercury runs to one piece. Our lips cannot separate, for our conscious selves are not there to tell them to part, but are far away lying dreaming together in an ecstasy. Celia, Celia, at such times I am not afraid of my age, my blindness, my lonely questioning pursuit. . . .

September 22.—Sometimes Celia and I are both together and at the same time completely childish. There is an extraordinary

lightness that comes from light or good digestion, or a fine sleep.
I don't know.

Celia has the gift especially. Even though she had been having a
row with someone half an hour before, she will quite suddenly
throw it off completely. I never knew anyone who begs pardon
and says she is sorry so easily—a thing I find it dreadfully hard
to do. She has one of the finest gifts the gods can give us—the
ability to see the other person's point of view. 'You were quite
right to be upset about that.' She has no meanness or sulkiness.
She simply falls out of one mood into another with no self-
consciousness whatever.

The day began with the sudden appearance of Simon Brennan.
He stood in his blue smock quietly beside Celia quite a long
time without her realizing it. She was writing letters before going
into the village. When she saw him she tried to scold him
severely, and said he must go straight back home again. Upon
which he whispered to her confidentially that his mother and
Dorothy had gone to Polchester for the day to see Gilbert back
to school and do some shopping.

So there seemed to be no harm in leaving him with me for the
morning. As usual he amused himself with old volumes of the
Illustrated London News. He lies, I understand, flat on his
stomach on the floor and then describes to me the pictures.

For instance: 'There's three ladies with very big dresses giving
a dog some sugar. There's a clock and fans on the wall, and a tree
in a pot. The room's ever so full.'

He believes that he is performing a very useful function for
me—*making me see*.

I was still under the influence of Celia's lightheartedness or I
would have been distressed perhaps by two things.

Lizzie Gayner came in about the housekeeping accounts and I
realized that something was wrong—*has* been wrong, in fact, for
a fortnight or more. How do I realize this? for she has said
nothing. In voice or movement, but especially in something that
is *scent* more than voice or movement, Lizzie has for many years

represented to me a kind of dried, ageing, immensely clean, good health. Her breath has the very faintest odour of dry hay, a little peppermint which is her tooth-powder. Then there is the starched cleanliness of her linen. Is there scent in a smile? Of course there is. It is as though the mouth took a step forward and the breath fanned your cheeks ever so slightly.

For a fortnight now Lizzie has not smiled. Now and then there is a tremble in her voice. Her hand is hot and the pulse beats in it. Something is greatly distressing her. I felt it especially this morning.

After she was gone Jim Burke came in and said quite abruptly: 'I expect I'll be off on my travels again very shortly, sir.'

It was a great shock to me. I thought he was very happy and contented with us. Simon was there, still faithfully reporting to me on the *Illustrated*, so I couldn't say anything. Anyway I wouldn't. But I asked him why.

'Just restless again.'

'Perhaps you'd better go,' I said. 'You're beginning to be useful to me. I don't want to be dependent on anyone.'

'Do you mean that, sir?' he asked, with a quick catch of the voice.

'Yes, I mean it.'

Then he began a long, silly, impetuous business about being weak, no good, biting the hand that fed him.

I dislike people to run themselves down. But I laughed and asked him whether he was robbing me.

'I might,' he said, 'I might.' And then he went off.

Finally Celia. She was full of things she had seen. Nothing is ever too unimportant or dull for her. But she must have someone to share it. She cannot bear to be alone about anything.

She had seen the oddest man in the village, in an old waterproof. He had three mongrel dogs at his heels. He spoke to her, saying that dogs were better than humans any day. He said that he was a music-hall performer staying in the village.

She was sucking a brandy-ball. She had a whole bag of them. Her lips were sticky when she kissed me.

CHAPTER VIII

At the Lamploughs'—The Moor—Misty Afternoon —At Garth House

CELIA WAS KINDLY by an instinct as natural as breathing. Just as when she was in a temper she wished to hurt her adversary by any means, however illegal, in her power, so when she felt kindly she would go to any distance, take any trouble, give anything away.

Her tempers were transitory, her kindnesses remarkably lasting. She was only unkind when she was unhappy or frightened or unable to deal with circumstances. She always wanted 'everything to be all right.' She expected, as a sort of justice, a perpetually happy tranquil world and, although her own generation told her again and again that, because of the older generation and a ridiculous monstrous War, everything was wrong, nobody was happy, the only mood was one of grasping selfish cynicism, she did not in her heart believe this. It *ought* to be a happy world. . . .

But about her kindliness there was no reasoning at all. If someone was ill, or had no money, or had lost some friend or lover, then Celia rushed off to help and never asked herself whether she were wanted or whether she *could* help, or whether she understood the psychology of the trouble.

So when she heard that poor Mrs. Lamplough had missed pneumonia by a breath and was weak and devastated after a sort of bronchial influenza, she hurried off to the Lamplough mansion, bearing two bottles of wine, a bag of tangerines, and a bottle of brandy-balls, the last a cure, to her mind, of every conceivable ill.

She did not really *like* Mrs. Lamplough very much: she knew that she was a wicked old gossip, and a liar of a fearful kind . . . still she had done Celia no harm, and it was entertaining to hear her talk about other people, and had she caught pneumonia she would almost certainly have died.

Mrs. Lamplough was delighted to see Celia; she was still in bed. Celia stood in the doorway bearing her gifts and sniffing with her nose. The room had that odour of camphorated oil, scent, and flannel that belongs to a lady's sick-chamber when she isn't very ill. The room was pretty but oppressively hot. Sitting up in a pink bed-jacket, wearing a white cap with a pink bow, her face soft and crumpled like a rosy apple pudding, her little eyes sparkling, rouge on her lips and rings on her boneless fingers, was Mrs. Lamplough.

Her voice was always of the soft and whispering kind, but to-day, because of her bronchial troubles, it was even more so. She asked Celia to come over and sit beside the bed as though she were about to tell her a most improper story. It was not out of her power to do so—but never with anyone whom she knew so slightly as Mrs. Julius Cromwell.

Celia, who loved to give people things, even when they hadn't the least desire for them, explained her presents.

'I would have come before, but oddly enough I knew nothing about it. You've been in bed a week, haven't you? What a shame! I brought you the tangerines, but don't eat them if you don't like them. Their advantage is that the skins take off so easily, and the disadvantage that they're full of pits. Julius sends the two bottles of port. He says they'll cure you in a day or two. And I added the brandy-balls, because I never can resist them if I'm ill. We have them sent down from Fortnum's. If your throat's sore, or you have a cough, they're perfect. There! I'll put them down on the table!'

Mrs. Lamplough caught Celia's hand in hers.

'That's sweet of you,' she whispered. 'You oughtn't to have bothered.'

'Does it hurt you to talk?'

'Not a bit! It does me good. I was only telling Henry this morning that I want a good talk with someone. I like to hear all the news, you know, although I don't believe in gossip, not malicious gossip.'

'No. Nor do I,' Celia said. 'At least, it's very difficult to tell where it *begins* to be malicious, don't you think?'

'Oh, I think one can *always* tell,' whispered Mrs. Lamplough. 'Never say anything you wouldn't like the other person to hear.'

'Oh, I don't know. That's *very* severe. We all say things about one another that aren't unkind exactly but that we wouldn't like other people to hear. I don't mind anyone saying what they like about me!'

'You don't?'

'No. Not as long as I don't know about it. What I don't hear doesn't worry me.'

Mrs. Lamplough settled herself in against her pillows. She had the face of an old baby who was waiting to be mischievous. Nevertheless her eyes were grave and she never let herself go in merriment. Although she swallowed greedily all that you had to tell her, she was intent on the next question that she would ask you. You could see her hanging all her questions on a sort of mental clothes-line. She liked a joke or a tall story. One of her favourite sentences, as she pressed confidentially your hand, was: 'My dear, I'm unshockable.' This, she explained, was because she had French ancestors.

She was always intensely sympathetic with her immediate confidant, always sharing his or her point of view, even though she abandoned temporarily other confidants. 'I know, dear,' she would say. 'I know. As a matter of fact, S. told me only last week that the real trouble is morphia. Yes, dear, I know it's horrible, but that would account for her being so queer the day you went there.'

She had, in fact, built up her life on the astonishing truth that people, while believing any horrors about other people, never face the fact that they themselves are discussed with the same ruthless devastation. Mrs. Lamplough made every friend feel a privileged listener. She enveloped her friends, when they were with her, in a sort of cocoon of false confidence, winding it round and round with her gentle whispers, her boneless fingers, her little pats and chuckles, and serious, rather melancholy eyes. She added to her innocent kindliness by the fact that she could not pronounce her *r*'s very firmly.

With all this she intended no harm, wished everyone well, loved her friends. It was Nature's intention that she should be at the centre of things—should notice more, hear more, have more wisdom about human beings than the ordinary man or woman. She meant no harm to anyone. Indeed, she often wondered why others were not as kindly, tolerant, indulgent, as herself.

She proceeded now to wind her cocoon round Celia, who looked very young with a little blue coal-scuttle hat perched on her dark curls, her pretty face smiling, her small body perched on the edge of a chair.

'And how are you liking it, my dear? Are you really *settled in?*'

Mrs. Lamplough gave a soft emphatic pressure to certain words as though she were digging them down as evidences, later on, of the plot she was constructing.

'Yes, thank you. It's all very nice.'

'And your husband?'

'Oh, Julius is very happy. Although he can't *see* the places, having been here as a child makes it all so real to him.'

'I suppose it does. We're all *so* excited about your being here, you know!'

'Oh, are you? I can't see anything very exciting about *us—* especially about *me!*'

Mrs. Lamplough's eyes sparkled.

'Your being *rich* is one thing. We haven't had anyone here with a penny in anyone's memory.'

Celia smiled.

'Even Mr. Brennan is waking up a little. I'm sure he's been asking your husband for all sorts of things.'

'No, I don't think he has. We're not, I'm afraid, very religious. That is, we don't go to church. And Mrs. Brennan doesn't like *me* very much.'

When Celia made this last remark it was exactly as though she had plopped a ripe, very sweet plum straight into Mrs. Lamplough's mouth.

'Oh, really! What makes you think that?'

'Everyone knows she doesn't.'

'That's because she's jealous.' Mrs. Lamplough nodded her head with infinite pleasure. 'She's been a kind of queen here for a long time. Silly old maids like Miss Vergil have flattered her to death.'

'Unfortunately,' said Celia, 'her small boy has taken a great fancy to my husband and will come round to visit us unknown to his mother. She came round to fetch him one day and was quite rude.'

'She was, was she?' said Mrs. Lamplough quite eagerly. 'She was *rude*, was she?'

The lady raised herself, leant a little towards Celia, and her hand descended on to Celia's. It was hot, formless, like a little muffin.

'One thing,' she said eagerly, 'I rather wonder at your husband doing was to engage that wastrel Jim Burke.'

'Oh,' Celia said, staring at her, 'he seems all right. Julius likes him.'

'All right! When he was with the Ironings what he didn't do! . . . However, it's really no business of mine.'

'What sort of things?'

'Well—no woman was safe from him, for one thing.'

Celia laughed. 'That was the fault of the woman I should think. Women can be safe if they want to be.'

Mrs. Lamplough delightedly pursed her lips. 'I'm not one for scandal. Again and again I used to stand up for him. But at the last—there was the maid at the Ironings' going to have a baby and——'

Celia laughed again. 'Anyway he's not dangerous in *our* house. Old Mrs. Gayner looks after the maids like a demon.'

'Does she? Does she?' Mrs. Lamplough drew in her breath. 'That's good, because your husband can't see what's going on and you're very young—much younger than he is. And he's so fascinating. That silly Phyllis Lock is madly in love with him . . . not that that matters . . . anything in trousers . . .'

Celia said: 'I don't feel that he's so much older. I love him so terribly.'

'Do you? Do you, my dear?'

Her hand now was clasped tightly.

'Yes. Of course I do. I'd been brought up to think that no one was any good, that fine character was a thing to laugh at. He's too fine for me—that's the trouble.'

'Is he? Is he?' Mrs. Lamplough whispered.

'I am always so afraid that I'm going to disappoint him. He trusts me too much. You know, someone who's blind is different from other people. He has to take a lot on trust. In our house——'

'Yes. In your house——?'

Celia had forgotten Mrs. Lamplough. She had been thinking of Julius, of their life together, of her own fears. She came back to another realization with a start—a realization that was visual rather than anything else—a picture of Julius and herself sitting in the lamplight close together, the dark walls safely about them, and Mrs. Lamplough was at the window, peering in, eagerly peering in. They were threatened, they were watched, they were overheard. Something evil was trying to get into the house.

She released her hand.

'I must be off. I should have a glass of that port right away.'

'Perhaps I will. It has been so *very* interesting, what you have told me. We are all so much interested.' She pulled a little at the pink bows in her cap. 'It has been the sweetest thing your coming in to see me like that. You've cheered me up wonderfully. Yes, and given me a lot of things to think about!'

Celia climbed into her Austin and drove straight out to the Moor, which was not what she had intended to do. It was yet early afternoon, a day of golden quivering mist, an early autumn day when there is a suspension of sound, so that, hearing a cart rattle on the unseen road, you almost put your finger to your lip and whisper, 'Wait. Wait a minute,' as you do before the first cry, subdued or challenging, of an orchestral symphony.

But Celia had never been taught to wait. Patience was not at all her virtue. She wanted to be somewhere by herself, or with some-one who would make her happy.

That old woman had disturbed her, frightened her. How? Why? What was coming? What was the matter with her nerves?

One thing the matter with them was that she had not enough to do. Somehow Mrs. Lamplough had shown her that. Her pic-ture of her life with Julius in the depths of the country had been a loving alliance, Julius depending on her, everyone depending on her, voices whispering: 'She's marvellous. All that she man-ages to do—and little more than a child!'

She laughed out loud in the car, for she had a good sense of humour about herself and she saw how very different facts were from flattering, egoistic fancy.

But there was *nothing* to do. Mrs. Gayner did the housekeep-ing, Curtis the car, Oliphant the valeting, Jim Burke the newspaper-reading. She did the loving, the sentiment, the emo-tion. . . . Oh yes, and they talked, but she fancied that although he did not think himself very clever, he thought that she was less so.

She drove the car forward furiously. He was right. She had had no education. She had been taught to dress, to drink, to pre-vent young men from reaching their ultimate but very temporary desire. That was all.

She had hoped that by now there would be promise of a child. There was none.

She knew, quite suddenly, what it was that she wanted. She wanted someone of her own age, her own kind, as bad and selfish and uneducated and stupid as herself, to whom she could pour out her heart. There was no one.

Why had that old woman with the pink bows in bed the power to hurt her? What if Mrs. Brennan *did* dislike her? She knew, though, that that did hurt her. She liked to be liked. She wanted everyone to say: 'Dear Mrs. Cromwell. Dear, dear Mrs. Cromwell.'

She was not at all accustomed to being disliked so quickly. But Mrs. Brennan really *hated* her. With us all, someone who hates us becomes to us someone so peculiar, original, unusual, that their portrait in our gallery is double-sized. Celia could laugh at herself, despise herself, be bored with herself, but she could see nothing in herself worthy of hatred. But Mrs. Lamplough knew of it and so, probably, did everyone else in the village.

Then Phyllis Lock! Mrs. Lamplough had said that she was in love with Julius. Well, the girl was a fool and everyone knew it, but—a blind man was so defenceless. Julius was so kind, so good to everyone. The Lock girl might misunderstand.

Then the curiosity that Mrs. Lamplough had shown! The sudden vision of her peering in through the window of Garth House. Imagination! But was not everyone in the place doing it? 'They are talking about us! They are spying on us! Everything we do is watched!'

Oh, stupid, stupid! What the hell did it matter if they all discussed, watched, waited?

But she herself was also watching and waiting. That was where the wrong was. She was not herself at ease. Julius had recognized it, for only two days ago he had suggested that she should pay London a visit, see her parents, have a good time. Why had he suggested it? Was he already tired of her? Why was it that she could never tell exactly what was in his mind?

Mrs. Lamplough had perhaps realized that. She had suggested that Julius' mind, imagination, went away, left them all. . . . But if Julius and she truly loved one another, that could make no difference. And they did. With every day they loved one another more. But within that love they were restless, uncertain, uneasy. Or *she* was. She was encountering some new experience for which her life had not prepared her. It was as though she, still a child, was encountering mature shapes, presences half seen and of another experience from hers.

She pulled the car up. She was at the Cross-roads. Through the tangerine-tinted mist the Church floated like the Ark. She got out of the car and stood on the road, feeling the grit beneath her shoe, then moved up on to the Moor and seemed in that mist, with that yielding life-giving surface beneath her, herself to be floating.

A lovely cold tang, as though something of exquisite freshness was kissing her cheek, met her. It was the first autumn roughness. The colours of the mist as now she looked into them were orange amber, the stiff raddled rosiness of puckered apples, the brittle crinkling saffron of the dying leaf, a sweep of palest gold from some tree dripping with yellow blossom, the dark glistening green of a mossy well-top, the dark purple thorn of a rose-stem, the purple, washed and shining, of a grape-cluster, the smoky furred green and crimson of a peach-skin.

All these colours seemed to throng the mist, for the afternoon sun was beating in the heart of it. Sounds, too, were in it like muffled guns, wood sharply broken, bells ringing in towers, oars striking the water, the plaintive yielding 'hush' of the tide as it withdraws from the shining sand.

There was no sound in the mist and there was every sound. Then, most unexpectedly, there was a voice.

'Mrs. Cromwell.'

It was Jim Burke with his bicycle.

'Why—what are you doing here?'

She was angry, as though he had been spying upon her. Then, she knew not why, she was pleased.

'My father, when he rang the bell for Early Service, used to say: "You never know your luck!"'

She felt that she must explain something—but what?

'I drove up to get a breath of air. . . . Mrs. Lamplough's in bed, ill.'

They were moving together, he pushing his bicycle over the springing rejoicing turf.

'Oughtn't I to lock the car?'

'There'll be nobody stealing it.'

'I'll be going straight back. I promised I'd be back for tea.'

She looked at him. In the mist he seemed naked, as though his blue coat, shirt, trousers were phantasmal. He was as strong and hearty a young man as she had ever seen. He must be about her own age.

'How old are you, Jim?'

'Twenty-six.'

They were approaching the Church, which seemed to float forward to meet them.

He said, grinning: 'You don't like me much, do you, Mrs. Cromwell?'

'Oh, I don't know! I didn't at first. You've got a very bad reputation, you know.'

'Only because I'm natural.' They were standing looking at the Church. 'I wouldn't like to hurt anybody, though. Only I don't believe in anything.'

'No?'

'What is there to believe in any more? Love of your country is vulgar, belief in God stupid, belief in man sentimental. There'll be another war shortly. We'll all be blown to bits.'

'And so?'

'Take what you can, while you can.'

'What do you want to take?'

'Food, women, work with your hands, everything that lives in the open air, sleep.'

'And that's enough?'

'Oh, not enough. It's a sort of makeshift for what ought to have been. We've been cheated.'

She felt happy in his company. She was talking at last simply, without affectation, to someone of her own queer lost generation.

'Cheated?' she said. 'I don't know. Who ever promised us anything? We're not very much, are we, to be given presents. Now my husband——'

'Mr. Cromwell! Yes, I'd do anything for him. I don't know how much it's his blindness, though. Without it he might be a very ordinary man, maybe. But that gives him something extra, something special. He sees further than the rest of us—or doesn't he?'

'I don't think he knows himself.'

He put out his hand and touched her arm.

'I'm awfully glad you don't dislike me, Mrs. Cromwell.'

She didn't move away.

'No. I don't. But I think it's a pity with your birth and education you've turned into a sort of loafer.'

'Now that's a snobbish kind of thing to say. Birth and education! You should know better than to use those words. Birth and education! As though birth means anything any more, and I'm educating myself all the time.'

'I used to think birth didn't mean anything any more. But now I'm not so sure. It means something if it means good manners. We, all of us, have been so rude and unkind for so long. We thought we were honest, courageous, said what we meant. Now that rudeness is getting as old-fashioned as courtesy seemed to us.'

'I don't think I'm rude,' he said gently. 'I don't want to hurt a soul, and if a lie makes them happy, why not? But I don't want to waste my time, because time's so short and there's nothing to come after.'

'How do we know?' she said. 'How do we know? Perhaps there is.'

'It doesn't frighten me if there is.'

'No,' Celia said. 'I shouldn't think things frighten you.'

He took her hand and kissed it and was gone with his bicycle. She heard him whistling in the mist. His lips had been warm and strong on her hand. She went slowly back to the car and stood listening for a moment before she got into it.

She stood in the hall of the House looking up the stairs. Then she heard the music from the study and went in softly, stood inside the door, swinging her hat in her hand.

The music stopped. There was a little pause while the record fell. Then it began again. He was sitting straight up in his chair with a pleased childish smile on his face. A flute ran up the scale. Then the music stopped. As it began again she went forward and ended it altogether. She stood looking at him defiantly.

'I want to talk,' she said. 'Tea will be here in a minute.'

He smiled and held out his hand.

'Only two more little movements. Beethoven's Serenade for Flute, Violin and Viola, Op. 25. They all go out into the wood at the Flute's invitation. The Flute is young, foolish and happy. The Violin and Viola not so *very* old, but think they are. Entrata. Then Tempo Ordinario. All in the wood sitting under the giant oak. Kind of *As You Like It* scenery. Flute, dear young thing, very chatty, but Violin talks even more and tells the Flute: "When he's *older*——" This makes the Flute reflective for a bit. But soon he's happy again. He *has* to be. It's his nature. Then Allegro Molto. Their minds are made up. They are all agreed. Lovely night. Stars between the trees. Why not go and serenade the second violin? There is a lamp in her window. They agree. Andante con Variazioni. Off they go. Under her window. They all play their best. But the Flute is so young, so gay, so irresponsible, he outbids the others. There is a face at the window and the

Flute's enchanting up-the-scale ecstatic question—Ta-Ta-Ta-TEE? . . . And then, darling, you stopped it all.'

He would go on sometimes like that—to her ridiculously. For what point was there in adding stories on to music? Music was music, wasn't it?

She put her arms round his neck, rubbed his cheek with hers.

'I went to Mrs. Lamplough's.'

'Was it nice?'

'Nice! No. Horrid. The room was suffocatingly hot. She frightened me.'

'How could she?'

'I don't know. She did. She said Phyllis Lock was in love with you.'

He laughed, kissing her eyes.

'She said I was too young for you.'

'She did?'

'No. She didn't *say* it. That was what she meant.'

'And then?'

'And then I went away.'

She knelt down with her head on his thigh.

'I love you so much—so very, very much. . . . And then I went on to the Moor.'

'Was it beautiful?'

'It was beautiful beyond anything—a gold trembling mist. Jim Burke appeared on his bicycle.'

'You like him better now, don't you?'

'A little. After a minute or two he went away.'

She broke out, clutching his hand in both of hers:

'Julius—isn't it awful?—I don't want ever to leave you. I mean not for an hour or two in the afternoon. That's the kind of wife I said I'd never be, clutching, possessive. It's just the kind of wife I am. I want *all* of you, *all* of you."

'You have all of me.'

'No, I haven't.'

'What *I* haven't got,' he spoke slowly, 'is your youth. I'm so old. I sit here and think how much older I am.'

She caught his head and his thick strong neck in her arms. She kissed him again and again, laughing.

'If you'd been younger I never would have fallen in love with you. I hate young men—stupid, conceited, ignorant. Aren't they? You know they are.'

'Yes,' he said. 'But when *you're* feeling young yourself don't you want them like that? Stupid and arrogant—your own kind.'

She stood between his thighs staring into his blind gaze.

'If you could *see* how I love you,' she said.

She slipped out a little later to see where the tea was, and someone was coming downstairs. Celia was in the shadow of the door.

It was Mrs. Gayner, fully dressed to go out. She walked softly, almost furtively.

She slipped past, opened the front door with great care, and vanished.

PART II

The Whisper

CHAPTER I

At the Rectory—In the Well

ON THE FOURTH OF OCTOBER Mrs. Brennan received notice that
one-third of Gilbert's school was ill with chicken-pox. The
school would be temporarily closed. This news was received at
breakfast time.

Daisy Brennan said:

'*Now* what are we going to do?'

Mr. Brennan, whose breakfast was always a joy to him, took
the last sausage and the last piece of toast, winked at Simon who
had observed this, and said:

'Do about what?'

'Do you realize that this means that Gilbert will be at home
without a break until nearly the end of January?'

'Well, dear, why not?'

'Why not? Why not? But what's he going to do with himself
all that time? Who's going to teach him anything?'

'Teach him?' Frank Brennan looked across to his wife with his
profile neatly turned. 'Let him learn from nature for a while.
It won't do him any harm.'

'Frank . . . Please . . . Be serious for once. Do you know Gilbert's age? Nearly fifteen. He's getting very difficult indeed. Last holidays he was rude and surly. He'll probably spend his time with the Cromwells, like Simon. A holiday of more than two months will be simply fatal for him. Who's to look after him? I certainly cannot. Is he your son or isn't he?'

'He certainly is.'

'Then have you a responsibility or haven't you?'

'Certainly I have. I won't attempt to deny it. The question is whether I fulfil it by sitting on the poor boy, forcing him to decline Latin nouns against his will, causing him to loathe his father so that he runs away from home on the first opportunity and marries a barmaid, or whether, like a *wise* father, I allow him freely to develop his personality, to observe and learn the simple things around him, to discuss them freely with me, to help me in one or two jobs and so lighten my burden a little. This, my dear,' he ended, putting the last piece of sausage into his beautiful mouth, 'seems to me by far the wiser way.'

Daisy Brennan looked across the table, as she had often done before, wondering what next she should say or do. Long years with her husband had taught her that he was unassailable. To lose her temper with him was fruitless. He simply caught her temper, enclosed it in a paper bag, and blew it up with a bang. Dignity was of no use, for he only winked and grinned. Tears were hopeless. He did not even lend her a handkerchief. Threats were absurd, for there was nothing to threaten him with. He was altogether outside her power. She was in the familiar position of a wife who was powerful outside her own family, powerless within it. Everyone beyond the Rectory thought her lovely, intelligent, charming, homage-worthy. Why then were her husband and children so unperceptive? Dorothy at least was not. She had heard the news with rapture.

'Oh, Mother, how lovely! He can learn with me. We can read the same books and Mrs. Mark has promised to teach me some French.'

'Mrs. Mark? What has she got to do with it? Simon, that's quite enough marmalade. Other people want it beside you.'

'I'm making a tunnel.'

'I've told you again and again to eat your food quietly and not make messes.'

'It's not a mess. It's a tunnel.'

'*Please*, Simon . . . Don't answer me back. It's such very bad manners.'

But Simon, who already knew his mother much better than she knew herself, only grinned and tilted his plate a little so that the marmalade should slide away from the bread.

'Why Mrs. Mark, Dorothy?'

'Oh, she's most awfully nice. She talks to me as though I were her own age almost. Do you know, Mother, she ran away with her husband——?'

'That's sufficient, Dorothy. Say Grace, Simon. You've been playing with your bread and marmalade long enough.'

Simon, with one eye brightly alert above his folded hands, said Grace.

Daisy Brennan followed her husband into his study. She knew well what he now would do—sit, his long legs stretched out, smoking a pipe, reading the *Daily Telegraph*, in front of the fire.

For once, however, he listened. Her voice was sharp, her distress real.

'Frank, things can't go on like this. Either you do something about it or I go up to London and leave you alone with the children.'

'Do something—about what?'

'The children. Dorothy will soon be grown-up. Gilbert is nearly fifteen. He listens to nothing I say to him. He is sulky and rude. Even Simon has been disobeying me, running off to the Cromwells at every possible opportunity. In fact'—her voice rose—'it is since the Cromwells came here that everything has been going wrong. Mrs. Cromwell has taken it into her head that she owns the whole place. I don't mind her being rude to *me*

—what else can a poor clergyman's wife expect?—but when it comes to stealing one's children, turning them against their own father and mother, indulging them——'

'My dear, what *are* you talking about?'

She saw that she had caught his attention. She rushed ahead so that not a moment might be lost.

'I'm talking about Celia Cromwell. Within a few weeks she has undermined all my work and position. You must admit, Frank, that I've been a good wife to you. I can't say that it's been easy. We've never had any money and you haven't given me much help socially. I don't blame you. That was *my* job. For years and years I've slaved. Because I *look* strong no one ever supposes that I can be tired. Be tired! Why, sometimes I've wondered how I can bear it another minute! You haven't helped me much about the children, either. When we found we couldn't afford a governess any longer I took on the whole thing. I've scraped and slaved so that Gilbert might go to a good school. Now after all these years this man and his wife come to live here. He's blind and rich—two interesting things. She's supposed to be pretty, although I can't see it myself. What happens? Everyone for miles round pays them homage, goes to their house to see what they can get. Even our own children . . . '

She was near tears. She looked superb with her bosom thrust forward, her handsome head thrown back.

He admired her. He loved her in his own way. But there had been many of these little scenes and he was longing to get to his newspaper.

'My dear, I still don't understand. I agree with you. You've been splendid. What we should all have done without you I don't know. But the Cromwells—what have they to do with it? I find him a fine fellow, poor chap. She seems harmless enough.'

'Harmless! She's seduced Simon already. It was after they arrived that Gilbert began to be rude. Even Dorothy——'

'Come now, Dorothy's an angel. I won't hear a word against her.'

'Yes. Everyone's an angel except me. . . . '

She controlled herself and said calmly:

'You just wait. There'll be a scandal in that Cromwell family that will make even you pay attention! Then you may be sorry that you've allowed your children to prefer *that* house to their own.'

He answered reflectively, picking up his paper and sticking his head into it.

'It's an extraordinary thing. Just because a man's blind he seems to have some extraordinary power.'

'It isn't because he's blind,' she answered. 'It's because he's got a wife years younger than himself and can't look after her.'

She ended:

'It's only the children. Nothing matters except the children. But if Gilbert treats me as he did before he went to school you'll have to do something about it.'

Dorothy told Simon that they must take care to make Gilbert as happy as possible.

'He'll be dreadfully disappointed. He was looking forward to this term like anything, playing football and making his mark.'

'What's "making his mark" mean?' Simon asked.

'Making his mark on the school. Now's the time when he's got to do it. He'll be fifteen soon. He wants to be a Prefect and Captain of the Football, perhaps.'

Simon stared at Dorothy as though she were some new species of sister handed to him for the first time.

'I think that's all very silly,' he said.

'What is?'

'Making your mark. I'm not going to school. I'm going to be a gardener.'

'Of course you'll have to go to school.'

'Why?'

'To learn things so that you can make a living when you grow up.'

Simon said: 'Gardeners make a living. You put something in the ground and later on you eat it. I shall be Mr. Cromwell's gardener.'

'But that will be years and years. You can't be his gardener until you're twenty. You're only eight.'

'Mr. Cromwell has a boy who's only fourteen and a bit. I asked him and he said, "I'm fourteen and a bit." I think it's silly making a mark at school.' He grinned. 'Mother hates Mr. Cromwell.'

'Oh no she doesn't!' Dorothy cried indignantly.

'Yes she does, *and* Mrs. Cromwell, *and* Jim Burke.' He lay down on the floor again, where he was drawing with coloured chalks. He wriggled his legs and laughed.

'I can do a ship with three sails. And now I'm going to do a mountain.'

When Gilbert arrived Dorothy took the greatest care not to be demonstrative. On every occasion when he returned from school she had a secret fear that he would believe in her a little less. It was natural that, as he grew, he would discover many people more interesting than herself. She did not complain of that but awaited the inevitable day with fear of the pain that he must give her.

She saw with delight that he needed her more than ever before. He was nervous about his mother. He looked at her shyly. On the morning after his arrival he spoke to Dorothy about it.

'I was rotten to Mother last holidays.'

'You were angry. You thought she'd been unfair to you.'

'No. It was more that I thought she didn't care.'

'Of course she cares, Gillie. She cares most awfully about all of us. But she likes us to show that we want her. Her feelings get hurt because she cares for us so much.'

'Yes,' Gilbert said. 'Last holidays I got awfully funny. I don't know what was the matter. I almost *hated* Mother. I thought she didn't care for us a bit but only for herself. Now, of course,

I see that's all rot. I'm going to show her that everything's all right.'

'I'm awfully glad.'

His face was eager, his slim body strong and taut.

'Dorothy, look here! I'm going to be home a long time now and what I want is for Jim Burke to teach me how to carve. Do you think he will?'

'Of course he will.'

'I want it more than anything—to make things with my hands. I tried a bit at school this term. I got some clay from somewhere and I did make a sort of man's head, but it wasn't right. I didn't know what to do. My hands were all ready, but when I wanted them to do something they did something else. I expect Jim knows.'

'Of course he does,' Dorothy said proudly.

That afternoon, a very fine one, Gilbert went off for a walk to think things out for himself. It had been a terrible blow to him when the school closed. This term had promised wonderful things. It was to be the bridge between childhood and maturity. Something had happened to him; what it was he did not quite know. Once, during the summer holidays, he had enjoyed a talk with old Mr. Lamplough, who had informed him that everybody was made up of gas and water and that there was very little difference really between a chair and a human being, except that a human being could reproduce himself, which on the whole Mr. Lamplough thought was a pity.

This had struck Gilbert very much, but it had not convinced him, because the changes of which he was aware in himself could certainly not be experienced by a chair, and no imaginable combination of gas and water could be as angry with his mother as he had been.

Thinking of this as he walked along, he wondered why, if he was only a mixture of chemicals, he felt this passionate desire to make something with his hands. The beautiful day was part of this, the scent in his nostrils, the pure colours of the sky and the auburn-amber foliage, the faint smoky light in the air as of silver and flame. He did not wonder very much. He was too happy, too free, his stomach was too healthy, his legs too strong. It was as though he was being swung along, almost flying in fact.

He made for the Well, the thick wood below the Moor, where the primroses always came first. He had known this wood since he was a baby. In the heart of it there was a small waterfall, a little pool, and a stream that ran, he believed, ultimately to the sea. He thought often of this waterfall, which seemed the centre of this country where he had always lived. When he was at Rafiel, watching the sea or bathing in it, he thought of the water-fall as the centre of the sea. If the waterfall ceased to tumble, then the sea would withdraw and all the land beneath it be dry. He had believed that, of course, only when he was very small, but the fancy still lingered with him.

At the entrance to the wood, by the side of the road, he saw a motor-car. Nobody was in it.

He entered the wood by a little path that he knew well and traced his way, treading over the dead leaves, and stopping some-times to wonder at the silence.

He cut himself a stick and, as he walked, peeled it with his pocket-knife.

He pushed some branches aside and came out on to the clearing and looked at the waterfall. Mr. Cromwell was standing there, leaning against a tree. He was quite motionless and staring into the sky, his head cocked as though he were listening. His body seemed very big and strong to Gilbert. His hands were still, his face was still; his open eyes stared upwards.

At first Gilbert thought that he would go away, but Mr. Cromwell had at once heard him, although Gilbert had made very little sound. His body was suddenly alive. He smiled.

'Hullo!' he said.

'Hullo!' Gilbert replied.

'That's a boy,' Mr. Cromwell said.

'Yes,' Gilbert answered, moving forward. 'I'm Gilbert Brennan.'

'I thought you were away at school.'

'I ought to be, but we've had chicken-pox and I've come home.'

Mr. Cromwell, who was wearing a large rough dark-blue overcoat, said:

'Come over to me, then we can talk better.'

Gilbert, rather frightened although he didn't know why, went over to him.

Mr. Cromwell leaned comfortably back against the tree again.

'When you're blind,' he said, 'you can hear leaves dropping. That's what I was listening to.'

'Can you really?'

'Yes. As they fall they make a kind of rustle half-way down as though they fought one last time for life. It's nothing to be depressed about, of course. If the leaves didn't die there wouldn't be new green ones bursting out in the spring. And that goes for everything and everybody.'

Mr. Cromwell put his hand on Gilbert's shoulder.

'Are you alone?'

'Yes, sir.'

'Not even a dog?'

'No.'

'Just going for a walk by yourself?'

'Well, you see, where the waterfall is I've always thought the best place of the lot round here, and I was awfully disappointed at the school shutting, and I'd only just got home, so I thought I'd come here.'

'You think this the best place of the lot, do you?'

'Yes, I do.'

'Well, for sound and smell I should say it is. How would you describe it now?'

'Just below where you are there's a rock with some pink lichen on it. It isn't pink exactly, but rosy. And under the rock there's the pool. It's small and now there are a lot of leaves in it and they've choked where the water runs away. There's a stream all the same, and it's quite blue now under the brown and gold leaves. There are two rocks like scissors and a yellow little tree.'

He was wrinkling his forehead and trying to be exact and detailed.

'Thanks,' Mr. Cromwell said. 'Where does the stream go to?'

'Right out to the sea. At least everyone always says so, and when I was a kid we used to think that if the stream dried up the sea would dry up too.'

Gilbert laughed as though the idea were extremely foolish, but as he laughed he felt as though he were betraying something or somebody.

'As a matter of fact that isn't such nonsense,' Mr. Cromwell said, quite gravely. 'Everything depends on everything else, and you can't be sure if one thing stops everything won't. . . . I must be getting back. Give me your arm.'

Gilbert proudly did so.

'You can just see me to the car. Would you like a drive?'

'No, thanks,' Gilbert said, 'I'm walking.'

'Of course you are,' Mr. Cromwell said. 'I forgot.'

Gilbert led him to the car with the very greatest care, but had a curious impression that Mr. Cromwell was leading *him*.

'You know, your brother Simon is a great friend of ours.'

'Yes. He's always talking about you.'

'Is he? That's very flattering.'

'You don't know Dorothy much, though, do you?'

'No, I don't.'

'She's the best of the lot. She *couldn't* be better.'

'You must bring her to tea one day.'

'Oh, may I? I want to see your house most awfully.'

'Yes, we'll settle a day.'

The car was there and Curtis now sitting in it.

Mr. Cromwell gripped Gilbert's shoulder a moment and climbed into the car.

Gilbert's adventures for that afternoon were not, however,

yet ended. Walking back to the village he considered Mr. Cromwell from every possible point of view. He liked him very much, but, unlike Simon, felt that he was strange. He was not strange to Simon at all, but there was something frightening and lonely about blindness.

Gilbert even stopped for a moment in the road, shut his eyes tightly and then walked along to see how it felt. The blackness was horrible. It was shot with flashing lights. He reeled from side to side exactly as when you play Blind-Man's-Buff. Mr. Cromwell had been blind, of course, for a very long time, and that made it better. Nevertheless it was beastly. It was the more beastly because Mr. Cromwell was so big and so strong. He was like a prize-fighter or a footballer, and *very* like Gilbert's greatest hero in the world, W. H. Hammond. Yes, *very* like Hammond. This made it much worse. Were you a measly little man you wouldn't want to do things, but Mr. Cromwell must always be longing to swim, play tennis, cricket, to box perhaps, or even to fence. He could swim, of course, and walk if he had somebody with him. But how beastly always to have somebody with you! Why didn't he have a dog? That was a grand idea. Gilbert might suggest it.

Thus thinking, Gilbert, looking ahead, saw *three* dogs and a very strange little man in a shabby waterproof walking with an odd skipping walk beside them. The dogs all trotted at his heels, keeping close to him. They were most certainly not beauties—in fact, mongrels.

One of them was a black dog who would have been a retriever had it not been for his tail, which was short and stubby; another was nearly a French poodle, and the third was a fox-terrier with a touch of Aberdeen. The semi-retriever was limping and on his face was a slight anxiety as though he feared that he might be left behind. The dirty woolly ear of the poodle was torn and raw. There seemed to be nothing the matter with the fox-terrier, who walked along, sniffing the air, bright and eager, a little *over-*

bright and eager, perhaps, as though at heart there was a creeping doubt.

The odd little man saw Gilbert coming and stopped.

'Good afternoon, sir,' he said.

'Good afternoon,' Gilbert answered politely.

The dogs also stopped.

Gilbert did not care for the looks of the little man. There was an odour somewhere in the air: his face was wrinkled and uneasy. There was furtiveness in every inch of him. He couldn't keep still, but tapped on the road first with one foot, then with the other.

'Are those your dogs?' Gilbert asked.

The fox-terrier was looking at him with burning pleading eyes, a sycophantic crawl-on-my-belly-if-you-want-me-to look.

'They are and they aren't, as you might say. The fox-terrier was given me. The farmer out towards Sizyn was going to shoot him because he said he was nothing but a nuisance. The black dog called Horace came limping up to me, and I don't know *where* he's come from. The sort of half-poodle hasn't a home either. He came down the road one day and some cottage people took him in, but they're mighty glad for me to have him. Funny when you come to think of it, for dogs are superior to human beings—at least, that's the way *I* look at it.'

'I've always wanted to have a dog,' said Gilbert, sighing.

'Have you now? Well, you can have any one of these you like to pick.'

'Oh no! Mother and Father would never allow me to keep one.'

The man looked at him, grinning, and so displaying some very ugly teeth.

'You never know till you try.'

The fox-terrier, as though he were aware that there was a possibility of something exciting, began to pretend that he had a game with a flying leaf. He barked shrilly, ran a little away and looked up at Gilbert.

They all walked on to the beginning of the village.

'What's his name?' asked Gilbert.

'I called him Benson because there was a man in the last hall I played in called Benson remarkably like him. He was a man who hadn't done too well in life because he was in prison for bigamy once. As a matter of fact he had three wives at one and the same time—three too many if you ask me."

Benson continued to run, look up at Gilbert and run again.

'There's nothing I wouldn't do for a dog,' the man went on. 'As a matter of fact, the pub where I am doesn't like them. I keep them in the garage and I must say they are as good as butter. More than I could say for the rest of the bastards.' Then as though he knew that he oughtn't to use such a word before a little boy, he coughed behind his hand.

'I know who you are,' he said. 'You're the Rector's son.'

'Yes, I am,' said Gilbert.

'I was talking to your sister one day.'

'Oh yes?'

'Look here,' the man said, 'I'll tell you what I'll do. I want Benson to have a good home. You take him and try him—see what your mother says. He's a clean little dog. Scrup'lous about the house. Does anything you tell him, too. Got a loving heart and beautiful manners.'

Gilbert knew that he was lost and Benson knew that he knew.

'I'll tell you what I'll do. You take him home and if they won't let you have him you bring him along to me. "Three Crows." That's where I'm staying. Get your mother to try him for a day or two and then she won't be able to resist him.'

Gilbert's heart was beating so that he could scarcely breathe.

'All right. I will.'

It seemed that it was not his own voice that had spoken these daring words.

'So-long. See you later.'

It was as though the little man had known him all his life.

Gilbert moved towards the Rectory.

'Go on,' said the man to Benson. 'There's your master now.'

Benson did not hesitate. He followed Gilbert, keeping close to him and wagging his tail.

When they were in the garden Gilbert hesitated. It might be more hopeful could Benson have a bath before he was presented. But a bath was a business and could not secretly be undertaken. Well, what did it matter? His mother would not consider the possibility for a single moment. There had never been a dog in the house. There never would be. Gilbert opened the door, walked into the hall. Benson ran forward, barked, and Mrs. Brennan was standing there.

'Hullo, darling, have you——?''

Then she stopped. She saw Benson. She could not help but do so, for he was smelling at her calves.

Gilbert began at once:

'I hope you won't mind, Mother, but I met a man and he said I could have this dog who's called Benson after a man the other man knew. We've never had a dog, have we, Mother, and this one is house-trained and everything, and anyway he could sleep in the tool-shed. I'd be responsible and as I'm going to be home a long time, now would be a good time to start with him, wouldn't it? I expect he's awfully good with mice.'

This last he added on the toe of the dramatic moment, because he knew that his mother hated mice as she hated snakes—saw, in fact, little difference between the two.

However, at any ordinary time, neither mice nor any other animal would have made the very slightest difference. Benson would have left this pleasant house as quickly as he had entered it.

It happened that Mrs. Brennan loved her son. She loved him with self-pride as well as with other things, and her self-pride had been desperately hurt. She wanted him back as he had been: she wanted him back with his old adoration, his old confidence in her, and his old obedience. She saw herself as the great divine goddess, pardoning, bestowing, Olympian, human. She scarcely was conscious of Benson, who, finding her ankles sterile, was pursuing, in a corner of the hall, a mice-suggestion.

She looked at her son and loved him. But she would not surrender too quickly.

'A dog? My dear Gillie!'

'I know, Mother, but——'

'And *what* a dog!'

Gilbert, amazed that his request had not been at once rejected, began at once to hope.

'You see, Mother, he can be most awfully useful. I don't know how we've got on without a dog so long. If he sleeps in the kitchen he guards the whole house, and you know that tramp there was hanging around last winter, and you said——'

'That's quite enough, Gillie. I don't know *what* your father would say——'

'Oh, Father always does what *you* want, Mother.'

'Besides, what kind of a dog is he?'

'He's a fox-terrier, of course.'

'He's got a funny head for a fox-terrier.'

Gilbert, shy of demonstration, nevertheless went to her and kissed her.

'Mother, thank you most awfully.'

Her heart beat ridiculously fast. For a grand Juno of a woman, the adored of the countryside, she was betraying absurd maternal emotion.

'Well . . . There, Gillie, that's quite enough. Mind you, if there's the slightest trouble with him, if he isn't perfectly clean——'

'Oh, but he is, Mother, he is! Oh, thank you, thank you! Hurray! Hurray!'

Transformed with happiness he rushed up the stairs, Benson barking, rushing after him.

At the top of the stairs was his father.

'Good heavens, what's this!'

'It's Benson, Father!'

'Oh, I see.'

And Gilbert rushed on.

He must tell Dorothy. Above all things he must tell Dorothy. In the schoolroom she was reading *Engel the Fearless* to Simon.

Benson, who like all mongrels was warmhearted, rushed at once up to Dorothy and made leaps at her. Dorothy was, of course, delighted.

'Oh, what a lovely dog! Whose is he?'

'He's mine. He's ours. He belongs here. He's been given me.'

'Belongs here? But *what* will Mother——'

'Mother says it's all right. Mother says I can keep him if he doesn't make a mess——'

'Oh, how lovely! Where does he come from?'

'There was a funny little man in the road. He gave him me.'

She knew at once about the funny little man. A strange shiver touched her body.

'Gillie, do you think it's all right? That's a horrid man. He spoke to me once.'

Gilbert was scornful.

'Of *course* it's all right. He'd been given Benson——'

'Benson! What a funny name!'

'That was the name of a man he knew once.'

Simon, always the realist, said:

'Who will feed him?'

Gilbert, very serious, went on. 'That's it. He must *not* become a kitchen dog. *We'll* have to feed him—always. When they're fed in the kitchen they get scraps and things and then they get fat and want always to be *in* the kitchen. He's got to be *our* dog.'

'Can he do tricks?' Simon asked.

'No, of course not,' Gilbert said impatiently. 'He's not that sort of dog.'

Benson was sitting with his tongue out, grinning and panting.

'He wants water,' Gilbert said. Looking at Dorothy he added, 'It was awfully decent of Mother, wasn't it?'

CHAPTER II

Garth House: In Julius' Study

JULIUS CROMWELL'S JOURNAL

October 23.—I have had a strange return of what I must call, I suppose, for want of a better word, my day-nightmares.

Before the War, when I was a young man, there was no one more normal than myself. So healthy was I that I simply couldn't understand any ill-health and I was a bore, I suppose, with my self-confidence and easy solution of everything. But even the healthiest has a queer morass of indecency, obscenity, abnormality, obsession, muddy and greasy, down in the cellars of his house. Freud's stock-in-trade. It wasn't until I was blinded that I realized mine.

I have been thinking these days of old Spencer. He lived about three miles from Bramgrove and was crazily enthusiastic about the French Neo-Surrealist painters. He would come and talk by the hour about them to me and I remember a good deal of it still—Chagall who painted flowers rising out of the heads of lovers, and dream landscapes where sea and land were utterly lonely and little stunted trees had giant leaves; Ernst who stuck pieces of cork and wire on to his paint; Miró and the later Picasso.

I never could see these pictures, of course, and I had no idea what Spencer was like except that he was *very* bony and had about him a scent of liquorice and tobacco: but I can hear his high rather piping voice as he described a picture of Chirico's, of giant trees growing in a room, of Dali's long sunlit plains with a woman standing, her stomach full of clocks, or something of Picasso's with a violin rising out of some melons. One landscape I remembered especially. It was by the sea-shore, and under the moon a man was moving towards a tower whose corners were women's breasts. A mirror stood all by itself near the sea and reflected in its glass a listening ear. I don't know what's happened to the Neo-Surrealists. They are all gone and forgotten, I daresay. I've long ceased to find any interest in them, but I remember that, during that time when Spencer used to come and see me, my subconscious created for me a world of dead slimy seas, deserted plains where clocks ticked and beautiful nude women carried eyes in their entrails and flowers were made of fur and sealing-wax.

Because I could not see these things with my physical eyes I saw them twice as intently with my spiritual eyes. I had only got to look down into my secret world and there were those seas and plains, deathly, eternal, the only sound the ticking of clocks, the only figures mechanical presences.

During the last fortnight these worlds have returned to me, and because my own real world all around me is going all wrong. How great a relief it is to me to write those words down! For weeks and weeks I have been hesitating to say them to myself. What is the matter with everybody—with Celia, with Mrs. Gayner, with Burke, even with Oliphant and Curtis?

Well, with Celia at least I know what it is—she is beginning to hate my blindness.

From the first moment that we entered this house I had some sense of this—no, before that, for I was aware of something in the car as we drove here. So opposite, isn't it, from what in stories or plays you would be told? There everyone has such burning sympathy for the blind, and the beautiful girl who marries the blind hero has no intention of doing anything else than look after him for the rest of his days with loving and devoted care!

So, I am sure, Celia originally intended. She is loving, generous, sympathetic. Too much so. Many women less sensitive than she would have devoted themselves to me and asked nothing better.

But Celia is beginning to find my blindness her enemy because

it won't surrender to her. Her youth and beauty are too ignorant and inexperienced to understand its personality. *Me* she has,
but my blindness is another force—not myself—that I myself can't
control and can only dominate at times. My blindness does not
want to be cosseted and protected and comforted and cared for.
It is proud and independent and is scornful often of myself. She
thinks that it is *I* who am scornful and independent!

The more she loves me and *wants* me, the more she *hates* my
blindness and resents it and is angry with it. The odd thing is
that everyone else in the house seems to be going queer because
we, she and I, are not tranquil. It is upsetting everything.

October 25.—'It is upsetting everything,' I wrote here two days
ago—and now indeed is everything upset. Celia and I quarrelled
this afternoon in good dead earnest. I behaved badly. I behaved
badly because I am a perfectly ordinary man. This afternoon I
was furious like an ordinary man and, like an ordinary man, I
wanted passionately to love her and to smack her at the same time.
The quarrel arose, of course, out of nothing—a little nothing
tremendously symbolic. The whole business of successful lovers
is to keep in step. A little in front, a little behind, just that much
out of step, and almost at once you begin to lose yourselves in
terrifying darkness.

The quarrel this afternoon was, like Othello's, about a handkerchief. It had a sort of stage-management. Half an hour before
tea Celia says (as she too often does), 'Is there anything I can
get you?'

I say: 'Yes, a clean handkerchief.'

She moves to the door. I hear it open and know that Oliphant
is standing there. I say: 'Oh, Oliphant will get it. Don't you
bother.' I tell him to fetch my handkerchief. He goes. She stands
there without speaking and I know that she is holding herself in,
trying not to shout. And I think to myself: 'How stupid! She is
about to make a row about nothing,' whereas I should have
thought: 'This seems to be about nothing, but it goes to the
very roots of our relationship. I must be very careful.' In fact,

if I'd thought of it, my darling Celia was standing there, like the woman in Dali's picture, her stomach full of clocks all ticking at once.

Neither of us spoke a word. No movement. Then the door opens and I touch Oliphant's cool firm little hand and the fresh crisp handkerchief is in my pocket. He goes out. She breaks then into a kind of schoolgirl cry:

'I wasn't good enough, I suppose, to fetch you a handkerchief. It must be Oliphant.'

Women want what they want so desperately that the end of their world is threatened every Tuesday and Friday of the week. But when they've got securely what they want they'll go through every torture, suffering, deprivation, quite tranquilly. Celia, because she wasn't sure of me, would plunge us both into hell over a handkerchief. If she had been sure of her possession of me she'd have suffered the stake and the fire without a murmur. Analyses of small unimportant love-affairs are stupid, but this Journal is for my own self-relief and clarity of mind. I want above all things to tell the exact truth. Later on everything may depend on it.

I tried to draw her to me. I am greatly dependent on touch. The first time that I meet anyone whom I mean to know I like their hand to rest for a little while on my arm or my thigh. Personality is perhaps more truly revealed by touch than by anything else, even for normal seeing persons. Had I held her in my arms there would have been no quarrel. Sexual intimacy between two persons who wish to know one another's hearts and souls has nothing gross. It is so spiritually revealing that the reactions that follow it are nine times out of ten disappointing. But Celia and I had passed all that. As with so many women, in my arms at night she was entirely relieved, all her doubts were over. This was especially so in our case because at night I did not seem to her blind. My blindness drew stealthily away. With the first beam of morning light it returned.

She knew now that physical contact would settle our differences—and she did not want them to be settled—so she stood away! When I realized that, I was angry. An ordinary man, like myself, when he loses his temper with a woman he loves feels suddenly that the whole of their sex is inferior, and he is the more angry because, in his earlier words of passionate love, he has let his own sex down. Only normal healthy men feel this, of course, but when I am in a rage I am a normal healthy man and a very stupid one. Plumb normality *is* stupid!

Our conversation then was ridiculous. Something—I don't know—like this, perhaps:

'Darling, Oliphant knows just where everything is.'

'And I don't, I suppose?'

'Why should you bother when Oliphant can do it so easily?'

'Bother! What a word! Why did I marry you?'

'Now, Celia, you're like a child.'

(Yes. Are not normal men in a rage stupider than stupid?)

I remember that here she said very gravely: 'No. That's your big mistake.'

She was so quiet that I said again, with a kind of tranquil patronage: 'Well, then, come! Let's have tea. It's all nothing.'

She replied quickly, drawing in her breath: 'Yes, it's all nothing. Nothing at all. Our relationship to one another. I've discovered that now. I've been discovering that ever since we came here. You want me for nothing but to be in bed with you at night. You have never thought, have you, that I'm a human being too? That I married you for something? I married you because I wanted us to be together and we're not together— never, never, never—except at night, perhaps for half an hour, when you want to make love. It isn't only that I'm nothing in this house, but I'm nothing to you either. All the time you're away from me, imagining your own things, seeing your own things, or listening to music you don't want me to share.'

I said, not too convincingly: 'I want you to share everything.'

'Yes, everything that is part of your need at the moment. But you don't want to share *me*, the kind of person I really am.

You push *me* away. But I'm a real person, quite as real as you are, although I'm *not* blind.'

She wished at once that she hadn't said that, and because I knew that I used it to hurt her.

'That isn't just,' I said very quietly.

We knew then that, through stupid unconsidered anger, we were both being hurried along into places where we should never go. But we couldn't stop. It was as though someone had taken us both by the shoulders and was hurrying us along.

'Just or no, it's true. Have you tried to help me? Have you made me share your own things? You know you haven't. You think I know nothing about books or music. I know more perhaps than you think.'

'I'm sure you do,' with a sort of cheap sarcasm. I was angry. I hated this row. Men hate rows. Women don't. That is women's advantage.

But if I was angry, she was angrier.

'You think this is all about nothing. You're saying to yourself "Poor child! What a baby she is!" ' (Incredible the fury and rage Celia put into this.) 'Well, you're wrong. It isn't all about nothing. It's about your conceit, thinking you're so superior to me that you needn't bother at all. I'm like a kept woman in your home. I'm a prostitute—that's all I am. I'm nothing in this house but a whore!' And she rushed out, banging the door behind her.

October 26.—This is serious, monstrous, ridiculous, absurd. After the quarrel we dined, saying polite nothings. Then we sat in the study and I turned on the Sibelius Fifth—which was stupid, I suppose, because one of the things we are quarrelling about is music, oddly enough. I couldn't hear a note of it and when it was over I began: 'Celia, darling——,' and at once she went out.

Later, I went up to bed and knew that she was there before me. When I lay down in my bed I stretched out my hand to take hers. As soon as I touched her arm she withdrew it. Then she said in the voice of the ice-maiden: 'Please—don't touch me.

I don't want to be touched. If you touch me I'll have my bed somewhere else.'

'I don't want to be touched.' And she said it like a child.

This morning I caught her as she was going out, led her into the study, shut the door behind us, put my arms round her and kissed her.

'Forgive me. Forgive me. I've been stupid, blundering. I'll be better. I'll be wiser.'

But she wouldn't surrender. Her lips were warm but dead. She said, quietly, as though she were repeating a lesson: 'There's nothing to forgive. It's just stupid,' and went out.

Now another mystery. Before I went up to dress for dinner Mrs. Gayner came in. She wanted to know about some sheets and blankets she was ordering from Harrods.

'You must speak to Mrs. Cromwell, Lizzie. I want her to be consulted about all those things. She has been feeling that she's left out a little.'

'I quite understand,' she said.

I put my hand on her arm. It was trembling.

'What's the matter?' I asked.

'The matter, sir?'

'Yes, Lizzie. You're in trouble. You've been so for weeks. What's your trouble?'

She withdrew from my touch.

'I think, sir,' she said, 'I'll have to leave.'

Oh, damn these women! Damn them! Whom do they ever think of but themselves? Here she had been with me for years and years. We had grown to be devoted friends. And now she says quite indifferently: 'I think I'll have to leave!'

'Don't be silly,' I said. 'That's nonsense.'

'I mean it, sir. It's no good as it is.'

'What's the trouble? Is it my wife? Are you getting on badly?'

'Oh no, sir. That's all right. She'll understand me in time.'

I knew, suddenly, that she was very unhappy—not only unhappy, but frightened.

'If it's not that, what is it?'

'I'm afraid I can't tell you, sir.'

'Can't tell me? But you've always told me everything.'

'It's my own private affair.'

'But your affair is mine. You know that there's nothing I won't help you about. Is it money? The other servants?'

'No, sir. Thank you, sir.'

I took her hand then and held it, for so I must do if I'm to *see* my friend. I told her that I was myself in some trouble, that things weren't easy, that I needed her as I had never needed her before.

Her hand was warm and trembling in mine. She said at last: 'Very well, sir. I can't leave you if you need me.'

I tried once more.

'But *what* is it, Lizzie? Is someone pestering you, are you ill?'

She said then: 'Mrs. Cromwell has discovered that the two silver cigarette-boxes in the drawing-room are missing.'

I laughed at that.

'She doesn't accuse *you* of taking them?'

'No, sir. I must say she trusts me.'

'Well, then, where's your trouble?'

'It isn't pleasant, sir, when things are missing.'

'Of course not. But if there's a thief we'll soon find him.'

'Yes, sir.'

I let her go. She was changed. She was a thousand miles away from me. Damn these women! I shall move into a monastery.

November 2.—This ridiculous business has reached a new stage. About a week ago Celia and I were lovers again after an interval of more than a fortnight. After that, until now, she loved me passionately at night and was stiff and schoolgirlish during the day. She is in a nervous, exaggerated state. I sometimes hope that it may mean that she is going to have a child.

Meanwhile, I am having a struggle with myself not to submit to her, utterly, completely, abjectly. To do anything she may order. To dismiss Oliphant and Curtis. To surrender to her dressing of me, bathing me, leading me everywhere by the hand.

I love her just now in a frenzy of this disturbed passion. For three nights last week we were like lunatics in one another's arms—as though we had never met before. We were hysterical, frenzied, as though we had not a moment to lose.

Finally we were unsatisfied. We had not really joined one another in those struggles and we knew it. Day by day I have had to walk as though on eggshells not to cause her unhappiness. That is humiliating. Against my surrender is my insistence that I should not surrender to anyone. I feel that I am doing what our Government is doing—surrendering all along the line to keep the peace. And I hate myself. I despise myself. And I love her so passionately that my heart all day is like toothache and my throat dry. I hate, I hate, I *hate* this submission and preoccupation. That world opened for me by my blindness is altogether darkened and obscure. When I was happy and free it was as though I lifted the latch and pushed the door back. I saw a noble landscape and what some writer called once 'The Great Good Place.' At least I knew it would be there when I had travelled in the right direction. It was like the third movement of the Mozart Trio, No. 5 in G major, where it is all lightness, haymaking, dancing round the maypole, forgiveness and love everywhere. Now I can see nothing. I think of her all day long. I am suspicious. I am even, God forgive me, jealous. For she *hates* my blindness. It is my blindness that is the villain. And how I ache to see, as never, never before.

This morning she was in the room. Jim Burke came in. I fancied that they stood looking at one another. And why should they not? The last man alive I would be jealous of is Burke. He is devoted to me. Devoted? An exaggerated word. He likes me. I trust him.

A ridiculous little dialogue occurred.

'I want to cut some of the trees down in the wood, Mr. Cromwell. They are far too thick.'

And Celia says quickly: 'Oh, not the holly!'

I say: 'What holly?'

Jim says: 'They're far too thick, anyway.'

There's a little silence, short, meaningless. But I feel that something is happening and at the same moment warn myself that if I begin to be suspicious of anything or nothing I'm a ruined man.

I say: 'Come with me into the garden, Jim.' Lest she should be offended I add: 'Come too, Celia.'

She says quickly: 'Oh no, I have to speak to Mrs. Gayner.'

Jim and I go out together. His hand is through my arm. He presses on it just below the shoulder. His hand is as strong as mine. We are two men together. There are no women in our world, and I have the fancy that he is glad as I. I have the fancy that he is suddenly relieved as I am. We are shoulder to shoulder. His grip on my arm tightens. We are walking on the lawn, strong and springy to our tread, and the sunlight on my face is thin with a ghostly warmth. We have never been so close as now, nor understood one another so well. It is almost—ridiculous thought—as though we were banded together against Celia.

We don't say a single word.

November 5.—Mrs. Mark has been all afternoon with me. Celia spent the day in Polchester, came back just before dinner, said she had a splitting headache and went to bed.

I go up in half an hour's time.

Meanwhile, I like Mrs. Mark. She is, it seems to me, just what I need at this moment. I imagine her as of middle height, grey hair, squarely built, quiet, determined, goodhearted, a little sententious.

This last she says she is.

'I am like the good moralizing daughter in the novel who, after sacrificing herself all her life to her parents, marries the hero.'

'Whose novel?' I asked.

'Anyone English before 1920. I've grown into the good, patient

Commère who solves everyone's trouble. A good, patient, priggish, nice woman.'

I told her that, to me, if she didn't mind my saying it, she stood for the past. When she was here the whole house had a double life. It was not only that I realized, through her, how important that other life had been, but that it was still resonant.

'Yes,' she said. 'I can hear Millie calling from the garden. There's a noise Henry used to make coming down the stairs.'

She went to the door and opened it.

'I'm feeling the worn places on the banisters—little smooth hollows. I know every one of them.'

'I want to tell you one thing,' she said, coming back to me, and putting her hand on my arm. 'I'm so glad it's you that took this place—the whole village is glad.'

I laughed and said that I made no difference to anybody.

She told me that no one could be unaware of me. It was as though I could see them all at their most secret. purposes, that there was no escaping me.

'Why, Celia and I feel that about *them!*' I cried. 'As though they were watching everything we do, overhearing every word we utter.'

'And so they are,' Mrs. Mark answered. She told me then an interesting thing. She had come down here to complete her life—it was to be the final rounding of her circle. 'Not that I'm expecting to die tomorrow, or any nonsense like that. I'm only sixty and, so far as I know, perfectly healthy. But I suppose the imminence of war makes all the old people feel the same. *Two* world wars in our lifetime! This surely must be the end for us. And so I wanted to see all this before I die. So I came. But death? Not a bit of it. Life, rather!' She caught my arm and held it, speaking excitedly like a girl.

'I'm in love again!'

'Good heavens!' I exclaimed, not very politely.

'Oh no! *That's* all over—long ago. I've only loved one man in my life. No. Dorothy Brennan.'

'She's a nice child.'

'She would have been my perfect daughter. There's something lovely about her. In *this* world—that such a child should exist! Life is rushing through me again. I have someone to care for, protect. . . . Oh, I'm not going to be a fool, you know. I shan't interfere. She's got her own mother. But I feel, somehow, that I *am* here to protect her from something, from someone. And that's connected with you too. If you hadn't come here, Dorothy's life would be different. You make us see things we never would have seen without you.'

I said to her before she went away: 'There's someone else you can help too—and that's me. I'm having my own difficult time.'

I like Mrs. Mark. She's generous-hearted.

November 7.—I had the oddest sense of Jim Burke for a moment this morning. He was standing quite close to me and it seemed to me that he was seized with some extraordinary passion —that he was standing there mastering it. I saw his eyes burning in a total darkness. I heard him sigh, almost groan. I could hear, I fancied, like thunder, the beating of his heart. His eyes and his heart. I wanted to help him. I nearly said something. Then he sat down and opening the paper remarked quietly: 'That filthy Hitler will ruin the lot of us before he's finished.'

CHAPTER III

Twilight Near the 'Three Crows'—Afternoon—The Holly Tree—The Rectory

SIMON BRENNAN discovered suddenly that life was of an absorbing and dramatic interest. Not that life had, during the whole of his eight years, shown the slightest sign of dullness. He had not, since he first drew breath, known a single moment's dreari-

ness. He had been angry, scornful, gay, sardonic, greedy, antic-
ipatory, grateful, disappointed, intriguing, adventurous, sleepy,
revengeful—never dreary.

He had always planned his life on his own lines, and anyone
who does that knows that he must outwardly acquiesce in the
foolish desires of other people. He had learned at a surprisingly
early age that to bend anyone in your direction you must flatter
him or her. He was already an excellent judge of character.

With all this he was not a horrid little boy. He was saved by
the possession of a warm heart. That would be a trouble to him
later on, as anyone who suffers from the combined impulses of a
sardonic mind and a warm heart well knows.

He was not, however, sardonic (sardonic children *are* horrible)
so much as determined. He saw his course clearly and pursued it.

Since the arrival of Julius Cromwell and the return of Jim
Burke the whole direction of his life was altered. He really loved
Julius Cromwell. This was the first human being he had really
loved as yet. He loved his sister Dorothy *almost*. He was hin-
dered from complete love by her too-ready submission to his will.
It would be too strong a thing to say that he despised her for
that, but he liked, and would always like, people whom he must
fight a little.

It is true that he didn't want to fight Julius Cromwell, but
he, by his blindness, his physical size, his mysteriousness, was
removed from all other men. When Simon climbed on to him
and leaned his head back against his great thundering heart he
felt immortal—or would have felt it had he known what im-
mortality was. Leaning against Julius' waistcoat he was in another
world, a world where magic rules. He was not, however, at all
a sentimental boy. He hated to be kissed and Julius never kissed
him. *He* kissed Julius and always as though the kiss might lead
to some new adventure.

Jim Burke was, in comparison, an ordinary person, but Simon
had always liked him. Jim told him all the things that he wanted
to know. The colours of birds, for instance. The Stonechat is

rose-coloured with a black head and a white collar. The Whin-chat is more sober in colour and has a light-coloured streak over the eye. And the distinctive mark of the Wheatear is a white patch just above its tail. The Yellow Wagtail has a canary-coloured breast and an olive-yellow back. The Grey Wagtail has a grey back and head and yellow on its chest.

You could, of course, get all these facts from a Bird Book that Gilbert had, but you didn't notice them when you *read* them. It was quite different when Jim Burke told you about them.

He had developed now a very clever technique about visiting the Cromwells. He knew that his mother greatly disliked his going there. He knew, too, his mother's habits exactly. Twice a week she went to a Sewing Party at the house of Somebody, unless Somebody came to the Rectory.

These affairs lasted for some three hours and during them his mother was altogether absorbed. He waited until Dorothy was engaged and then he slipped away, taking care always to return before his mother should enquire for him.

If the weather were fine he occupied himself in the garden with Jim Burke. There was always plenty to do. When it was wet he was with Burke or Curtis in the garage or potting-sheds. He at once discovered that it pleased Mrs. Cromwell if he was defying his mother. When she saw him she said: 'You naughty boy, Simon! Go home at once.' He said: 'Mother's at the sewing party.' Then she laughed and gave him a brandy-ball. But, of course, his real objective was Julius Cromwell. On a fine after-noon Julius motored, walked, or pottered about the garden.

Sometimes Simon was lucky and met him when he was starting for a walk, either with his wife or Oliphant. Then Simon said he was just on his way home and would go with them part of the way. He always added: 'Mother's at a sewing party.' He made up to that neat, silent little man, Oliphant, who had, he knew, very much influence with his master. He ran joyfully along beside Julius, like a little dog.

But best of all were the days when he found Julius in the

garden, or the wet days when very slyly he penetrated the study. Then he would say softly: 'Hullo!' and Julius would turn, looking with his blue eyes away above that small body, and say sternly, 'Simon!'

Simon would say: 'Mother's at a sewing party.'

'That doesn't make it any better. You know you oughtn't to come here.'

'I only looked in.' Simon had picked this mature phrase up from somewhere.

Then Julius laughed and picked him up, and Simon leaned back against the waistcoat and heard the heart beating.

Often Mr. Cromwell was listening to music. Simon didn't mind this. The sounds were pleasant and soothing. He liked the sweet soaring note of the violin and especially when it went high above all the other instruments. Mr. Cromwell would say:

'That's the Mendelssohn Unfinished Quartet. The Andante has one of the loveliest themes in the whole world. Mendelssohn isn't sentimental as people think,' which meant nothing at all to Simon, but he was flattered.

Always he kept his eye on the clock, for, like Cinderella, he had his fatal hour of return.

On a certain afternoon in November, when the dusk was beginning to sweep through the valley in a violet-grey haze, Simon was in the Garth garden. A bonfire of dead leaves was burning and crackling at the end of the lawn. Simon was hiding in the wood, for he thought that Jim Burke was coming. He would spring out on him and surprise him.

Julius was alone in the study listening to the 'German Dance' movement in the Quartet in B flat major by Beethoven.

Celia was coming in from her afternoon walk. She stopped at the end of the lawn to watch the little gold and sullen red tongues of flame as they sprang from the bonfire and mocked the sky. She thought that she would walk to the house through the wood. She was very unhappy.

Jim Burke, pushing dead leaves into the bonfire, saw her cross the lawn and followed her.

The afternoon was not cold. So, at least, Mrs. Gayner thought, slipping out of the house, keeping close to the hedge as she hurried along the road.

There is, some thirty yards before you reach the 'Three Crows,' a narrow path that leads off from the main road between fields. In the late spring and summer it is a famous traditional resort of lovers, for the trees overshadow it and there is a fine private stillness here, save for the birds and the murmuring human voices.

It is desolate now. Across the dun stubbled field the light fades into a milky white, and from this stalks and barren stems and gaunt leaves protrude with contorted, frustrated gestures as though they were making some last desperate appeal. A band of red gapes above a black-bellied cloud. If anything moves it moves stealthily. The air is close and sulky.

Mrs. Gayner found her son waiting for her. She kissed him as she had kissed him when he was a little boy, on the cheek and then on the mouth. When her gloved hand touched his thin body she felt such a trembling of love within her that the road with its bare trees was suddenly misted.

"All right, Mother. That's all right now."

'Why didn't you come last week? I haven't seen you for a fortnight except once passing you in the road.'

'I couldn't get away, Mother.'

'Get away from what? You aren't doing any work that I know of.'

'Well, there you're wrong—see?'

'What *are* you doing then?'

'I've sold a dog and some other things.'

'Yes.' Mrs. Gayner moved away from him a little. 'I know what you've been selling. Those cigarette-boxes.'

'Look here, Mother, I told you I hadn't taken them, didn't I?'

'What do you lie to me for? That last time you came to see me when Mr. and Mrs. Cromwell were out at the dinner-party, you slipped into the dining-room and took them.'

'I did not. See?' He did his little shuffle on the road. 'It's blasted hard on a fellow when his own mother thinks him a thief.'

'I *know* you're a thief, God help me. And everything else that is bad.'

He suddenly slipped his hand into hers. She could not help but hold it and press it. It was so thin and so slight.

'Look here, Mother, have you brought me the dough?'

'I've brought you enough to get to London with. I've written the address of the place you're to stay at there. To that address I'm sending you your ticket for the s.s *Andromeda* that goes to Jamaica, and a few pounds more. I've written to my cousin, Mr. Jacobs, in Kingston, and he'll give you something to do. I know he will, for he's a kind man and wrote to me about you last year, as I've told you.'

There was a silence. The little man shuffled about on the dry leaves. At last he said:

'Gee, Mother, I don't understand you. I'm the only son you've got and I've come to live near you and here you are pushing me thousands of miles away just as though you hated the sight of me.'

'It isn't you I hate, Douglas,' she answered passionately. 'It's your character. And why you've got that character I can't tell. It isn't all your own fault, I suppose, but being what it is I'm not going to have you robbing the man who's been better to me than any other human being, as long as I live. And I'm not going on with all this secrecy either.'

'I hate that man,' he said reflectively. 'I bet he knows who I am and all about me. I bet he knows I'm here with you now. He fair gives me the creeps. They all say in the village he sees more than any man that's got the use of his eyes. There was a man in the same lodging as me in Coventry once, just the same. If I was to steal anything from him,' he added, 'it would be only fair. What's he got everything in the world for and me nothing?

There's a time coming when we'll be all equal, just like they are in Russia.'

'You and Mr. Cromwell equal!' she answered scornfully. 'But never mind that now. Are you going to London tomorrow? Answer me that.'

'I don't know.'

'You don't get a penny unless you do.'

'Oh, don't I? That's all you know. What would your Mr. Cromwell say if he knew you'd got a son like you say I am? What would he say if he knew I *had* taken those cigarette-boxes?'

'He'd understand. He'd do anything for me.'

'Mrs. Cromwell wouldn't then. I know all about it. She's jealous of her husband, she is, and would like to get rid of the lot of you—that snarky companion that dresses him in the morning, the chauffeur, and all of you. *I* know.'

'It doesn't matter what you think you know, Douglas. You don't get a penny unless you're off to London tomorrow morning.'

'Well, I'm not going—see?'

She looked at him and then looked away at the desolate ghostly scene, at the chill dark that approached like an enemy.

What was she to do? He looked as though he hated her. He was thin and cold and badly clad. She longed to put her arms round him, lead him to a roaring fire, place before him all the best food and drink in the world. But he was bad. He was a liar and a thief and ungrateful. These things made no difference to her love for him.

'You can't do anything by staying here. You know you can't, Douglas. I can't go on keeping you. I haven't got the money.'

'I'm going to stay,' he answered. 'I like it here. I can't leave my dogs, anyway. They'd just be killed if I went away. Nobody wants them but me. Besides—there's a girl.'

'A girl?' She caught her breath. 'Oh no——'

'You needn't worry, Mother. I'm not going to touch her. She's the parson's daughter.'

'Miss Dorothy? Why, she's a child!'

'She's lovely,' he said. 'I'd do anything for her. She won't come to any harm from me, but I like to look at her. I like to see her walking out. She's so serious and she's kind. She's like a spring flower.'

'Don't you frighten her or speak to her or anything!' Mrs. Gayner said fiercely. 'If you do, I'll tell Mr. Cromwell and have you sent away.'

Something touched him. The distress in his mother's face perhaps. He kissed her.

'Don't you worry. I'll think about going to London. I will, straight. A man can't make up his mind all in a moment. I've got to find homes for the dogs, haven't I? You must see that. It wouldn't be decent. . . . ' He shivered. 'It's dark almost. You'd best be getting home.'

Celia stood for a moment watching the bonfire. She remembered no time in all her life when she had been as miserable as she was now. She was furious with Julius and loved him more than ever before. She loved him but he had eluded her. He was separated from her by all these people who surrounded him—by Oliphant, by Curtis, by Mrs. Gayner.

She was lonely with a new loneliness. She had not a friend in this horrible place. She hated Garth, she hated Glebeshire. And they hated *her*. Headed by the loathsome Mrs. Brennan they all hated her. In every place before they had loved and admired her. She had been surrounded by friends of her own age.

She remembered how Gerda Mills had said to her when she heard of the engagement: 'Why, Celia! He's old enough to be your father, *and* blind.' Those had been the attractions then. She had fancied herself weary of the young and crude. He was blind and would need her. Physically she had adored him and physically she adored him still. But she had no contact with him. The physical contact was nothing unless she had other contacts as well. What she needed was a friend, and he shared his friendship for her with all these others. Oliphant was always there, and if it wasn't Oliphant it was Curtis. The odious Mrs. Gayner was for ever spying on her, creeping up and down stairs, watching her. Julius poured out his heart to her. Celia was a child to him, inexperienced, only to be teased and cuddled. But she was *not* a child! She was a mature, experienced woman. If Julius thought he could keep her out of everything, if he thought that she would be content to satisfy only his physical needs, then he was badly mistaken and must be shown that he was.

Because she loved him she liked to hurt him. The only way that she could show her power over him was by hurting him. He would not allow her any other power.

She walked slowly across the lawn. She realized, as though she were looking at another person, that she was in a silly hysterical state. Her eyes were filled with tears for no reason at all. She was angry and she was miserable.

Had Julius quite suddenly appeared in front of her, crying out: 'Oliphant, Curtis, Mrs. Gayner, are all gone, darling! I knew you didn't like them, so I have dismissed them all,' she would have run to him, hugged him, hugged him, knelt at his feet, allowed him to do what he would to her.

And yet she did not care so very deeply about Curtis, Oliphant, and Mrs. Gayner. They were figures symbolizing the barrier that his blindness had built up. To think that she must live for ever with this blindness, this intangible, hateful blindness that detested her. For ever and ever! She was young and had all her life to live. What was he doing now? Listening, in all probability, to his beastly music. Quite happy, perfectly satisfied! Not thinking of her, not needing her. . . .

She entered the wood. She saw the holly. How dark the leaves, how white the bark in the thickening dusk! The leaves were ferocious. And behind the tree Simon was waiting to leap out. But he would not until Jim Burke was also there.

She heard the steps crunching the crisp fallen leaves and turned. 'Jim—hullo!' She was pleased. He had become in these last weeks

her friend, because he was almost of her own age, was just what
he seemed, was friendly and honest and—might be anything.
That fascinated her—the things that he might be. When he read
the papers to Julius of a morning he read them as though he had
a perfect education. He read them with a little of the parson,
a little of the actor, a little of the casual friend in the tone of it.
And yet he preferred to be a sort of under-gardener.

She knew also that he was in love with her. No one else was—
no one else in the whole world. And no one else was young. He
was attractive, always clean, however grubby his hands might be
from his work. His control of his body pleased her. He was so
very fit that he needn't give his body a thought. She had considered what he would be like without his clothes. It was a pity
that he must wear clothes.

'Hullo!' he said, and grinned. 'I'm just going to the garage.
Like to come?'

'No, I don't think so. It's nearly tea-time. Funny it isn't colder,
the sky looking as it does.'

'It's always close in this little wood, whatever the weather.'
He stared into her face. 'You're not looking very gay.'

'I'm not feeling very gay. Do you feel very gay always?'

'No, I'm damned if I do. Sometimes I'm like a dog with a tin
can to its tail. Sometimes I'm like a man shut up in a cell. Sometimes I've got no head, only a stomach. Sometimes I could howl
like a tom-cat on the tiles.'

She smiled.

'You *are* eloquent!'

'What's the matter?' he asked abruptly. 'Don't tell me if you
don't want to, but your being happy means a lot. I watch you
sometimes and think: "Is she happy or isn't she?" '

'Why should it matter to you whether I'm happy or not?'

'Oh, I don't know. It just does.'

It was growing darker and he moved towards her, staring into
her face.

'I'm glad someone cares!' she said bitterly. She moved as though she would go away.

He touched her sleeve. 'Don't go for a moment. We never talk. Not since that day on the Moor. I've seen for a long time that you were unhappy. I told Mr. Cromwell that I must leave; I couldn't bear to see you as you were. He doesn't want me to go.'

'Yes, he likes you very much.'

'And I like him better than any man anywhere. What's the matter between you two?'

She didn't reply.

'I oughtn't to ask. But I simply can't help myself. You don't have to answer, though.'

'What's the matter,' she said slowly, 'is that. when we were married I thought I'd be able to look after him. But I was wrong. He's surrounded by people who look after him. If we hadn't any money and lived in a workman's cottage alone, then it would be all right.'

'Yes, I understand. You're lonely. No people of your own age about—except me,' he added.

'Well—there it is. It will be all right. It's a comfort to say something to somebody.'

'You can always talk to me. Because I think the world of him. It wouldn't be right to talk about him if I didn't like him. At least, that's the way I see it.'

'No. It wouldn't be right.' She sighed. 'I suppose most people are unhappy about something.'

He came very close to her. She could feel his breath on her cheek.

'But I don't want *you* to be unhappy. I can't bear it. I lie thinking about it. I want to make you happy. You're so beautiful and so young, it isn't right for you to be unhappy. It isn't right, and it mustn't be.'

The words came from him breathlessly. He caught her shoulders in his hands, kissed her on the mouth, turned and went out of the wood.

Young Simon Brennan had, on this particular afternoon, mistaken the hour of his mother's sewing party. For this reason or that, it was to be at four-thirty instead of three-thirty.

Dorothy, standing at the window of the school-room, watching the blue-grey dusk, was thinking about Jim Burke. She was wondering what Jim Burke was doing.

Gilbert, seated on a tip-tilted chair at the table with the shabby green cloth, was wondering about Jim Burke too. But in quite another fashion from Dorothy. He was wondering when Jim would give him another lesson. He had in front of him, piled on a sheet of *The Times* newspaper, a heap of putty. Jim had given him already one lesson; his sharp skin-tight face with its ardent eager eyes was drawn into the work as though face and putty were one. Jim had not had time to show him very much. The fact also was that Jim did not know very much, working by the light of nature rather than reason. But Jim had told him enough to make certain things more obvious. For instance, a head must have proper proportions, and these proportions must be decided before the work was begun.

Benson, the dog, lay on the floor, his head on his paws, his eyes fixed on his master. In his muddled, neglected life he had never, before this, belonged to anybody. Now, quite beyond any question, he belonged to Gilbert Brennan.

Gilbert felt for him a burning love which was part of his ardent repressed nature. He wanted to love all the world; everything was appearing to him as though for the first time; but he was desperately shy and full of pride and terrified of rebuffs. He seemed to many people a sulky, rather ill-mannered boy. But Benson would not rebuff him nor would he think him ill-mannered. Benson worshipped him. In Benson's eyes Gilbert could do no possible wrong. Even Dorothy thought that Gilbert could do wrong and sometimes told him so. It was a new experience to him to have this worship and it touched him deeply.

Dorothy turned from the window and came to see what Gilbert was doing. She realized that although as yet he knew nothing at all about it, there was something in the movement of his slim strong fingers that meant a talent.

'Gillie—do you think Jim really cares anything about us?'

'Care about us? Of course he does.' His eyes were bent over the table.

'No, but I mean—would it matter to him if we died tomorrow?'

'Of course it would.'

'I do hope so.' She sighed. A month or two ago she would have said what was in her mind—'I love him most awfully.' Now for some reason she did not.

There was nothing wrong in loving Jim Burke, but now, for the first time, she wanted to keep it to herself. She thought of love as something that you felt when you wanted to protect and defend somebody, and to help him in every possible way. She loved her family and she was beginning to love Mrs. Mark, but that was something different. It was as though Jim Burke were surrounded with a ring of almost blinding light.

'You know that horrid man who gave you Benson——'

'There's nothing horrible about him.'

'Oh yes there is. Everything is horrible about him. That waterproof he wears and his eyes and his teeth and the way he shuffles along——'

'Well?' Gilbert was moulding the putty. It was a funny-looking head, but all the same he felt behind his fingers a new power. This power was the most exciting thing he had ever known. His fingers couldn't *do* anything yet, but soon they would. It was as though they were alive with separate life.

'He spoke to me again this morning—when I was coming out of the Post Office. I do wish he wouldn't.'

'What did he say?'

'Something about he might be going to London, and he hoped I was well, and was the little dog all right?'

'What did you say?'

'I got away as soon as I could. I *hate* him. I wonder who he is and what he's doing. He said something about Mr. Cromwell. He said he didn't want that blind man coming along spying things out.'

Gilbert stood up, stretching his thin arms.

'Of course it doesn't look anything *yet*. But Jim said I wasn't to put in the eyes and mouth until I'd made the general shape right.'

As soon as he rose, Benson rose too. Now the whole of his body was moving and his eyes pleaded with Gilbert—to do what? It didn't matter so long as they did it together.

The door opened and Simon came in.

It was obvious at once that something had happened to him. When Simon was excited his whole personality was bent to one purpose—namely, to realize his excitement to the full. He was not emotional or sentimental so much as running at full power. When, at the age of four, he was given his first train he said nothing, not even 'Thank you,' but at once, without losing a single moment, set himself to doing everything with a train and railway lines that could be done. He was a realist with a wonderful power for disregarding everything that was not to the point.

He had never as yet in his life seen any human being kiss another as Jim Burke had kissed Mrs. Cromwell. He had never as yet seen any human being look at another human being as Jim Burke looked at Mrs. Cromwell. He did not, of course, think it shocking or immoral. He supposed that anybody could kiss anybody; himself he hated to be kissed. But he had not remotely supposed that Jim Burke would want to kiss Mrs. Cromwell. Jim Burke was not, in his experience, a kissing person, and was all the better for that.

There had, however, been something very strange in the kissing of Mrs. Cromwell by Jim Burke, something very strange also in the way Jim had rushed from the wood, something very strange in Mrs. Cromwell's face as she stood there afterwards without moving.

Simon had crept away and then run home. He wanted to tell someone about it and discover what it had really meant. He would ask Jim Burke as soon as he saw him.

He said very little to his brother and sister. He went to the bedroom that he shared with Gilbert to take off his overcoat. Coming out he encountered his mother, who was going downstairs to receive her guests.

'Why, Simon! Haven't you had your tea?'

'No, Mother.' Then he said slowly, 'I've been in Mr. Cromwell's garden.'

She was in a great hurry and so could not be as cross as she ought to be.

'You naughty boy—I told you——'

He was staring at her with excitement.

'I was in the little wood and Jim Burke was there and Mrs. Cromwell. I was hiding to give Jim a surprise, but he kissed Mrs. Cromwell and ran away.'

Mrs. Brennan stopped on the top of the stairs.

'What!'

So there *was* something exciting about Jim kissing Mrs. Cromwell! He was right.

'Jim kissed Mrs. Cromwell and ran away!'

'Jim Burke . . . !'

She stood staring at her small son as though she were in a trance. Simon knew nothing about trances, but he did know that delightful warming self-approbating sensation of being the bearer of important news. At the same time, very oddly, he was uncomfortable. There was something in his mother's face that frightened him. *Why* should Jim Burke kiss Mrs. Cromwell? That was what he wanted so eagerly to know.

Now he was suddenly wondering—why should Jim Burke *not* kiss Mrs. Cromwell? His mother's face made him ask himself that question.

The ladies had already arrived. After a little pleasant conversation they settled down to their tea.

Mrs. Lamplough was sitting in a chair by the fire. Daisy Brennan touched her arm.

'Alice, come over here a moment. I've something to tell you.'

They went together to the window.

'You won't believe it, but it's true. My Simon . . . "

Miss Vergil called out:

'Now you two! What's the mystery?'

Very soon they all of them knew.

CHAPTER IV

In Celia's Room—The Winter Afternoon—At Mrs. Mark's Cottage

CELIA STOOD LISTENING with all possible intentness. As she had expected, the Voice came from the heart of a golden cloud. She had always thought that it would. God's Voice in a cloud. She must not miss a single word. The Voice had the tone and measure of a singing-master who had once taught her or tried to teach her; it was rich, resonant, and patient. It was also, as she had not expected, quite conversational. It was friendly, just as the singing-master's had been. He had attempted once, she remembered, to kiss her.

'I am not saying,' the Voice continued, 'that you are entirely to blame. Allowances will be made. But it *is* entirely your own affair. You can't say that you haven't had plenty of warning.'

The Voice paused as though it expected her to say something. But she did not speak.

'You have, of course, been shockingly educated. Simply not educated at all. A great deal of that has been your own fault. You were not at all a stupid child, and if you had not been so lazy and selfish you would have protested against the kind of education you were getting, or rather not getting. There was plenty of good education to be had. You might have learned at least one language properly, read some books that taught you something. You might have tried to learn what music was really about. You had some natural taste. You were too idle and self-willed to bother.'

The Voice paused again. Celia said nothing. There was nothing to be said.

'You disliked being made love to, especially by old men, but your vanity was exorbitant. That night you spent with young Fellowes you did not enjoy at all. The bottle-parties you went to really disgusted you, especially the one at Mrs. Highman's, but you were frightened to seem peculiar. No one else was shocked, so you mustn't be either. All very stupid.'

The Voice paused again. It was getting very cold and there were shadows like gigantic mailed figures in the mist that clung about the mountainside.

'However, you are at last in real danger. I am warning you. I shall do nothing whatever to stop you. I gave you freewill just as I gave it to everybody else. If you do the wrong thing it will be nobody's fault but your own. I am warning you.'

Celia thought that perhaps she should say, 'Thank you very much.' She said nothing. Her teeth were beginning to chatter with the cold.

The Voice became suddenly more tender.

'But, my dear child, I cannot tell you what happiness it will be to me—and indeed to all of us—if you avoid this danger. I have a great tenderness for you. I shall have the same tenderness whatever you do. It is yourself that you will punish, and most bitterly. This is your last chance. Pray consider . . . pray consider . . . pray consider . . .'

The Voice faded away. The cloud was no longer golden, and there was much movement, confusion behind the mist. She was now so dreadfully cold that she must do something about it. She was naked. She rose to her feet and found Jim Burke standing there. He was naked also.

'How foolish!' she said aloud. 'He was only my singing-master.'

'Certainly he was,' Jim Burke said. 'Come with me and we'll forget all about him.'

This was the moment. She saw quite clearly that thousands of eyes were watching her through the mist. There was intense silence. They were waiting to see what she would do.

'Why shouldn't I?' she cried aloud, defying them. 'Why shouldn't I have some fun?'

She caught Jim Burke's hand, but she wasn't happy. He caught her in his arms, but his body burnt her as though with fire.

'Oh, don't!' she cried out. 'You're hurting me!'

'I don't care!' he shouted. 'I've got you now. You're mine! You're mine!'

'I'm not!' she cried. 'I belong to Julius!'

But it was too late. The wind rose and shrieked about them. They were rushing down the mountain at a terrible speed and she knew that, in a moment, they would be destroyed. Horrible things were there waiting for them.

Her terror was frantic. She could not see Jim Burke. She could not stop her falling. She fell, she fell, she fell!

She screamed:

'Julius! Julius! Save me! Save me!'

She woke up.

She felt at once his arms about her. He had slipped out of his bed into hers. He held her closely against him, pushing her head back a little so that he might kiss her mouth and stroke her forehead. Above everything else she loved the touch of his hands on her forehead. His hands, his hands! She clung to him. Her eyes were wet. Passionately they loved. Completely they were mingled, and when at last they drew apart it was only their bodies that were separating.

They lay now very quietly, their hearts hammering but wrapped in a great peace. Her head was on his breast, her hand on his thigh: his hand very gently enclosed her neck, stroking it a little, moving downwards to the hollow of her back.

They began quietly to talk.

'What was it? A nightmare?'

'Yes. I dreamt that God was warning me. His voice was like a singing-master's I once had.'

'Warning you of what?'

'Of being an idiot! And I *was* one. I was nearly lost. I went rushing down to perdition.' She said nothing about Jim Burke.

'And then you called out for me?'

'Yes.'

'That was one sensible thing anyway!'

She sighed. He laid his hand above her heart.

'Don't sigh. The danger is over. You're safe.'

'I don't know that it is. At night everything is all right. We love one another. We trust one another. Oh, Julius, you are a darling at night!'

He kissed her.

'But in the day it is all different. As soon as it is dark we run towards one another with cries of joy as though we had lost one another during the day.'

'In all married life,' he said, 'it is either the day or the night that is more difficult—unless both are so easy that they amount to nothing at all. Darling . . . I can ask you now, what has been the matter all these last weeks? Why have you been so nervous? Why have you been suddenly so angry with me? Tell me—tell me truthfully—do you find my blindness more than you can endure? Are you frightened when you see years and years of it stretching ahead of you? Did I do you a terrible injustice by marrying you?'

She answered at last, in a low trembling voice: 'I'm not good enough . . . I haven't any character . . . I'm just rotten.'

He caught her and held her so close to him that she felt the pulse of his heart beat against her ribs.

'Darling, darling! You *have* character; you have everything. Only trust yourself as well as me. . . .'

But she drew back from him a little and said again, very low:

'Would you forgive me, whatever I did? Would you still love me, whatever I did?'

He did not answer. She was suddenly aware of his blindness.

At last he said:

'I don't know . . . I can't tell. I don't know myself well enough. I don't know how I'd behave.' Then quite sharply he asked:

'What do you mean? Whatever you did?'

'If I stole, if I went to prison, if I were unfaithful.'

'I don't know. I can't tell how I'd behave.'

She went on in so low a voice that he could scarcely hear her:

'Because I would love you just the same. If I did something terrible it wouldn't be because I didn't love you.'

He sighed as she had done.

She went on:

'The trouble is I don't know myself. I love you so awfully that it might drive me . . .'

He said almost with a cry:

'What's the matter? Are you frightened of doing something?'

'That's the trouble. I'm frightened of everything. In the day-time I'm all by myself—I've never been so lonely in my life before.'

To his horror she began to cry, submissively, like a child. He caught her to him in an agony of distress.

'You mustn't cry! You mustn't cry! Dearest, dearest—you mustn't! You mustn't! Lonely? How can you be lonely? When I am with you always, loving you always——'

She interrupted: 'No, no! You are not with me always! In the day you're not. Often you go away from me and from every-body. Then I have no one else. No one here—no one of my own age who understands what we're like—all of us who never had any proper life.' She was quiet. She sat up, away from him, staring down at him although it was so dark.

'I've never told you, Julius—but I slept with a man when I was seventeen.'

'I've never asked you, have I?' He pulled her down to him.
'I understand more than you think. I know the kind of life you
had. I know how much older I am. . . . We have to be tested,
both of us. We don't know what we really are yet. I'll pull
you through. You'll pull me through. Only tell me everything—
everything. Then I'll help you.'

'Yes. You help me,' she murmured. 'I'm nearly asleep. Help
me, Julius. Help me.'

On a certain afternoon early in December Celia decided to
call on Mrs. Mark.

It was the first day of winter. In Glebeshire winter is seldom
severe. It is a season there of mists, of sudden bursts of sunshine
as warm as early summer, of drifting rain that seems, even in
December, to be encouraging violets and primroses; above all,
of winds from the sea that blow the chimney-smoke athwart the
sky and carry the salt spray on to lanes and fields far from the
shore.

But today was winter. The sky was snow-blue, the air still
with a sting of frost. Scent was keen. You could smell the leaf-
mould of the hazel. There had been a night-frost and, in spite
of the sun, patches of faint silver lay like spider-web still on
the field. The silence was winter's silence. A dog barked; somewhere a motor-engine purred; a bird sang, stopped, and sang
again.

Celia was made happy by the weather. When she encountered
Phyllis Lock at the end of the village she felt very friendly. She
thought Phyllis Lock a silly young woman, but she was sorry
for her because she had so awful an old mother. Phyllis was
wearing a frightful coat of bright green. Celia knew that her
own little flame-coloured hat and short fur coat beautifully became her. She felt therefore more kindly towards poor Phyllis.

'What a lovely day!'

'Yes, isn't it?' Phyllis stared at her with all her mouse-coloured
eyes.

'That is because of my hat,' Celia thought.

'How are you? I haven't seen you for quite a while.'

'No, we haven't—I mean I haven't . . .'

Phyllis had a laugh so meaningless that the kindest thing was to call her nervous. She was not, however, nervous of anyone or anything.

'How is your mother?'

'Very well, thank you. *What* a lovely day!'

'I hope you'll come to tea one day.'

'Thank you. I certainly will.'

Then, with an intentness that was more than polite, she said: 'How is Mr. Cromwell?'

'Very well, thank you.'

'Oh, I *am* glad!'

'Why—had you heard that he had been ill or something?'

'Not at all. Oh no, certainly not. We all like Mr. Cromwell so much, you know.'

Celia laughed.

'Of course you do. Well, I must be going on.'

'Yes. So must I.' Phyllis stared at Celia's hat so passionately that Celia almost offered to give it her. But it would look terrible on Phyllis. Everything did.

'Well, good-bye. Mind you come to tea soon.'

'Yes, I will. Thank you very much. What a lovely day, isn't it?'

So Celia went on beyond the village pleased about her hat. But what a girl! Now that she thought of it Mrs. Lamplough yesterday had also stared, but Mrs. Lamplough was awful and Mrs. Brennan was awful and Miss Vergil was awful. Why were there no nice women in this dreadful place? No one save Mrs. Mark, and she did not belong here.

Celia was as suddenly depressed as five minutes before she had been happy. They did not like her, these women. Mrs. Brennan, of course, hated her. They liked Julius. That had been an odd remark of that silly girl's. 'We like Mr. Cromwell'—as though she had said: 'We don't like *you*, though. None of us do.'

What did she care? What did it matter if a lot of silly old women in a silly little village disliked her? But she did care. She wanted to be liked, to be gay, to be popular. Why did they not come more often to see her? That was Julius' fault. He did not care for dinner-parties. He wished to sit alone with his music. No one liked her. No one loved her. Yes, poor Jim Burke loved her. That was very wrong of him. She had not spoken to him for at least three days after he had kissed her. But it was very warming that someone should love her, and, because she loved Julius so dearly, there was no danger in it. She knew how to manage Jim Burke as she had managed so many other young men before him. And he *was* young! Young as all her friends had once been. And he could see when she wore pretty clothes and looked her best. Could see and admire. Of what use was it to say: 'Julius, I am wearing a flame-coloured hat. Julius, this dress is blue like the sea'? Julius only knew that she was there when he touched her.

There were tears in her eyes. How she wished, oh, *how* she wished that Bobby Hills or Diana Maurice or Stephen Ludlow would appear in the road at that moment. What fun they would have! How words would rush out, how they would laugh, the jokes there would be!

Why did she not invite Diana or Bobby to come down and stay? Julius would not like it—or, if he did, *they* would not like it! Dull for them, a place like this. Dull for them, dull for everybody. And here, instead of Bobby or Diana, was Mrs. Mark's cottage.

She rang the bell. Mrs. Mark herself appeared.

'Why, Mrs. Cromwell! How delightful!'

Celia was depressed, she was lonely, she was therefore on her dignity. She felt warm towards Mrs. Mark, but, because the old ladies in Garth did not like her, she would be the grand Mrs. Cromwell. She was, in fact, as she walked graciously into the cottage, like a child dressed up in her mother's clothes.

And she found other children there—the three Brennan children seated at the tea-table. She drew back.

'Oh, I didn't know——'

'It isn't a party. It's just that they came over to tea. We're all delighted for you to join us.'

'No, no. How are you, children? I'll come another time. It's your own special party.'

'It isn't in the least.'

Celia saw Simon staring at her, then grinning. She saw Dorothy smiling shyly. She saw Gilbert, whom she knew very little, staring apprehensively, his hand on the collar of a ridiculous mongrel dog.

She saw also one of the most magnificent teas she had ever beheld. There was a large china dish with yellow roses on the cover that must hold muffins or crumpets or both. There was a big saffron cake. There were brown buns with sugar like snow spread on them, glass dishes with blackberry jelly, strawberry jam and gooseberry, a comb of honey, a loaf of brown bread, crusty and dark, a square of butter as yellow as ducklings, and a lovely 'tumble' of Glebeshire cream with the crisp pale covering and the golden luxuriance beneath it.

Now the weather had made Celia very hungry. When she saw a cake, three tiers of it, rising to a postman carrying letters in red and white sugar, she could only stare like a baby.

'You see, it's Dorothy's birthday and Mr. and Mrs. Brennan have to be in Polchester, so——'

'That's a nice shy girl,' Celia thought, 'I've always liked her,' and, impulsively, as she did everything, she unclasped the necklace of tiny seed pearls round her throat, went up to Dorothy, holding it out.

'My birthday present is very late but most sincere.'

'Oh no, I couldn't—I really—I mustn't——'

'Please. I bought these once in Paris to give to a friend in London. They are of no value, but I knew she'd like them. And when I got to London I found she'd married her bank manager, a horrible fat old man, and I was so disgusted that I wore the necklace myself. So you see they were *meant* as a present!'

This was a story invented on the urge of the moment, and had not a word of truth in it save that the pearls had been bought in Paris. But Dorothy had never owned any jewelry save a ruby ring out of a cracker, which, unknown to anyone, she had long treasured in a drawer. But this! A pearl necklace!

'Oh, I couldn't! I couldn't! Mother won't let me!'

Celia smiled grimly.

'Don't tell your mother who gave it you. Just say it was a present.'

But the mention of Mrs. Brennan reminded her of her married dignity again. She pressed the necklace into Dorothy's hand and then sat down rather stiffly. She knew that the party had been gay just before she entered and was gay no longer. She wanted to throw her flame-coloured hat on the floor, make them all dance in the middle of the room, and then sit down to devour the largest tea of her life. But she was Mrs. Cromwell whom Mrs. Brennan, the mother of these children, hated, so she was grand and stiff and ceremonious.

She fancied, however, that Simon, who for some reason looked especially wicked with a napkin under his chin, knew just what she was thinking.

'I do hope you're hungry,' said Mrs. Mark.

'Moderately,' Celia said with delicacy, eyeing the dish with the yellow flowers.

'Because we are all ravenous. And I do hope you'll stay and play games with us afterwards.'

'Oh, well, I shall have to be getting along, I'm afraid. Just one cup of tea, and then . . .'

To her horror, after saying this, quite another voice spoke straight from the heart of her stomach. This voice said urgently to Simon: 'Take the cover off that dish, Simon. Is it muffins or crumpets?'

Simon took the lid off the dish. They were crumpets so buttery that the very sight of them suggested dripping chins.

But all was not yet well. The children showed a very delicate politeness, as though Celia were their guest as well as Mrs. Mark's. Only Simon knew her. Dorothy had heard enough to know that her mother and her mother's friends disapproved of her. She could not, as she looked at her daintiness, the exquisite colouring of her face, the smartness of her little hat, her youth and yet her absolute maturity, believe that she was anything but perfect. Dorothy had never before seen, close at hand, any lady who was like the pictures in the *Tatler* and the *Sketch*.

She had always thought her mother beautiful, but now there was a dreadful temptation to betrayal. No, no. Mrs. Cromwell was of the Town, her mother of the Country, that was the difference. But *why* did her mother and Mrs. Lamplough not like this lovely creature? Another temptation to treachery. Could it be that they were jealous?

Dorothy noticed another thing, and that was that Mrs. Mark was completely at her ease with Mrs. Cromwell as her own mother could never be. Mrs. Mark was in appearance very ordinary, a squarely-built, white-haired, elderly lady. But Mrs. Mark was what Dorothy's mother was not—secure in some inner confidence, so that flame-coloured hats and plucked eyebrows could not shake her.

Gilbert, for his part, was thinking of Julius Cromwell. Ever since that meeting with him in the Well he had been thinking of him. He wanted very much to see him again, but he had none of Simon's assurance. Mrs. Cromwell was all right. She was pretty and her clothes were smart, but was she nice to Mr. Cromwell? Did she look after him and help him when he moved about, and be at his side when he wanted something? If she did not, Gilbert thought poorly of her.

For the rest, he was preoccupied with the behaviour of Benson. It had turned out that Benson was a 'One Person' dog. Now this no one could have told. Some dogs were and some dogs were

not. It had touched Gilbert most deeply that Benson cared for
nobody but him. It seemed that he was the one and only human
being for whom Benson had been waiting. If Benson had been
a handsome grand pedigree dog it would not matter so much.
But Benson was a dog wanted by no one, thought beautiful by
no one (and indeed he was not beautiful); it was therefore something very wonderful that this neglected dog should need him,
depend upon him, trust him. However, sentiment apart, the
point just now was—how would Benson behave? For this was
Benson's first party, his first visit, since Gilbert had acquired
him, into society.

From the moment that they entered Mrs. Mark's sitting-room
Benson thought only of food. He could not see the things on
the table, but he could smell them. It was as though he had never
smelt food before. He sat close to the table-leg and stared fer-
vently upward. His body was stung into a passion. When someone said 'Benson' he turned his head for a brief instant, but
immediately it swung back again. Behind his desire there was
still, in all probability, his love for his master—but of the two
devotions, which would be the stronger?

'No one is to give Benson anything,' Gilbert said firmly.

'Who is Benson?' asked Celia.

'He's my dog.'

'What a funny name!'

'The man who gave him to me said he called him that because he was like a man he knew once.'

'Funny!' Celia said. 'I knew a boy called Benson once. He
could do tricks and he produced a rabbit out of a hat at our
house once and it was nearly killed by my mother's cat.'

Dorothy and Gilbert did not think this funny. They were
distressed about the rabbit. But Simon wanted to know more.

'Did the cat kill the rabbit?'

'No, it didn't kill it. But it tore a lot of its fur and scratched
its eye. . . .'

Things were not going well. Mrs. Mark wished, in her heart,

that Celia Cromwell had come on any other day but this one.

The situation was saved, however, by Celia's extraordinary appetite. Celia had been brought up, like all her generation, to worship slimness and had gone through much suffering. Today the sharp air, the wonderful food, the presence of the children, made her throw away all her caution. The children watched her with amazement. They had always believed that only *they* were greedy, that grown-up mature persons ate chiefly from a sense of duty. Now they beheld Mrs. Cromwell eat crumpets, three or more, then spread brown bread with cream and blackberry jelly, then devour honeycomb, then saffron cake, and then say, quite brightly, 'Dorothy, it's about time you cut that cake!'

'Have some more blackberry jelly first,' Simon, who had been watching her efforts with delighted amazement, said huskily.

'I think I will,' Celia answered.

Dorothy got up to cut the cake. She blushed when she had to do anything in public. Her mother had told her so often that she was awkward—told her with kindly irritation—'Now, Dorothy, *really!* Look what you've done!'

At one time she had envied quite desperately the girls of whom she read in stories, who were for ever drilling in gymnasiums and told to hold their backs straight. If only *she* had gone to a boarding-school, she had been wont to sigh! But now it appeared quite plainly that she was clumsy by nature and that no school in the world could have cured her.

Oddly enough, both Mrs. Mark and Celia were thinking quite the opposite of this, as they watched her. Her body beneath the village amateurishness of the pink frock showed the immaturity of the child, but it had strength and poise and the naturalness of any young lovely thing. Her eyes were large, dark, and serious: her dark brown hair fell in two strong plaits, one on either side of her slim white neck. Her mouth, her most beautiful feature, was open a little with the excitement of the moment and was half afraid to smile.

'She has lovely arms and legs,' Celia thought, longing to tear that cheap frock off her and dress her properly. The little necklace of pearls seemed so very grand above the badly-cut collar of the dress.

'Speech! Speech!' Simon cried. He got this from *The Cock-House at Fellsgarth*, which he was at the moment enthusiastically reading.

Dorothy's hand that held the knife trembled a little.

'I can't make a speech, but it wouldn't be right not to thank everybody, and I do very much. Mrs. Mark has given me a cuckoo-clock and I told her before that I wanted one more than anything, so that isn't fair, and Gilbert has given me his first head he's ever made out of clay, and that makes me very proud.'

'And I've given you some scissors,' Simon interrupted.

'Simon's given me some scissors which I wanted very badly. Other things I've had are a pot of chrysanthemums from Jim Burke and a Bible from Dad and Mummy. And then there's this.' She fingered the tiny pearls. 'I don't know what to say. I think, perhaps——' She paused, very confused, then cleared her throat and went on, 'Mrs. Cromwell was so kind and she saw I had a birthday when she hadn't expected me to have one, and so perhaps she gave me the necklace because she was so kind. She was surprised and didn't really mean— What I mean is, it's so wonderful and much too good——' She hesitated. She looked around her, her eyes full of tears.

Celia jumped up, put her arms round her and kissed her.

'Come on,' she said. 'Don't be an ass. Of course I want you to have the pearls. I'm most awfully pleased, as a matter of fact. Come on. Cut the cake. Simon just can't bear waiting.'

So the cake was cut and they all cheered and the sugar post-man was given to Simon.

Afterwards they cleared all the tea-things away and played games. If they were all children Celia was the most childish. She threw her hat on the floor. She played the piano for them to dance to; she hid with Simon in a cupboard in Mrs. Mark's bedroom during Hide-and-Seek, and some very strange feelings stole over her as she held his thick strong little body close to her (for the cupboard was small). Would she have a child one day? That would put everything right.

Simon was engaged in wondering whether he dared ask her why she had kissed Jim Burke. The thought of his mother's face stopped him. In some queer fashion he had the idea that he must not tell anyone else of that adventure lest he should hurt Mr. Cromwell.

But how mysterious were grown-up persons! He did not like women and was relieved when Dorothy opened the cupboard door and discovered them. He had been terrified lest Mrs. Cromwell should kiss him. She seemed to be a very kissing person.

The best of it was, however, when they acted charades. Celia now was really splendid. She threw herself into this as though her very life were threatened. She did 'Shipmate' with Gilbert and Benson. In the first syllable she pretended to be seasick over the side of a chair. In the second she dressed Gilbert in a shawl, gave herself a moustache with a burnt match, and tied a handkerchief round Benson's head. When they acted the whole word they all pretended to be sailors rolling out on a spree and Benson barked his head off.

When it was all over she stood in the middle of the room, the moustache giving her a wonderful piquancy, clapped her hands and cried:

'I know! I know! We'll have a wonderful Christmas party at Garth House and ask everybody, and we'll have charades, wonderful charades!'

Her eyes shone, her cheeks flushed, her body danced with happiness. All the children clapped their hands.

Gilbert was especially happy, for Benson had behaved, from first to last, like a perfect gentleman.

CHAPTER V

A Night of Splendid Stars—At the Rectory—Mrs. Gayner's Room—In the Garden

DAISY BRENNAN, like many another, was a disappointed woman. Only child of an adoring mother, she had been taught to consider herself unique—unique in beauty, intelligence, goodness, and charm.

So long as she could believe that these graces were really hers she was happy and kind. She believed in them all until she married Frank Brennan, for her beauty was undeniable, her circle stupid, her nature on the side of the angels, and her charm resilient so long as she was not crossed.

She was heroine of her group in Surbiton and her mother adored her. Frank Brennan was curate at the church in Surbiton where she attended, and they fell in love with one another instantly. Because they were both virtuous marriage was the only cure. At the end of the first year Daisy discovered that she had married the laziest man in England.

This discovery reacted on her in a number of ways. She was herself lazy and three childbirths made her lazier. She was also bewildered by her husband. She could not tell whether he loved her or no; one day it seemed that he did, another he was, it appeared, unaware of her existence. This uncertainty gave him a great fascination for her. She remained in love with him because of it.

She also loved her children so long as they loved her, which, when they were small, they most certainly did. Without ever saying so, she gave them to understand that she was a wonderful woman. She had, wherever she was, a number of admirers, and these admirers said to the children: 'There's no one like your mother, dear. You're lucky to have such a mother.'

It was not until they had been two years at Garth in Roselands that she discovered that she was a disappointed woman. It happened one night when Frank suddenly leaned in the bed towards her and said: 'We're not worth much, the pair of us. We don't deserve to be alive really,' and then turned on his side and went to sleep.

She never forgave Frank this little speech. There had been a terrible conviction behind his words. He had never said anything unkind to her before. When in the morning she asked him what he meant by it he asserted that he had never said it, or, if he had, that it must have been in a dream and he was speaking to somebody else. 'Probably my double, my dear. Everyone has a double, you know.'

She was not to be deceived. Someone—and after all, the person who knew her best, who had lived with her, eaten with her, slept with her, whose children she had borne—thought her a woman of no value. *This* was the direction in which life had taken her when she might, had everything worked properly, been Queen of a London salon.

She saw, for a brief space, with clear eyes. She saw that she left her duties to Dorothy, to the cook, to the governess, that her religion was a humbug, and that her intelligence had died of atrophy.

She saw that the ladies of Garth and their compliments were nothing to be very proud of. She cried, and catching Gilbert to her breast, asked him whether he loved her, and when he, his eyes frightened, said that he did, she answered solemnly that he mustn't, that she wasn't worthy of her children's affection, that she was much better dead.

It is the fate of all of us, however, that we should be allowed only brief moments of vision, and Daisy Brennan very quickly saw herself as a misunderstood woman who had married the wrong husband, been plunged into dreary seclusion, been robbed of all her proper destiny.

Beneath this foolishness there was a good, kindly, well-meaning girl who had never, in spite of the years, grown into a mature woman. When things went well with her she was generous and warm of heart. She concentrated upon the adoration of the Garth ladies and the devotion of her children.

For a time things went very well. She shared activity, she was kind to the villagers, and she found that she was still in love with her husband. Sexually she was a one-man woman; physical infidelity quite truly shocked her. She listened to the funny and sometimes coarse stories that Miss Vergil and Mrs. Lamplough and Fred Ironing occasionally told her, and laughed with the narrator because she wanted to appear a woman of the world, but she neither liked them nor approved them. Modern novels really revolted her and she was passionately prudish about all the processes of nature. All this was natural to her because she had no sense of humour.

So things went on until there was the shock of Gilbert's extraordinary behaviour about Rafiel. This was quickly followed by Simon's passion for Mr. Cromwell. Even Dorothy, the quiet obedient faithful Dorothy, felt a devotion for Mrs. Mark.

She could not endure that her children should not think her the most wonderful person in the world. This was not only vanity but also the apprehension of a very real love. If her children deserted her, who was left? Then it appeared that Mrs. Lamplough, Miss Vergil, Phyllis Lock, found Mrs. Cromwell lovely, smart, a woman of the world. They didn't *like* her, of course, but the more they disliked her the more they were fascinated. So, very quickly and very naturally, her hatred for Celia Cromwell became a motive force in her life. Celia was, to her mind, a poor little, almost dwarfish thing who, because her husband had money, was able to dress smartly and astonish the natives. What an injustice was here! Daisy Brennan, with her magnificent figure and carriage, was born to astonish London. Because she was married to a poor clergyman she could not even astonish Garth in Roselands and must take second place as soon as this little upstart arrived.

It became evident very soon that Celia Cromwell was one of

these loose modern girls. She went with her poor blind husband to church on Sunday (*and* the clothes she wore on these occasions!) but you could see, from her conceited, arrogant look as she sat there, that she was a heathen. Daisy Brennan had seen her lip curl scornfully one Sunday at a passage in one of Frank's sermons—and this also showed her ignorance, because Frank always chose his sermons from the very best preachers!

Being irreligious she must also be immoral. Girls of this post-war generation never had any morals! Lucky for her that her husband was blind. And he, poor simple man (no one could help but like him), what must he do but engage Jim Burke, have him in the house to read the daily papers! Jim Burke, a man scandalous with women, a scamp and a vagabond.

Then there came the episode of Simon. Celia Cromwell insulted her when she went, as any mother would do, to rescue her child. To confess the truth, Daisy Brennan was a little nervous of her son Simon. She could never be sure of his thoughts and he looked at her now and then in the very strangest way. Gilbert and Dorothy were simple enough, but Simon, no. He reminded her at times most unpleasantly of her husband. Father and son had the same impenetrability. Finally there came this dreadful thing—Celia Cromwell and Jim Burke kissing in the Garth garden. Her innocent child had seen it, which made it the more disgusting!

Within twenty-four hours everyone in the village knew it. No one was surprised. They knew their Jim Burke. The villagers for the most part took a philosophical view. What would you expect of a young pretty girl, always dressed in the latest London fashions, married to a blind man old enough to be her father?

Sexual looseness was not regarded very seriously in Garth. The record for illegitimate children in Glebeshire was as high as anywhere in England, and ever since so many poor vigorous young men had been killed in the last war, you might expect the men who remained to be in lively demand.

But Miss Vergil and Phyllis Lock, ignorant of positive experience, took their adventures vicariously, and Mrs. Lamplough had never found Mr. Lamplough a very satisfactory husband.

Daisy Brennan was the only one of them all who was deeply and truly revolted.

There arrived one morning in the post an invitation from Garth House for a Christmas party. Not only were Mr. and Mrs. Brennan invited, but the three children also. An afternoon party.

At first Daisy Brennan was determined that they should none of them go. They should not accept hospitality from that wicked woman's hands.

On further consideration she was less certain. Everyone would accept. She liked and admired Mr. Cromwell. She was also curious and inquisitive. She would see how that wicked woman behaved on such an occasion. Moreover she enjoyed parties. But the children should not go. On that she was determined. She had been horrified when she discovered that Celia Cromwell had been present at Mrs. Mark's on the occasion of the tea-party. Dorothy had shown her the pearl necklace and she had wanted to order that it should be instantly returned to Celia Cromwell. But this she had found, to her own surprise, she had been unable to do.

Dorothy's joy had struck a chord in her own heart. She realized that Dorothy had never been given anything of value in all her life before. Had she had the money she would have showered gifts upon her children, who were part of herself and were good children and she loved them.

She hated Celia the more, however, for giving her girl something so much better than she could ever give her. She found herself kissing Dorothy and promising her, rather incoherently, that one day she would give her something very much better.

'You poor child!' she said. 'It isn't your mother's fault that you don't have lots of pretty things.'

Dorothy, surprised by these demonstrations and very happy that her mother loved her, was determined to do twice as much for her as she was already doing.

'You love your mother most, don't you, darling?'

'More than anyone in the world,' Dorothy said.

That was a night of splendid stars. No one in Garth could remember to have seen a night like this in their lives before.

'It's a crackling blue-smoked frost,' old Lamplough said to himself, striding along to spend the after-dinner evening with Julius Cromwell. He meant that a pale-blue shadowed haze hung about the hedges, and under it the rime sparkled on the grass.

On the moor farms, in the hamlets towards Rafiel, about the village of Garth itself, people came to their doors and said: 'Oh, look at the stars!'

In the doorway of a cottage not far from Sizyn Church the woman of the house stood, gazing up, a baby of six months, wrapped in a shawl so that only two eyes and a nose protruded, in her arms.

'Look at the stars, baby! Look at the stars, baby!' and the two eyes bright like diamonds stared up at the stars and then closed again in sleep.

At Miss Vergil's they were playing bridge—the Ironings, Phyllis, and their hostess. Miss Vergil was dummy. She had strolled to the door.

'I say, come and have a look! You've never seen such a sight!'

When the round was over they crowded to the door. Mrs. Ironing said:

'I always think that stars are like diamonds.'

Miss Vergil, moved beyond caution, put her arm round Phyllis and drew her close.

'Don't, dear!'

'Why not?'

'Fred will make fun.'

Then they forgot everything, for the stars blazed their personalities to nothing—and it was thus that they were at their best.

Daisy Brennan, their meal over, drew her husband to their door.

'Did you ever see such a sky?'

He was lighting his pipe.

'It's a sharp frost.'

'Yes, you can almost hear them crackle. Brr! it's cold.'

She followed him into the library. He sat in his old leather armchair, picked up a novel, stretched out his long legs, yawned, sighed with satisfaction (for this was an hour that he loved), and then, as she was standing in front of the fire looking at him, was forced to say:

'Well, my dear, what is it?'

'It's this.' She handed him the Cromwell invitation.

'Oh, so they're giving a party. Well, what about it? We're free, aren't we?'

'I don't want the children to go.'

'Oh, poor kids—why not? With all those stars shining too!'

'What *do* you mean?'

'On *such* a night—Shakespeare believed in stars.'

'Frank, please be serious.'

'I'm perfectly serious. Poor kids, why shouldn't they go? They don't get such a lot.'

'To that wicked woman! No. I altogether refuse.'

'Wicked?'

'Yes, you know perfectly well.'

'She kissed Jim Burke—or so our youngest son says.'

She was angry. Her voice shook as she answered:

'You condone adultery. You're a clergyman. You——'

'In the first place, we don't know that there's been any adultery. Kissing to Mrs. Cromwell's generation means nothing whatever. Further, I am quite certain that Mrs. Cromwell loves her husband. Further, as to my being a clergyman—I'm the rottenest in the Church of England.'

She said nothing.

'Does it ever occur to you, Daisy, that I'm sometimes ashamed of myself, that I'm shy of looking at the stars?'

She answered hotly:

'No, why should you be ashamed?'

'Oh, no more than the rest perhaps. All of us who have slipped our job. I'm not accusing myself. But at least I'm also not accusing anyone else.'

'It's your duty, Frank. Here is the grossest immorality——'

'Come, come! Jim Burke has kissed Mrs. Cromwell. Would you care to see the full sheet of all my thoughts—yes, every one —since I got up this morning? If you did you'd leave this house tonight. Not that they're worse than the rest. Does God go on forgiving, do you think? Over and over again? Every minute of the day? Or is there something in the idea that as He made us so He must suffer us?

'And, to return to this particular instance, do you really imagine that at an afternoon party with every old maid of the district present our children will have the chance of being perverted, ruined? I think not. And anyway your friend and crony Mrs. Lamplough is more dangerous than Mrs: Cromwell will ever be.'

She hated him in this mood.

'I don't want them to go.'

'They're going. I wish them to go. And that far-seeing man, Julius Cromwell, will protect them. In his house they are always safe.'

'Far-seeing! Why, he's blind!'

Her husband grinned up at her.

'Give me a kiss. You are a better woman than you appear on the surface.'

She kissed him because she loved him. She hated his moods but loved his unattainability. And she had learnt, after many years, that when he said a thing, he meant it.

On this night too—but not seeing the stars, for the curtains were drawn—Mrs. Gayner sat writing to her sister.

MY DEAR ALICE,

It's been quite a time since I've written but I've been terribly busy and there've been all sorts of troubles. I know you're silent as the grave, aren't you, dear, but things have a way of getting back as I used to find in the old married days, and although you're far away you never know, do you?

Since I wrote last I've made another very determined effort to get Douglas off to Jamaica and this time I thought I'd done it, for he comes in here one night—and every time he climbs in by that window, he knows where they keep that ladder in the tool-shed, I'm off my mind with terror—and begins to cry, laying his head in his arms just as he used to do when he was a little chap, and I couldn't get anything out of him for ever so long. He's got a room now with a Mrs. Gibbings at the far end of the village and it seems that she had an old Sealyam (I've spelt that wrong, I'm sure) that was all mangy and everything and, poor thing, it died. Douglas it seems had been nursing it and was heart-broken at its dying. All the same he's been stealing again—I know he has —and I pressed it upon him that he must get away before the police nab him and he brings disgrace on me as well as himself. I thought he'd decided but next day he's still here and cheeking the woman at the post-office. She goes so far as to ask me if I know who he is, saying that no one in the village can bear the sight of him. And yet, Alice, if they'd seen him with his head on the table crying his heart out over a mangy old dog they'd have thought different.

I'm just out of my wits and I'm sure I'm not myself for the sleep I'm not getting and the little I'm eating. I believe I'd be driven to tell Mr. Julius all about it were it not for Mrs. Crom-well. I can't say that things are any better between her and me than they were and I put down much of this to the girl Violet who, I'm certain, tells her lies about me, for the girl hates me and that's the truth. And now I'm telling you things, Alice, you're not to repeat, even to yourself, but it's a help to me to write to you about everything just as it is.

They are saying in the village that Mrs. Cromwell was seen kissing the young man Burke who I told you is helping Mr. Julius with the newspapers and such things, and they say even worse than kissing. That it's anything worse I don't believe for a single

*moment for Mrs. Cromwell loves Mr. Julius as anyone living in
this house can very well see, but this Burke has no morals at all
as everyone knew from when he was living in this village before.
And yet you can't help liking him for he'll do anything for you
and is so young and strong that if I was forty years younger
I'd fall for him myself. Where the trouble really is is that Mrs.
Cromwell and Mr. Julius are not hitting it off as they should do.
She's been used to a gay life and plenty of friends and it's a dull
life for her here and Mr. Julius likes to sit quiet and listen to his
gramophone. It's strange how two people can love one another
truly and aggravate one another all the day. He's not a saint and
never was one, and he raps out at her in a way he shouldn't. It's
my idea he feels his blindness twice as much since he married her
because she's wishing all the time he wasn't blind. She's never
learnt to put up with anything she doesn't like and it's a new thing
to her. But what I think, Alice, is that love is a very strange thing
and however long you live you'll always be surprised at the many
different kinds of love there are, like mine for Douglas and you,
and Mrs. Cromwell's for Mr. Julius, and Douglas' for his dogs,
and that nice lady Mrs. Mark for this house where she lived once
so that she's always coming over to have a look at it and puts her
hand on the banisters as though she'd take them away with her.
Just one small place like this village and all the kinds of love there
are in it—it makes you think, doesn't it?*

*The funny thing, Alice, is that I'm doing all I can to send my
Douglas out of the country, and yet if he goes I don't know what
I shall have to live for, I really don't—only the Lord Jesus will
show me what to do as He has always done.*

*All the trouble there is in the world just now and the trouble
there is in this house is because God is forgotten and He must
bring us back by suffering . . .*

There was a knock on her door.

'Come in,' she said, pushing the sheets under the blotting-paper.
The door opened and to her great surprise Jim Burke stood

there. He was wearing a white soft collar, a dark-blue suit. His brown skin made a fine contrast. He was as handsome and as healthy and as cheeky, Mrs. Gayner thought, as anyone she had ever seen—and she wouldn't mind if he kissed her.

'Hullo, Jim! What is it? You're a stranger here. Anything wrong with your room?'

'No, Mrs. Gayner, thank you. You're busy. I'll come another time.'

'Only writing to my sister. That can wait. Sit down.'

He took a chair and sat down, she noticed, like a gentleman, easily and lightly for a boy with his thick back and heavy thighs. His hair rising from his temples was almost white, blanched with the open air. His nails were beautifully clean and neat. Why wasn't she twenty again? Just as well perhaps that she wasn't!

'What is it?' she asked again. 'Anything I can do?'

'No, I don't know that there is. Something I ought to tell you, though.'

Oh dear! More trouble. As though there wasn't enough in the house already!

'Something to tell me? I don't want to hear it if it's unpleasant.'

'I think I ought to.'

He leant on the table towards her and smiled at her kindlily.

'I've been having a talk with your son.'

'Oh . . . !' She half rose, her hand at her throat.

'Now, Mrs. Gayner. Please.' He put out his hand and, for a moment, touched her soft one.

'Don't be frightened. I won't give you away.'

'How did you know?'

'Well, he stole my gold pencil.'

'Oh dear! Oh dear!'

'Wait a minute and I'll tell you. We were sitting in the "Three Crows" having a drink. Of course I'd seen him about a lot. I'd noticed he was very decent to the mongrels he'd have at his heels. A perfect passion for dogs he's got, and I liked that in him. Otherwise——'

'No. He isn't very likeable, Douglas isn't,' she sighed. 'I love him because I'm his mother, but in general he isn't very likeable.'

'I'd been writing an address for a man on a bit of paper. I turned to have a drink and when I looked back my pencil was gone. I knew that your son, who was sitting next to me, had taken it. I happened to put a great value on that pencil so I waited until he went out and followed him. Outside I caught him round the collar and asked for my pencil. Of course he said he hadn't got it, but I frightened him and he gave it me. I still held on to him and pretended I'd hand him over to the police, which of course I never intended to do. Then he told me he was your son.'

'Oh, what am I to do? What am I to do?' Mrs. Gayner cried. 'It's only got one ending.'

'Yes, it's only got one ending, Mrs. Gayner. He must leave here. Out of the country. I've got friends in America. Perhaps I could do something.'

'I've been trying. I was ready to give him the money for Jamaica, where I've a cousin who would help him, but he won't go.'

'Why don't you tell Mr. Cromwell? He thinks the world of you. He's ever so kind. Better he should hear it from you than from someone else. He's bound to know sooner or later.'

'Yes, I've thought of it often and often. But there's Mrs. Cromwell. She doesn't like me, I'm afraid. If she knew——'

At her mention of Mrs. Cromwell his face for a moment lightened.

'I'll turn it over in my mind. You mustn't mind my knowing, Mrs. Gayner. I shan't tell anybody.'

'No, of course I don't mind, Jim. It's a kind of relief. It's been awful having it all to myself.'

'Does he come here?'

'Yes, I'm afraid he does.'

'When does he come, and how?'

'At night. This sort of time. There's a ladder in the tool-shed, the one that's half ruined and isn't locked at night. He comes in by the window.'

'That isn't so good. Do you give him money?'

'A little now and again.'

She looked at him quite beseechingly.

'Well, you tell me if you're in trouble. I've been about the world quite a bit, you know.'

He got up and smiled.

'Don't you worry. Rum, isn't it? All the wasted love in the world.'

'Oh, but it isn't wasted! I'm all he has.'

'Yes, I know. And a nice way he repays you. There's other sorts of love too. Even in this small place there's enough different kinds of love to run the world with—and yet all the world's thinking of just now is hate.'

'I don't know what's coming to everybody.'

'Oh, it will be all right one day, I expect. Love!' His hand was on the door. He shrugged his shoulders. 'When it catches you you can do nothing whatever—nothing at all. It burns like a fire in your very stomach. I thought I knew a lot by now, but I never knew what love was—not until now. Well, so-long. Don't you worry.'

After he was gone she took out her letter again. But she couldn't continue it. She sat staring in front of her, thinking of Douglas.

Downstairs Julius and old Lamplough stood at the window of the study. The curtains had been drawn back. The stars blazed down over the dark deep well of the lawn. Celia was standing a little behind them. Julius had his hand on Lamplough's arm.

'I'm off to bed,' Celia said. 'The stars make me sleepy. Besides, I know that you two talk better without me.'

She held out her hand.

'Good night, Mr. Lamplough.'

He bent over her hand with a courtly old-fashioned gesture.

His dark shabby velveteen jacket smelt of snuff. She saw his nose like the spout of a teapot. She and Julius had had a dreadful quarrel at dinner-time. About what? About the cooking of cabbage.

She was angry and rebellious and for twopence would cry out in childish rage, whether Mr. Lamplough were there or no. He disliked scolding women. In truth he disliked all women save the beautiful and completely dumb. His sharp old eyes regarded her. He was glad that she was off to bed, but sorry for Julius, because he was well assured that there was a 'Mrs. Caudle' lecture for him in store. And he liked Julius better than any man he had ever known.

When she was gone he returned to Julius, but this time he put his hand, the veins of which stood out, purple and swollen, on Julius' shoulder.

'Pity you can't see them. I can't remember ever a night like this one. It must be some special keenness of the frost.'

'The funny thing is,' Julius said, 'it is as though I could smell them—a whiff of gunpowder. They are dangerous, Lamplough. Dangerous. War leans on the edge of the sky. Don't you feel it?'

'Perhaps I do. But I'm too old to care.'

'Not about mankind?'

'Mankind! Not I! Why, you're the only human being I've liked for years. I'm nearly dead. I loathe and despise mankind for the mess they've made of this enchanting, entrancing world. These stars! Why are we made to feel their beauty and majesty so desperately?'

Staring so intensely that it was as though he would leap through the window, glass and all, he recited:

> *"Thou shalt measure the stars:*
> *Orion and the Pleiades*
> *Shall send thee embassies;*
> *Thou shalt chart the cities of Mars;*
> *Thou shalt sift Aldebaran*

> *As gold dust in the pan;*
> *Algol shall undusk*
> *For thee his demon trouble . . .*
> *In vain! All is husk,*
> *To be cast out with the stubble."*

He repeated, with bitter, trembling-voice scorn:

> *"In vain! All is husk,*
> *To be cast out with the stubble."*

'Where is that from?'

'I don't know. I learned it years ago. My useless brain is stuffed with rubbish.'

'Give yourself a whisky—me one, too.'

Lamplough filled the glasses, while Julius lay back, his legs stretched out.

'Sit down, you bitter old man, and give me some advice.'

Lamplough, looking, with his scanty grey hair on end, like a malicious bird, sat down.

'I'm very good at advice. Having made a complete mess of my life I'm an excellent counsellor.'

'We're friends, aren't we?' Julius said. 'Lately we've been meeting a good deal. I like you very much and trust you.'

'Thanks. As far as you are concerned I'm trustworthy.'

Julius stared into his own world.

'You say you've made a mess of your life. I don't suppose you have. None of us can tell until it's all over. But I'm in a fair way, I think, to make a mess of mine.'

'How?' asked Lamplough.

'I love my wife with heart, soul, body, everything I have. I love her more every day I live. I have reason to believe she loves me. And yet, with every day in this place, we are drifting further apart.'

'You haven't been married very long.'

'No, I know that, and all about the first year being the hardest, and the rest of it. At the same time I *don't* know it, for my other marriage had no difficulties at all. It was supremely happy, and yet I didn't love Elinor as I love Celia. I've spoken of this,' Julius went on quickly, 'to no other living human being.'

'I know what you're thinking. That I'm married to the worst gossip in England.'

'No. I wasn't thinking that. I shouldn't be talking at all if I didn't feel I was talking to myself.'

'That's a great compliment,' Lamplough grunted.

'The trouble is I'm in a fog. I came down here the happiest man in the United Kingdom. It seemed to me that nothing could go wrong. But how queer a thing marriage is! They always tell you that the difficult time in marriage is after the first physical passion has worn thin. But in that way Celia and I are more in love than ever we were. Our *bodies* are all right. But our *souls*—Do you believe in souls, Lamplough?'

'How can I but believe? If men had only bodies they'd have settled down long ago. The strongest would rule the weakest and after a bit of fighting that would have been the end of it. I believe in a cruel malicious God whose sport we are.'

'That's too simple, I think. I don't feel that I'm anybody's sport. That's the devil of it. Some way, somehow, if I'm intelligent, brave, generous enough, I can put this all right. I suppose I'm not. I suppose I'm not fine enough.'

'And your wife?'

'Oh, that's simple! Celia reacts to her feelings. If she's hungry she eats; if she's angry she's angry; if she's generous she's generous. If she's disappointed she's disappointed. She's bitterly disappointed now.'

'Why is she disappointed?'

'She married me with the romantic notion that she was going to help me. She was, of course, in love with me as well, but it was my blindness that touched all her generosity and kindness. I was so crazily in love with her that I thought of nothing but that. I knew that my blindness made me queer at times, but I thought that she would get used to that. You see, Lamplough, before I was blinded I was just like anyone else. I lived physically and, except for a love of music, hadn't an impulse that wasn't physical. But blindness leads you into strange places. Another world grows up in you. It becomes intensely interesting. It makes the outside physical world shadowy, or rather it takes that outside world and makes it part of the inside world. I can't express myself. That's the trouble. I try to write things down in my Journal but the *expression* is always eluding me. I know what I mean but can't write it or say it. I haven't the equipment. But I tell you one thing: I know that if I don't hold on to the physical world —the world of food and sleep and trees and walls—I'll lose contact with everybody. As it is I sit too much by myself, listen to music too much, get suddenly impatient if Celia interrupts me, want to get finished with meals and walks and people so that I can sit back and let my mind go and penetrate through. . . .' He shook himself as though he were dreaming. 'There it is, you see. That's the danger. My love for Celia is the one great thing that keeps me sanely in touch.'

'Well, that's all right then,' said old Lamplough, 'as you love her so much.'

'No, it isn't. It's just *that* that she can't understand. She's been brought up anyhow. No religion, no codes. There's no reason for her why she shouldn't do anything at all that she wants to. Any kind of spiritual world seems to her nonsense. She's got the creed of her post-war generation that there *is* no creed, that life's a cheating business with no purpose, and the only thing to do is to get as much out of it as you can. At least that *would* be her code if she were not so kindly, sweet-hearted, childlike. As it is, she finds herself tied to a man fifteen years older and up against a physical deformity that she hates, can't deal with, that, she feels, separates her from me. I shouldn't—' his voice trembled—'I shouldn't have married her. It was a crime. I didn't know it, but now I see it.'

'Yet you love one another,' Lamplough said.

'Yes, that makes it harder, for never before have I loathed my blindness as I do now. If I could see—if I could see! Oh God, if I could see!'

There was a silence, then Lamplough said: 'I think that's melodrama, Cromwell. You're damned lucky to love one another as you do.' He hesitated then said slowly, 'I married my wife thirty-five years ago because I wanted to go to bed with her. She had yellow hair then like a canary and was soft and playful like a kitten. I compare her with the animal kingdom because that's where she belongs. And for twenty-five years I've hated her—hated everything about her—her lies, her mean gossip, her creeping little eyes, her lisp, everything.'

'If that's so,' Julius said, 'why didn't you leave her long ago?'

'Because I'm as bad as she is. I'm mean and think it's cheaper the two of us together. I'm lazy and can't be bothered to look after myself. I rather enjoy my hate, I think. I look at her across the table and think: "You're a filthy old bitch, you are," and then ask her, quite gently, to pass the butter. If I had a little more courage I'd murder her. As it is, she thinks I'm rather fond of her. Yes, that's the position, and when I hear you go on as you do, I want to say "Love each other. Go on loving one another. Don't mind what happens. Love one another. And to do that you've got to respect one another." '

He got up rather clumsily and went over to Julius, put his hand for a moment on his shoulder.

'She'll grow. She's fine. You're fine. You can't go wrong.'

Just before he went away he said:

'Take your blindness as a gift, not a penalty. I said just now I believed in a malicious God. And so I do. He's beaten *me* and is proud of it, I don't doubt. But don't *you* be beaten. Don't give Him that crumb of satisfaction. Be wise and patient. Wisdom and patience. They are the things. And when I'm hanged for murder remember what I've said. Can I help you upstairs in any way?'

Julius laughed.

'Oh no. I'm very clever at it.'

'All right, then. Good night.'

CHAPTER VI

Garth House—Afternoon—Everyone Present

DOROTHY AWOKE on that particular morning knowing that something very special was in store for her. She woke often with this sense, and when, fully awake, she tracked the prescience to its reality she found often enough that it was something very small —a book that she knew she would enjoy, the promise by the cook of ginger pudding, or an expedition with Gilbert and Simon.

'Oh, it's the party!'

She jumped out of bed to run to the window, to find that it was the most sinister of all possible days. Rain was pouring down from a sky so heavy that it seemed to be composed of muddy mattresses. However, what did it matter? It would be indoors and the grimier the exterior the more cosy inside.

There was the promise of a party for her so seldom, but never in her life had there been promise of *such* a party! Everyone had been saying, for weeks, that it would be a wonder. Moreover, it would not be for Dorothy this time a terror, as parties at the Lamploughs' or Mrs. Ironing's often were.

The annual children's dance, given by the Ironings, was always a terror. Dorothy loved to dance and danced very well, but in the district around Garth there were simply not enough boys, and the boys there were could not, for the most part, dance. What happened was that someone like Fred Ironing kindly asked you to dance, and you were pressed in a kind of despair against his soft and heaving stomach. Or, worse than that, you must dance with another girl—as though anything could be sillier! Moreover, Gilbert was always unhappy at these dances, and any pleasure that Dorothy might have felt was stolen from her by glimpses at Gilbert's unhappy face.

At the Cromwells' it would not be only dancing, there would be games and charades. Then there was an especial atmosphere about Garth House because Mr. Cromwell, whenever he met you, was so friendly that you could not feel lonely or desolate. Then both Gilbert and Simon loved Mr. Cromwell, so that they would be happy.

And, somewhere near at hand, there would be Jim Burke.

Dorothy collected her sponge, soap, and towel and made a dash for the bathroom. How lucky! She was there first, and as she lay in the bath, listening to the rain thundering on the roof, she felt so happy that she looked upwards, smiling, and tortured her eyes with soap.

While she was drying herself there came the knock on the door and Simon's husky voice demanding, 'How much more time are you going to take?' and, according to custom, she shouted: 'I'm just coming out!'

When she was back in her room she spread her party-dress out on the bed. She was forced to confess that it was shabby. It was three years old and she realized with a sudden alarm that she was growing out of it. This was a child's dress and she was a child no longer. She threw off her old yellow woollen dressing-gown and looked at herself in the glass that was cracked down the middle.

She tilted it back so that she could see the whole of herself. She was frightened. It was a stranger that she seemed to see there. She passed her hands down her body as though to reassure herself that it really *was* her body. A strange emotion, half of fear, half of pride, surged through her. She hurried, as though she were ashamed, to dress herself.

At breakfast their father said: 'The party's all off. Mrs. Cromwell's got scarlet fever.'

The dismay in the children's faces made their mother say: 'That's too bad, to tease them like that.'

'How do *you* know?' He went on, 'I may have just had a message. Anyway Simon can't go. He's wanted by the police.'

This cleared the air.

'I'm going to be a policeman one day,' Simon said.

'Why?'

'Because you can imprison people for lots of things, and then, when they're in prison, you can go to their houses and take what you want to. Besides, you see lots of murders.'

He walked about that morning with his head in the air. Ever since he had caught Jim Burke kissing Mrs. Cromwell and had observed the sensation that his news made, he had considered himself as a very exceptional detective.

He prowled around and watched people. He decided that everybody did many things that others were not to know. He discovered that there were many things that you must never mention. In fact the world was twice as interesting as it had been before.

A party must be an ideal situation for noticing things. He wished no unkindness to anyone, for he was warm-hearted and friendly, but his curiosity was widely awakened. He was especially interested in Mrs. Cromwell because of her behaviour at Mrs. Mark's tea. Above all he regarded himself as the great friend and protector of Mr. Cromwell, whom he adored. He saw himself, in fact, as Mr. Cromwell's private detective. He intended to enjoy himself. He knew that the food would be excellent. The only adverse circumstance was that he hated to wear his navy suit. He looked such a ninny in it. No one had told him, but he knew that it was so.

The rain had ceased when they started off and the sky had broken its grey with little furrows of blue.

Inside the drawing-room Dorothy stood lost in wonder.

The room had been cleared, but on the walls were still hanging the old water-colours in their gold frames, to give everything a friendly air. The light was soft and glowing. Garlands of red-berried holly were hanging from wall to wall and at the far end by the window was a magnificent Christmas tree.

Tea and coffee were being carried round by the maids.

This was not a children's party, so Dorothy was not embarrassed by a confusion of little boys in Eton jackets and girls in white frocks, all standing about self-conscious and either arrogant or sunk into shyness. Instead everyone she had ever known seemed to be there. There was a tumult of voices and she heard Mrs. Ironing, who was heavy in dark-red velvet, say, 'It's been raining like anything. When it does rain it does rain, doesn't it? But after all we must expect rain sometimes, mustn't we? It can't be dry all the year round.'

Very soon she saw Jim Burke, in his dark-blue suit, helping with cake and bread and butter. Almost at once he was passing her and he stopped.

'Well, I never! Why aren't you having some tea?'

She looked at him smiling at her and knew that she loved him so that she would do anything he asked her. If he said: 'Now go on! Run all the way to Rafiel,' at once, in her party-frock, she would run.

He perhaps felt something in her serious gaze. Among all those grown-up people, all talking and gesturing falsely, this child in her shabby frock ('Why doesn't her mother buy her a new dress?' he thought, quite angrily) was apart and better than they. Or so he felt. But there was something else he was feeling very much more strongly, someone else at whom he was constantly looking, whose voice he was always striving to hear.

'We've only just come,' Dorothy said.

'Have you? You're late.'

'That's because I couldn't find a clean handkerchief,' Simon said promptly.

'Look here. If you want some food, go over to that little table near the Christmas tree. There's no one sitting there.'

'Oh, thanks most awfully,' Gilbert said politely. What he longed to ask Jim was whether he would give him another lesson in modelling soon. He hadn't seen Jim for several weeks. And Jim remembered!

Before he hurried away he said: 'What about the modelling? I'll be over one of these days soon.'

'Oh, thanks most awfully!'

Wasn't Jim a marvel? To Gilbert, who was shy of asking for anything, this seemed a miracle. After Benson, Jim was next.

The three children reached their table, but to their horror old Mrs. Lamplough sat down at the same time.

'I'm not going to stand any longer. I'm an old woman. Much better to have a sit-down tea.'

She peered at each of them in turn, screwing up her little eyes to see them better.

'Your mother and father here?'

'Of course,' said Simon, who hated her.

'That's not a very polite way of answering. I'm sure your mother taught you better than that. You're getting a big boy now, Simon, and manners are manners. Too big for that sailor-suit, *I* should say!'

'Shall I get you some tea?' Gilbert said, because he felt that it was right.

'No. A maid will bring me some. I suppose so, at least. I can't say that things are very well organized.' She was peering about the room with her little eyes. 'Everyone seems to have come. Can you see who that is standing next to Miss Vergil?'

'That's Major Richardson, I think,' Dorothy said.

'Fancy! Coming all the way from Dundyke! They must have motored over. Hired, I expect, because I hear that things have been going so badly with them they've had to put their car down. There's poor Mrs. Wintringham. She looks terribly ill, doesn't she?'

'What's the matter with her?' Simon asked.

'Hush, Simon! You mustn't!' Dorothy said.

'Why not?'

'Little boys,' Mrs. Lamplough said, 'mustn't ask questions.'

Then they saw Julius Cromwell. He was standing, with Celia's arm through his, talking to Miss Vergil and Phyllis Lock.

'By gum!' Simon said, 'this chocolate cake is scrumptious.'

But something drove him. He wouldn't be happy until he had spoken to his friend. He jumped up, nearly knocking Mrs. Lamplough's elbow, and pushed his way through and caught Julius' hand.

'Hullo, Mr. Cromwell!'

'Why, it's Simon!'

Phyllis Lock kissed him.

'I tell you what it is,' Mrs. Lamplough said, 'Simon's getting out of hand. I've known you children since you were born so I've a right to say something. I shall speak to your mother.'

'It won't make any difference,' Dorothy said, hot in defence. 'Mother and Father want Simon to be quite natural. And he's as good as anything.'

'It isn't much use being good if you haven't any manners,' Mrs. Lamplough said. But she wasn't really thinking of the children. Her eyes were never still, up and down the room, taking everything in.

This was Celia's afternoon, or, at least, she was determined to make it so. Before she had married Julius it was an occasion such as this that had been her especial glory. So many hostesses were baffled by the sight of other people driven together under one roof and standing, hostile, critical, waiting for everything to go wrong.

Such an occasion lit some fire within her so that she felt that exaltation alive within all of us when our personal talent is precisely demanded. This was the thing for which she was destined. To make everything go, to see that everyone was happy. Since they had come to Garth there had been no opportunity to show the whole neighbourhood what she could do. This was no vainglory. She *liked* people to be happy. She could not pretend now, as she looked around her drawing-room, that this was a very intelligent or lively set of humans. They were making a lot of noise with their chatter, but, really, what a collection! Poor old Major Malpas with his purple nose and game leg, Mrs. Ironing in her velvet, Miss Vergil with brass buttons all down her flat chest, old Lady Drumacre with her lorgnette, Mrs. Brennan, a Juno in a small pork-pie hat; that old horror Mrs. Lamplough in her dingy bonnet! She had to confess, without any prejudice, that her own two men were like eagles to crows. That poor boy, Jim Burke, who looked at her as though he could eat her (she did hope that nobody else was noticing!), and, of course, Julius with his splendid body and grand head. He was the centre of everything always. Her love for him hurt her heart; she did not mind if Jim kissed her again. She could imagine it was Julius adoring her.

Then she actually forgot him. She remembered nothing but her determination to make the party go. She determined perhaps a little too much. Glebeshire is, inland at least, a sleepy somnolent county. Canon Ronder of Polchester used to say of it, in the old days, 'The Lotus Land—all minor characters can end their days peacefully here.' In any case, even in 1938, when the world was rocking, Glebeshire was not very greatly disturbed, nor wished to be. Nearly everyone had lived there since the Conquest. Time was not. Innovations were unpleasant.

Perhaps three-quarters of the men and women in the room that afternoon felt something a little unpleasant about Celia's excitement, her drama, her manipulations. They were accustomed to parties where old ladies literally fell asleep in their chairs and no one thought the worse of them for it, where friends danced lazily with one another and talked a little scandal, where there were set out some bridge tables, where no one was very definitely host or hostess.

But Celia made a little speech. She stood near the Christmas tree and clapped her hands. Then, when everyone was silent, she cried out in her clear child-like voice:

'Now we're going to dance to the gramophone. And everyone has to dance! There's room for everybody!'

People did not want to be *told* to dance. And did she not look strange, standing up there, in that wonderful rose-coloured frock that fitted so overclosely to her figure, did her eyes not shine quite unnaturally, need her voice be pitched to that excitement? It was, after all, a very pleasant party. The room was pretty, it was interesting to see this handsome blind man in his own house, it was comfortable to feel for an hour or two surrounded by riches, even though they were somebody else's. Then, as usual, it was agreeable to meet old friends and chat a little, amusing to notice clothes and behaviour. What was the need then for all this direction and ordering, especially as Mrs. Cromwell was little more than a girl and didn't, in any case, belong to Glebeshire?

Nevertheless excitement of a kind—excitement half rebellious, half acquiescent—*did* pervade the room.

It was Julius' handsome, completely up-to-date gramophone that played. These modern dances were easy, and even though you couldn't dance at all you could make some sort of a show of it.

Celia went about the room urging everyone to dance, speaking to them as though she had known them all her life! She danced herself with young Johnny Hope from Rasselas, and how beautifully they did it! No one else in the room could approach them, so perfect, so easy, so graceful and casual were their movements. So young, in fact, they both were.

Julius had danced for a little while with Celia, she guiding him with great skill; then he retired quietly to a corner, sat down on a little sofa set back against the wall and listened to all the sounds, the music, the voices, the stirring of the feet that came to him in a coloured web behind his eyes. He was very happy. He was a shy man. He had been blind for too long to be self-conscious because of his disability, but he was self-conscious in another way. He thought that he must be dull to anyone with sight who did not know him very well. He understood completely the gruffness and irritations of the deaf. It is not only that the blind and deaf are shut off from human activities, but they must of necessity be continually imagining the many active things that human beings must be wanting to do. 'You run along now, I'm perfectly all right,' Julius was always beginning to say.

Above all, he could not endure to be pitied. He had reached an amazing sensitiveness to the slightest hint of pity whether in movement or voice. He was not only shy, but he was also proud.

That was why he did not care for the company of strangers. It was not that he did not love human beings, but rather that he loved them too well. He refused to have either their pity or their boredom, and he often imagined these things when they were not there.

But now he was happy, for he was host, successfully, in his own house. His guests were enjoying it all—he could tell from their voices and their laughter—but they did not drive themselves in upon him. He hoped that in the general gaiety he was forgotten.

He had been greatly proud when he had heard Celia's voice announcing the dancing—her young freshness, her own clear happiness, these things, through her voice, made him see her beauty.

'Dear Celia. Dear, dear Celia.' He was thinking of her so intently that he was irritated when he found that someone was sitting down on the sofa beside him.

A hand touched his arm and a voice said: 'It's Katherine Mark.'

'Oh, I'm so glad!'

He turned, smiling, towards her.

'You didn't *look* pleased when you heard me sitting down.'

'I didn't know it was you.'

'I had to come and tell you how beautiful Celia is looking, and how happy.'

'Yes. I could tell from her voice just now that she was happy.'

'The whole thing is the greatest success.'

'Is it? I'm so glad.'

'Of course I don't know what parties are usually like round

here. Pretty dull, I expect. We used to have parties forty years ago in this very room and they *were* dull.'

'Didn't you liven them up?'

'No. I wasn't good at that. I was too shy. I'm shy still, for that matter.'

'I'm shy too.'

'Yes, I know you are. When Millie came back from France the parties were brighter. She was gay enough for anything! But Mother was afraid to unbend and Aunt Aggie was a terror and Father used to go away to his study and work at his writing.'

'Are you enjoying this?' he asked.

'Immensely. I love to see people happy. I am getting especial pleasure from watching Dorothy.'

'Dorothy?'

'Dorothy Brennan. You know, Mr. Cromwell, it's wonderful to reach the age when you can love someone without being possessive. Being possessive is the root of all evil. I'm still a little possessive about my son, I'm afraid, but not in the least about Dorothy. She is a darling—quite unaware of her own merits, generous-hearted, enjoying everything.

'Yes,' he said, nodding his head. 'Being generous-hearted is the thing. It's almost everything. And being possessive *is* the devil, you're quite right.' Then he added, quite shyly: 'Look here, Mrs. Mark, will you call me Julius?'

'Certainly. If you'll call me Katherine.'

'Let's shake hands on it.'

They did so.

She said: 'You know, you have the most beautiful hands.'

'Oh, nonsense!'

'Hands mean a lot to me. They're an index to character.'

'Everything is. We give ourselves away all the time.'

'Yes, we do, don't we? And yet our bodies are nothing. Only a kind of wrapper on the box.' She laughed. 'When I was a girl I used to think it would be dreadful to be old. Forty, I used to think. To be forty, how awful! And now I'm sixty and my opinion is it's the best age. You're not decrepit and you've lost some follies, and you don't expect more than the daily charms, and the daily worries seem less important. Even, later on, to be decrepit needn't be so very bad.'

'Aren't you lonely?' he asked.

'Yes, sometimes, but God is much nearer. By God I mean some kind of company that you can't see, only feel. And feeling is much more certain than seeing.'

She got up.

'Mr. Lamplough seems to want me about something. He's making signs to me.'

After she was gone he too stood up. The gramophone was playing the 'Blue Danube' waltz, which even now, after so many years and endless repetition, was fresh and lovely—the most beautiful waltz in the world.

A voice said in his ear: 'You should watch Jim Burke with your wife. There are fine goings-on.'

The children had enjoyed the dancing. Dorothy had had a wonderful time, for after Simon had insisted that he should be allowed to bump around the room with her (he had no idea of dancing at all), Johnny Hope, who had been performing so wonderfully with Celia, approached her and asked if she would give him a dance.

This seemed to her so incredible an adventure that, for a moment, she could not speak. Then she said shyly, 'Thank you very much,' and advanced into the room as frightened as a mouse who scents cheese but fears a trap. There *was*, however, no trap. Johnny was a very nice young man who, finishing his dance with Celia, said, 'That girl over there's got a sweet face.'

'That's the parson's daughter.'

'Why, of course. Last time I saw her I was in Etons and she had a torn stocking. I'll ask her to dance.'

Johnny was so good a dancer that anyone could dance with him.

Dorothy knew an enchantment. She found that there came to her new adventurous steps; she did what it was brilliant and clever to do before she had thought of doing it.

She knew that everyone was looking at her. She knew that as, before her glass, she had realized the change in her, so others too were realizing it.

'That's the Brennan girl. How she's growing! Why, she was a schoolgirl when I saw her last.'

And *how* she hoped that Jim Burke was aware of her! A word of praise from him would make her afternoon joy complete.

Gilbert, too, enjoyed himself and his pleasure came from an unexpected quarter. It was old Mr. Lamplough who, watching the dancing, saw also the thin-faced little boy with the large serious eyes, quite alone and, in some undefined way, rather fiercely on his guard.

'Well, young Brennan, you look very thoughtful!'

Gilbert turned sharply and was rather frightened at the near neighbourhood of the bent-shouldered, hook-nosed, shabbily-coated old man who had hairs growing out of his nose and large purple veins on the back of his hands.

'How do you do, Mr. Lamplough!'

'How do I do? How do I do? Why do I come to these silly affairs? To enjoy myself? Dear me, no! To please my wife? Not that either, I'm afraid. But because my friend Julius Cromwell likes me to be here. Why are you not at school?'

'There was chicken-pox, so we were all sent home.'

'Chicken-pox! And what are you doing with yourself? Idling, I suppose.'

'I'm not learning much, I'm afraid. I read some French with Dorothy, and do Latin exercises.'

The old man smiled, and when he smiled his ugly face was quite hideously kind.

'Take my tip. Don't you worry if you *are* doing nothing! I was very diligent at school, and very intelligent too. With what result? I've done nothing with my life whatever.'

'You know a lot about Shakespeare, don't you, sir?' Gilbert asked politely. He had been told that this was so.

'I *do* know a lot about Shakespeare. And all perfectly useless. I'm like an ant who is for ever climbing up a stone that is too slippery for him. Shakespeare is slippery, my boy, damned slippery. He isn't a man at all. He's the whole planetary system. However, never mind about Shakespeare. What do you do with yourself all day?'

'Oh, there's plenty to do! There's the garden, and helping Dorothy and Mother, and I'm trying to model.'

'You are, are you? Model what?'

'I can't do anything yet, sir. Jim Burke's shown me a little, but he hasn't much time.'

'Humph! I've got one or two books that might help you. I'll leave them at the Rectory.'

'Thanks most awfully, sir.' This was so encouraging that he went on, 'I've got a dog too.'

'Oh, have you? What sort of a dog?'

'He's mostly fox-terrier. He's a bit of Aberdeen, too. He's a mongrel.'

'They are the best—always most intelligent.'

'Yes. Benson's *very* intelligent. He's almost human.'

'Everyone always says that about their dogs, as though it were remarkable. As a matter of fact, I sometimes think that human beings are dogs, and dogs are human beings. Is he a one-man dog?'

'That's exactly what he is, sir. He doesn't really care about anybody except me, and I suppose that's selfish, but I like it all the same.'

'I should think you do. That's what we're all looking for. You must bring him to see me one day. We will take a walk together.'

'I should like that very much, sir. Thank you.'

Simon joined them.

'Well, young man, what have you been up to?'

He was very hot and grinning.

'This beastly suit tickles me.'

'Take it off then!' Mr. Lamplough said.

This was a new idea to Simon, and a fascinating one.

'Mother says it's wicked to be naked.'

'A fig-leaf! A fig-leaf's all you want. Fig-leaves are so large now in England that they cover religion, politics—everything. We're false when we're clothed and hideous when we're not, so it's a bad choice either way.'

Simon wriggled his shoulders but hadn't an idea of what the ugly old man meant. Nor did he care. For Celia was speaking again.

Julius stood there, not a muscle in his body moving. No one approached him just then, for all were listening to Celia. He heard her voice through a cloud of darkness. She was saying that now there would be charades. Chairs were being brought, sofas were pushed forward. She was saying that she would lead the first one with Johnny Hope, Winifred Hope his sister, Fred Ironing, Phyllis Lock, Colonel Baines.

His brain leapt to life. Who was it who had spoken to him? He had not recognized the voice. It had, in all probability, been disguised. How cruel and malicious a thing! Like an anonymous letter it must be entirely disregarded. But, like an anonymous letter, it left its sting. How monstrous a thing from a guest in his own house! It had been a woman's voice.

They were sitting down, laughing and chattering.

Someone said to him: 'Wouldn't you like a chair, Mr. Cromwell?'

He smiled. 'No, thanks. I'd rather stand. I can see better.'

Jim Burke . . . Jim Burke . . . Jim Burke. But he liked Burke and trusted him. Celia? At the thought of her it was as though water moved over his heart and rocked it. Celia was faithful. She loved him. He would stake his life on her honesty. His life? Certainly. His life was worth very little to him if she were dishonest.

If one person said this to him, others were thinking it. Perhaps everyone in this room. . . . No. It was a gossiping foul-minded woman. Mrs. Lamplough? Yes. Very likely Mrs. Lamplough. But he could not see. If he could see, all would be clear in a moment of vision. One look at Celia's face . . . But now he was doubting her. How shameful a thing! Because a dirty-minded old woman had whispered in his ears.

One of those passions that he so greatly dreaded was hovering near him. A mood when all the blacknesses bred in his blindness swept down upon him, when the world clouded so that he could see nothing real but only the fancies that belonged to his blindness. He dug his nails into his palms. He must control this. No one must detect anything, either now or ever. He must give no one the satisfaction of knowing that he was touched. In the room now, with him, was the woman who had whispered to him. She was watching him, hoping for some sign.

They had begun their acting. People were laughing at their appearance. They had dressed themselves, he supposed, in odds and ends as you did in charades. He heard Celia's voice, clear as a bell. She said: 'But I told you, James, that I cannot *bear* cucumber.'

Yes, for the woman to have whispered that, they must be talking. There *must* be some talk. And it sprang from nothing. Celia was young, heedless. She had been kind to Burke as she was kind to everybody. Here, in this country community, anything was suspicious, and because he was older and because he was blind . . .

Everyone was clapping. The first syllable was over.

'Very good, wasn't it?' some man said to him. 'By Jove, your wife can act!'

'What do you think it was?'

' 'Pon my soul I don't know. First I thought it was "hash." All about cooking it was, anyway. But "hash" makes a damned bad beginning to a word.'

The thing was, of course, to dismiss it utterly, as though it had never been spoken. But there was a wild trembling in his mind that, for the moment, he could not control. Jealous? He had never been jealous since he was a boy. Jealous? Jealous of Celia?

They were back again, but now he heard the voices in a mist. Broken sentences. 'Your cabin must be the one——' 'Oh, I do hope it won't be——' 'Yes, the steward told me——' Something to do with a ship.

Celia loved him. She had been bored a little and cross a little, but she *loved* him. On that he must fix his mind. As though he could doubt it . . . some filthy old woman . . .

With a rush the anger was upon him. The words were forming in his brain. He would call out to them all sitting so smugly watching this foolishness: 'I'm blind! I'm blind. I can't see! Think of that, you idiots. How would you like it? What would you do? I can't see my wife. You can see her and I can't. Even when I am in the same room with her I can't tell what she's doing! I'm in darkness, perpetual darkness, for ever and ever and ever! Isn't it funny? You can see my wife and I can't! You're laughing. You're clapping your hands . . . and I can't see. I don't know what you're laughing at. I can't see my wife. What do you think of that?'

'If you ask me,' the man said, 'I think it's "bedrock." '

He moved very cautiously, touching a sofa-end, a chair, a picture-frame, and found the door.

He slipped out of the room.

CHAPTER VII

Garth House: In Julius' Study

JULIUS CROMWELL'S JOURNAL

January 3.—I listened to someone on the wireless this morning who very chattily ('My dear, it was exactly as though he were sitting over a fire in the same room with you') told us that there are three ways of keeping a diary—World Events, Self-Analysis, small daily detail—'had roast beef for dinner, a bit tough—saw first primrose—moon on its back tonight forebodes rain'—but, liking none of them he would keep no diary this year.

I don't like any of them either. World events are horrible. I see no way out. Our country is pusillanimous, the very thought of Hitler makes me bilious. Anyway, what do I know of what is really happening?

As to self-analysis, I am a regular conventional man placed in irregular abnormal circumstances. I know that I am on the edge of a real disaster as many, many an ordinary married man has been before me. I love my wife and am, God forgive me, jealous of her. I ask God's forgiveness, because jealousy is the vilest, meanest of all the human passions. I am determined not to surrender to it and I surrender every hour.

So far I may be said, in the external sense, to have behaved decently—yes, extra decently. Celia has for the most part, I think, been happier in the last two weeks than at any time since she came here. And that is because I have been more considerate, more careful to please her. And I have been careful to please her in a sort of spying way. My motives seem good, but behind them I am asking, will she give herself away now? Shall I tempt her to some sudden confession? Foul, foul! In all my life nothing fouler.

There come at times hours of the most radiant light, the most perfect confidence. Every suspicion seems to have cleared away. I see with the utmost clarity. How could I have suspected her for a single instant? As she talks to me a great weight is lifted, as though by a divine hand, from my heart. I can see my other twisted self and look on it as an obscene madman, just as one does for a brief while after yielding to some sensual temptation, in the reaction from some basely satisfied moment of passion. I remember a soldier in the War telling me that he went to a brothel chiefly for the wonderful sense of purity, simplicity, clarity that was his for a brief while after he came away. The intervals when one moves out of Jealousy's company are like that.

But Jealousy is very strange. He leaves you in order that he may return where you least expect it.

This afternoon for example. It was a faint dim day of the New Year, warm and comforting. Not a breath of wind. We motored to the wood called the Well to look—or she was to look—for primroses. They are found here sometimes before Christmas. We were both very happy. Her hand was on my arm and sometimes I put up my hand to touch hers. She prattled on about her childhood, about her incredible mother whom death has relieved from being the most ridiculous old lady ever seen. She was capable of changing her clothes a dozen times a day and she used to dress Celia up in the most fantastic things, tear bits of ribbon off her, put them on again, kiss her and be enraged with her all in a moment, and then suddenly, dressed herself only in her vest, sit down in a chair and go on with a library novel, eating chocolates by the dozen at the same time. Celia was rather fond of her and, when she went for a year to a finishing school in Paris, missed her badly. 'She was always having lovers,' Celia said. 'I suppose it's from her that I get my dreadful infidelities.'

And at once I was changed. I could have caught her round the throat and throttled her.

'What do you mean?' I asked her. My voice was choked.

At first she noticed nothing. She had left me; she was looking for primroses. Her voice came from a long way off.

'I've told you,' she said. 'I've only misbehaved once in my life and I hated it. But if I hadn't married you——' She called out: 'Oh, there they are! The darlings! A whole clump of them! Wait, Julius! I'll pick you such a bunch!'

We walked back to the car and she noticed that something was wrong with me. I could tell at once that she was frightened and, because she was frightened, she was angry. My sane self talked to my insane self. 'Now, that meant nothing. You were happy. Go on being happy. There's no reason for any change.'

But my body would not obey my reasonable mind. My heart was beating. My arm trembling. We were walking apart. We were silent. I tried to force myself into the easy happy tone of half an hour ago. The words would not come. With the increasing silence my anger, my misery, my physical pain of heart and throat grew more active. We drove home in silence. She went up to her room without a word. She hadn't given me the primroses.

January 7.—I said the other day in this Journal that I was a normal ordinary man in abnormal unordinary circumstances. I am coming to believe that every man born of woman is as *un*ordinary as every other man. It is circumstances that betray the truth.

Now take Boss, the butcher in Garth. When young he must have been a boy of wonderful physique. He is short but his strength of shoulder, arm, and thigh must have been terrific. He had, however, first an adoring mother, then a kindly orderly wife. (Very nice woman, Mrs. Boss.) He has grown, as butchers do, stout.

He makes a decent living, has three nice children, and a loving faithful wife. His contentment is supreme. He is too lazy to run after other women. He plays darts and bowls and would be drunk on occasion if it were not for Mrs. Boss. He told me the other day that his digestion is perfect and he never has a cold. He is proud of his garden and his politics are summed up in the two phrases, 'We don't want foreigners meddling here' and 'I'm a Socialist really.'

That's Boss as he is. But imagine a handsome stranger invading Garth and making love to Mrs Boss. (She is still, they tell me, very personable.) My guess is that Boss would appear suddenly to be a man of almost maniacal intentions. His temper would be frightful, he would drink like a fish, he might, if things went far enough, commit suicide or even murder. Everyone would then say how changed he was, 'You wouldn't know him for the same man,' and so on. Not at all. He is the same Boss. He has now latent in him cruelty, obscenity, abnormality, frenzy. He will probably escape through life in safety unless disease touches his brain. 'There but for the Grace of God goes . . .'

These are platitudes. Of course. I am not an original, I see nothing for the first time as painters, writers, musicians, philosophers of a good class see things. But a platitude is for oneself no longer a platitude when it is experienced in one's own life.

This morning Jim Burke, as usual, read me the morning papers. I thought of him with devilish malignity and great affection. I like no one, save Celia, to lead me about, be close to me, put his hand through my arm as I do Burke.

But when he had been reading for about half an hour I said: 'What's the matter with you, Jim? Something's on your mind.'

(There had been no sign of his being different. I said this to test him.)

'I'm all right,' he said.

'No. I've noticed it for some while past. Something's on your mind.'

He said nothing, but began to read again.

Once more I interrupted him.

'Stop for a moment. Never mind the papers. I want you to tell me.'

'Don't you think,' he said at last slowly, 'that sitting there as you do you imagine things sometimes?'

'Perhaps I do,' I answered cheerfully. 'But you know they say that if you're blind your senses are much more alert than an ordinary man's. There's something in that.'

'The village thinks so anyway.'

'Thinks what?'

He laughed. 'That you can see farther than people who *can* see. They say that it's as though they were living in this house and you could see all they were doing and thinking.'

'Do they really?' Then I said: 'Come here. Sit close beside me. Put your hand on my knee.'

After a little hesitation he did so.

'That's better. Now I'm really talking to you. What do the people in the village say about us, Jim?'

'What do you mean—*say* about you?'

'About Mrs. Cromwell and me. We've been here quite a long time now. I'd like to know what they *really* think.'

'Oh, they like you—they all like you. They think you're a fine man.'

'I'm glad of that. And Mrs. Cromwell?'

He hesitated. I felt his hand tremble ever so slightly.

'Some of them like her—some of them don't.'

'Why don't they?'

'The old maids.' His voice was suddenly hard. 'And Mrs. Brennan. That lot. They're jealous of her. They think she's stuck-up.'

I laughed. 'That's a funny idea.' Then I went on lightly: 'Do they consider us a devoted couple?'

'Why, of course—anyone can see that!'

'Do *you* think we're a devoted couple?'

I could feel that he was annoyed with me for asking these questions. It would seem to him in bad taste.

'Do *I* think? What does it matter what *I* think?'

'It matters a lot. You've lived in this house quite a time. You're sensible. You've travelled about the world a lot. You have watched human nature.'

He broke out: 'Well, you *are*, aren't you?'

'Certainly we are. I only would like to know how it seems to you?'

He took his hand from my knee. He sprang to his feet.

'Here! Why are you asking me these questions?'

I realized that he was greatly agitated.

'Don't get so excited. There's no reason to be excited.'

'I tell you what!' he went on. 'It's as I said—you sit there imagining things.'

'Perhaps I do. Perhaps you'd be the same if you were blind.'

His voice softened.

'Perhaps I should. It's a damned shame. You don't know how sorry I am.'

'I don't like to be pitied,' I said.

'I'm not pitying you. I like you better than any man I've ever known. There's nothing I wouldn't do for you. No, nothing.'

'That's all right, Jim. Don't let's get sentimental.'

'It's not sentimental. It's just how I feel. You go probing and probing until I don't know where I am.'

'All right. Let's get on with the reading.'

It has not been strange in the circumstances, I suppose, that my mind should have dwelt much on the question as to who it was whispered in my ear on the afternoon of the party. It is not strange either that I should at first have decided that it was Mrs. Lamplough, she being the core or heart of the village gossip. So I asked the Lamploughs to tea.

When Celia heard that I had done this she was angry. (She is constantly angry now, angry in a kind of self-defence way and ever since the primrose-picking exhibition.)

'That's unkind of you, Julius. You know how I hate her.'

(I take great pleasure in remembering for my Journal the exact words of past dialogues. My memory for trifles now seems prodigious. I wonder whether it is so with all blind people. Perhaps that is the real reason why chess masters can play so many boards at the same time—that they are blindfolded helps them rather than hinders them.)

In any case I can recall this conversation with Celia most vividly and how Jealousy, like a fat blowzy woman, wheezed in my ear: 'Has she been kissing Burke, do you think?' Vulgarity, bad taste, flaring clothes, eructations, cheap scent—all these things are part of Jealousy's furniture.

'Whatever did you ask her for?'

'I want to know something.'

(I couldn't resist saying this. I don't know myself. Three months ago you couldn't have persuaded me that I would act like this because some foul-minded bitch—or perhaps not a woman—whispered a line of dirty gossip in my ear. But then, you see, I'm in *love* with Celia.)

'To know something? What on earth can· Mrs. Lamplough have to tell you?'

'Well, my dear, she's the village's prize gossip.'

'Gossip? What do you want with gossip? I thought you were above such a vulgar thing!'

'A blind man is above nothing. He is constantly wondering.'

'I know you are. That's what I——'

She quite suddenly came over to me, put her arms round my neck, her cheek against mine. Her cheek was wet with tears. With what agony I loved her then. Yes, *agony* . . . for the pain constricted my heart and my bowels.

'Celia! You're crying!'

She put up her hand to her cheek and mine.

'No. It's nothing. I hate Mrs. Lamplough so.'

When they came Celia was out. I had to apologize.

I had, of course, never seen Mrs. Lamplough but her clothes always smelt of moths. The purr of her voice was pure animal. I mean a physical sound without humanity.

I was amused, after his declaration of the other day, that old Lamplough should be so charming to her. He is certainly afraid of her.

'Have one of these rock buns, my dear. They're charming.'

'Alice says, Julius, that Sizyn Church wants some looking after. It's being neglected.'

She spun an unbroken web of chatter.

'It certainly does. Frank Brennan is the laziest parson in the whole of the British Isles *and* he knows it, which makes it worse. However, perhaps it's just as well for Daisy Brennan that he is. If he had some energy the village girls might be in danger, because he's still good-looking and his religion is *most* queer—not a religion at all, if you ask me. I wonder the Bishop hasn't something to say to it, but he's as lazy as Frank, if you ask me. They say his eldest boy—the Bishop's, I mean—is simply going to pieces at Cambridge—wine, women, and song. His College bills are simply *awful*, I hear, and, as it is, the Bishop's had to strain things financially to send him there, and Mrs. Crawford's health is just being undermined by it all. I was told in Polchester the other day that she's under drugs half the time, and her two girls are just running round Polchester without anyone bothering where they go or who they go with.'

'Try some of this blackberry jelly,' Lamplough suggested. 'You'll like it.'

I, quite suddenly, knew that it was not she who had spoken to me at the party. There was something in her voice that could not possibly disguise it from me—no, not for one sentence.

Then she asked: 'How are you finding Jim Burke, Mr. Cromwell?'

I knew that she was waiting passionately for my answer.

'Oh, I like him. He's a good fellow.'

'I'm glad that you find him so. That's more than he used to be.'

'I expect gossip exaggerated things.'

'Well, I never listen to gossip myself, but it was more than gossip when he was with the Ironings. However, I believe in giving everyone a fresh chance.'

How odd her voice! It has the property of hypnotism. You listen in a kind of trance, loathing it, but wanting it to go on. But this time I did *not* want it to go on. I had found out what I wished to know. I got rid of them early. I know that she went away deeply insulted because Celia was not there. I suppose, when you come to think of it, she was right.

January 10.—That I am extremely unhappy is nobody's fault but my own. Things have not been made easier in these last few days by the fact that Jim has seen fit to show sulks.

This particular kind of sulks, I believe, is the especial property of real true-blood Englishmen. Being by nature inarticulate it is a real relief to be in a mood in which no words are necessary at all. Burke's politeness is intolerable and he answers me in monosyllables. The answer to all this, of course, is to send him away, and some of the time I think this is the solution. But I care about him, that's the nuisance of it. I am at heart, I suppose, unsure of myself and perhaps have always been so. This unsureness makes me want to secure the affection of everyone round me. I can't bear to have anyone under my roof who dislikes me. But Jim and Celia both must just now find my moods intolerable. I say to myself: 'Get rid of him. Everything is settled as soon as he goes.' But, of course, nothing is settled by his going. If there has been any infidelity to me the fact of the infidelity is there whether he goes or stays. And I must know. *I must know.* If I say to him, 'Jim, are you in love with my wife?' and he says, 'Yes, I am,' and I say, 'You'd better go then,' and he says, 'Of course. I asked you to let me go long back,' where am I better off? And I cannot ask him: 'Is my wife in love with you?' Moreover I know that she is not. Of course I know it as I know that my heart beats in my breast. But does that preclude infidelity? Things that, because of her upbringing, are nothing to her are to me at the very root of our relationship. He is young and vigorous. Only to know. *To know.* To ask her once: 'Have you flirted with Jim? Has he kissed you? Has he taken you in his arms?' Oh, God, God! help me to be a real man, wise, beneficent, generous-hearted. But I am not—I am as mean, spying, underhand as any other of the multitudes of jealous husbands who have, from the beginning of time, known this unworthy wretchedness.

And, just now, everything is against me. I have a fancy that Celia's maid, Violet, is somehow in this business. At any rate there is a feud between Mrs. Gayner and her. Mrs. Gayner wants her to go, says she is impertinent, lazy, always stirring up trouble with the other servants. But Celia won't hear of her going and is now at open war with Mrs. Gayner.

Apart from all this, Lizzie herself is no longer at my side as she has been for so many years. She has her own secret, although what it can be with so upright, loyal a woman I cannot imagine.

My worst and most maddening irritation is that I fancy that if

I could see I could settle all this trouble. Could I once look into Celia's face, I tell myself, everything would be resolved. I would say, 'Do you love me?' and she would say, 'I do,' and it would be all over.

As it is, when she speaks to me, I imagine a hundred different nuances. I fancy that she is looking away as she speaks, or is frowning or scornful. And she is afraid of me, of my sudden moods, my unaccountable silences, my abrupt questions.

January 12.—I am ill. I have been ill for half an hour. I am very seldom ill, have not an ache or a pain. But half an hour ago, as Celia began to read to me, a pain, a little pain, crept into the skin of my forehead between my eyes. I asked her to stop reading. Once again she was hurt by my abruptness, and went up to bed. A quarter of an hour ago I took out this Journal and as I began to write my whole body began to be invaded. Little pains are running about it like messengers. Someone is turning a knife inside my forehead. My legs and arms ache as though they were not *my* legs and arms at all, but have been forced on me by an enemy. I am shivering, but my head is like a hot thunderstorm. It is so long since I have been ill that it seems impossible that this can happen so suddenly. An hour ago I was perfectly well.

January I don't know what.—I have no decency to be writing. When I was laid here I insisted, half delirious as I was, that my Braille Milton and my padlocked Journal and a photograph of Celia should be put on the table beside my strange bed.

Celia was in her dressing-gown. Lizzie Gayner found me trying to crawl upstairs to my room. She and Oliphant undressed me. I remember that as she buttoned my pyjama-jacket over my bare hairy chest I fancied that it was my mother again and sleepily said: 'Good night, Mum.'

I was in bed when Celia came in. I remember little more. It has been a sharpish attack of influenza. There is a danger of pleurisy. I have spent most of the days in dreaming, but Lizzie Gayner said half an hour ago: 'Now straight off to sleep, mind.' And here I am, the moment she was gone, finding the key in my match-box, unlocking the Journal, and sitting up with my head like a swollen apple-pudding, writing from my favourite poem of all poems:

> *Ye valleys low where the milde whispers use,*
> *Of shades and wanton winds, and gushing brooks,*
> *On whose fresh lap the swart star sparely looks,*
> *Throw hither all your quaint enameld eyes,*
> *That on the green terf suck the honied showres,*
> *And purple all the ground with vernal flowres.*

How lovely it is with the old spelling which I made Celia once repeat to me from an early Milton that old Colebrooke gave me. And how silly Celia thought it. 'Spelling it like that just makes it absurd!' And how hot, dirty, sweaty, choked, and rheumed I have been all day, and how simply repeating 'That on the green terf suck the honied showres' refreshes and *washes* one with a kind of crystal shower. How too this notion that poetry is only for the aesthetes breaks down. There never was less of an aesthete than I (perhaps a *little* aesthetic on the music side). But those words are *physical*. My body is gross, heavy, unclean. There is something else, though, that if washen and reclothed rises from this bed and sits singing in the window, urged thither by Milton. And this foul room! And my dream. My dreams of all day and all night. Vast caverns 'immeasurable to man,' or whatever it is, with the too-familiar Beethoven Fifth booming away where the sea will shortly rush in and an old witch—Mrs. Lamplough—naked-dugged, thick, glistening, oily black hair, digging in the sand for oysters, and that dreadfully supercilious fellow on the *Weekly Round*, whom Jim reads out to me of a Sunday morning, sitting on a rock near Mrs. Lamplough and telling her in that lazy, superior voice of his that Milton is lacking in 'symphonic rhythm,' or some such nonsense, and little Simon Brennan wallowing in the green-blue pool at the mouth of the cavern, cocking a cheeky eye at Lamplough meanwhile and deliberately splashing his untidy clothes with sea water!

Now the odd thing is that I have full vision in my dreams. Is my picture of young Simon anything like the reality—and the critic whom I never give a thought to save for a brief moment on Sunday, does he really look the self-satisfied, lazy, untidy beggar I see him as? And the orchestra playing the Fifth Symphony all in evening clothes, a cross between waiters and artists, with a wave nearly knocking Adrian Boult off his rostrum! Such a noise! The trumpets blowing, the drums banging, the sea roaring ever nearer and nearer, and Headache, a large green crab with hairy claws, making a peck at me every now and then, threatening to lie across the whole of my face and eat into my nose. But, above all, I must not betray myself in my dreams. Nothing of Celia, nothing of Jim. No shout, no cry, no murmur. I said to Lizzie half an hour ago: 'I haven't been talking nonsense, have I?' I fancied that she was looking at me with rather a pitying tenderness? Although I can't see her, I know she has so good a face, that old woman—goodness without a single afterthought, goodness for no ulterior motive. Goodness because she can't help being good. I can write no more. My hand sweats on the paper. Out, light that oppresses my eyeballs. Now for the brilliant, peopled darkness!

CHAPTER VIII

At Garth House—Afternoon and Night

To ALL OF US, even the most insensitive, there come days, or only hours perhaps, when danger threatens us so nearly that every step taken, every word spoken, seems full of risk. Not definite and named danger; there is rather a general danger in the air.

It was so for Celia on this 14th of January. At the moment of waking, looking round her and expecting to see, as she still did, Julius sleeping in the bed beside her, she said aloud, still only half awake: 'I've got to be very careful today.'

The room was dark. Violet had not yet arrived to call her, she came and drew the blinds back, in the January half-light; at that moment the furniture seemed to settle itself down as though it had been alive and stirring in the dark.

'What's the matter, Violet?'

'Nothing at all, ma'am.'

'You look as though you'd got out of bed the wrong side.'

Violet made no reply but busied herself about the room.

'I wonder you stay here,' Celia went on, drinking her tea.

'Why, ma'am?"

'You don't like it here.'

'I like to be with *you*, ma'am.'

'That's very nice of you. We're neither of us very popular, you know.'

Violet looked at her as though they had a secret understanding, which was annoying because of course there was nothing of the kind. It might be that Celia, bored and out of temper, had on occasion chatted to Violet with more familiarity than was wise. But Violet was young and pretty and always on the side of her mistress. They had common ground in their dislike of Mrs. Gayner.

'You know that funny little man in the village, ma'am?'

'No, of course I don't. What little man?'

"The one who always goes about in a waterproof with a lot of dogs at his heels.'

'Oh yes. I've seen him.'

'He was in the garden last night.'

'What!'

'He was, ma'am, really. I saw him myself. It was my night off and I spent the evening at the Raglans'—he's a farmer at Konstans, two miles from Sizyn.'

'Well, well, get on.'

What had this wretched little man to do with her? And yet he *had* to do with her. Everything was dangerous.

'Well, ma'am, young Will Raglan drove me back on his motor

bike. It was eleven or thereabouts. I was just going indoors when I heard someone moving. I stayed hidden in the porch and he hurried past me. There was half a moon and I saw him as clearly as I see you. He hurried along, down the drive, and out at the front gate.'

'What an extraordinary thing! All right. I'll wear the blue. That's all. I'll turn the bath on myself.'

'I thought I ought to tell you, ma'am.'

'Yes, of course.'

In the afternoon she encountered Miss Vergil near the Post-Office.

'How's Mr. Cromwell?'

'Oh, he's better, thank you.'

'Out of bed?'

'Oh no. He had a touch of pleurisy.'

'Old Greening isn't bad, is he? When you think he's been here thirty years.'

'No. For a country doctor.'

Miss Vergil, who was looking, in her man's hat and severe tweeds, like an old soldier in mufti, muttered with her gruff casualness:

'Mrs. Cromwell, I oughtn't to say this, I suppose—damned cheek no doubt. I know you don't like any of us, and I daresay you're right, but I'd rather be friendly than not. What I mean is, if I ever can be any sort of help you can rely on me.'

'Thanks very much,' Celia said, surprised.

'Yes. I've made a muck of my life on the whole. Not that that interests you. But you can trust me. So-long.'

And she turned and walked, as though she were on parade, down the street.

That was nice of her, Celia thought. The first one that's been decent. But this too seemed like a warning. What did May Vergil mean? Why should Celia need anybody's help? She didn't *want* anybody's help. What she wanted was kindliness, affection, some-one whom she liked to comfort and console her and tell her that she was beautiful. And, at the same time, she knew that what she wanted was that someone should tell her that she was no good, a failure, a wife so unsatisfactory and ignorant and weak that her own husband had grown to despise her and neglect her and wish for any company rather than hers.

At home again she took off her things and went in to see her husband. He was fast asleep, lying on his side, his mouth a little open, helpless as a baby. Mrs. Gayner was sitting near the bed. She got up when Celia came in. Celia shook her head and then motioned with her hand towards the door.

The two women went together into the passage.

'He's sleeping.'

'Yes, I see that he is. You go back, if you don't mind waiting a little longer. I'll be with him when he has his supper. After that, when they've made his bed for the night, he'll be all right alone. He's got the bell there. He's ever so much better, isn't he?'

'Oh yes, ma'am.'

'Has the doctor been?'

'He came just after you went out.'

'What did he say?'

'He seemed pleased. He said the chest was almost right and he thought Mr. Cromwell could get up for a little tomorrow.'

'Ah, that's good! . . . Mrs. Gayner.'

'Yes, ma'am.'

'Something worries me. Have you seen a little man in the village, he always wears a waterproof and goes about with a lot of dogs?'

'Well, ma'am, I'm not sure . . .'

'Oh, you must have seen him! A horrid little man, and they tell me in the village he's up to no good. They all wonder what he's doing here. He doesn't seem to work and yet he has money.'

'Yes, ma'am.'

'The point is that the village people suspect him of stealing, although they haven't caught him out yet.'

'Oh yes, Mrs. Cromwell. I think I *have* seen the man.'

'I'm sure you have. Violet says she saw him in the garden last night. It was her evening out. She came back about eleven and he passed her as she was going in.'

'How could she be certain?'

'There was some moonlight. She saw him most distinctly. I don't want to bother Mr. Cromwell with it just now. But it rather frightens me all the same. Jim Burke sleeps in the house. I shall tell him to keep a look-out.'

'It certainly *is* upsetting,' Mrs. Gayner said.

'If you hear anything will you let me know?'

'Certainly I will.'

Celia had her dinner alone and her uneasiness increased. She hated to eat alone. Nothing made her feel so melancholy and deserted. After dinner, she went up to see Julius again and talked to him for a little. Then she went back to the study and began to read a book about Marie Antoinette. This she did partly because she was so ignorant and must improve her mind, partly because she was a little like Marie Antoinette herself and felt a real sympathy for that poor mistaken lady.

The door opened. She looked up and saw Jim Burke standing there.

In her heart she was delighted to see him, although she would most certainly not tell him so.

'Hullo, Jim!'

'Hullo! I came to tell you that everything is locked up and all right.'

'Oh, Jim, I wanted to tell you. Violet saw that awful little man who has the dogs in the garden last night.'

'What was *she* doing in the garden?'

'It was her night off. About eleven. He was after no good.'

'All right. I'll watch for him.'

Very casual he is about it, she thought. He looks cross.

By the door he said:

'What have you had against me these weeks?'

'Had against you? Well—yes. I haven't forgiven you yet.'

'I forgot myself. That's all.'

He stared at her as though his eyes were beyond his power to control.

'I suppose you hate me,' he said slowly.

'I don't hate you. Of course I don't.'

He came into the room a little way.

'I don't mind—I don't mind anything—if you're kind to me.'

She was firm. But she did like him very much and she had perhaps punished him sufficiently.

'We'll say no more about it.'

'I'd do anything for you—anything. If you told me to kneel down——'

'Now, Jim, don't be a fool. I don't want you to kneel down or anything else. Good night, and keep an eye open for that horrid little man.'

He said no more. He turned his eyes from her and looked about the room. Then he went out.

After his supper, when Celia had left him, Julius fell into a light sleep. He was asleep and yet not asleep; he was dreaming and yet not dreaming. Someone was playing his favourite of all the Beethoven Sonatas, Opus 31, No. 1. 'How much better,' he said, 'than the "Moonlight." The trouble is that hardly anyone can play the last movement.' This time it was played superbly, malicious, humorous happiness falling in a shower of notes, touching his eyes, opening them, so that he stared in passionate delight at the room he had never seen before, stared with wonder at the high white walls, the wide-open windows, and beyond them a night sky of stars such as old Lamplough had once seen in his company.

But it was the enchanting little melody of the Scherzo that somebody was singing, the melody that Beethoven repeats so often, that is never monotonous.

'How loving, how tender Beethoven really must have been,' he said. 'And he was deaf as I am blind.'

'But you are blind no longer,' Lamplough said. 'You have succeeded in breaking into that other world at last. You knew it was there but never gave yourself time enough in your search for it.'

'So many other things intervened,' Julius said, moving about, staring with passionate delight at the grass that, although it was night and the stars were blazing, gleamed like water into the far distance. He listened to the Sonata, to the wild but perfectly ordered riot of notes that suddenly paused and waited with an enchanting delight of anticipation.

'Now that you know this place is real you'll never again doubt its existence, will you?' old Lamplough asked quite anxiously.

'Will I be able to see now always?' Julius asked.

'Yes, if you like. It's your own affair. It depends on your faith in reality.'

'Then,' Julius cried radiantly, 'I need never be anxious or afraid again. Is Celia coming?'

'If you can persuade her.'

'How happy she will be that I can see after all. There will be no trouble any more. She won't be lonely or restless now.'

The music had stopped and, following it, there was so full a peace as Julius had never known. The great white room opened into a courtyard and there he saw many figures moving. 'How long it is,' he thought, 'since I have seen a face! What a weary time it has been! And now I shall be able to watch Celia's eyes.'

As he moved through the room towards the courtyard he woke up. He lay on his back, exceedingly happy, humming the little melody from the Scherzo. 'That, at least, is real. I could go down now to the study and play the whole Sonata through on the gramophone.'

He lay looking into the darkness. 'There is such a place, there is such a world. It is real and true to me in·this darkness. How wonderful it was to see, even though it were only a dream. Perhaps if I sleep again the dream will return.'

But now his brain was awake. He turned on his side and from his repeater learned that it was half-past eleven.

He was much, much better. The dry sharp pain in his chest was gone. He pressed his hands on his body, his chest, his arms, his legs. His body was cool again and strong.

'This illness has been a good thing. Something was wrong with me that this illness has cured. I know what I will do. I will take Celia on a cruise. We will go to Italy and Greece. Although I cannot see, the sun will warm me and she will be so happy. People will all love her, not be jealous of her as they are in this little place. She shall flirt if she pleases. I will lie in my chair and feel the sun on my face while she dances. It will be a little like the white place of which I have been dreaming.

'First we will have a week or two in London and I can go and hear some music. I can enjoy the theatre if she is at my side to tell me what is happening.'

He rolled over, luxuriating in the new awareness of health that he had.

'It was my fault. To bring her here and keep her all through the winter! I have been selfish. For some reason I love this house very much. Katherine Mark has made me feel its past life and when I am alone I am not alone. But Celia has not felt it. She is so much younger and I have buried her here.'

He raised his arms above his head, yawning in his happiness. 'How clearly I see everything now! How mean and doubting I was to be jealous! And what Hell it was! That is all over. Burke is a good fellow and is fond of me."

He sat up. An idea came to him. He smiled in the darkness. Carefully he got out of bed, felt for his soft wool slippers, walked gingerly to the chair where his dressing-gown was. He was weak, of course. His legs trembled a little. He felt his way to the door. He stood there, smiling. Then he opened it.

Celia could not sleep. She turned on her light and tried to interest herself in Marie Antoinette. She hated to sleep without Julius. She had grown so happily used to that company. Even though she had quarrelled with him all the evening she had only to grin at him as he lay, his eyes closed but his hand stretched out towards her, for everything to be tranquil.

'I'm an awful fool,' she said suddenly out loud, addressing Marie Antoinette, who was flirting with Fersen. 'But then I'm young, ill-educated, spoiled. How can I improve myself?'

The trouble was that she was not sure whether she wanted to! Her youth was so very charming and would be gone so soon. And how often her youth had saved her. At seventeen or so she had flirted with an elderly but famous painter, and had been saved from things 'worse than death' only because, not liking some exhibited painting of his, she had written to tell him so and had added, 'And you see, dear, I am so very jealous for you.' These few words had infuriated the famous painter so beyond measure that he had hated her from that instant. Yet she had meant so well!

She had not, she decided, lying back with her arms behind her head, yet reached the moment when youth and age discover a common understanding. That awful moment when she will suddenly cry with conviction 'I too will be fifty' and the many millions of the Fifties are waiting in serried ranks, their ears cocked, to hear that cry.

No, she had not reached that crisis. She still could not understand the aged. She *loved* Julius, she thought, leaning over and considering the empty bed, but did not understand him. At that she was miserable and lonely again. She wanted someone—almost anyone—to take her in his arms and comfort her. The Indecencies which lie so very close, cheek by jowl in fact, to the Proprieties, invaded her mind. But she did not care. She lay considering the very incoherent, improper, loving, mean, generous, selfish jumble her mind was.

She heard the click of the door. She turned sharply, sitting up. It was Jim Burke. He stood just inside the door. He was wearing only a shirt and trousers. His shirt was open at the neck. On his feet were shabby, faded, red bedroom slippers. His hand was still on the door.

'He's mad,' she thought. 'I'll call for Julius.' But she did not.

At last in a whisper she said: 'Jim Burke. Are you crazy? Get out of here.'

'Yes,' he answered, 'I'm crazy.' He closed the door very quietly and came into the room.

'If you don't get out this second I shall call Mr. Cromwell.'

'No. Don't. I was afraid you'd lock your door.'

She was now really frightened—frightened and furious. Suppose that Mrs Gayner or Violet——

Her heart hammered at her voice and it trembled a little.

'I give you a minute, Jim Burke. Otherwise I'll raise such a row in this house·that——'

'Don't. Don't,' he said very gravely, as though he were giving her advice for which she had asked. He crossed the room and stood near the window looking at her. The only light in the room was from her lamp beside her bed.

'I had to see you where no one would disturb us. You've been unkind to me for weeks so that really this is your own fault. I couldn't help kissing you that day and I can't help loving you, although I think Mr. Cromwell is the finest man I've ever known. You needn't think I've been happy over it. I haven't at all. Most unhappy. Never remember in all my life being so unhappy. But it isn't to do with ourselves whether we love anyone——'

'You crazy fool!' she broke in. 'Stop talking nonsense and get out of here. Don't you see that anyone can come in at any moment? If I ring this bell——'

He smiled but continued to stare at her in her black silk pyjamas as though she were wearing nothing at all. 'There was a play once I saw in London had just that situation in it. Irene Vanbrugh, the actress's name was, and I kept her photo for quite a while.'

He came closer to the bed.

'All I'm going to do,' he said, 'is to sit on this bed and hold your hand and perhaps give you a kiss. Nothing more. I wouldn't hurt you for anything—and besides, I think Mr. Cromwell's the finest man I've ever known. Tomorrow I'm going away. I've been meaning to go for weeks, because I'm really so very unhappy being close to you every day and being able to do nothing about it. I'll kiss you once and after tomorrow you will never see me again.'

Her eyes never left the door. She could think of nothing but the danger of someone hearing a noise and coming to investigate. Mrs. Gayner's bedroom was directly above hers.

She was looking away from him, staring at the door, as she said:

'Please, please! We'll talk in the morning. We'll settle everything in the morning. Someone can hear. Mrs. Gayner's room is over this one. Please! Please!'

He came and sat down on the edge of her bed, which was the outside of the two.

'Don't be frightened. No one can hear us with the door shut. Everyone's asleep, aren't they?'

He put his hand out and touched her arm.

She saw the handle of the door turn. She switched off the light.

Julius thought: 'I will go in very quietly. I will kiss her very gently. I will lie down perhaps for a little but not wake her. Then I will go back to my room. She will never know that I have been there. Perhaps she will dream that I kissed her.' So he opened the door very softly and closed it almost without sound. He stood there, his body trembling a little, for he was weak. He listened for her breathing and could not hear it. That meant nothing. She could sleep so very gently.

He took some steps forward and then stopped. He had the fantastic notion that someone was in the room, someone as well as Celia. He shook his head, smiling. He had noticed often that his senses had become so acute since his blindness that a room would seem to him full of people and there would be no one there. A little wind rattled very gently the blind. He moved forward again and again listened. He stood taut, listening with all his faculties. There was no sound save the movement of the blind, but his apprehension of a human being came rather from a consciousness of pressure on the space of the room. He had often felt the pressure of furniture in a room, and then, when someone entered, the pressure would be different. He knew that Celia must be sleeping or she would have heard the opening and closing of the door, however slight the noise had been.

He felt now that someone was behind him and turned abruptly, knocking his leg against a chair. This noise would surely wake her and he listened. There was no sound save the reiteration of the blind.

He stood thinking. He must not frighten her, but if she was awake, why did she not call out?

Then his second personality, his blind personality, angered him. 'There is someone here. There is someone here.'

He turned back, found the door again, and began to move along the wall, touching it with his hand. Some fear, a sense of horror quite foreign to him, was attacking him. He had known this on many occasions, especially in the years that followed immediately his blindness. He would be quite alone in a room and would be sure that someone was going to attack him. It would be the remains of his war-nerves. He would turn suddenly, throwing out his hands, and there would be nothing but air. He would be enraged and cry out and even fight with his fists in space. But many years had taught him discipline. There was nobody there— of course there was nobody there. But he would make sure.

His nose was sharp. He could smell substances that to the normal man had no odour at all. It seemed to him, sniffing like a dog, that there was a man's odour here—something of tobacco and earth and a man's clothing. At that thought his heart jumped and was still. A man! A man!

He began now, stealthily, as though he were tracking something down, to move along the wall. He knew everything in this room, the exact position of everything. Here was the long wardrobe. He traced with his fingers its shining surface. Here the small writing-table with the little clock and the leather blotter. He moved on. He was beside the far window now. He stroked for a moment the curtains, then thrust his arm behind them. No one was there.

He moved on, and here was his own smaller wardrobe where his suits hung. He opened it stealthily and pressed his hand among the clothes. No one was here. He came to the other window, opposite the beds, touched the curtain and, with the next movement, his hand was against a cold throbbing cheek.

He paused there and drew a deep sighing breath. Then his hand moved, almost caressingly, over the face. He felt the cheek, the forehead, then the hair.

'Burke,' he said.

His brain was amazingly clear. This was a familiar scene; he had been through it, it seemed to him, before. In plays and novels you 'crashed' your fist into the fellow's face. His arms, though, had fallen to his sides. All he said was: 'What are you doing here, Jim?' He did put his hand up again and felt the neck and the breast-bone. His fingers lingered there a moment. Then, perhaps because he wondered whether Burke were naked, he touched the shirt and the belt of the trousers.

'Why are you here?' he asked again.

The well-known familiar voice answered: 'I came to ask Mrs. Cromwell something.'

'An odd time, wasn't it?'

'I meant nothing. Mrs. Cromwell didn't know. . .'

'You'd better get out.'

'Yes, Mr. Cromwell.'

Someone moved quickly across the floor. The door opened, was closed.

Julius turned towards the bed. He was fearfully tired. His legs shook so that he was not sure of himself and he sat down on the edge of the empty bed.

'You awake, Celia?'

'I didn't know he was coming, Julius. I didn't! I didn't! I was reading. I couldn't sleep. He came in and stood there looking at me and began to talk a lot of nonsense. I was furious and told him to get out. But he wouldn't. He said he was going away tomorrow and wanted——' She stopped.

'Yes. Wanted what?'

'Wanted to kiss me before he went. He said he'd been in love with me since he came here and it was terrible because he thought you the finest man he'd ever known. That's why he was going away.'

'I see. Has he ever been in here before?'

'No. Never.'

'Has he ever kissed you?'

There was a long pause.

Julius said again: 'Has he ever kissed you?'

'Yes. Once.'

'When?'

'Several weeks ago. In the garden.'

'I see. Were you angry with him?'

'Of course. Furious.'

'But you didn't tell me.'

'No. I didn't want to make a fuss.'

'And you've been quite pleasant to him since then.'

'No. That's what he said upset him—my being unkind to him.'

'I hadn't myself noticed that you were unpleasant.'

'Julius, you must, you must believe—I didn't—I couldn't—I love you so much.'

This was all horrible to him. He must get away. He must be by himself, quite alone.

He got up.

'Somebody told me——'

'What did somebody tell you?'

'That you and Jim Burke——'

'There was nothing to tell. Nothing, nothing.'

'Somebody thought there was. Would he have come in here like this if he hadn't thought——'

'I don't care what he thought. He's mad, crazy. I ought to have told you, I know. I was frightened. I thought you'd be angry.'

'And that I would send him away? Of course I would have done.'

He stood, thinking.

'Good night,' he said.

After she heard the door close she began to cry, miserably, with childish crying. She lay down, burying her face in the pillow and crying into it.

PART III

Light in the House

CHAPTER I

From Five to Six—At the Rectory

WITHIN TWENTY-FOUR HOURS the news was everywhere. Mr.
Cromwell had discovered Mrs. Cromwell in bed with Jim Burke,
had thrashed him 'within an inch of his life' (the settled 'scandal
phrase'), thrown him out of the window. Jim had disappeared.

The only quite certain fact in the whole matter was that Jim
Burke had disappeared. No—there were two more facts. Someone
had seen Jim Burke entering Mrs. Cromwell's bedroom and only
ten minutes later Mr. Cromwell entering it.

Beyond this nothing was *really* known. *Who* had seen these
entries? Some said Violet, Mrs. Cromwell's maid, others that it
had been Oliphant, others Curtis.

From the house itself there was no word. That Jim Burke was
gone was true. Nothing else. It has been said before that Garth
in Roselands was not an especially moral village—neither more
moral nor less moral than any other place. The business of sexual
intercourse and its casual results—this was considered a common-
place. Did a girl have a baby, then there were many factors to
be studied. If the man married her all was well: if she went and

had her baby somewhere else all was nearly well. What the girl must *not* be was 'bold-faced.'

Now Mrs. Cromwell was held, at once, to be 'bold-faced.' She was from London, she was young and pretty, she wore smart clothes, had her eyebrows plucked, was rouged and powdered (although this, of course, all the village girls were too), was 'a damn sight' too free-and-easy with everybody. Moreover her husband was blind, poor gentleman. Moreover the scandal involved Jim Burke, who, as everybody had long known, was a libertine and a worthless man. No lady who *was* a lady should have lowered herself . . .

Mingled with this was the Newer Socialism, and a very odd one it was. We were all Socialists now, but we still liked Ladies to behave and Gentlemen to be Gentlemen. We wanted everyone to share and share alike, all big houses to go, no one to save money that might be given to the poor workingman—but, at the same time, we liked to admire someone, and how could you admire your own lot who had slept and eaten and drunk with you, whom you knew to be wastrels or idiots or dullards?

Most especially had Mr. Cromwell been allowed privileges, for he was so handsome and big and wore bright colours when he was out, a blue scarf with a brown jacket for instance. He was blind and so he was mysterious; he was courteous and friendly—'a proper gentleman.' 'A gentleman that *was* a gentleman.'

And now this painted, loud-laughing, self-pleased girl from London had deceived him with the bad boy of the village. She had not even chosen someone like Johnny Hope or even old Ironing to be gay with.

Within those twenty-four hours the whole village condemned her. There was not a voice that murmured in her favour. Even Mr. Boss, the most tolerant of God's creatures, growled that 'it shouldn't 'ave been that Jim Burke. If she was a bit restlesslike let her go up to London.' In higher social circles scandal was, as it ever is—packed with pleased superiority, news excitement, and a comfortable satisfaction that 'something had happened at last.'

They had not, of course, liked her from the first. They had never liked her. They had expected something just of this kind. Their dislike of her was greatly heightened by their liking for Mr. Cromwell. His blind staring blue eyes, his broad kindly face, his whole personality pervaded them. They were all in love with him. It was as though they entered Garth House and sat around him, cheering him, reassuring him, comforting him. In actual fact they did not catch a glimpse of him.

Four days after Jim's disappearance they were all at the Rectory —the usual time—four to six. Gladys Ironing, Alice Lamplough, May Vergil, Phyllis Lock, their hostess Daisy Brennan.

In Daisy Brennan's heart there was working a true and power-ful horror. She was forced to consider the physical facts—that Mrs. Cromwell had been found in bed embracing Jim Burke. That Julius Cromwell had discovered them thus.

There was, of course, no proof of any kind, but imagination ran ahead, as it always does, of information. Everyone knew that this was what had occurred. A detailed description was ready. There could be no doubt of any of it.

Daisy Brennan confessed her mind.

'I shall never speak to her again. However long she remains here, I shall never speak to her again.'

They were working round the table. Mrs. Lamplough almost sunk under a black coal-scuttle of a hat (she was like some white-faced snail, moving her head, stealthily, from side to side under her shell). Phyllis, very girlish, was wearing no hat, and would impatiently shake her flaxen locks as though to say: 'How young I am! My youth is beating at the window of my heart!' May Vergil beside her was wearing a soft white collar and a buff waist-coat. She looked like an ageing male impersonator. Mrs. Ironing would look up at the window, stare at the sun as though she had never seen it before, and then murmur something about her sew-ing or life in general. Daisy Brennan, her head up, her chest out, was Offended Morality on her charger Indignation. She repeated:

'If we let a thing like this pass——'

'A thing like what?' May Vergil asked.

Her question made everyone jump—spiritually jump. For everyone had been comfortable. Daisy Brennan was pleased at her indignation. Phyllis Lock pleased at her own excitement. Mrs. Lamplough darkly pleased at wrong-doing. Mrs. Ironing pleased and safe because they never laughed at her when some general topic commanded them. Everyone had supposed that May Vergil was pleased too. It was clear from the rasp in her words that she was not.

'May, dear,' said Phyllis.

Miss Vergil fixed her martial eye on Mrs. Brennan.

'I want to know, Daisy. A thing like what?'

May Vergil was in a temper. Everyone knew the sign. The fourth brass button on her waistcoat trembled ever so slightly. However, Daisy was no coward.

'A thing like what, May? A thing like adultery—a thing like the pretty' (oh, what scorn on that word!) 'young wife of a fine fellow who was struck blind in his country's service committing adultery with a common young man in her husband's employ.'

'Now, now. Stick to facts, Daisy. Who *says* that she has committed adultery?'

Now *saying* a thing in so many definite words was dangerous. Daisy, who felt indignant at this most unexpected behaviour of May Vergil's, whose voice therefore trembled with a sense of ill-treatment, answered:

'Who *says?* Why, May, everybody.'

'And *who* is everybody? Such statements are slanderous, you know.'

Phyllis Lock began to feel very uncomfortable. She hated it when May was in one of her 'policeman' moods.

Daisy threw up her head and took a firm stand.

'I'm not one, as you all know, to say anything against anyone that isn't true. Everyone will grant me that. I've no intention of discussing the facts. I simply say that Mrs. Cromwell is not a fit woman for my children or for anyone who believes in decent behaviour to know.'

'Ha!' May Vergil had a peculiar little snort all her own when she was hot on the track of a criminal. 'That's all I wanted to know. You have no facts, Daisy. No one has any facts. All that anyone is certain of is that Jim Burke has left the village, and *that's* a good riddance. As to Mrs. Cromwell, anyone with half an eye can see that she's devoted to her husband. In any case it's *their* business, not *ours*.'

Daisy Brennan was furious. Her bosom rose and fell most handsomely. She had never been scolded by May Vergil in public before.

'I have always thought, May, that you are pretty lax about these things. You say it isn't our affair. It *is* our affair when we all live together in a small place like this and are all meeting constantly. The whole village knows about this. What will all those who look up to us say when they see——'

'Look up to us my foot!' May Vergil broke in very rudely indeed. 'My dear Daisy, have you *no* idea of the things they say of us behind our backs? Do you really imagine that they think us all saints and angels? What they think of *me* everyone knows. That they think you and Frank the laziest pair in England—everyone knows that too!'

This was indeed *too* much! Daisy Brennan was so angry that she saw everything and everyone double as though she were intoxicated—and especially Mrs. Lamplough's sharp little eyes, alight with pleasured malice.

'I don't think, May, that personalities are quite the thing! I don't think——'

'To hell with what you think!' May Vergil rose so abruptly that her chair fell over behind her.

'I only want to warn you, Daisy, that you'll be getting yourself into an action for slander. You'd better look out. Mrs. Cromwell is a charming woman and, so far as I can see, she's done nothing whatever but give that oaf Jim Burke a flea in his ear for damned impertinence. So-long—and mind your step, the lot of you!'

She banged the door behind her. There was general consternation. This was most serious. This was a real breach in the social life of the community. Everyone went home long before the appointed time.

Yes, most certainly, one thing *does* lead to another. The lives of at least five people might have been altogether different had the little Pardoes not happened to pay a call directly after the ladies left the Rectory.

Daisy Brennan stood alone in her drawing-room so very angry that her legs trembled and her throat was dry as hayseed. May Vergil! Before them all! To call her 'the laziest woman in England,' to say that Mrs. Cromwell was charming, to charge them all with deliberate lying!

Her anger was, as anger almost always is, mingled with self-pity, and behind the self-pity was uneasiness, dismay even. *Had* everyone in the village been saying that Frank and herself were lazy? She knew of course that lazy they were—or rather, building up her defences, she agreed that Garth was a place where energy was wasted. Suppose that Frank *did* begin to preach his own sermons instead of reading a *much* better sermon of some more brilliant clergyman's, who would be benefited? Mr. and Mrs. Boss perhaps! And, for herself, if she were lazy in some ways she was energetic in others. She was charming to everybody and would be happily beneficent had she only the money to be beneficent with.

But the root of her anger was her shocked astonishment at May Vergil's indifference to immorality. She had always thought that there was something strange about May. Now indeed she was sure of it. And yet, before the coming of the Cromwells, how friendly in her dry sarcastic way had May always been, how greatly had she admired Daisy Brennan—or so it had seemed!

And to be insulted in that way before Mrs. Lamplough! This was a sharp sword piercing Daisy's bosom. For Alice Lamplough would now be so very happy—triumphant, even. The story would be everywhere before another day was done. Daisy would never speak to May Vergil again. She also would never speak to Celia Cromwell again. And yet there they were, all so close together, unable to separate, meeting every day. . . .

At that moment through the half-open door Benson looked in. The children had gone for a walk with their father—a great occasional event which they hugely enjoyed. At the moment of departure Benson could not be found, and their father had refused to wait, sadly to Gilbert's disappointment.

Benson, returning from a sterile rat-hunt in the garden, was amazed to find that Gilbert was nowhere. Without Gilbert he was lost, without Gilbert he was alone in a world of enemies. Beyond that there was always, when Gilbert was gone, the awful fear that he would never return. Who could tell with these strange mortals whether they would return? So he pattered about searching, and, choosing a very wrong moment, peered into the drawing-room.

Daisy, seeing him, hated him. She had never liked him. Her good-natured weakness had pandered to Gilbert. His hair was disordered, his eyes sycophantly anxious, his nose plastered with mud. She gave him one look and he fled.

A moment later the little Pardoes were introduced. They were always known as the little Pardoes because, both physically and spiritually, they were little indeed. Mrs. Pardoe was the widow of a clergyman who had been Vicar of St. Mary's Moor and been knocked down by a steam-roller and killed. Always such ludicrous accidents were happening to the Pardoes. Who else *could* be run over by a steam-roller? He died penniless, and now Mrs. Pardoe and the two children lived at Christiansland, two miles from Garth, helped by a reluctant brother who sold cotton in Manchester and grudged his sister every penny. Mrs. Pardoe was very poor and very obsequious and her children had learnt to be obsequious too. They were very small, very white in the face, suffered from adenoids, and watched everyone with anxiety.

When they visited Daisy Brennan they came as though to the Queen of Sheba, and Daisy liked that. She was always kind to them and gave Mrs. Pardoe old clothes discarded by Gilbert and Simon.

Now she ordered tea and suffered her anger to be changed into graciousness. Lucy Pardoe sat on the very edge of her chair, breathed heavily and, when she felt it to be safe, stared at all the beautiful things in the room, for to her they were beautiful, especially the large screen with red dragons painted on it. Laurence Pardoe, who was as thin as a match and wanted to run away to sea at the first opportunity, hated these calls. He felt dimly that when his mother paid a call on anybody it was because she wanted something. Mrs. Pardoe herself was like a little mouse for whom a fierce cat was always just around the corner. But Mrs. Brennan was kind and it might be that there would be a pair of shoes or a jacket enriching her family before the call was over.

Conversation consisted in Daisy Brennan asking a series of questions, such as: 'And how have you all been?' 'How is the garden doing?' 'Tell me what fun you've been having lately, children.' To these questions Mrs. Pardoe, who was always running ahead in conversation to make sure that no peril was lurking, would answer:

'Oh, Mrs. Brennan, what a lovely bowl of primroses! In that blue bowl—so lovely, such perfect taste—a blue bowl—the spring flowers. Yes, we've been quite gay, haven't we, children? and Lucy recited "It was roses, roses all the way," didn't you, Lucy? Browning's "Patriot," but of course you know. A mother is always prejudiced, isn't she, Mrs. Brennan? Or am I perhaps exaggerating? In any case although she was nervous at the beginning she quite regained her confidence before the end—didn't you, Lucy? It was for Foreign Missions. In the Church Schoolroom. I *am* so sorry to have missed the children. Is Dorothy growing? I expect she is. Such a lovely girl!'

'Yes. Their father insisted on taking them out for a walk.

Quite a rare occasion and the children love it. But of course if
we had known . . .'

'Oh, dear Mrs. Brennan. No. No. Oh no indeed! That's just
what I said to Lucy. "We'll go along as it's a fine day and just look
in for five minutes." We didn't mean you to bother about tea—we
didn't, indeed. And we mustn't stay. Just a bite and we're off!'

But the tea was being brought in and the Pardoes, without
knowing it, followed the rather rickety little table that held the
bread and butter, the plum cake, the strawberry jam, with anxious
eyes, for other people's food was always better than their own.

Daisy Brennan, noticing the wide staring eyes of Lucy Pardoe, thought: 'Poor child! It isn't her fault that she's never learnt
manners, and she really does look hungry. I wonder if they'd be
insulted if I offered them the plum cake to take home. There
isn't a thing upstairs! Or would those old flannel trousers of Gilbert's not be *too* shabby?'

And at that moment Benson actually shuffled (for his walk,
when he was embarrassed, *was* a kind of shuffle) into the room.
The fact was—he was desperate! He had been from end to end
of the house looking for his master, pushing his muddy nose into
every room, sniffing at a shirt of Gilbert's that lay on the bedroom
floor, suddenly pricking up his ugly ears and listening at what
might be Gilbert's step. Gilbert was not in the house. He had gone
for a walk without him. All that remained was that room with
the hateful woman inside it. On an ordinary occasion he would
have been too anxiously nervous to venture for a second time.
But now every risk must be taken. So in he came with that air of
one who has committed an awful crime, the air of all frightened
innocents before the ruthless enemy.

At once Lucy cried: 'Oh, what a lovely little dog!"

Lovely! That was the last word to apply, but to Lucy Pardoe
all dogs were lovely, all food appetizing, all possessions acceptable.

'Do you like him?' Mrs. Brennan said with a beaming patronage.

'Oh yes,' Lucy said, shrinking into herself, for she had seen, after one glance from her mother, that she had forgotten her manners.

'Well, you can have him!'

Here was a solution. She hated the dog, it was doing Gilbert no good, she would tell Gilbert that on his next birthday he should have a *real* dog—a puppy of good breeding.

'Oh no!' Mrs. Pardoe broke in. 'We couldn't really. That's just like your wonderful generosity, Mrs. Brennan, but we couldn't really. Lucy, I'm surprised at you! Well, just a half cup! Such delicious tea—only half a cup.'

'You'll be doing us a kindness. Gilbert picked him up in the road somewhere. He's quite good about the house, no trouble really, but it takes Gilbert's mind off his work. He's at home because of the chicken-pox, you know. He's not much to look at, I'm afraid—the dog, I mean—the children call him Benson.'

'Dear me, what a funny name!'

'It is, isn't it? Certainly you must have him. Lucy seems to have taken quite a fancy to him.'

At the moment of departure Benson refused to go. He stood with his feet firmly planted, looking with agonized despair across the village green. However, a piece of cord was discovered, and the Pardoes departed, leading, with little chirrups of reassurance and comfort, the unhappy Benson.

The children greatly enjoyed the walk with their father. He was always at his best when he was alone with them. He strode along and Simon ran ahead with spirited bursts in order to keep up with them. Their father talked without ceasing and much that he said they did not understand. He constantly adjured them to do always what pleased the people in power. He told them always that if they wanted to succeed in life they must placate the people in power persistently until they became people of power themselves. Then they could trample on everybody in their own turn. They understood that he was being scornful, and felt, in a curious undefined way, that he was asking for their consolation.

It was one of those spring days when everything has an especial clarity and colour—not an April day of sunlit cloud and sudden glittering rain that is gone as it comes, but a day when the air is warmed with a hidden light. The young green of the trees has the sharp 'cut' look of carved jade, and the fields are freshly coloured—a new amber, a pearl iridescence between˙ hedges of a faint moth-green. The birds cry shrilly to one another as though startled by their discoveries. A dog from somewhere ran frantically at the little stream that chuckled beside the road, as though he believed that for an hour or two only would the waters be so fresh and so crystal. It was a day when, if you are a doubter, you may suddenly wonder whether after all there may not be a first cause, a planned universe, a settled destiny for everyone.

But Dorothy and Gilbert were not very happy, in spite of the beauty of the day and their pleasure at being with their father.

Children live in a world so far removed from that other where grown persons are active that they can discover events only by spying, conjecturing, putting two and three together and making six of them.

Something had happened. One event at least was clear. Jim Burke was gone. Gilbert was very sorry, because he liked him and because now he would not teach him modelling. But there was more than that. Gilbert, like all sensitive adolescent boys, was very lonely. He longed for affection but was shy of inviting it. Jim Burke was a friend, although in this friendship there was none of the strange radiance that there had been in his meeting with Mr. Cromwell in the Well. But Jim Burke *was* a friend and he had none other save Dorothy and, of course, Benson.

He was pleased when his father turned abruptly and started back towards Garth.

'Time to go home! Time to go home! Tea! Tea! Mustn't be late for tea!' . . .

For Dorothy there was alarm, threatening danger in the air. Why had Jim Burke gone so suddenly, in the middle of the night as it were? Had there been a quarrel? About what were her elders and betters whispering? Something to do with the Cromwells. Everything was to do with the Cromwells now.

She felt that she could not live without Jim. Love had, for her, as yet, nothing obscure or confused about it. You loved someone as Molly loved in *Wives and Daughters*, or Jane Eyre loved Mr. Rochester. You were ready to give up everything and follow the beloved faithfully round the world. It would be terrible to give up Mother, Father, Gilbert, and Simon, but since that day of the party at Garth House she had known that she would follow Jim Burke to any place that he ordered.

She must discover where he was, why he had gone. Had he money, food? Was he perhaps needing her, thinking her faithless? She hurried beside her father, seeing nothing but Jim's face, hearing nothing but his voice.

She was taking off her things in her bedroom when her mother abruptly entered.

'How late you are! It's too bad of your father.'

'It was such a lovely day. Father said——'

'Never mind your father. It's nearly six o'clock. The Pardoes have been here.'

'Oh, poor Mother! And you were all alone.'

'Well, never mind that. Dorothy, there's something I want to say. You must give that necklace back to Mrs. Cromwell.'

'Oh, Mother? Why?'

'Never mind why. There are good reasons. And if Mrs. Cromwell talks to you anywhere you're to say as little as possible and come away.'

'What has Mrs. Cromwell done?'

'Never mind what she's done. It's enough if I say so.'

Dorothy was standing very straight and still, her hat in her hand. She said at last, staring into her mother's eyes:

'No. I can't do that.'

'Can't do what?'

'Give the necklace back.'

'But of course you must if I say so.'

This was only another incredible event in an incredible day. Dorothy who had always been so pliant, so willing, so obedient!

'Mrs. Cromwell gave it me. It's mine. I thanked her for it. It isn't yours, Mother, and Mrs. Cromwell didn't give it to you. I don't know what Mrs. Cromwell has done, but it would hurt her very much.'

'My dear Dorothy! Am I your mother or am I not? There are some things you mustn't know. You are little more than a child. If I tell you it's right to do something, then it *is* right!'

Dorothy began to tremble. She felt sick. But she repeated:

'No, Mother. I'm awfully sorry, but I can't——'

The door burst open. Gilbert stood there.

'Where's Benson? I've looked everywhere. I've whistled.'

Daisy Brennan looked at both her children.

'What's the matter with you? Have you gone crazy? Tea's an hour late as it is.'

'Mother, where's Benson?'

She felt for the first time in her life frightened of her son.

'Now, Gilbert, don't make such a fuss. It's perfectly all right. Your father and I will buy you a dog on your birthday.'

'*Buy* me a dog?' His voice was breathless. 'Where is he? What has happened?' His voice dropped. 'Is he dead?'

'Of course he isn't dead! What an idea! The fact is the Pardoes came to tea. Poor little things! They never have anything and you have so much. Benson came in and they liked him, so I said they could have him.'

She didn't meet Gilbert's eyes. She went to the door.

'Now, children, that's enough of all this. Come and have your tea.'

But Gilbert caught his mother by the arm. He shook her. He screamed: 'You gave Benson to the Pardoes? You gave him to the Pardoes?'

She shook herself free so that he stumbled.

'Gilbert, you're forgetting yourself! Really! I'm ashamed.'

'I'll never forgive you. Never! Never! You've done a beastly thing! Beastly! Beastly!'

He ran past her, out into the passage, stumbling, tumbling, down the stairs.

CHAPTER II

Thunder Cloud—Rain by Sizyn

IT HAD BEEN always Celia's practice to sulk when people—parents, loving young men, female friends—were angry with her. With a quick facility she discovered that she had been wronged and, after that, sulks were both charming and effective. We are, it is true, always wronged in one way or another because we regard ourselves as 'something very special.' That is a point of view that even those who love us very much indeed cannot altogether accept.

Celia loved Julius and therefore she realized that something very terrible had occurred, whether she were wronged or no. But wronged she was! She had committed no crime. She had not been even indiscreet. If Julius and silly Jim Burke chose the same moment in which to visit her bedroom, was it her fault, and was there not something ludicrous about it? Every farce had enjoyed that situation for centuries.

It was because she loved Julius that the situation was not only ludicrous. She realized that at once. Jim Burke was already forgotten. Her whole attention was concentrated on Julius.

She went to his bedroom on the morning following the absurd affair. She kissed him, and, because he could not see her, put as much dignity into her voice as it would hold.

'Julius, I haven't slept at all. I'm very unhappy. But I had nothing to do with his coming into my room last night. I was horrified. I understand that he's gone. No one has seen him this morning.'

She realized then that she had to do with a Julius whom she had never seen before. For some while he did not speak. At last, staring at her and beyond her, he said:

'Please! Please!' Then he raised his voice. 'It's not a thing to discuss. Now or ever.'

She shrugged her shoulders.

'Oh, well, if you are going to believe all the silly chatter. They hate me, you know. Those old women in the village. They'll get up some other scandal in a minute. It doesn't matter *what* I do, they'll talk all the same. It's your place to defend me.'

He picked up the newspaper on the bed.

'I'll do what's right.'

She thought of offering to read to him. He would miss Burke. But she was going to be proud, a woman in the wrong. So, without another word, she left the room.

But what was she to do? It was so difficult with a blind man. Celia, angry, hurt, wronged, was so distressing a sight to anyone who loved her. But when she *wasn't* a 'sight'? When he could not see her eyes dim with tears, her lips trembling, her pitiful helplessness?

In her room she found Violet.

'They tell me Jim Burke's gone.'

'Yes, ma'am. He has.'

'Why? Do you know? Did he have a quarrel with Mr. Cromwell?"

'I'm sure I don't know, ma'am.'

She hesitated. She was sure now that Violet knew everything.

'What are they saying downstairs?'

This was disgraceful—to discuss servants with servants. But she must know.

Violet said vehemently: 'Mrs. Gayner says that Jim was rude to you, ma'am.'

'Oh, she does, does she?'

How she hated Mrs. Gayner! Then, carried away by her own sense of injustice and loneliness, she burst out:

'Well, he was. Most impertinent. I told him to leave the house.'

'Yes, ma'am.' Violet added, quietly: 'I never liked him. Full of cheek he was. And he had a dreadful reputation from his last place. I don't know what the master ever engaged him for.'

'Was he ever free with you, Violet?'

'Well, ma'am, he would have liked to be. But he didn't dare. I saw to that.'

When Violet had gone, she sat on her bed, and the old fright that had first come to her in the car on that first day of driving into Garth, returned to her.

This was terrible. She had, by her own words, placed herself on a level with Violet. She was alone in the house. She had not a friend here. She jumped up on the impulse of leaving at once and returning to her parents in London. That is what she would do! Shake herself free of this horrible place where everything had been wrong from the beginning. She would be again with her own people, her old friends who understood her and knew that she was good and faithful. She began to open drawers, to pick out clothes and throw them on to the bed.

She stopped, standing in the middle of the room. This would not do. If she left now everyone would say that she was guilty. What did that matter? But it did matter. She would face them all. She would show them that Julius loved her, believed in her. But did he?

She felt as though she were trapped. But she was not one to be so easily beaten!

'May I read the papers in the morning to you, Julius?'

'That's very kind of you.'

Before she began she asked for directions:

'How do you like them? Do you want a summary of the news, then the leaders, and then some gossip?' She smiled gaily, remembered that smiles were of no avail and felt exasperation. Suddenly she realized that this was all in very bad taste, reminding him of Jim Burke as nothing else could do. It was too late now to retreat.

'Read the things that interest you most,' he said.

He was sitting upright, leaning a little forward, staring. She fancied that he would not listen. He was, in the way that she most detested, lost in his own world. She had read the papers already to herself that morning. It was exquisitely boring to read them all again.

She began. It was as though she were reading in an empty mausoleum.

'Any country that still rests under the illusion that Hitler's word is to be trusted must have felt some anxiety when it learned . . .' She tried to find some news. Each item seemed more trivial than the other. 'Is this the way you like it?' she asked.

'Thank you. Yes.'

At length she ceased. He said nothing at all.

She went over to him and laid her hand on his arm.

'I'll do it better another day.'

'That was very good indeed.'

The next thing that happened was that she lost her temper with Violet and dismissed her.

She rang for Violet and Violet did not come. She rang four times. That evening, as she was dressing, she asked her where she had been.

'I was out, ma'am.'

'Was it your afternoon off?'

'No, ma'am.'

'Why were you out then?'

'I went down to the village. I was away only half an hour.'

'You should have told me you were going.'

'Yes, ma'am.'

Violet looked at her. It seemed to Celia an impertinent look.

'What's the matter with you?'

'The matter, ma'am?'

'Yes, you've been very strange lately.'

'I am very sorry, ma'am.'

Celia lost her temper.

'I'm not going to have it. You were excellent at first, but now

I don't know what's come over you. You can't even speak to me politely.'

Violet made no answer.

'What's all this about? Has something upset you?'

'Nothing at all, ma'am.'

'You *were* a human being. Now you're an automaton. You'd better tell me what it's all about.'

'I don't understand, ma'am.'

'Yes you do. Perfectly. If you're not happy here you'd better go.'

Violet said slowly: 'I'm not happy here. No one is.'

'Why?'

'We never know where we are with you, ma'am. I'm sure I've done everything I can to please.'

Yes, her look was insolent. It said: 'I know a lot and you know that I do.'

'Well, you'd better find another place.'

'Very good, ma'am.'

But as soon as it was done Celia regretted it. What a foolish thing! She had been friendly with the girl and told her many things that she should not. The girl would gossip, talk maliciously. She told Mrs. Gayner.

'I'm going to send Violet away.'

'So I understand, ma'am.'

'You never liked her, did you?'

'No, ma'am, I didn't.'

'Find someone else—a quiet country girl is best.'

'Yes, ma'am. I daresay it won't be difficult.'

To her own surprise she found that she had a sudden impulse to confide in Mrs. Gayner, to make a friend of her.

'Mrs. Gayner, do forgive me if I've been tiresome sometimes. I *know* I'm tiresome. It's the change from London perhaps. This is a very quiet place, isn't it?'

'It *is* quiet.' Mrs. Gayner smiled. 'Why don't you have a trip up to London, Mrs. Cromwell? It would make a change.'

'Perhaps I will. If I can persuade Mr. Cromwell to go.'

She realized that Mrs. Gayner herself didn't look very happy.

'You wouldn't like a little holiday yourself, would you? It must have been quite a business settling in here. Have you any children—or friends that you would like to see?'

Mrs. Gayner paused.

'I have a son, ma'am.'

'Oh, how interesting! I didn't know. Where is he living?'

'He moves about. His job takes him to different places.'

'Wouldn't you like him to stay with you here for a little?'

'He couldn't get away, I'm afraid, ma'am.'

'Well, mind you tell me if you want a little holiday.'

'I will, ma'am. Thank you very much.'

Not much further there. Mrs. Gayner hated her, she supposed, as did everyone else in this house. This beastly house! This beastly house! The house itself hated its own silence. What it wanted was life, noise, singing, a family of children. It wanted to be the house that it had been when Mrs. Mark had lived in it. Celia had tried to wake it up. She had given her Christmas party. People in the district had invited them to dinner, but Julius hated dinner-parties. And yet he enjoyed things like the picnic he had given at Sizyn!

'Julius, the days are getting much warmer now. Let's have an afternoon party. We can have them in the garden.'

'Very well, dear, you ask them.'

'No,—but would *you* like it?'

'Very much.'

'Do you think people would like to come?'

'I'm sure they would.'

For weeks now there had been no physical intimacy. Once more they slept in their twin beds side by side. She would not ask him to take her in his arms, but she longed for it. Oh, how she longed! She touched his arm. He made no movement. Soon it must all come out. This truce could not continue.

One day she walked into the village and saw Phyllis Lock coming towards her. Celia smiled and hurried her step, but Phyllis turned down a little lane between cottages. So that was it, was it? They were cutting her.

But, a day later, she encountered Miss Vergil, who was very friendly.

'I wonder whether you would have tea with me one afternoon, Mrs. Cromwell.'

'I should love to. You'd better not ask anyone else though.'

'Why not?'

'They are all cutting me.'

'Oh, nonsense!'

'It's certainly absurd, but it's a fact.' She looked into Miss Vergil's face, as taut as a brown skin drum. 'What do they say I've done?'

'They think you flirted with Jim Burke, and Mr. Cromwell turned him out of the house.'

'I didn't, of course. But what business of theirs is it anyway?'

'You know what little places like this are.'

'It all began,' Celia said slowly, 'with someone whispering in Julius' ear at our Christmas party. I wish I knew who it was.'

Miss Vergil was greatly interested. She had not heard this.

'I thought,' Celia went on, 'that it must have been Mrs. Lamplough. But Julius is certain that it wasn't.' She broke out passionately, 'Why *can't* they leave us alone? I've never harmed anyone here. I only wanted to be friends.'

But Miss Vergil was thinking.

'I wonder who that was—a caddish thing to do. I wonder . . .' She ended: 'Pay no attention. People have said things about me all my life. Do I care? Of course not. You *will* come to tea, won't you?'

'Of *course* I will.'

This encouraged her. She had two friends at least, Mrs. Mark and Miss Vergil.

On a fine afternoon she asked Julius whether he would go for a walk. Her hand through his arm they wandered up the leafy lane towards the Moor. She was determined that she should establish some connection with him—an angry one, a brutal one: anything to bridge this dreadful gulf.

She chattered brightly.

'How warm the sun is, Julius! In this southern part of England it is like another country. It has taken a little time, but now I'm getting to love Glebeshire.'

'I'm glad.'

'People used to tell me in London that it was stuffy, unless you were right on the sea. Do you know, in all these months we've never been to Rafiel. Shall we go one day?'

'I'm afraid Rafiel is spoiled.'

'The sea must be the same. They can't touch that.'

'Charabancs go down there every half-hour. Curio shops, cafés everywhere.'

'It must have been lovely when you were a boy.'

'It was. The most perfect place.'

'Oh, now we're coming out on to the Moor. How lovely it is! All silvery! How I wish you could see it today!'

'I can smell it.'

'Yes, a rich warm scent like toffee. No. Not toffee—that's too sticky. There's the salt of the sea in the breeze—as though it were only a yard away.'

'So it was once.'

'Mustn't that have been strange? Old Lamplough described it to me once. Slippery rock, marsh, and huge slimy animals crawling up and down.'

Julius said nothing. He looked weary.

'Shall we sit down for a moment? Here's a good place,' she said.

They sat down: he leaned forward, resting his beautiful hands on his stick. She loved his hands. She wanted to take one between hers, feel its warmth, the strength of its bones, shiver with delight as his fingers closed about hers. Would she dare? No, she must not. A lark was singing. A little cloud like a silver-edged mushroom went over the sun.

They started homeward. She had achieved nothing. She was very miserable.

'You know that Violet is gone? Mrs. Gayner and I agreed that she was impertinent.'

He said nothing.

'Mrs. Gayner runs the house splendidly.' She hoped that this would please him.

'I'm glad you like her now.'

'I was very silly. I didn't at first.'

They walked for a long time in silence and, during the silence, her resentment mounted and mounted as though a horrid growth was enlarging, with every footstep, inside her body.

They were almost home again when she burst out:

'What have I done? Why won't you say? I'd rather you were furious and turned me out of the house. I've done nothing. That's the ridiculous part. It wasn't my fault that Jim Burke came into my room. I've done no wrong. I haven't! I haven't!'

'Please, Celia! It's no good.'

'Why is it no good? Aren't we married? Didn't we—don't we love one another? If you don't love me any more say so and I'll go back to London.'

He said very slowly: 'I can't help myself. You must give me time.'

'Time? Why should there be any time? It's weeks now. It's dreadful. I'm all alone here. If you don't love me—if you don't love me——'

The words choked her. They were at the gate of the drive. He walked forward.

She cried so that anyone might hear:

'It isn't fair! I'll go home! I'll go home!'

And she ran down the drive into the house, leaving him to find his way himself.

After that she was as miserable as it was possible for a young woman to be.

She was furious. She was furious. She repeated it to herself over and over again. She said it aloud, sitting up in bed. The early grey morning light showed his humped shoulder as he slept, peacefully breathing like a happy child. 'I'm furious,' she said, and waited to see that shoulder turn. But it did not. She pictured to herself that scene when he would hold out his arms and she would cross to his bed and be enfolded.

In actual fact he came every night from his dressing-room, touching always the same things, the chair-corner, the shelf above the wash-hand stand, pausing always before he moved on, stood above the bed, threw off his blue dressing-gown, slipped into bed.

'Good night, Celia.'

Sometimes she replied. Sometimes she did not.

What must she do? So easy were she not in love with him. But easiest of all were he not blind. *Now* she knew why it was that she had been afraid coming in the car for the first time by Sizyn—lest, on one horrible day, he would be able, by the strength of his blindness, to slip away from her. Now that day had come. Because of his blindness she could not seduce him, could not frighten him, could not insist that he kept contact with her. And, of course, the more that he eluded her, she, loving him, loved him the more.

One night she tried to seduce him. He was like a dead man. At one moment he sighed. At that sound she was so bitterly humiliated and so wildly enraged that she slapped his face. He made no reply.

'I'm sorry,' she said. 'I forgot myself. I will never do it again.'

'I can't help myself,' he said at last. 'I can't escape from myself.'

She returned to her bed and lay there, wishing that she might seduce all the men in England if only he could know that she was doing it.

But that didn't last. All she wanted was that they should be friends. She had nothing to confess. If only she had!

At last one day she made a set speech:

'We can't go on like this, can we? I had better go back to London.'

'Perhaps you had, for a little while.'

'I don't understand you. Only a little while ago you loved me better than anyone in the world. Nothing's happened really and yet now you don't love me any more. How can that be?'

'I don't know.' He shook his head in a kind of despair. 'It isn't as you say either. If we could both wait——'

'Then I'm going to London.'

'Yes. For a little while. Perhaps that would be better.'

But she didn't go. She found to her own surprise that now, more than ever before, she didn't want to be away from him. She wanted to hurt him, strike him, knock him down, insult him, but be near to him. Now that his body was removed from her she loved it much more dearly. She loved everything about him—all of him. But nothing was of any use. You cannot love flesh that is dead to you.

At last one day, on a heavy thundery afternoon, she took the Austin and drove herself up to Sizyn Church.

On a day like this Glebeshire is under a curse. All the weight of Heaven's anger lies like a mailed fist upon it. The sky is steel and relentless. Over the sea there was a grape-purple cloud like a looped curtain, and the grey line of the sea was a smudge of disgust. The land from the sea to the Moor never stirred. No tree was allowed to be friendly, every roof was threatened. The Moor is inhuman at such a time and this is what it wishes to be. It is ashamed of men.

The Church was white and the stones of the running wall sharp and cruel. Behind the Moor, opposing the sea, grey heavy clouds slowly rose and hung, like wreaths of unblown smoke, in silent sinister preparation.

Celia got out of the little car and wondered why she had come there. She had a wild notion that she would drive on, just as she was, to Polchester, catch some train to London there. She could send for her clothes. She could write to Julius saying that she would come back when he wanted her. But someone else—Mrs. Gayner perhaps—would open her letter and read it to him. She could not bear that. She knew that if she was lonely now she would be more lonely yet in London.

She looked about and saw, to her surprise, a boy standing beside a bicycle quite close to her. It was young Gilbert Brennan. She knew very little about this boy. Her only contact with him had been at Mrs. Mark's tea-party, and of that contact all that now remained was the memory of an ugly mongrel dog. There was, however, something desolate about the small thin-legged figure, his ugly school cap a little crooked on his head.

'Hullo, Gilbert! How are you?'

He touched his cap shyly. When he came close to her she saw that he was sorry that she was there, and she determined to go away at once.

'I only came out for a little drive. There's going to be a thunderstorm.'

'Yes, there is.'

'You'll get awfully wet if you don't bicycle home.'

'I don't care if I do get wet.'

'I hate getting wet myself.'

He turned away. She saw that his hand was trembling on the handle-bar. Then she saw that his upper lip was trembling also. She was at once touched to all self-forgetfulness. He was very unhappy and alone.

She moved forward towards the Church, which, now that a black cloud hung over it, was lit with a white iridescence.

'I suppose,' she said, 'it's a bit dull sometimes when you ought to be at school.'

He nodded.

'Aren't there other boys you can be with?'

'I don't want to be with anybody. That's why I came out here.'

There was an awkward silence. She had no experience with little boys. She thought of something to say.

'Where's that funny dog you had at Mrs. Mark's? He ought to be with you.'

He turned and she was surprised at the fierce bitterness in his gaze.

'He's gone.'

'Gone! Why, did he run away?'

'Mother gave him away.'

'Why?'

'I don't know. It was when I was out walking with Father.'

'Didn't she like him?'

'I don't know. I thought she did.'

He went on, speaking with little sharp gulps:

'It was some beastly people called Pardoe came to call and one of them said she'd like Benson who came in just then looking for me because we couldn't find him for the walk and he was missing me, and Mother said the Pardoes could have him. And they took him away tied with a piece of string and he put his feet down and kept looking round for me. I know because Mrs. Boss saw them and she told me.'

'I suppose your mother thought you didn't care for him.'

'Of course she knew. She knew I loved him.'

'Then I don't understand——'

'And what was worse was that I was all Benson had. He's a one-man dog and I know he's thinking of me all the time and perhaps he won't eat his food and the Pardoe children are awful. They are really. They don't know anything about dogs at all.'

He held himself erect as though he were making an oath.

'I'll never forgive Mother. Never! I won't as long as I live.'

She said at last:

'How far away do the Pardoes live?'

'Oh, not far.'

'Why don't you go and see him then?'

He looked around him, dropped his voice and spoke as though he were telling her the secret of his life.

'That's what I'm going to do. And I'm going to take him away,

too. I came out here on my bicycle to think about it. And if
Mother won't let me keep him I'm going to run away.'

He looked at her with a sudden fearful suspicion.

'You won't tell anyone?'

'But of course not.'

'Do you think—would it be stealing?'

'I suppose technically it is. But they won't say anything—the
people who took him, I mean.'

'Suppose the Pardoe children have got very fond of Benson?'

'If they have, you had him first.'

'Of course I did.'

'And if, as you say, he's a one-man dog, he'll be miserable
away from you. You've got to think of the dog's happiness.'

'Yes, of course.'

She said, smiling:

'I shouldn't run away.'

'I will if Mother doesn't let me keep him.'

'We can have him for a little while and you can come and see
him whenever you like.'

She thought amusedly, 'Here, what am I doing? Encouraging
theft, defying Daisy Brennan's wishes, interfering between mother
and son.' And she was glad that she was!

The rain began to fall, heavy sulky drops.

'Now the rain *is* beginning to fall. Let's go into the Church.'

The door was unfastened. They sat down side by side in one
of the pews. The famous window was dark, and yet the colours,
the snow-white of the hawthorn, the purple lettering, the brown
of the priest's robe, glowed against the blackness. A flash of
lightning struck it like a sword. A peal of thunder broke the
tension.

'Are you afraid of thunder?' she asked him.

'No, of course not.'

'Some people are, all their lives.'

She seemed to him very little older than himself. He was quite at his ease and his unhappiness was less acute. He spoke low because he was in church.

'I don't *understand* Mother,' he said. What an intensely feeling little boy he was, she thought. 'She doesn't want me to have things or make any friends or anything. She's always stopping me and saying she's hurt.'

He pulled himself up. It wasn't right after all, whatever he felt, to talk like this about his mother to a stranger. But he had talked about it all to nobody. There was something deep inside him that he could not understand, something new. He would never think about people in quite the same way again, and instinctively he knew it.

Celia was thinking of the day of the picnic, when she and Julius had sat together in this Church and had loved one another.

She looked at the window and the figures were blurred. Julius and she, so little a time ago, had sat there together. And now—they would never sit there together again. Things would never be right, never, never.

In spite of herself the tears began to trickle down her cheeks. The Church was very dark, but Gilbert saw them. They were terrible to him. He did not know that grown-up people cried. He was terrified. Why was she crying? She was unhappy too, and, he suddenly realized, more unhappy than he. He wanted to run away. What ought he to do?

The rain crashed down upon the roof. She said never a word. She did not wipe the tears away. She sat staring in front of her.

Without knowing that he did it, he put his hand into hers.

CHAPTER III

In Simon's Room—On the Road

SIMON had made a small room in the attic entirely his own. No one knew or cared about this place. It was the smallest room of three, but it had a good-sized window and a deal table and two very rickety chairs. Against one wall and piled high to the edge of the sloping roof were many faded volumes of old magazines—the *Cornhill*, Mrs. Henry Wood's *Argosy*, bound clumsy *Illustrated London News*.

On the low wall opposite these volumes Simon had pinned a curious assortment of pictures that had come his way—aeroplanes in flight, the King, Queen, and the two Princesses, a vigorous presentment of Jack Doyle the boxer, and a lovely lady whose name Simon did not know (Miss Patricia Burke as Principal Boy). This last he admired because of her smile, which he thought sporting and comradely. On the deal table was a stuffed bird that Jim Burke had once given to him, the wooden soldier that he had gained at the picnic, and an empty cigar-case that Mr. Cromwell had given him.

His greatest possession, however, was his 'Detective Book.' This was a large, brown-covered exercise-book in which he scribbled so illegibly that he could not himself read what he had written. It was illustrated with tremendous pictures of ships, motor-cars, bleeding corpses, and men with terrific noses. In a mysterious fashion he believed that this book was of the greatest importance and would one day be of national significance. The rusty lock to the door possessed a key, and this he kept always about his person.

What he greatly enjoyed was to enter this room very quietly, lock the door, balance himself on one of the rickety chairs, and either write in the 'Detective Book' or sit, with a face of grim seriousness, 'thinking.' His thoughts were not very connected and sometimes he fell asleep with his head on the table.

He liked also to gaze from the window and watch, far below, the movements of people in the garden. It gave him a tremendous sense of power to watch people who could not see him. He hoped that one day he would see something really tremendous—something to equal that great occasion when from behind a tree he had seen Jim Burke kiss Mrs. Cromwell.

Until now his life had been one long sequence of gaiety and enjoyment. He had experienced no real troubles beyond a cut finger, the toothache, stomach-ache, and the inevitable little stupidities of his elders. In the last month, however, trouble had come to him, and trouble with which it was not easy to deal.

In the first place, he was not seeing Mr. Cromwell. He had been to Garth House twice in the last three weeks and on neither occasion had he been welcome. It was not that Mr. Cromwell had been unkind. He had greeted him as he had always done. Something was wrong. For some reason that he could not understand he had not dared to climb on to Mr. Cromwell's knee; he was not sure that Mr. Cromwell had been aware of his presence.

It made a serious difference that Jim Burke was no longer there. Oliphant and Curtis and Cotterill were not his friends in the way that Jim had been.

But there was something deeper than this. Although he was only eight years old he had already a quick sense of atmosphere. There was trouble in that house. They were all unhappy. Mr. Cromwell was unhappy and Simon did not know how to help him.

So he went there no longer, and knew the first unhappiness of his life. And the less he saw of Mr. Cromwell the more deeply he loved him.

As bad as this was the unhappiness in his own family. His mother was unhappy; Dorothy was unhappy; Gilbert was unhappy. His mother's unhappiness did not distress him very greatly, for she was often unhappy for very slender reasons. He realized that sometimes she liked to be unhappy because then other people took notice of her. He knew all about this because he had tried it himself and found it very successful.

Dorothy was unhappy because Jim Burke had gone away. He thought this very foolish: he was himself sorry that Jim Burke had gone away, but there were plenty of interesting persons and things remaining in the world. He was, however, very fond of Dorothy although he a little despised her because she was a girl and made open demands on his affection. He would like to find Jim Burke for her if he could.

But his real disturbing distress was for Gilbert. Gilbert was unhappy because his mother had given Benson to the Pardoes, and this Simon could understand completely, partly because a dog *was* a dog and partly because he hated and scorned the Pardoes. With respect to Gilbert in general Simon felt a protective instinct.

He knew that Gilbert 'felt things' in the way that he himself never did. If their mother spoke sharply to Gilbert at a meal, for being greedy about apple tart, or not wiping his mouth, Gilbert went first red and then white. Simon never minded in the least if admonished. Grown-ups thought this admonishing to be their duty and liked to see themselves in important positions. Had Simon been older he would have expressed his feelings in the Norman proverb: 'Hard words break no windows.' As it was, he enjoyed greatly seeing how far he might go.

It was quite different with Gilbert. He was sensitive to everything. But Simon, who enjoyed teasing his mother and Dorothy, never teased Gilbert. He respected him because Gilbert always told the truth, was, in spite of his shyness, brave at crises, and admired Simon. If anyone else teased or scolded Gilbert, Simon was angry, and it was for this reason that he felt little respect for his mother.

When his mother had scolded Gilbert, Simon 'thought out' a new way of teasing her.

In this matter of Benson he was altogether on Gilbert's side, and for every possible reason, to annoy his mother, to damage the Pardoes, to make Gilbert happy, he was determined to recover Benson.

After a very serious 'thinking' in his attic and a number of scribbles and screamingly funny drawings of the Pardoes in his 'Detective Book,' he went to find Gilbert.

It was just after luncheon, a fine water-cloud silver-blue day.

Dorothy had gone off by herself. Gilbert was kicking his heels in the garden.

'Hullo, Gillie!'

'Hullo!'

Simon looked very small and square in a blue blouse and diminutive grey shorts. He had, as frequently after a visit to the attic, a smudge on his cheek. Gilbert, very miserable, looking at him, thought him 'a very decent kid.' Because Simon's nose was pug and his cheeks round and fat he always looked a little like a clown.

'Are you going anywhere?' Simon asked.

'No, I don't think so.'

'Well, I am.' Gilbert knew that Simon loved his mysteries and that he liked them to be enquired into but not penetrated.

'Where are you going?'

'Wouldn't you like to know?' Simon said, grinning.

'Yes, I would.'

'Nobody shall. It's a secret.'

'What did you tell me for then?'

'Just because I wanted to.'

'Oh, all right then.'

This kind of badinage continued for a little and Simon said:

'Gillie—don't you miss Benson like anything?'

'Of course I do, you ass.' Gillie kicked furious dents in the lawn.

'I bet the Pardoes don't know how to look after him.'

'I hate the Pardoes.'

'So do I.' Simon looked at him mischievously. 'Why don't you go and take him away?'

This was what Gilbert had been asking himself ever since his conversation with Mrs. Cromwell. But he was of the Hamlets of this world. So soon as action was proposed to him he saw many reasons against it.

'I don't know. Perhaps I will one day.'

'If you brought him back, would Mother let you keep him?'

'I don't care what Mother does,' Gilbert answered fiercely.

'Where's Dorothy?'

'She's gone out by herself.'

Simon moved off.

'Where are you going?'

But Simon didn't answer. With the manner of a sleuth, stepping lightly, looking cautiously about him, Simon disappeared.

Safely on the village green he was pleased to see that there was no one about. He moved away down the road. He was, for his age, a most excellent walker. It was a cool day and there was a pleasant breeze from the sea. He was greatly pleased with himself.

He was yet better pleased when, half a mile along, he came up with a cart, filled with sacks, drawn by a plodding horse, and Mr. Seabanks, a farmer and a friend of his, seated somnolently in front of it.

He greeted Mr. Seabanks and asked for a lift. The Seabanks' farm was less than a mile from the Pardoes'. Mr. Seabanks, a stout, heavy, red-faced man, lifted him up, sat him down and asked him a question or two. Where was he going? How were his father and mother? When was he going to school? Simon had long ago learned that the way to baffle questioners was to ask them questions in his own turn. This he did. He asked about pigs. He asked about Mrs. Seabanks. He asked about Mr. Seabanks' lumbago. This last was of real interest to him, for he had once been taken by Mrs. Seabanks to see Mr. Seabanks in his bed and had then learned that, because of lumbago, Mr. Seabanks was unable to move and had to be turned in bed by Mrs. Seabanks. Mr. Seabanks liked to talk about his lumbago.

'Strikes you like a knife, you may say, before you can say "Jack Robinson." There you are, can't move, not even to eat your vittles.'

Once Mr. Seabanks asked suspiciously why Simon was going so far from home, but Simon answered that it was a secret.

'You're young to have secrets. Does your mother know?'

But Simon grinned and when the Seabanks' farm was in sight, requested to be lifted down, thanked his host very politely and started up a side lane.

Now began the exciting and enchanting part of his adventure. He not only felt like a detective, he *was* a detective. He walked up the lane, then turned into a road, ran for a while, keeping close to a hedge that he might not be seen, passed some cottages, hesitated for a moment, unsure of his way, then saw a familiar cross-roads and, with infinite pride, turned up to the right where the Pardoes' house was. He had every reason to be proud, for he had been to the Pardoes' on only two occasions, but wherever he went now he always noticed things and laid them up in his mind. You never could tell when you would need such evidences.

The Pardoes' house was a mean little place with two protuberances like large inquisitive ears and a chimney like a swollen nose. Above the door were panes of coloured glass and in front was a small gritty lawn: also two poverty-bare garden beds.

In the middle of one of these garden beds Benson was sitting!

Simon could not, for a moment, believe in his luck. He stood back in the hedge and stared at Benson. This dog had never been a beauty; now he was a disgrace. It was clear that his coat had not been brushed for many days, but, more than this, his spirit had died within him. He sat up on the dirty garden bed, gazing in front of him with lackadaisical indifference. While Simon watched, Benson thought that he would examine some part of his person, but his indifference was such that when he was half-way there he stopped with one leg half-raised and drooped. He possessed not even that fragment of energy.

There was no sign of life anywhere. The little breeze blew through the hedges, somewhere a woman called sharply, no human being was to be observed.

Simon acted quickly. He crossed the road, unlatched the little gate, and whispered 'Benson.' Even as he did so he caught the dog in his arms, held him tightly to his chest and moved back across the road behind the body of a stout and friendly oak.

He was but just in time. The front door opened and Mrs. Pardoe, attended by Lucy and Laurence, appeared. They looked, as always, untidy and entirely without either charm or spirit.

'We had better take Benson with us, I suppose,' Mrs. Pardoe said. Then she began to call, like a little tuneless whistle, 'Benson! Benson!'

Simon, in an agony, stroked Benson's untidy head. Benson neither moved nor uttered.

'Well, really, how tiresome! And we are late as it is! Benson! Benson!'

The children, without interest, began to peer about.

'See if he's in the house, Laurence.'

Laurence vanished.

'I don't want to go to Mrs. Tibblethwaite's,' Lucy began.

'Now, Lucy, enough of that. If Mother says yes it *is* yes.'

'Anyway we'd better not take Benson. Mrs. Tibblethwaite has a cat.'

'Has she? Dear me! I didn't know.'

'Mother, I don't want to go to Mrs. Tibblethwaite's.'

'Lucy, if you say that again I shall punish you.'

Laurence appeared.

'I can't see the beastly animal anywhere.'

'Laurence, you are not to use that horrid word. I've told you before. Never mind about the dog. Lucy says Mrs. Tibblethwaite has a cat. Now, children, come along. We're late as it is.'

They moved off, a dismal trio. They turned the corner.

Benson licked Simon's face.

'Oh, Benson, they called you a beastly animal!' He imitated Mrs. Pardoe, 'Now, children, come along.'

He put Benson down and, turning from the main road, started for home.

'Where's Dorothy?' Mrs. Brennan was asking Gilbert.

'I don't know, Mother.'

'And Simon?'

'I don't know, Mother.'

His cold politeness infuriated her and made her miserable. Life now seemed to be advancing towards her like a masked man threatening her with some awful disaster. She was hemmed in by discontent, malice, and all uncharitableness—she who only six months ago had been the lovely, radiant Daisy Brennan whom everyone loved.

'It's tea-time. And that.isn't the way to speak to me.'

'I'm sorry, Mother.'

'But don't you *know* where Dorothy and Simon are? Did they go out together?'

He looked at her and she turned away. Boys of fourteen were horrible, mysterious, undecipherable. And one's own son the worst of all!

She went out.

Five minutes later Simon appeared in the doorway. He whispered: 'Gillie, quick!'

'What is it?'

'You'll see!'

He ran up the stairs to the attic, Gilbert following. He put the key in the rusty lock. He drew Gilbert in and shut the door behind them.

Lying on his belly, his eyes bright with excitement, his ugly tail wagging, was Benson.

Early on that same afternoon Dorothy had gone out. She wanted to be by herself. She must think, understand if she could some of the troubles and longings that now besieged her.

Ever since the day of Jim Burke's disappearance it had been as though she were living inside Garth House.

The only person who would understand this was Mrs. Mark, because she too lived, in her heart and mind, inside Garth House. She had said once to Dorothy:

'You are my youth. I recapture it in you. Not that I was like you—I was much more rebellious than you—but because I, an old woman, am fond of you I am young again through you. You don't mind that, do you?'

Of course she did not mind it, although she did not understand it. Grown-up people were very strange, but Dorothy was now growing towards them. She had realized that ever since the day when she had looked at her body in the mirror. And this 'growing towards them' was deep inside her feeling for Jim Burke, which was different now from the thing that it had been even a month ago.

This change in her feeling for Jim Burke was mixed again in her thoughts about Julius Cromwell. She thought about him a great deal. She felt as though she knew him and he knew her.

He sat in the centre like a god and they were all grouped round him. He was sightless and yet, because he was physically blind, he saw into all of them, knew what they were doing and thinking.

What had happened on that night in Garth House? She had asked her mother and she had asked Miss Vergil. Both had told her that 'she was not old enough yet.' She had discussed it with Gilbert, and Gilbert had said that 'Mr. Cromwell and Burke had a row about Mrs. Cromwell. Simon saw Mrs. Cromwell and Jim kissing, you know.'

Here there was a mystery. It was silly of Jim Burke to kiss Mrs. Cromwell but surely nothing very terrible. Although now when she thought of it and visualized it to herself, new emotions were aroused in her; the beating of her heart was intense, her longings for Jim were sharp and hurting. She ached for Jim to kiss her and then they would go away and live together; she would have children and work for him. But none of the explanations that her girl friend had once offered her meant anything to her. She and Jim would kiss one another, he would put his arm around her, they would walk into space and she would be for ever happy.

She longed for this so desperately that she was sick with longing. She had the absurd conviction that Mr. Cromwell, sitting blind in Garth House and listening to music, as Simon said that he did, knew all about it.

But this concern with people outside her own family was quite new to her and led to great confusion. As though her own family were not preoccupation enough!—for her mother was now always out of temper, Gilbert, since Benson had been given away, kept to himself as though he were encased in armour, Simon was mysterious.

Her loneliness was the terrible thing! She would have talked to Mrs. Mark had she not been afraid of Mrs. Mark's affection for her. No one else before had ever told her, to her face, that she loved her. She was embarrassed by this, and shy because she was sure that soon Mrs. Mark would be disappointed in her. She would do some dreadful thing and Mrs. Mark would say: 'Oh dear, I didn't know that you were like that!'

Now, in her ill-fitting clothes, she walked quickly, she did not know where. Always now when she walked, with others or by herself, she looked for Jim Burke. She was certain that he had not gone very far away. He liked everyone in Garth; that was where his friends lived. He would find some work on a farm or in Rafiel.

She had walked without looking about her, and quite suddenly, as though she had been set down there from an aeroplane, found herself in a deserted place near a village called Couper towards Rafiel and the sea.

From here you could outline the long grey-silk stretch of water and two black rocks called the Sentinels. Around her the wind sighed and moaned, and she went into a little wood to escape it and to see whether there might be early primroses. It was dark here and the sky through the trees was like moss. Some animal moved. Twigs crackled. Two dogs ran forward, and then, to her horror, as though it were an evil dream, she saw advancing towards her the little man in the shabby waterproof whom she had always hated. She could not escape. One of the dogs was already sniffing at her feet.

The little man stood looking at her and grinning.

'It's Henry Sharp,' he said. Then as she didn't speak he went on: 'You know me, don't you? We've talked before. I gave your young brother a nice little dog.'

She moved to go. He turned sharply and stood in front of her. He was breathing fast, and his breath, stale-drink-tainted, very slight like a whispered warning, attacked her.

'No. Don't go. We're all alone here and can have a talk.'

She was frightened in a way that was quite new to her. This was unreal and yet very actual—as things are in dreams.

'I can't stay, I'm afraid. I'm late as it is. I must go home.'

'Must you—really?' He smiled into her face, anxiously as though he were asking her a favour. 'No. Must you? Can't you stay just five minutes?' He shuffled his feet.

'I'm afraid not. Good afternoon.'

But he did not move and she could not turn back because that would lead her only deeper into the wood.

'You're too proud to talk to me. That's it—see?' He had an odd way of saying excitedly 'See?' and he would do his little shuffle with his feet on the dead leaves. The two dogs were roaming in the undergrowth, and the sound of breaking twigs and the snuffle of dogs on the hunt were familiar and homely. Set in the heart of this homeliness was terror.

'I don't know why, I'm sure—why you should be too proud to talk to me. I'm all right—see? I've been on the halls in tip-top towns too. Song and dance. I gave your young brother a dog—and for nothing—didn't ask him a bean.' He smiled and came a step nearer. 'I like you—see? Always have—ever since I first came here. Always had a fancy to you. But I've never said a word—have I?'

'No. That is—no.'

'Well, then—what are you grousing for, eh? You're a nice girl. Ever been kissed—by a man, I mean?'

She looked about her, and up between the trees. No one. Only the blue-moss sky and the dogs snuffling, padding with their feet.

She had courage and she said, even smiling:

'No. I must go home. Really I must. We'll have a talk some other time.'

'No time like the present, that's what I say.'

He was staring at her. His small inquisitive eyes moved about her face, then to her neck, then down, over her body, to her feet. His voice was increasingly breathless, and his feet shuffled as though in a secret, excited rhythm of his own.

'I'll only kiss you. That's all I'll do. Christ, I've been wanting to do it . . . ever since the first time I saw you. Give us a kiss. It isn't anything. Really it isn't. You'll like it. I promise you will.'

For the first time in her experience of life she was aware of a man's physical self. She was aware and felt a deep recoiling horror, as though, quite suddenly, a veil had been lifted from all existence. Her childhood was ended as he touched her arm.

He caught her hand in his warm, dirty, damp one, bent forward and kissed it. In his little eyes there was a look of modesty, of reverence. When he raised them again they were greedy and almost closed.

'You're lovely—you are really. Not everyone's fancy perhaps. But mine. I like you, see? I think you're lovely, see?'

She had snatched her hand away and turned; she took some quick steps and stumbled. He caught her with his arm and at his touch she began to tremble: she could not move.

Only, in the middle of this nightmare, she saw that one of the dogs was lying, stretched out, his eyes fixed in adoration on his master's face.

'There. You'd have fallen if I hadn't caught you. There's nothing to be frightened of—see? You wouldn't be frightened of me, would you? I'm only going to kiss you.'

Like a small child she pushed at him with her hands.

'Leave me alone. Please, please, leave me alone. Oh, please.'

But he had touched her and was trembling. The back of his hand was against her neck. He caught her shoulders. He pressed his mouth, which was a live trembling thing, independent of his body, against hers. Her head was flung back, she half turned, fighting against him with all her force, and fell. As she fell she uttered a shrill beseeching cry. He stumbled on to his knees.

'Don't cry! No! No! Don't cry! I won't hurt you. You're lovely, see?'

His hands hovered above her. Then, as happens always in plays and story-books but very seldom in real life, he was caught by his miserable collar and thrown back, sprawling, into the bushes.

For the second time Jim Burke had made a quite unnaturally prompt and accurate appearance.

The little man picked himself up, turned and ran for his life, the dogs capering joyfully after him.

'Just like a tale in a book, and the second time,' Burke said, grinning at her. He pulled her up with his strong hand. Her hat lay on the ground: she was crying: tear-streaks stained her cheeks.

'When I catch that bastard I'll break his neck. Sorry! Let's sit down for a moment until you recover yourself.'

They sat down.

She stared at him. She could not believe. She blew her nose.

'I don't know . . . It can't be real . . .'

'Easily explained. I'm working at Couper Farm. Been there a week. I saw that little swine passing with his dogs and I followed him because I wanted to give him a letter—that he could deliver by hand. I was at the edge of the wood when I heard you cry. So it isn't so wonderful.'

She caught his broad thick arm. 'Oh, Jim! Jim! It's a miracle. I've been thinking of you all the time—all these weeks. Wondering where you were. Every time I went out.'

With her hat off, her hair untidy, the tear-smudge on her cheek, she looked a child again. He saw that she had lost all control. She was crying and sobbing. He put his arm round her.

'There! There! It will be all right in a minute. I know you were frightened.'

But, when she felt his arm about her, she caught his head in her hand and kissed him on his rough unshaven cheek and his mouth.

His body grew rigid. He held her for a moment tightly against himself. He stared out above her head, one hand clenched. Then with great gentleness he got up, moved away from her, stood kindly looking at her.

'You're only a kid. You don't know about anything.'

She knelt on the rough grass. There was a hole at the knee of one stocking. She examined it. Then she looked up.

'Jim—I've been wanting to tell you for ever so long, I love you more than anyone in the world—more than Mother or Gillie. I'll go with you anywhere if you like me to, and we'll have children. I'll keep the house when you go out to work.'

He looked at her and his face clouded. He was no saint. He had suffered greatly in those weeks. He was (as it seemed to him) in passionate love with a woman and he knew the sexual frustration of being near to her but not seeing her. With men of his kind there is no more positive sexual irritant. He looked at Dorothy, her face raised to his, her maturing body, her inciting helplessness. He lowered his head and stared at the ground. Then he looked up, smiling.

'What a kid you are! You don't know a thing about it.'

'I do. It isn't a new idea. I've loved you for ever so long.'

He knelt down beside her, touching her hair for a moment.

'No. You think that. You don't know. You'd be wretched if you went away with me, my handsome. You'd hate me in a week for the things I'd do to you.'

She shook her head violently. But she didn't touch him now.

'No, I wouldn't. You could do anything you liked.'

'Anything I liked!' He repeated her words mockingly. 'You're wrong there. Anything I liked! Have you ever seen me tight? I'd say not. And you know nothing about men, nothing at all. The bastards they are.' He took her hand and patted it. 'There's another thing. I'm in love with someone, terribly in love. I'd be cut into little pieces for her—small, small pieces.'

She stared at him, then down at the hole in her stocking.

'I see,' she said.

'Will you do something for me? Do this for me. Will you?' He felt in his pocket and produced a damaged envelope. 'Will you give this to her when no one's about? Will you? There's nothing wrong in it. But I must see her. I must see her when she's alone and ask her to forgive me.'

Dorothy took the envelope.

'It's Mrs. Cromwell.'

'Yes, it is.'

'It's her you love.'

'Yes, it is.'

'But it's wrong. She's married.'

'I know she is. My God, don't I know!'

'And Mr. Cromwell's blind.'

'Yes. And he's the best friend I ever had. I'd do anything for him.'

Dorothy sighed. She put the letter into her dress.

'Very well, I'll give it her.'

'That's a good girl.' He kissed her, but she didn't respond at all.

He got on to his feet and pulled her up beside him. He picked up her hat. She put it on.

'Now I'll see you to the road. You'll be all right then.'

She didn't reply. She walked quietly, without saying a word, at his side.

CHAPTER IV

In Julius' Study

JULIUS CROMWELL'S JOURNAL

I suppose that there is nothing more ill-advised than for a human being to write down on paper, even though no eye but his own will ever see it, the filthy depths into which his soul can sink. Pepys, Rousseau—oh, well, they were professional fellows. They watched their misbehaviour greedily with one eye while the other watched the public. Pepys wrote in cypher—but did he not hope that, one day, that cypher would be publicly translated?—and so, after a hundred and fifty years, it was.

But I have nothing in common with any professional. I am an ordinary if ever there was one—half beast, half aspiration towards something other. As I write now I am altogether miserable—miserable with that worst of all miseries, cowardice and self-contempt. It is perhaps that I may blow up a little courage into myself that I write this down. I may find a scrap of that quality lost somewhere in the general mess.

One of the dreadful things in this affair is my discovery of myself. Like most men, I have, I suppose, always wondered in my heart how I would face the supreme test. That didn't come, as you might have expected, in the War. I was young, in marvellous health. I liked the comradeship, the surrender of oneself to orders, even the adventure of imminent death.

It didn't *really* come, I can see now, with my blindness. I knew some dreadful hours, but everyone was kind and I had a pride in pulling myself to meet this situation. I had Elinor.

It has come now. I have been miserable enough for weeks past, but nothing to the misery, the abandonment to every horror, of this present. Last evening was the worst of my life. Celia had gone to bed. I sat there, quite tranquil, empty of any sensation, wondering whether I would go too. Then the abomination of desolation rushed in upon me. My heart began to beat furiously as though I had just been told some fearful news. My head was hot and constricted, my brain twisted, like metal wrecked by a bomb. I sat staring into darkness, possessed by awful visions. I saw the world torn by a fearful devastating war, and this time the evil powers everywhere triumphed, as I think they may do, for, during these twenty years, we have been slack, unimaginative, slothful, careless. I saw everything for which good men have been working and hoping for hundreds of years ruined, smashed in a night.

I heard, as though it were literally in my ears, a dreadful wailing and lamentation go up. I heard myself crying with the others: 'Why didn't we foresee? Why didn't we take thought? Why have we thrown all the good things away?'

Then I sank to further perceptions. I was dreadfully afraid. I have always rather prided myself on my courage. I have often said to myself, since my blindness: 'You stood that very well. You're really a fine fellow. Quite exceptional. You're ready for anything.' (I didn't know that I said this. But I did.)

Now I saw that I had really no pluck. After all, even though I was blind, I was better off than most. I had possessions, money, comforts, and people delighted to tend me: a few people loved me. Two or three thin layers of confidence and self-pride. Now they were gone, pierced through in a moment, and I had thought them so very solid.

As my heart raced my terror grew. Destruction was coming to the world and I couldn't face it. I wanted to hide. I had always said to myself that nothing could touch my inner self, but now my inner self was revealed for the first time, and it was a wretched, puling, pink, naked little thing. I have written often in this Journal about the interesting discoveries I would make as I went down and down into my very self—that Good Place with the stars and the peace and God above all. But now for the first time I was really 'going down' and there was nothing there but horror.

These terms, 'horror,' 'destruction,' 'smashed in a night,' are melodramatic unless they are actually true. But I think 'horror' is true of the suddenness of this discovery of oneself. It is as though a king had been magnificently leading his army against fearful odds, exhorting them, encouraging them, and then, quite suddenly, lays down his arms, betraying his country, his men, his friends, and his allies. It is betrayal of that kind that I am now feeling. I am none of the things that I thought I was. I am not brave nor faithful nor honest.

It is not that I have surrendered to jealousy or known panic, but that I see myself as a poor rotten creature and *don't care that I am so!*

How fantastic to me during this last week has been my idea of God. My notion that a benevolent Power had given me free will and was proud if I exercised it rightly!

Benevolent! There's humour for you! Religion is, I suppose, a confidence in the reality of the spiritual self. I have no spiritual self. Now, in my darkness, I can see nothing but my physical being, a grotesque object with all its processes ugly and grotesque. The act of eating—the pushing of grass and flesh into a hole in one's face. The act of sexual intercourse—leaping up and down with cries and groans, the sweat of human bodies, the dull apathy after the act is so briefly concluded; the act of defecation, the gradual dropping of one's body into ugliness and decay; the *pains* of the body, the torture of toothache, of rheumatism, of sinus, the little daily ordinary pains; the final rotting or burning, and in a week forgotten save by one or two. Our little cheats to salve some of this rottenness. Our pretence that music or painting or literature can make up for these. Our greed for food or drink. Our pretended love of nature, when behind it there is unceasing fear. The betrayals and falseness of friendship. Day after day we rise and clean our bodies and cover them with clothes and clutch at our alleviations to hide our fear.

Oh, I know that often enough I have cheated myself that there were pleasures and delights. But they pleased me only because I thought myself a fine fellow. I was the centre of the picture— brave under misfortune, charming to everyone, admired by all, wearing bright clothes, clean as a pin, strong as a lion. Have I not felt myself, since I have been here, the centre of everything, drawing all the neighbourhood into the comfort and safety of my splendid personality, even a child like little Simon Brennan? When he has climbed on to my knee and laid his head against my heart, have I not been proud as though I were a king of men?

I have even flattered myself over my jealousy of Celia, thinking myself very superior to her and indulgent towards her. But now not only am I a coward and base, but all around me are cowardly and base as well. The hideous Nazi doctrines are perhaps the only doctrines human beings are fit for—cruelty, disregard of all cries for pity, the elimination of individuality because human individuality is worthless, despicable.

I am sleeping again in the room where I was ill, that room I know to be hideous although I cannot see it. Celia said never a word when I said that I would sleep there. I woke last night after hideous dreams and I heard a voice in my ear saying: 'You are not fighting. If you don't fight now you are lost and many others beside you are lost also. It is now or never with you.'

As a novelist would write—'my mouth curled with scorn.' Fight? What is there to fight? I have not even surrendered, because there is nothing to surrender. And yet I lay there wondering. How long ago and sentimentally pathetic seemed those days when I had fancied that there was something to fight for! Those old words of William James that I had quoted to myself so often: 'Life *seems* like a battle . . . something eternally lost or gained.' And those words I have often repeated to myself—'Be still and know that I am God.' At least I am honest at last. It is not God that I know now but myself.

I wish to be honest here—no romance, symbolism, sentimentality. As I lay on my back staring into bitter blackness—I would like, at some more tranquil time, to put on record the colours into which I peer, colours created by sounds, by smells, by touch. The colour of a marble-cold shoulder, hard, smooth, strong; and of a woman's shoulder, soft, yielding, and moving towards one instead of resisting—these are two violently different colours. The colour of a voice—purple with an edge of Chinese white, or grey shot with an unexpected orange light so that the speaker becomes attractive unexpectedly to you and you smile . . . so, as I lay, staring into blackness, I saw a man in armour. Oh, I have often seen him! He is, I fancy, my memory of one of Bellini's

Madonnas, seen when I was twenty and with my father on my first visit to Italy. The one in Venice, the Madonna standing in front of an orange-rose curtain, and the two Saints, one on either side—one with a beard, the other in armour, holding a staff, round-cheeked, his helmet jewelled, light on his breast-plate, very strong, broad-shouldered, and with eyes and set mouth of absolute fidelity. Some servant about the place whom Bellini made to sit to him for an hour or two, but he has been with me always after that Venice visit, and especially since I was blind.

With what reality did he appear to me last night! I didn't want his company. I was scornful of him when he came. It is just that company that is so exasperating to me at present. He is the kind of romantic sentimental symbolism with which I have so long been cheating myself. 'Oh yes,' I say to him, as he stands there with his white staff, the red cross painted on it, with his solemn childish eyes, his plump cheeks, his rather too-fearless mouth, 'it's easy for you. You are a common soldier with no imagination. All you have to do is to obey. You have never considered the rottenness of the world. You are guarding a child and are yourself a child. I have put away childish things. And what use anyway will you be against Hitler's soulless robot mechanized army when it comes rattling across the world?'

He replied to me: 'None of these things are your affair or mine. You had better get up from your bed and fight. If you don't there will be many others lost beside yourself. We are never alone in a battle, you know. So you will find out after you have lost it and betrayed those depending on you.'

But I wasn't to be taken in by imaginary painted saints any more. Or I thought I was not. Even now I am not quite sure, though.

A strange thing has happened. Why will they not leave me alone?

Yesterday afternoon I was sitting in the library. The sun was beating on my head. I had turned on the famous Schubert Quartet in A minor, Opus 29. Almost *too* familiar, isn't it, especially the little Minuet? And yet it survives its deadly popularity. It is so very gentle and kind, and as always with Schubert, even in the most hackneyed things, you feel the wisdom behind it. That stocky, bespectacled man—*the* symbol above all dead or living men of everything that the Nazi spirit is trying to destroy, and that is indestructible. Anyway, I was listening to the last movement, the Allegro Moderato, when a warning voice is suddenly heard. Again I was reminded, 'You must *fight* for these lovely things if they are to be secure. Not anybody. But *you. You* must fight.' And, with irritation, I got up and turned it off before it was ended. At that moment there was a knock on the door and Violet's successor—Nancy—a *very* simple girl, said:

'Miss Brennan is in the hall, sir, and wishes to see you. Only for a minute, she says.'

'*Miss* Brennan?'

'Yes, sir.'

'Not Mrs. Brennan?'

'No, sir. Miss Brennan.'

'Ask her to come in.'

Dorothy Brennan. I didn't know her at all. I have only ever had a few words with her. A nice simple girl, they tell me. The door opened and closed and a very sweet child-like voice said:

'I beg your pardon.'

'Is that Dorothy Brennan?

'I'm very glad to see you,' I added, smiling. 'Because I *can't* see you, draw a chair up.' She did. 'That's right. Give me your hand.' She did—a soft, young girl's hand but strong in spirit, with character. I held it for a moment, then released it.

'Now. That's splendid. Will you have some tea with me? I was just going to have some.' I could tell that she was very nervous.

'Oh no, thank you, Mr. Cromwell. I must get back. I don't know whether I'm doing the right thing.'

'I'm sure you are.'

'It was Mrs. Cromwell I really wanted to see.'

'I'm afraid she's gone into Polchester for the day. But anything I can do——'

'It's a letter I was asked to give her. I don't like keeping it. I thought you might give it her.'

'Of course I will.'

'It's from Jim Burke.'

As soon as she said that I felt an irritation so acute that I could have shaken the child. At first I felt nothing but this irritation. It was one more evidence that I could not keep my life to myself. Imbeciles, idiots, children, must intrude upon it!

Was this child so simple that she could not understand that she must not hand private letters about in that simple way? Was Jim Burke himself so simple that he had not said to her: 'See that you give it only to Mrs. Cromwell. No one else must have it'? Was the child so immature that she had heard nothing about this miserable village scandal, had not heard from her elders that Jim Burke had made trouble in this house? Had she been so innocently brought up that she knew nothing about sex life, about love between men and women?

I held the letter in my hand and knew a monstrous exasperation.

'Did you see Jim Burke in the village then?'

'Oh no, Mr. Cromwell, it was on the way to Rafiel. I had gone for a walk and met Jim Burke.'

'What was he doing there?'

'He had been working on a farm for some weeks.' She hesitated, and went on: 'There's a horrid little man who goes about in the village with a lot of dogs. He gave Gillie one. He came and frightened me, and Jim Burke was there just as though it were in a book.'

She laughed—the gayest, most natural, merriest laugh. And I knew when I heard it that she herself loved Jim Burke and that she knew nothing about sexual love at all. I knew too, at that moment, why Mrs. Mark loved her. How involved we all were together!

'So he rescued you, did he?'

'Yes, I suppose he did. The funny thing is that he has done it before, and about the same little man.'

'Who is this horrible little man?'

'I don't know. No one seems to know anything about him except that his name is Henry Sharp.'

'And was he really rude to you?'

'He tried to kiss me.'

'He did, did he? We must have him locked up.'

'Oh no! Although I *am* afraid of him. But not to lock him up. Don't you think, Mr. Cromwell, being locked up in prison is the most awful thing than can happen to anybody?'

I said—and I can't think why, because really I'm not senti-mental about myself: 'That's the way I am—being blind.'

'I know.' Her voice sank to a sort of reverential gravity. 'I've thought of it often and often. To tell you the truth, Mr. Crom-well, I can't get you out of my head. I'm always thinking of you. I hope you don't mind.'

'Mind? Of course not.' Then I asked her: 'You're fond of Jim Burke, aren't you?'

'I love him more than anyone in the world.'

'When you say "love," Dorothy, what do you mean?'

'I would go with him anywhere, do anything for him—if he wanted me.'

'Do you really mean that? You know, living with someone, after the first romantic feelings have passed away, isn't so easy.'

'I know it isn't. Father and Mother quarrel often, but they love one another really. They couldn't bear to separate.' She sighed— a most child-like sigh. 'However, he doesn't want me. I suppose I shall be an old maid and look after Gillie's children and Simon's. I don't mind a bit. There'll be heaps to do.'

'You know, Mrs. Mark is very fond of you?'

'Is she? I'm ever so glad.'

But it didn't mean a great deal to her emotionally. I was sorry, a swift instant, for Mrs. Mark.

'I must be going back. Good-bye.'

'Good-bye.' I held out my hand. She put hers in mine, most trustfully, most friendlily. She caught her breath and I could see (although I couldn't see) her shining eyes. She said huskily: 'I think you're wonderful. We all think so.'

She went away with a kind of rush. I stood looking into darkness after her.

I felt something in my hand. Jim Burke's letter. Why, I had forgotten all about it! Yes, I had forgotten all about it.

Celia came in and I gave it to her.

'There is a letter for you from Jim Burke.'

My voice did not shake, neither did my hand. My body was so passionless that it might have been made of soap or butter. I was passionless. Celia was to me like the well-known signature to a document. The affair had been completely settled already. The signing was of no particular importance.

'Where did you get this?' Celia asked me.

'Dorothy Brennan brought it. She met Burke by accident in the country somewhere and he asked her to give it to you. You were out, so she gave it to me.'

I felt the edge of the paper against my hand. She was trying to give it back to me.

'I don't want to read it.'

'Oh yes, you had better.'

I heard her tearing it to pieces.

'That was a pity. I should like to know how Burke is.'

She answered furiously:

'That's clever, isn't it? Pretending you don't care! And you care damnably. You're miserable. I'm glad you are. You deserve it. It's I who haven't done anything! Not a thing! Not a thing!'

And she rushed out, slamming the door. Soon, when the war comes, as it will, we shall have something real to trouble about.

Meanwhile—this seems real enough to be going on with!

CHAPTER V

Seagulls—At the Rectory—Seagull on Wet Grass

AFTER A DAY OR TWO of violent storm—the thunder of the sea quite sharp and audible, like the cracking of biscuits—flurries of seagulls haunted the village with screams and cries. After ten days of storm a long day of pause and hush and stillness. The light was smoky after the rain; all the colours were dull but the sky was blue, very open and spacious, with dusky clouds, thin, transparent, and lit like the scaly windows of lanterns. Because the air was so very still the sea could be heard murmuring as though with its fingers on its lips.

The seagulls remained. Especially did the village green appear the right place to them, for they rose and fell above it. Then, strutting on the grass, their red beaks lifted, they seemed to carry the village in their cold scaly eye and place it on the edge of the sea, spray floundering against the shop windows, and the chimney-smoke reeking of bacon and sea-weed together.

Simon, his small stout legs firmly planted, watched one large seagull of dazzling whiteness with a beak of fresh shining crimson, stride about the green like Judge Jeffries in some devilish assize.

Simon knew that it was forbidden him to stand about on the village green doing nothing. His mother had told him again and again how common it was. But he did not mind if he *were* common. He *liked* to be common! Young though he was, he had already discovered that the common had much more fun, day by day, than the refined.

He stood watching the seagull, because he had so very much to think about.

There was the excitement of Benson. For a whole week he had

been confined (with certain surreptitious excursions) in Simon's attic, and no one, save Gilbert, knew that he was there. How had he been able for so long to keep this secret? Ah, this was the lovely thing! For Simon it was the very salt of life—to sustain a mystery, to be spending half your life in a manner unknown to your so-called betters, to be engaged on detective work (Benson's meals, his outdoor exercise, his physical habits—all these had to be arranged for), to know something (viz. that Benson was in the attic) that your elders did not know—all this was honey and manna to Simon's spiritual stomach.

Very gratifying too was the behaviour of Benson; for that dog, mongrel of mongrels, begotten in a hedge, delivered in a ditch, nevertheless showed now the greatest character and astuteness—even, miraculously, human. He knew just what was occurring and that his beloved master's happiness depended on his discretion.

He never complained at his inactivity, and when, after dark, he was released for a short time, he did, with swift grinning eagerness, all that he was supposed to do, then raced about, not barking as was his natural habit, and rejoiced finally at being carried against his master's chest secretly up the stairs, never uttered a sound, only once or twice turned his head and licked his master's cheek.

Simon greatly approved of his discretion and did not mind at all that Benson's heart was entirely Gilbert's. Simon had no liking for sentiment that was aimless self-luxury. He liked everything to have its proper place and point.

This brought him to his sister. Dorothy was changing under his eyes. He had seen it coming for a long time. This change was to him no new thing, for he had watched a number of girls of his acquaintance 'go funny' when their chests changed from flat masculine to rounded feminine.

He did not, as yet, bother himself very much about the sexes. He observed the physical differences as he observed the crimson beak of the seagull, but these physical differences seemed to him of no importance. One was made one way and one another. A nasty fat schoolfellow of Gilbert's, aged fourteen or so, had attempted once to enlighten Simon (then aged seven) as to 'what was what,' but in the middle of the sticky narration Simon had seen a bullfinch, recently introduced to him by Jim Burke, and had wandered off, following it from tree to tree. He would be always, perhaps, one to whom observation would be more than feeling. And yet he *had* a heart, as this conversation with his sister showed.

For she had returned from a walk on that very afternoon when Simon had rescued Benson, in great distress. Two days later she summoned Simon into her bedroom. She only did this when there was something of the greatest importance to discuss. Simon stood just inside the door, his head cocked a little on one side. Yes, she was different. She had grown up, he decided, and, quite suddenly, he realized that she was his sister and that she had always been wonderfully good to him and that he loved her. There was something now about her as she looked at him, her eyes distressed, her whole being asking him for help, that made him for once respond romantically. He *would* help her. He would do anything that she asked.

'Simon, I think perhaps I've done a dreadful thing.'

'What's the matter?'

'This is what happened. I went for a walk by myself, and that horrid little man that gave Benson to Gillie—you know?'

Simon nodded his head.

'He came up and spoke to me. And then he tried to kiss me. It was horrid and I screamed and fell down, and Jim Burke suddenly appeared.'

'Jim Burke! Oh, golly!'

'Yes, it was just like a story. He knocked the little man down and he got up and ran away. Well, then——' She paused and looked at Simon with some doubt. 'You won't tell anyone, Simon? You swear it? No one—not Gillie—no one?'

'I swear it,' said Simon rather hoarsely.

'I told Jim,' Dorothy said very solemnly, 'that I loved him

more than anyone in the world and that I would go away with him anywhere he liked.'

'Oh, you didn't!'

'Yes, I did. Anyway I do, so why shouldn't I say so?'

'And what did he say?'

'He was most awfully nice but he loves someone else.'

'Yes, I know. Mrs. Cromwell.'

'Yes, Mrs. Cromwell—and of course Mrs. Cromwell's married, so of course he couldn't do anything about it."

'No, of course not,' Simon said.

'But he asked me to give her a letter. I said I would.' She hesitated. 'This is where I think I was awfully silly.'

'Didn't you give it to her?'

'No, I didn't. I went over yesterday and Mrs. Cromwell was in Polchester. So I gave it to Mr. Cromwell.'

'Oh, I say!'

'Yes. Do you think I did a wrong thing? You're very young, Simon, but somehow I can tell you and I couldn't tell Gillie.'

'What did Mr. Cromwell say?'

'He was most awfully nice. I liked him terribly.'

'I like him better than any man anywhere,' Simon said proudly.

'Yes, and Gillie says he does too. He asked me if I liked Jim Burke and I said I loved him and would go with him anywhere, and Mr. Cromwell said that sort of thing wore off, and I said that I'd be an old maid and would look after you and Gillie always.'

'I shall look after myself.'

'But the point is,' Dorothy went on, 'was I wrong to give the letter to Mr. Cromwell? What do you think, Simon?'

'Did he read it?'

'No, of course not. People don't read other people's letters.'

'Then it's all right.'

Dorothy sighed. 'I don't know. You can never tell with grown-up people. What I think, Simon, is that Mr. Cromwell is awfully unhappy.'

'That's what I think too,' Simon said. 'He doesn't want me over there any more.'

'I know. I don't think he wants anybody. He's so beautiful. He was wearing a blue tie and he sat staring in front of him. He was most awfully kind, but I couldn't do anything.'

'No. There's nothing we can do.'

Not only was Mr. Cromwell unhappy, Mrs. Brennan was very unhappy too. She had never been so unhappy in her life before. Everything had been stable and settled with her until the Cromwells had come to Garth.

But it was not only the Cromwells. The earth seemed to be trembling under her feet. She was not a woman who had ever taken much notice of politics or of world events. But now she was forced to consider them. Everyone was considering them; not only her immediate friends, but the villagers, the farmers. It was as though a dark cloud hung just beyond her personal door. She did not know what the dark cloud threatened, but for the first time in her experience it threatened her herself. She had always been sure of her own safety. Little quarrels with her husband or her friends had seemed at the time important, but now, quite suddenly, they were important no longer. Some general unsteadiness was shaking even the little world of Garth.

One night she asked her husband: 'Do you think there really will be a war?'

'Very likely.'

'How will it affect us?'

'It will affect everybody. We are all bound together so closely in these days.'

That was what she was feeling. 'We were all bound together.' The quarrel between Mr. and Mrs. Cromwell (and according to that girl Violet, who was now living in the village, the trouble had been really shocking), Gillie's sulks, Simon's rudeness, the bad behaviour of May Vergil—all these things were working together as symptoms of a more threatening danger.

She was simple, she was ignorant, she was weak. She had been fortunate, as are so many child-like people, to reach mature years safely without herself being mature. She had been covered up and protected because the other people around her were not mature enough to find her out. Of all her personal contacts only her husband was mature, and he was too lazy, and perhaps too fond of her, to expose her childishness.

Circumstances—her dislike of Mrs. Cromwell, her trouble with her children—had revealed to her that she was quite alone—alone as everyone is alone. But she did not know enough about anyone else to realize that others, that all men and women on the earth's surface, were alone. She thought that she was unique.

She was frightened. She awoke in the middle of the night and was frightened. She was frightened in the middle of a meal, during a walk, shopping. She asked others whether they thought there would be a war, and when they said 'Yes,' she said: 'How dreadful! Why do the Germans want a war?'

'Because they want to destroy us.'

The Germans wanted to destroy her! She was helpless. Nobody loved her or cared whether she were destroyed or no.

A dreadful incident was about to bring this forcibly home to her.

Gilbert's secrecy about Benson grew with every day more unpleasant for him. Unlike Simon, he had no pleasure in mystery. His intense shyness did not mean that he was not honest. It was because of his honesty that he was reticent. He would not be false about his emotions, and, because of that, he must conceal them because they were so easily wounded.

He was, of course, conscious of none of this, but he now found himself involved in deceit on every side. Except for his mother, the two most important contacts he had experienced during this last year had been with Mr. and Mrs. Cromwell—the meeting with Mr. Cromwell in the Well, the meeting with Mrs. Cromwell at Sizyn. By these he had been admitted for the first time to grown-up intimacy. It was a great leap in his development when he sat in the little Church, his hand in Mrs. Cromwell's and she crying.

He had a great capacity for loving in his nature and he had the passionate creative feeling of an artist. He might be now only a small boy carving clumsily an obscure head from a lump of wood, but as the honey-coloured chips flew, he saw with his eyes into far distances. He was a young son of Praxiteles.

Now all these feelings of bewilderment—love, creation, Benson's devotion—centred round his love of his mother. He loved her and he hated her. He hated her because he was deceiving her and she had forced him into that deception. He hated her because she wanted to swallow him up. He loved her, whether he liked it or no, because he loved her.

During all this week of the hiding of Benson he was on the edge, at every meeting on the stair, at every meal, of exposing the mystery. He detested secrecy and he hated this one the more because Simon was enjoying it so greatly. There was something in Simon that he could not understand any more than Rupert Palatinate would have understood Mazarin.

But if he had loved Benson before he was given away, he loved him twice as dearly now. For that dog was human. The race of men and women is divided between those who say of a dog: 'There is really no difference between him and a human being. He as good as talks'—and those who don't.

Benson revealed now, under duress, his soul. He could not enjoy confinement, all day long, in Simon's attic. He must know every evening, at his ten minutes' release, an intense joy, and yet, running in the darkness on the lawn, he never uttered a sound, never barked with joy, never yelped with sensuous pleasure at the intricate and diverting evening scents and odours. One soft word from Simon or Gilbert was enough for him. And yet, so far as he could tell, this captivity might be for all time. He would not complain while Gilbert was there.

Only one compensation he had—he was fed sumptuously.

Bones, scraps, biscuits, vegetables were for ever being brought to him. He began to fatten.

Clearly this situation could not continue for very long. It did not.

One evening, warm and scent-laden, when the spring was hinting that she had her hand on the handle of the door, Gilbert, who should have been in bed, crept out from the decayed conservatory on to the lawn and let Benson loose. At once he disappeared into the warm stirring darkness. Gilbert stood looking at the stars and wondering from whom he could learn more carving. The Easter holidays would soon be here and after them he would return to school. He understood that great changes had taken place since the break-up in the autumn. He learned from listening to his parents that the school had been in a very bad way, that the old head master was gone and that there would be a new one. It would be altogether a fresh start, and he felt in his bones that his place in it now would be very different.

He would be older, he would be in one of the upper forms, he would win, at least, his Second Eleven colours in cricket, perhaps, if the bowling were not very strong, his First. He swung his arm round, as he stood there. His slow bowling had certain possibilities because he used his brains. He thought of Mr. Cromwell. He would like, before he went back, to talk to him about all this. Mr. Cromwell would be the very man to give him interesting and trustworthy advice . . .

Benson returned out of the darkness. Gilbert picked him up and stealthily passed through the conservatory into the passage. On the turn of the stairs his mother was standing.

Well, it had happened. He was glad. The deception was over. He caught Benson more tightly to him and stared.

'Gillie! But why aren't you in bed?' Then, taking it in: 'The dog——'

'Yes. He's been here a week.'

'A week?'

'I've been keeping him in the attic.' He was resolved that Simon should not be mentioned.

'Come with me.'

He followed her into the drawing-room.

'Put that dog down.'

He put Benson down.

She sat, leaning forward, and looked at her son. At that moment she hated him. This was the climax to her long-strengthening sense of betrayal.

'Now. Tell me, please—why have you disobeyed your father and myself?'

'I haven't disobeyed. He was fetched back. He was my dog. You gave him away, but he was *my* dog.'

'You knew that your father and myself didn't want him here—I stood him as long as I could—then his dirty habits made him impossible.'

'He hasn't any dirty habits.'

She was intensely moved with disgust for her son. Her hands shook. She was not a cruel woman, but there was something now in his small cold blind face that made her tremble with rage.

'Come nearer.'

He came nearer.

'How long do you say that dog has been in the house?'

'A week.'

'You have been hiding and feeding him all that time?'

'Yes, I have.'

'What a horrid thing! Dirty! To keep a dog—' She broke off. 'But the wickedness. You'll have to be beaten for this. You've never been beaten. We've been too gentle with you. The disobedience . . .'

'I don't mind being beaten.'

'The dog shall be destroyed.'

A quiver ran through his body.

'If you kill Benson I'll kill *you!*'

'You'll do *what?*'

'You shan't touch Benson. You can do what you like to me. I don't care. But if you touch Benson——'

She got up. She caught Benson in the neck, lifted him. She did not know herself what she was going to do. A moment later Gilbert threw himself on her. He caught at her arm. She threw Benson across the floor and he landed, greatly to his surprise, against a little table, which fell over. Gilbert was beating at her with both hands. She slapped his face.

They stood apart, both breathing heavily. Benson, who found nothing in life extraordinary, sat on a piece of broken china and began industriously to lick the inside of a leg. It appeared to him, perhaps, the polite thing to do.

She had never struck any of her children before. She was horrified. Gilbert also was horrified. A new bond, that was to alter all their relationship in the future, was formed by their mutual horror. For they loved one another.

His face was grey-white save where she had struck him. He did not move but stood as though at attention.

'I'm sorry . . .', she said, looking at him with puzzled eyes— but she was really seeing only herself. 'I didn't mean . . .' Then she said abruptly: 'You'd better go to bed now.'

He picked up Benson and without a word went from the room.

She sat on the sofa and put her hand on her heart. It was racing most dangerously. But for once she didn't care about her physical symptoms. All her principles of living were disrupted. Those principles were that she was an English lady and must never forget it, that she was superior to other English ladies who did so forget, that she was fine and stately and beyond all possible disorder. Now she had behaved like the commonest woman in the village. She suddenly cared nothing for her position or the proprieties of being an English lady. She discovered that she loved her husband and her children beyond and above everything else on earth.

After a while, still bewildered and scarcely knowing what she did, she crossed the passage and knocked on her husband's door.

He was sitting, with his feet stretched out, smoking, reading a novel.

'What is it, my dear?' he asked with the voice of the husband who, at this particular moment, wishes that he had never married. He looked at her. Then he put down his book.

'What is it? Something's the matter.'

She sat down and began to talk quite incoherently.

'I've struck Gillie—in the face. He's been very naughty. But I lost my temper. I don't know what's the matter. I said this morning when those seagulls were squawking all over the place that something was going to happen. It's that dog——'

'Now, my dear,' he said, 'begin at the beginning. *What* seagulls? *What* dog? What's Gillie been doing?'

'What has Gillie been doing?' She repeated his words, staring across at him, bewildered. 'You'll never believe when I tell you. He stole the dog back and has been keeping it upstairs, unknown to any of us, for a week.'

'Well, that shows you——'

'Shows you what?'

'That you can't keep a good man down. You shouldn't have given his dog away in the first place.'

At any ordinary time Daisy Brennan would, at this point, have been so rightly irritated by her husband that she would have risen and left him. Now all was different. She was not irritated. She scarcely heard him. She was thinking of Gilbert.

'He was standing on the stairs clutching the dog. You can imagine the shock I got! In the first place I thought Gillie was in bed, and secondly, of course, I never expected the dog. I'm afraid I was dreadfully upset.'

'You should always sleep on things. Soundest of all rules.'

'How could I sleep on it without some sort of explanation? I took Gillie into the drawing-room and asked him what he'd done.'

'Well?'

'He was terribly rude. He told me he'd fetched the dog back because it wasn't mine to give away.'

'There he was quite right.'

'But when I said that of course we'd have the dog destroyed he said a most dreadful thing.'

'What did he say?'

'He said if I touched the dog he'd kill me.'

'I suppose he was in a rage just as you were.'

'No, but what a thing for a son to say to his mother!'

'Oedipus complex—or something like it. Well, go on.'

'I picked the dog up and Gillie flew at me. Beat at me with his fists.'

'Didn't think he had it in him.'

'Then I threw the dog away and slapped Gillie's face.'

'How do you mean—you threw the dog away?'

'I threw it against a table, which fell over.'

'What did Gillie do when you hit him?'

'Do? I don't know. We looked at one another.'

'Did he say anything?'

'Not a word. I said "You'd better go to bed now," and he went —with the dog.'

'I see. And that was all?'

'Yes. That was all.'

Brennan looked at his wife and she seemed to him a child like his other children. Although he had been married to her for so long, he had never realized that until now. He realized another thing—that, through all these years, he had completely failed in his duty to her. Behind this little conversation of theirs he had felt that she was looking at him in quite a new way, that she was saying to him, 'I don't know where I've got to. I'm bewildered, distressed. I've just done a thing that I would never have believed I could do. Please help me. Only you in the world can.'

He knew, too, that this moment, here and now, was a test of their whole life together. If he failed now, he would lose her and perhaps himself. And he might fail because he was such a lazy man.

He said easily: 'I shouldn't worry about it, my dear. Let Gillie

keep his dog. He'll be going back to school soon. He's been un-
settled by staying so long away. As to smacking him, that's what
every mother does to her children sooner or later. He's a decent
kid really.'

But he hadn't helped her at all. He saw that at once. She continued to stare at him in the same bewildered, perplexed fashion.

'It isn't that. I can't explain . . . I've been frightened for
months. I've lost all confidence in myself. What is it?'

'What is what?'

'Why am I frightened?'

'It's nothing,' he said reassuringly. 'Everyone gets like that
sometimes.'

'Why am I frightened?' she repeated.

'I suppose there's a general nervousness. People are afraid of
a war.'

'Yes. We're all afraid. God doesn't seem real.'

'He's real all right.' He puffed at his pipe. 'It's we who aren't
real enough.'

She began to cry. Tears rolled down her cheeks. She sobbed
out uncertain words. 'Those seagulls this morning. I thought they
were threatening me. I've been thinking for years I'm a fine
woman. And I'm not at all. I hadn't known—how much I loved
you—you and the children. Nothing else matters.'

She went over to him, knelt at his feet, came close to him. His
pipe fell; he put his arms around her.

"Darling—don't cry. I've been to blame. I love you, too. We'll
be all right. A new life. Oh, God, give us, through adversity, a
new life.'

On the early afternoon of that same day May Vergil had stood
at the door of her cottage watching three seagulls quarrel angrily
over a small crust on her lawn. One of the gulls limped and was
always late for the fair. The other two, their prize divided between them, flew off with deep powerful drives of their wings.
The lame one, seeming to May Vergil oddly to resemble the

character that, in all fiction, she most detested, Tom Pinch, stood virtuously, his head cocked, looking as though he were in search of a church organ and the pleasant practice of a hymn tune.

'He's a prig and a hypocrite,' she said, going back into the sitting-room, where Phyllis Lock was eating chocolates. She had been lunching with her friend.

'Who is?'

'A seagull with a lame leg—on the lawn.'

'You don't like people with lame legs, do you?' Phyllis said, and felt really clever.

'I don't like people who make themselves sick with chocolates—after a decent lunch, too.'

She took the box away.

'Miss Quilter brought the box yesterday. I told her that when she knew me better she would abstain. I forgot you were coming today.'

'Miss Quilter? That's that fluffy yellow little thing from Rafiel. A new friend. I'm jealous.'

'You have no need to be.'

May Vergil stopped opposite her friend and looked at her. Phyllis giggled.

'I hate it when you look at me like that.'

'You've no need to be jealous about anybody. You know that.' She put her hand for a moment against Phyllis's cheek, then drew it swiftly away.

'Why? Why? Why?'

'Why what?'

'Why have I loved you for so long? Why have I loved you at all?'

'That isn't very complimentary.' Phyllis pouted. 'I'm sure I'm very fond of you too.'

'Yes, yes,' May said impatiently. 'That isn't the point. For years I've cared for you, looked after you, protected you, prevented you as well as I could from making a fool of yourself over rotten men. . . . If I hadn't held you back you'd have tried to flirt with Julius Cromwell.'

'Well, I haven't—so why bring it up?'

'No. But what do you *see* in men? Cromwell is one of the better kind, I admit. But most of them!—stupid, conceited, rough, and when they've kissed you once or twice it's all over. Marriage—children, perhaps that's different. But you don't *want* to be married, Phyllis. All you've ever wanted is something physical, and even that mustn't be dangerous. If Cromwell kissed you you'd be in Heaven, but if he offered to spend the night with you you'd be horrified. There's a very vulgar word men have for women like you.'

'Really, May! I don't know why I stand it!'

'You'd stand anything—any kind of insult. You're ignorant, weak, silly!'

'May! I won't——'

'I've wanted to say this for months. I've been blind—a bloody fool if there ever was one.'

Phyllis stared up at May and her eyes brimmed with tears, as they did very easily. She was fond of May.

'There's another thing. I've been meaning to ask you if you know who it was.'

'Who what was?'

'Ages ago. It was the Christmas party that the Cromwells gave. It meant a lot to me, that party, because, although I didn't talk to them much, I got to like them both enormously that afternoon. They were so kind, so human, so normal. . . . They were what I wanted.'

'He is.'

'So is she. And although I've seen very little of them since, I've been conscious of them. They've changed me. I'm going up to London, Phil, and start something worth while. I'm sure a war's coming and there'll be plenty to do.'

'What! And leave me?'

'Yes—and leave you. High time I did. What I wanted to ask

you was this. Celia Cromwell told me one day that all her trouble
with her husband began because someone at that party was cad
enough to whisper in Cromwell's ear that his wife was misbehaving with Jim Burke. It was a woman.'

'What a filthy thing to do!'

'Yes, wasn't it? Who do you think it could have been?'

'Alice Lamplough.'

'I don't think it was.'

'But it couldn't have been anyone else. It was just the sort of
thing she'd do.'

'It wasn't you by any chance?'

'Me! May! Of all the rotten things!' She got up. 'I'll never
speak to you again for this.'

'Swear to me it wasn't you.'

'Of course it wasn't.'

'Swear—Oh, Phil, please!' May Vergil's voice softened. 'Please,
Phil! I've been haunted by this. I haven't dared to ask you lest
you should lie to me. But if you'll swear it wasn't I'll believe you,
and I can't say—you wouldn't understand—how happy I'll be.'

'Of course it wasn't. Do you think I'd——?'

'No. But swear. A good old-fashioned oath. Swear. "I, Phyllis
Lock, swear by everything I value that I didn't——" '

Phyllis broke in furiously:

'I won't swear! You're bullying me as you always do. I won't
be bullied. I won't. I'll leave the house and never speak to you
again.'

'Then it *was* you!'

Phyllis sank down on the sofa and began to cry.

'I didn't mean to. . . . I said it before I knew what I was saying. I was in love with him. I am still. It was such a shame that
beastly woman carrying on with a servant. . . . Oh, May, you
won't tell anyone, will you?'

'No, I won't tell anyone.'

'I suppose you'll never speak to me again?'

'I'm not your friend any longer, if that's what you mean.'

'Oh, May. . . . You can't give me up. After all this time—such a little thing.'

'And now you'd better go home.'

'Yes, I suppose I had. You promise not to tell anyone?'

'I promise.'

Phyllis got up, gave one look at May which said: 'You'll be all right tomorrow. You often lose your temper, but you're always all right afterwards.'

She picked up her hat and trailed away.

May Vergil said: 'That's the end of that.' Her odd ugly face had the rigidity of an unescapable but nevertheless resolute loneliness.

There was a thin quick shower of rain. The grass of May Vergil's lawn was gleaming wet. The seagull was still there, hopping slowly from place to place. A little man, with two mongrels at his heels, slouched by. He stopped at the gate and saw the bird. Stealthily he came into the garden and advanced to the lawn. The gull, oddly, did not move.

The man knelt down on the wet grass and examined the leg. The bird was quite still, watching him with a bright strong eye.

'It's a cut. It wants watching.' The bird seemed not to be frightened of the dogs. The man picked up the gull and furtively, as though he had stolen something, which indeed he so often had, crossed the road, the dogs following at his heels.

CHAPTER VI

*Third of March—A Stormy Night—At Garth House
—Walk Through Wind and Rain—At Garth House*

THE RELATION between a man and woman who love one another is never static. When trouble comes, as it had come now with the Cromwells, the movement is often so swift that, like a retiring army before a swiftly advancing enemy, the ground cannot be defended before it is lost.

So it was now with Celia Cromwell. This was her first experience of love. She seemed to be fighting an enemy hooded and masked. This was no exaggerated metaphor. It really seemed to her that Julius was her enemy, and she could neither see him nor touch him. With every day's increasing hatred of him she knew that she loved him more.

Not only was he elusive but she was also unable to keep contact with herself. When life moves quietly we think that we are such and such. These temptations we have, but we have dealt with them. We have established ourselves securely for ever. Our religion is formed, our social behaviour is established, we are wise and controlled and safe. Then a wind blows, someone knocks on the door, a sentence is spoken and, in a moment, there is no security.

The only thing that she wanted in life was to re-establish her relations with Julius. But for the first time in her relationship with any human being she was baffled. The one thing that she would not do was to throw herself at his feet and ask for his pity. Why should she when she had done no wrong? With every hour the distance between them grew. With every day a new self was growing within her old self—something crazy and wild. Instinctively she was terrified of her own craziness. She had thoughts and impulses now so abnormal that she had no rule of life or morals with which to control them.

For every one of us there is a territory so dark and dangerous that we refuse to consider it. And yet without preparation we may be swept into it and see with terrified eyes roads, fields, hills, so new and dangerous that our very terror of them bewilders us.

It was this terror and darkness and newness that she felt increasingly. Many times she was on the brink of going to him, taking his hand and saying:

'I am sorry. I have been to blame. Forgive me. Please, please, forgive me.'

It was his blindness that always stopped her. The full realization of the fear that had come upon her on that first drive into Garth was fully realized. For his blindness was entirely established. It was the mask that he was now wearing. He had gathered it about him like a dark enveloping cloak. Because of it he had always distrusted the world that he could not see. Had he ever seen her with physical gaze he could not have distrusted her. Men can read the soul through the eyes. But if they are blind, however strongly they believe, there are constant clouds of circumstance, created in a world to which they do not belong, that darken that belief.

They must be very lonely from time to time.

Also, young though she was, Celia realized that Julius was engaged in some terrific battle with himself. It was not only that he was distrustful of her but also that he was distrustful of himself.

In the early days of their marriage he had told her that he could not believe that she loved him. He so much older and blind. 'You will come to hate my blindness and then I will hate myself. I'm not only this fine loving husband. There is another man as well who is mean and cruel and revengeful. It is only my belief in you, my darling, that keeps the other man down.'

She hadn't understood him in the least. She knew him through and through, soul and body. But she understood now that she was dealing with that other man and that he was dealing with him too. It was for her to help him in that battle if she knew how. But she didn't know. She was terrified of this other man who was veiled from her. His blindness became abhorrent to her, and yet she knew that, were things otherwise, she could love him all the more because he was blind. If he had brought his blindness to her and surrendered it and said: 'I give it you with the rest of me because I love you,' all her maternity and protection would have taken him in and cared for him. But he didn't say that. He said: 'I am blind and don't trust you. So keep away.'

With every day through that horrible spring her impulse to go away increased. But her imagination was vivid enough to see that away from him her unhappiness would only increase because she loved him.

Once, when she had been very young, she had thought for a brief while that she loved a young man. On a Sunday he had taken her to luncheon at Ranelagh. Just before luncheon they had had some ridiculous quarrel and, on an impulse, she had gone home. The dreariness of the rest of that Sunday she had never forgotten, for it had rained, she was alone, she had nothing to do, and the young man seemed to her twice as desirable as in fact, on reconciliation, she found him.

But the knowledge that she could not leave Julius drove her crazy. If she went to London perhaps he would not care: she would sit there waiting (as she knew she would) for a letter or a telegram, or best of all, the opening of a door and his figure inside it. That waiting would be terrible and might lead to a complete separation—if he did not care.

But he *must* still love her. He could not suddenly cease to love her over so ridiculous a cause, when so little a time ago he had loved her so dearly. That other Julius loved her, but this one perhaps did not. This *blind* one that sat in the chair, or walked touching a table so lightly, or sat opposite to her, feeling with his fork for a potato.

Then came a dreadful day—the third of March. When she woke she heard every window in the house rattling and every door. The rain beat on the house with a passion of curses. It drove down upon the lawn as though it were sadistic in its punishment. It was a nervous storm. At the moment of waking she felt it. She looked out from her window. The sky was leaden and, across the grey, white spumish clouds drove in fury. She turned back into the room, shivering. She felt so strong an apprehension that it was like an act challenging fate to put on her clothes. 'Something will happen today. Before night something dreadful will have happened.'

Her body was cold and hard, shrunken within itself, separate from her clothes.

When she came into the dining-room the fire was smoking.

'What a horrible day!' she said.

'Isn't it?' Julius smiled. 'But it's March. We must expect it.'

'How did you sleep?'

'Very well, thank you.'

The room was intolerably cold, and she went over to the fire to stir it into flame. A little bluster of spiteful thick smoke shot out at her.

'I'm afraid this fire is smoking horribly.'

'It always does when the wind is this way.'

She wanted to say to him: 'Do you feel this? Are you nervous as I am?' But he did not seem to be nervous. His fingers moved with their beautiful trained adroitness. He always seemed to be neater about his food and his drink than a normal man who could see.

They did not speak. Her hands were trembling. His were beautiful, strong, and steady.

She said at last:

'I don't know what's the matter with me. I feel nervous and jumpy.'

'That's the wind. It's a beastly wind. One of the drawbacks to this coast.'

After breakfast she saw Mrs. Gayner as usual. Mrs. Gayner too was nervous, but then for a long time she had not been her quiet self.

'Mrs. Gayner, is there nothing we can do about these fires?'

'I'm afraid not. When the wind's this way they always smoke.'

'I'm a mass of nerves today—as though something were going to happen.'

'I feel it myself, Mrs. Cromwell. I always do when the wind's this way.'

She was alone all the morning. No one came near her. She tried to write some letters but abandoned the silly business. It was as though she had been placed out of contact with everyone living. She picked up a book—a heavy brown volume on the table at her elbow! *The Letters of D. H. Lawrence.* There had been a time when it had been the fashion among her friends to read Lawrence, as though there were a new gospel here. And perhaps there was. She could never be sure, because so much of *The Rainbow* and *Women in Love* bored and wearied her, and sometimes there were magnificent things.

But now she read on and on and it was as though Lawrence screamed in her ear, telling her that catastrophe was on the way. She could not understand why he rejected everything and every-body—rejection, hate, misery. And then would come some passage of natural description so lovely and quiet that his voice dropped to a loving encouraging whisper. He rejected all living human beings. He said again and again with sickening reiteration that he trusted no one. His dearest friends he would embrace at one moment and reject with loathing at the next. Everything revolved around himself. He was sick, he was poor, he was betrayed, and he said so over and over again. But he had genius, that strange gift of seeing everything and everybody for the first time, as though no one had ever lived on this earth before himself.

But his own thin nervous cry increased her own fear. He was right. The world was dreadful because the people in it were dreadful—dreadful and menacing.

In the afternoon she thought that she would drive over to see Mrs. Mark. She would be sure to be indoors on such a day.

She put on her hat and coat and then stood, in the middle of her bedroom, hesitating. Mrs. Mark wasn't the person she wanted to be with. Mrs. Mark was good and kind and broadminded, but she was dull—not always dull, but dull for Celia on that day.

She would be affectionate and consoling, but she was a century old and belonged altogether to the past. At that moment the storm was so violent that the floor seemed to rock under her feet. There went the past! It was gone, it was gone! Some horrible new world was preparing, a world made after the Nazi German fashion, where there would be no mercy nor kindness nor understanding of the individual.

She took off her hat and coat and wondered what she was going to do. She felt such a despair as she had never before known. She looked in the mirror and it seemed that she saw two figures there: one Celia behind another Celia, and the second Celia she had no mastery over. The second Celia might commit any folly, any madness.

As she went down the dark stairs, hearing the rain like the loud snapping of fiddle-strings against the staircase window, she heard the second Celia say to the first Celia: 'I must get out! I must get out!' And the first Celia answered: 'Leave me alone! You are driving me to something crazy.'

During dinner they spoke very little. The curtains were drawn, the fire was not smoking, the storm now was like distant drums.

'I'm afraid I'm not very gay tonight,' she said, smiling, and then remembered as she so often did that he could not see her smile.

'A day like this is awfully tiring.'

She watched him while he peeled an apple. He must, she thought, have East Anglian blood in his veins—the fairness, the thickness, the heaviness, the sense of yellow light and fragrance, Scandinavian, Viking . . . and, at that instant, he looked up and stared across the table at her. His blue loving eyes stared into her face. His loving eyes that yet meant nothing, said nothing, because they saw nothing. But it was now as though they opened—the strangest thing! As though he could see again! She, although she had been married to him for so long, found it difficult to believe that he was not gazing at her with all his soul, loving her, wanting her, needing her.

She did then a very odd thing. She remembered that, soon after they had come to Garth, one night she had jumped out of bed and hidden in the room, teasing him. At last he had caught her and covered her with kisses.

Now, without a sound, she slipped out of her chair and into one at the side of the table. His hearing was so much acuter than the hearing of any normal man that he would, she thought, detect her. But he did not. He continued to stare in front of him at the place where she had been, the candlelight shiny on the raised half-peeled apple in his hand.

So he had not been staring at her! She knew, of course, that he had not, but there was something terrible now in seeing him continue with those wide blue eyes to look into space as though he loved a ghost. When she heard the door open she slipped back into her seat. It was the maid bringing in the coffee.

'Coffee, Julius?'

'Thank you. I'm just ready for it to-night.' He crunched the apple with his teeth. His eyes closed for a moment as he drank his coffee.

'Do you mind if we have a little music?' he asked.

'Oh no,' she said, hating it. 'The storm's worse than ever.'

His broad back bent over the gramophone. 'Help me, my dear, will you? We'll have the Brahms Trio in E Flat major. You'll find it in the Brahms drawer. Yes, that's the one—For Pianoforte, Violin, and Horn. The Horn comes in as a kind of consoler, comforting: "Things aren't so bad—never so bad as you think." That's what the Horn says. Sort of thing you want on a night like this. And the Finale's grand—Allegro con brio—The Ride to Hounds. Grand. Ah, yes.' He sank down, listening with a happy smile to the first notes of the Andante.

'Ah, yes. Now you're happy,' she thought savagely. She hated him—or at any rate, the second Celia hated him as he sat, curled up now in the chair, huddled, a great mass of body, piled up, his head back, his strong neck brown and bare so that it would be a real pleasure to squeeze it. And she had once been held by those arms, naked breast to breast, and now in her rose-coloured evening dress that he could not see she stood staring at him, while the great curve of his thigh bulged over the arm of the chair, and his groping blind fingers beat time, in the air, to the music.

One disc rattled down. The Scherzo began.

'I'm going to bed.'

'Oh, just wait for the Ride to Hounds.'

'No. I'm tired. This beastly day . . .'

'Good night, then.'

'Good night.'

On the stairs the storm raged about her. From some distant part of the house a door furiously banged.

Most unexpectedly she fell at once asleep. She was awakened by a sudden flinging open of a window because the catch had been snapped by the storm. Wind and rain poured in. She got up to close the window. She looked at her clock. It was a quarter-past two. She saw that there was a little pool of water just below the ledge of the window and, as she stared at it, a frenzy of loneliness, unhappiness, terror, seized her.

She could not stay here! She could not see Julius again. He would play music when she was so unhappy. She saw his thigh hunched over the side of the chair and his naked throat stretched out between chin and collar.

She threw off her nightdress and stood staring at the little pool of rain. The pool enlarged. It covered the floor. It invited her to step into it and to allow the water to rise and close, like a velvet clasp, above her throat.

She dressed, and while she dressed she talked to herself.

'He plays music. He rides to hounds. He plays music. I'm so unhappy that I don't mind if the water does rise. And it's all about nothing. I love him but I've lost him. And I've lost my make-up box. I've lost my make-up box. I'm going away and never coming back.'

She ran out of the house and the wind knocked her back against the stone pillar of the steps. She ran crookedly through the streaming dark into the garage and got the small Austin. She drove out into the road with one window of the car wide open, and the rain slashed her in the face and the eyes.

She drove towards the Moor and Sizyn. She was going perhaps to London.

But she didn't go to London, for just above the Well Wood the car ran into a signpost and turned over.

She climbed out, and, through the rain and storm, began to run.

Although Celia did not know it, that had been also a terrible day for Julius. He too had felt the nervousness of the storm, the irritability that came from the ceaseless racket and driving hostility of the rain.

He reached, on that day, it seemed to him, the lowest depths of his own darkness. He had experienced before times when it was suggested to him, as though by an evil spirit, that man's whole trust in goodness was a fantasy.

He was a man neither philosophic nor of a penetrating intellect. He had believed in goodness because of the lovely things in life—affection between human beings, physical passion, music, the sun, the moon, flowers, all scents (now so especially valuable to him), bodily health, kindliness, the brave spirit in ordinary men, the progress of justice, men of good will. Because of these things he thought that the experience of life—in spite of evil, pain, betrayal, fear, greed, selfishness—fell with so preponderating a weight on the side of good that there must be a ruling power of love and hope. There had been also an assurance within him of a deep, progressing life towards some future good, finer and stronger than anything this life afforded.

All this was perhaps very simple, and clever men might call it the immature experience of a child. But he was not a child in his own experience: he had suffered and withstood and sometimes conquered like a man.

Throughout this day the belief had grown in him—strengthened by many weeks of unhappiness—that he had, his life long, not only been cheated but had, wishfully, cheated himself. Another war was threatening the world and might soon be upon them all, with the added horrors of modern mechanism and science. There was no true evidence that there was a root of goodness in human life. Men cheated themselves with their little toys and pleasures. What if this belief in greater forces was illusory and if men, poor pitiful stupid men, were only like ants in an ant-heap, blindly tumbling, one upon another, to destruction? If men were indeed alone, then he had no hope, for they were not able, of themselves, to live wisely, to conquer greed and fear.

This awareness of a ghastly, unmeaning, unreasoning loneliness was terrifying, and he saw only the powers of force and mechanical might remaining supreme. The end of civilized, hoping, progressing man!

In the tiny figures of himself and Celia he saw the symbols of man's powerlessness. They had had everything on their side—good dispositions, wealth, health, love—and they had failed because they were not wise enough to trust and compromise their selfishness.

He was to blame. He had fallen, for so little a reason, into a slough of suspicion and jealousy.

He could not raise himself out of it. It was as though he were held down by some strong evil power to which he had submitted almost without a struggle.

After Celia had gone to bed he sat there, unable to move, unable to think, so unhappy that it resembled an illness that had seized him. When he had been really ill he had had evil dreams. Now he was hemmed in by something that was no dream but a reality of negation, of powerlessness, of weakness of all will.

He sat on without moving, looking into a darkness shot with horrible colours and beset by a misery so chill that his body trembled with cold although his head was on fire.

Two o'clock struck but he did not hear it. He felt in his mouth and throat a loathsome taste as though he had swallowed some evil thing. He thought that he would get a whisky and soda from the dining-room. He moved through the room, into the hall, and opened the dining-room door.

Then he stopped. Once again, as on that night in Celia's bedroom, he was aware that someone was there. He felt against the wall and switched on the light.

'Who's there?' he said. There was no answer. He felt a relief in his heart. There was some action to be taken and any action was better than the horrid passivity of the last hours.

'Who's there?' he said again. 'Is it you, Mrs. Gayner? Who is it? Come on, I know someone is there.'

Something dropped to the floor. Someone rushed at the door, but he caught with his hand a thin trembling shoulder, and then held strongly a small body constricting, writhing, then limply submitting.

A whining voice, crowded with terror, was revoltingly pleading.

'Oh, Mr. Cromwell, please! Let me go. I didn't mean anything, truly I didn't. I came in for a drink, truly I did. It's an awful night and I was perished. Oh, Mr. Cromwell, I didn't mean any harm. I'm telling you gospel truth, straight I am.'

'Who are you?'

'You know me, Mr. Cromwell. You've spoken to me once. Sharp's my name—Henry Sharp.'

'What are you doing here?'

'I told you, Mr. Cromwell. I slipped in for a drink.'

'At *this* hour? What were you doing round here, anyway, in the middle of the night?'

'I'm always walking around night-time, I am really, Mr. Cromwell. I'm like that. And I walked into your garden and——'

But Julius had been passing his hand over the thin trembling body. From a pocket he drew out what he knew to be his two silver match-boxes, and a small paper-knife that he also knew—one of agate and gold.

'So you've been stealing things?'

There was no answer. The body trembled in his grasp like a bird's.

'Why? Why come here?'

The man whispered: 'I didn't mean . . . I came in for a drink as I said. I haven't any money.'

'Who *are* you?'

'He's my son, Mr. Cromwell—more shame be it said.'

Mrs. Gayner was standing close beside him.

He drew her in, shutting the door behind him. 'Quietly. I don't want to wake Mrs. Cromwell.' He had let the man go. 'Now, Mrs. Gayner, what is all this?'

'This is my son, sir. He lives in the village and comes to see me at night. He's been doing it for a long time. Because he's a thief and no good I've told nobody, and he's kept it dark too, living in another name. That's why I haven't told you and Mrs. Cromwell.'

'Ah!' Julius said. 'That's what's been the matter with you!'

'Yes, sir.' Lizzie Gayner began to sob, little dry sobs like the rustlings of twigs.

Julius said: 'Come, Lizzie, sit down here beside me. Let me have my hand on yours. Your son can go. I'll do nothing about this.'

'He's gone,' she said quite simply. 'He slipped out when you moved from the door, sir. He's like that,' she added.

'Well, he can't stay on in the village after this.'

'No, sir. I'm sure, sir. You're quite right, of course. And I mustn't stay on either.'

'You not stay on? Why ever not?'

'You and Mrs. Cromwell wouldn't want the mother of a vagabond and a thief as housekeeper.'

'Nonsense! Whatever difference does that make? Why didn't you tell me long ago? Aren't we friends?'

'Of course, sir. But I was so afraid you'd send me away—and my heart's here. I couldn't live away from here, I think.'

He felt her terror beating now in her breast. He touched for a moment the sleeve of her woollen dressing-gown.

'I would never have sent you away. How could you dream of it? But tell me about this dreadful boy of yours. Has he no profession—no trade?'

'Well, sir, he was on the halls—dancing and such. Then when that failed he came here, where he knew I was. He had been a gentleman's servant but lost that through stealing. He can't keep his hands off other people's things—and that's the truth. I tried to get him abroad. I found him the money and a place with a relation of mine in Jamaica. But it was no use. He wouldn't go. And in a sort of way I was glad he wouldn't. Although I've been in a terror and miserable of your knowing, I was comforted too, having him so close all these months.'

'Why! Are you fond of him after all he's done?'

'Fond of him! Oh, Mr. Cromwell, he's all I've got! I know he's no good and worthless and a thief, but he's terribly good to animals and to me sometimes. I love him, whatever he does, however he behaves. He's my son and my only one, and I'll never turn from him whatever he may do.'

At her words a sudden longing for Celia sprang like a bright fire in Julius' heart. 'A bright fire.' It was like that. A quick illumination, shining, leaping, that will come to any man at any time about another human being. 'Why have I been fooling like this, missing the true place, the right word, the only meeting?'

'I don't see how you can love him——'

'Loving has nothing to do with reason,' Mrs. Gayner answered. 'Why, Mr. Cromwell, my husband was, in a way, a really bad man—that is, he couldn't keep away from girls—any girl—it didn't matter whether she was plain or pretty. He must have her. It was like a constant irritation. But I had to love him. And he loved me in his own way. When you love a person you love a person. At least, that's the way I look at it.'

'Yes, I see. I hadn't seen it that way, or thought I hadn't.'

She got up. 'I must go back to bed, sir. You've been most kind and it's a great relief to me that you know now.'

'Yes, but he can't stay here—in the village, I mean.'

'No, sir. Of course not.'

'We'll manage something.'

'Yes, sir. Thank you, sir.'

He stood up. 'Lizzie, do you know something?'

'No, sir. What, sir?'

'You're the best friend I have in the world.'

'Oh, thank you, sir. But it isn't true. You have Mrs. Cromwell.'

'Yes. I have Mrs. Cromwell. But, as you say, that's different. That's love.'

'I'm very glad—very glad, I mean, that you two have come all right again, sir. I hope that isn't impertinent. She's very young and most lovable—and she adores you, sir, if I may say so.'

She had been scarcely gone when the telephone bell rang, loud, insistent, as it does in the middle of the night. He went to it and the voice at the other end was Jim Burke's.

When he heard those very familiar, soft, rather drowsy tones his whole body stiffened. So this night was the night, was it? In a swift second of vision he knew that the events of these hours were arranged like the hoops for the horse-jumps at the Circus. *How* he jumped was his own free affair and his action now depended on all the other actions that had gone to build up his character in the past.

'Well?' he said.

'Oh, Mr. Cromwell, is that you? I *am* glad I've got you. I'm at Raglan's Farm near Sizyn.'

'Well, well—what is it?'

'Mrs. Cromwell is here—soaked through. She's ill. She's been wandering over the country.'

The enemy, almost defeated, had one last thrust. She knew Burke was there. She went to meet him.

'Yes, Mr. Cromwell. I've been working at Raglan's for the past week. Raglan found her in a swoon at the door. Mrs. Raglan put her to bed. I thought I should tell you, lest you should be anxious.'

'I'll come at once.'

CHAPTER VII

March the Fourth—At Raglan's Farm—Dawn by Sizyn Church

HE ROUSED CURTIS. They went straight to the garage and got out the car.

He noticed that the storm had died away. A heavy blackness

lay upon the earth and a hushed stillness as though the world were recovering itself after its whipping.

He did not think as they drove; he had a picture before him of Celia, wet, swooning, knocking on Raglan's door. He went into no question as to why she had gone, what had driven her to that. No thought as to her guilt or his—only a driving, all-possessing urgency to have her safe under his care.

Curtis drove the car into the yard. Julius jumped out, and Raglan met him and helped him to the door. Inside the kitchen Mrs. Raglan told him that they had given Mrs. Cromwell a warm bath and put her to bed. She had been passive in their hands as though she had been sleep-walking. She had said nothing at all, only shivered and turned her head from side to side. Now, they hoped, she was sleeping.

Julius stood, knowing from their voices that Mrs. Raglan was tall, Raglan short. Mrs. Raglan kind and business-like. Raglan a little bemused and out of his element. They showed no kind of curiosity; they might have known Julius all their lives. He remembered that when he had got out of the car Raglan had come to him and led him into the house with a touch that was protective, caring, as he might use to a strayed sheep that had been rescued. He heard the door open and Jim Burke's voice. There was no embarrassment between them.

'I want to see her for a moment,' Julius said, and an instant later he felt Burke's hand on his arm, exactly as it had been so often at Garth.

'I left Curtis outside in the car,' he said as they climbed the stair.

A door was opened and then he heard Burke cry out:

'She's gone!'

He clutched Burke's arm.

'Gone!'

'Yes. She must have slipped out. There's the nightdress Mrs. Raglan lent her. She must have put on the wet clothes she was wearing.'

'Quick!' He plunged blindly back into the passage. 'Why didn't someone watch her? My God, anything may happen!' He would have fallen headlong down the crooked stair had not Burke caught him round the waist.

'Steady! Steady now. Hold on to me. We'll find her! It's all right! Don't be disturbed now. She can't have gone far.'

Even at this moment he felt again Burke's comradeship. There had never been any man he liked so much, nor anyone who knew so exactly what he was and how he was.

In the kitchen he heard the Raglans' exclamations but didn't wait for them.

Raglan said: 'Shall I come with you?'

'No, I'll take Burke.'

'I have a torch. A big one. It lights everything up.'

'Give it him then.'

With Burke's arm through his he passed, almost running, through the yard.

'How far can she have gone? How long since anyone saw her?'

'When I telephoned to you Mrs. Raglan had just been up to see her.'

'Ah! Not so long. We'll find her if we cover the Moor. She'd be walking and stumbling. Oh, God! in those wet clothes. What have I done?'

They walked together like one man down the road that led to the Moor. Burke flashed the torch. Julius was in a fever. He clasped Burke's arm and clenched it, stumbled in his eagerness, breathing as though he had run a distance.

'There's no rain. The storm is over. Any sign of dawn?'

'No, not yet. Although it's coming earlier now it's March. We'll find her. Don't be scared. She'll be all right.'

'But when you saw her—was she ill? How did she look? Didn't she speak at all? Not a word?'

'No, Mr. Cromwell. She sighed. I heard her sigh. But she seemed all dazed. Mrs. Raglan said when she was giving her her bath she was like a child. Let her turn her over and dry her just like a child.'

'There! Jim, don't you hear something? A voice crying.'

They stopped. Jim flashed his torch. There was a silence as though they were underground, and then, like a door opening, came the rhythm, an undertone, of the sea. The air was fresh and brilliant with the recent rain.

Julius suddenly called, 'Celia! Celia!' and there was such a loving urgency in his voice that Burke, who also loved her, started as though it had been his own voice.

'Come on, man! Come on!' Julius cried, catching down at Burke's warm dry hand. 'What are you waiting for?' And he began to talk, with a wild incoherency and yet with purpose too.

'She'll be weak after that bath and the bed. She won't be able to go far. After all, she's only a child. I know you were in love with her, Jim. Maybe you still are. I don't care. All the world can love her. Everybody! Everybody! Because she loves me with all her heart and soul. Don't you see that she does? She wouldn't have run away and lost her head else. She was desperate because she thought I didn't love her. I was jealous, Jim—jealous of you. I was in a black cloud of jealousy.'

'I want to tell you, Mr. Cromwell,' Burke said. 'I want you to know that I would never have done her any harm. And she didn't care for me—not a jot or tittle. As you say, she was very young and I was mightily to blame. You don't know how I blame myself. Besides, there's never been a man in my life I've cared for as I have for you, Mr. Cromwell. Only I loved her and I do love her. I can't help that, can I? God knows, I didn't want to. But something puts that kind of love into our hearts and we're mad for a time. I'll never see her again after tonight, so there's nothing for you to worry over.'

'When we find her,' Julius said, 'everything is all right. Nothing will be wrong again. I'll look after her and care for her and love her. We all have a devil in us, Jim. It's all in *Lear*. This night and the heath and the storm. Everyone lost in the darkness. Flash your torch. There's someone crying out. Listen! Listen!'

They stopped again. Burke, knowing the night and the country so well, was aware that it was the pause before the beginning of the dawn—the pause when, as though it had never happened before, the darkness prepares to break before the power of a new world. He felt it everywhere, the slight stirring, the faint rustling, a great universal preparation for departure.

It was strange to him, too, hearing Cromwell's voice, broken, urgent, revealing his very spirit. For Cromwell had always been controlled, in perfect self-command, a blind man standing strong in the fortress of his own blindness.

Now Cromwell had revealed himself totally, he was keeping nothing back, and Burke felt that he would do anything for him, anything in the world that Cromwell demanded.

They were now in the middle of the Moor, on the way towards Sizyn.

'Here. In that hollow. Let me see. There's something white there.'

Burke went over, flashing his torch. No. It was nothing—a slab of white stone. He felt, for a moment, the hopelessness of this. She might have gone anywhere, down the road away from the Moor, or along the Rafiel road. She would be found in the morning. It would be better to go back to the farm and wait for the day. But he could not say that. He no more than Cromwell could wait passively, doing nothing.

'I know!' Cromwell cried. 'I know where she will go. Come on, man. Come on. Sizyn Church. We had a picnic there once—don't you remember?—and she and I sat in the Church, talking of ourselves. She'll remember that. She'll be there. Come on. Come on.'

He dragged Burke by the arm. 'It's as though I could see,' he said. 'Everything. Every stone, every blade of grass. There's a light everywhere. When it's dark I can see and hear and smell. That's what they do for blind men, Jim. A kind of compensation, isn't it? God's never so hard as you think He is. He's given me sight in the dark so that I can find her.'

Was the dark less heavy? Burke thought that it was—as though one veil had been withdrawn from the many that remained. Yes, it must be so, for quite suddenly he saw, grey against black, the tower of Sizyn Church.

'That's the Church,' he said. 'We're almost on to it.'

Cromwell broke from him and ran, stumbling, forward, crying, 'Celia! Celia!'

He was right. She was there, huddled up against the rough stone wall. How did he know? Burke saw him stiffen, point in front of him with both hands and then run straight forward. Burke himself could see nothing but the faint line of the Church, the grey stone wall, and, he wasn't certain, a donkey against the wall there. But all these—the Church, the wall, the animal—were shadows against shadows. The dark was less heavy than it had been ten minutes earlier. That is all that one could say. But Cromwell had known no doubt, was kneeling on the grass. Burke joined him. Mrs. Cromwell was there, huddled up, her face turned towards the wall.

Burke took a long look at the little form, shapeless, colourless in the moving dark, part of the wall, of the soil, of the sky. There was centred all that he loved in the world. All that he loved in that moment of time. There would be many other moments for him.

Perhaps he realized this, for he looked up at the sky and all about him like a dog sniffing the wind. The freshness was good. He could quite clearly feel the pulse of the coming light like a bird driving through the air. After the storm it would be a lovely day.

'Can I do anything, Mr. Cromwell?' he asked.

There was no answer.

'Is there anything I can do?'

There was still no answer. So he shook his head like someone who suddenly and unexpectedly finds himself free. He stretched out his shoulders.

'So-long, Mr. Cromwell. So-long then.'

He strode off and never gave a look behind.

The turf was sodden wet, but Julius gave no heed. He had taken Celia in his arms. She lay without moving, her eyes closed, her damp clenched hand unconsciously against his. A flood of words came from him.

'My darling, you shouldn't have done this. Running away! It wasn't kind. But it was all my fault. Mine. Mine. All mine. And I've learnt my lesson. I have indeed. I've learnt my lesson.'

She moved, raised her head and let it fall. He felt her movement. Her action made him realize the sort of fool he was, pouring out sentimental nonsense and forgetting her state. He had been walking in a waterproof and this he wrapped round her. Her clothes, although stiff, were not sodden. Mrs. Raglan must have dried them. She was not cold. Her cheek to the touch of his hand was warm and soft. He had brought brandy and he forced some between her lips.

She swallowed it but still lay, her eyes closed, against his chest.

He stood up, holding her like a baby in his arms. He moved forward and came against the stone wall. Then he had an idea. He knew that the Church was always open. The porch was to the left; he walked with cautious steps, holding her carefully against him. He could not now stretch his hands out to guard himself, but it was true that he had a stronger sense of things in the dark than people who could see. It was as though, like a fool and a drunkard, there was protection somewhere for him. His shoulder knocked against the stone of the porch. He turned and pushed with his knee against the door. It was latched and he leaned forward with his burden, felt for the latch with the ends of his fingers, jerked it open and moved in.

The little Church was cold but not damp. It seemed to receive him friendlily. He felt the pew-end and sat down. Then he took her and cradled her on the seat within his arm.

He sat there in silence. Her breath stroked his cheek. Her hand was in his. He was filled with unutterable love and gratitude.

She stirred and took her hand from his. She sat up and said in the voice of a startled child: 'Where am I? What is it?'

'We are in Sizyn Church,' he said. 'Just for a moment, resting before we go home.'

'It's Julius.'

'Yes. It's Julius.'

She snatched herself from him. She tried to get up, but sat down again.

'But I'm not going home. I'm not going back.'

'Where are you going?' he asked.

'I don't know, but I'm not going back.' Again she tried to get up and this time she succeeded. She would push past him, but with his hand at her breast he held her.

'Wait. Rest a little. Whatever else you do, rest a little now. Afterwards you can do what you want.'

'The car broke down or I would be near London by now. I ran into a post.'

'Never mind about the post. How do you feel?'

'Rotten.'

'Will you have some more brandy?'

'No. I'd be sick. I have a dreadful headache.'

She put her hand to her head like a child. He could not see that. He knew it was better for the moment not to touch her, so he sat apart.

'Why are you running away like this?' he asked her.

'Because I hate you and I hate Garth and everyone in it.'

'Were you hurt when the car hit the post?'

'No, I don't think so.' Then she asked again: 'Where are we?'

'In Sizyn Church.'

'What time is it?'

'I don't know. It will be dawn soon.' He waited and then added very gently:

'I have the other car at Raglan's farm. Won't you come back to Garth for an hour or two and rest? Then you can go back to London if you want to.'

'No. No. No.'

'Very well then.'

After a silence, she began in a trembling voice:

'Why did you come after me? Why can't you leave me alone?'

'You're my wife. I love you.'

There was silence again.

Julius said:

'Won't you at least come back for an hour or two, Celia? Change your clothes, have a bath. Then you can go up to London by train.'

'I have such a headache. I can't think. When I walked from the car I didn't know where I was going. I saw a light in a house. Then I think I fainted.'

He reached out and took her hand. She didn't resist.

'Listen, my darling. You're as free as air. You need never see me again if you don't want to, although I shall be very unhappy if that's so. But I want you to understand this: It's all my fault. I was jealous and couldn't put myself out of it. I couldn't speak. I wanted to, but I couldn't. And then, when I knew you'd run away, it all cleared. In a moment I cared for nothing in the world but you, and so I always will.'

Her fingers stirred a little in his hand.

'How did you know I had gone away?'

'Jim Burke telephoned from the Raglans'.'

'Was Jim Burke there?'

'Yes. Didn't you know?'

'I don't remember anything.' Her voice was infinitely weary.

'You're terribly tired. Please, please, Celia, come back to Garth for a little.'

'No. No. I'll never go back to Garth.'

'Why do you hate it so?'

'I've been so unhappy there.'

'Will you come to the car at Raglan's, then, and Curtis shall go back and fetch some things.'

'No. I like it here. Although the seat's very hard.'

He took off his coat and spread it under her. To his surprise and joy she allowed him to do this, and even once more lay back against him. He thought she was falling asleep but she said:

'We don't love one another any more. Why do we pretend? Our marriage has been a dreadful failure.'

'I don't think it has,' he said quietly. 'We both wanted to have our own way perhaps. Because I'm blind, both of us imagine things. We hadn't wanted to depend upon one another but only on ourselves. But I see now how interdependent we are. We all are. All the world. The world hasn't realized it yet, but it will.'

'I don't care about the world. You thought I could be unfaithful to you. At the first chance you thought it.'

'I was jealous. Most men are, some time or other, when they love a person.'

She sat up, shaking her head. He felt that she had some of her real vigour again. Her voice was stronger.

'No. We aren't suited. That's the trouble, Julius. We aren't suited.'

'Don't you love me any more then?'

She didn't answer. Instead she gave a little cry.

'Oh, the light's coming in! The Church is waking.'

She stared at the trembling grey colour that began to wash the walls of the little Church. It was going to be a lovely, glorious day. The window seemed to move forward towards her, the hawthorn blossom, the monk, the donkey with his silver bells. The sun was not up yet, but everything was preparing for its rising. Already a faint shadow from the purple glass streaked the chancel. Beyond the two side windows white shadows in the sky warmed very gently with an invisible light.

'Look, Julius! The sun is coming. Forgive me. I had forgotten. Oh, you look so tired!'

Then she threw herself on his breast. She drew his head against her cheek. She kissed his eyes. Then his mouth.

'I love you! Of course I love you! I've never stopped for a single moment! But you were angry and you didn't trust me any more, and they all hated me. Julius, hold me close. Not now only.'

Always. Let me never be alone again. I'm not strong enough.
Darling Julius! Darling, darling Julius!'

She caught his hands, his beloved hands, and held them.

'Oh, how silly we've been! How silly and how unhappy!'

He held her in his arms against his breast. His blind eyes looked
out, over her body, to the Window. He felt the light warm upon
his face.

CHAPTER VIII

In Julius' Study

JULIUS CROMWELL'S JOURNAL

I HAVE perhaps found nothing stranger in this life than the way in
which the Past huddles back into the Past—not only huddles but
rushes back the moment it *is* the Past, flings itself on to the general dust-heap and becomes nothing but waste. I mean by the
Past anything that is unimportant enough to *become* the Past—
everything and everyone still alive—that is, the Present and the
Future.

My old nurse, for instance. She was called Minnie Bax. She had
flaming red hair and was as thin as a neatly-rolled umbrella. She
would smack my bottom with relish and then kiss my little
round tummy. She sucked peppermints and loved a fat butler up
the street. She must have been pretty then. I saw her once kiss
the butler's two chins when we were out promenading. I remember that of all extraordinary things she had a tattoo of an anchor
on her right thigh. I used to see it when she undressed. She said it
belonged to a sailor once. Well—does all this mean anything?
Yes, that Minnie Bax is alive and the Versailles Treaty dead as a
door-nail. So we live on, buttressed with love and reality. For I
loved Minnie Bax and she is so real to me that I can feel her wed-

ding ring hitting my behind at this moment. But all the rest, all that we do not discard, what queer rubbish it is!

All the 1914–18 War—what remains of it but the heroism, the unselfishness, the comradeship? And now we darken under the cloud of the next one—and of that, too, only the creative things will remain.

I love Celia—oh, how I love her! And yet a short time ago, in that rubbish-heap past, I was hidden from her by the ignominy of that battle between the jealous animal in me and the seeing spirit. Had I lost her—as I so nearly did—how many others, how much good life, would have been lost with her!

I am going to take her with me. We are going travelling—to Greece perhaps—somewhere, and she will tell me of the beauties that I can't see, and I will let her go with the handsomest traveller in the Seven Seas and never know a tremor.

But, for a moment, to be practical, I am haunted by the three Brennan children. Not by their actual presence, for only Simon has been here, but by the constant pricking sense that I owe them something. I would love to have a child of my own, and still may, thank God. These are not children of mine, although that odd tick Simon seems maliciously to adore me and to feel that he belongs to me. He was here two days ago and sitting on the floor. He caught my leg with both his hands to draw my attention, and said:

'Why have I always got to do what other people tell me?'

'Because they are older and know better.'

'I know better what *I* want.'

'Yes, but you're not alone on this globe.'

'No, but there's nobody else like me, Dorothy isn't, nor Gillie, nor Mother or Father. You aren't.'

'No. We're all different. But we've got to live together.'

'I don't see why. I can live by myself.'

'No you can't. You can only do that if you don't love anybody, and from what I've seen of you you'll love plenty. The moment you love anybody you're not alone.'

He laughed.

'People are awfully silly. They don't know you're watching them, but you are.'

'Luckily,' I said, 'you're silly too, and people are watching *you*. We're all bound up together. Everything we do affects everybody.'

He caught my hand in his rather sticky one.

'You'd better go and wash your hands,' I said.

'You'll always be here, won't you?' he said. 'When you're quite old I shall come and see you just as I do now.'

'As a matter of fact Mrs. Cromwell and I are going away very soon. We're going travelling.'

He started away from me like a wild animal. I felt his urgent dismay.

'It's all right. We'll come back again.'

He still didn't say anything.

'You can be fond of someone just as much when he's away as when he's with you. More, sometimes.'

'Where are you going to?' he asked.

'Greece perhaps. Lots of places.'

He sighed with satisfaction.

'You can send me postcards. Those coloured ones. They'll have stamps too, won't they? Don't send them to the others. Send them only to me.'

'All right. But aren't Dorothy and Gillie to have any?'

'Oh, I suppose so. But it doesn't really matter. You don't like them as you do me.'

The Brennans have given a farewell tea-party for Celia and me. It was an odd experience. I wrote the other day in this book something about the creative things being the only things that remain. It isn't the fearful losses at Passchendaele that now remain, but the resolve created by those losses that nothing like that shall ever happen again. Something just as bad will happen in the next war, I don't doubt, but it won't be *that*. I see Hitler's bogy sort of

power and cleverness. He'll bring tremendous ruin with him before he finishes. But it is all destructive. The idea of Nazi Ger-
many ruling the world has neither bigness nor spiritual grandeur
enough. So it must ultimately fall. Even Napoleon's idea wasn't
big enough. A St. Francis vision, even a Calvin vision, is big
enough creatively, not a Napoleon, and oh, how much less a
Hitler-Goering-Himmler!

All this big stuff comes down to a little tiny scene, as in *The
Dynasts* you move from vast planetary systems to the Wessex
peasant ploughing his English soil—to wit, tea-party for us at the
Rectory.

My point is that for me it was a creative moment which will,
as long as I am alive, outlast all the Hitlers. A creative moment for
me indeed, for it seemed to me that I myself had created everybody present! I was, I must confess, radiantly happy.

Such a capacity for happiness have Celia and I! And yet we per-
mitted ourselves for weeks most desperate miseries.

She has told me how, when she left the house that night, she was
mad with unhappiness. When the car hit the post she remembers
thinking, 'I hope that's killed me,' and, after that, she was really
crazy, feeling that she had lost not only me but all life. She wanted
to die. She preferred to die.

And when she ran away from the Raglans' she had a knife with
her and meant to kill herself at Sizyn Church, and fell asleep
instead!

All incredible nonsense to her as she lay in my arms last night.
A brainstorm, you call it. But it wasn't. It was simply that we
both lost contact. Not only with one another but the central force
of life—call it God or what you will. To that, I know now, we
must always hold. All of us. Not only because we keep touch
with God, but still more perhaps because we keep touch with one
another. Contact. Contact. 'Only connect . . .' as some writer
keeps saying somewhere.

The last thing I meant though, here, was to indulge in amateur
metaphysics. The grandiloquent point I wanted to make was that

everyone at the Brennan tea-party—Dorothy, Gilbert, Simon, Mr. and Mrs. B., the Lamploughs, silly Fred Ironing, the two old girls Phyllis Lock and May Vergil—seemed to belong to me, to have been created by me. Only Mrs. Mark, who was created by the house I now own, didn't belong to me. A phantasy. I had never seen any of them. I had my own idea of them from their voices, their scents, the things they said.

Dorothy Brennan for instance: 'What I really want now, Mr. Cromwell, is to learn typewriting. I must *do* something, mustn't I?'

Gilbert: 'Do you think, Mr. Cromwell, when I go back to school, they'd let someone in Polchester teach me carving?'

Simon: 'I don't want you to go away.'

And I: 'What about the postcards?'

'Well, of course, that's a pity, but I'd rather you stayed and I didn't have the postcards.'

Mrs. Brennan: 'I'm very happy, Mr. Cromwell, and it's all due to you.' (What she meant I haven't the least idea!)

That silly girl, Miss Lock: 'I want to make a confession, Mr. Cromwell. It was I——'

But I stopped her.

'No confessions. I'm a conjurer. I can make my rabbits tell me everything.'

I knew she was staring at me and her mouth was open. Her breath smelt of peppermint.

'I believe you can, Mr. Cromwell.'

And Miss Vergil: 'When you get to the Island of Thasos, Mr. Cromwell, you will find an altar to Pan half-way up the hill. Place some flowers there for me.'

'Certainly, Miss Vergil.'

'My gratitude to you for releasing me from a ridiculous obsession.'

And old Lamplough, taking me by the arm to the window: 'I've told her everything, Julius. Not what a mean skinny common informer she is, but of that night when I was with you and the stars blazed. You couldn't see them, but you *felt* them, and I told her what a poor pair of mortals we were and that we stayed together simply because no one else would have us, and that one day the stars would blaze again and she'd go out like a twopenny dip.

'I told her to read *Troilus and Cressida*—Shakespeare's version. The most Elizabethan of all the plays, isn't it? And to study Thersites and Pandarus. To learn even one lesson in horrid baseness before it was too late.'

'And what did she say?'

'She said she was a virtuous woman, far too good for an old horror like me. But I frightened her. Thanks to you, Julius, she'll always be a little bit frightened now before she dies.'

'Why to me?'

'Because she thinks you're even better than she is at knowing what's going on. She thinks you have unholy powers, Julius.'

And lastly, Brennan himself: 'You know, Cromwell, it's an awful thing to believe in God and not do a thing about it. All right if you don't believe. But if you do—I've been blind for years—another kind of blindness from yours.'

I wanted to get away then. My illusion of grandeur was over. I had created nothing. We were all only half-made. There's every kind of thing still to be done.

Sometimes I can frighten people. Why, I cannot imagine. On this occasion it has been useful, for I understand that the loathsome Douglas Gayner left London yesterday morning for the West Indies. I was in his company once more for five minutes before he left this place. His mother was with him.

'I always knew you could see in the dark,' he said.

He had, so far as I can tell, no redeeming trait except, as his mother continues to insist, his kindness towards sick animals. A fellow-feeling, I suppose. In a well-organized state, citizens below a certain standard of morality will be anaesthetized—public morality, I mean. And as to that, I'm not sure that I'm not below it myself. Given certain conditions and circumstances—enough hunger of those dependent on me—would I not steal? The especial physical attraction, some drink, the certainty of secrecy—might I not yield? Enough torture and would I not give even Celia away? I think not. I tell myself no. But my experiences of the last few months are not encouraging. The most astonishing specimen of humanity known to me is the completely self-assured human—often a convinced Christian. Did not Christ Himself cry 'My God, my God, why . . . ?'

But what I want to put down here is the love of Mrs. Gayner. Simply to record it so that if a day may once again come when I am false in my heart to Celia, I may remember what I wrote on this page. For it was Mrs. Gayner's words that night about her horrible son that saved me. For me, as I suppose for most men, there must be an element of admiration in my love—there must be something for me to admire. Not so with the best women. The more despicable the object, the more faithful the love.

Listen to Lizzie Gayner as I fill her chair in her room, her cat upon my knee.

'You could have gone to London to see him off, Lizzie.'

'I didn't wish to, sir. And I'm glad he's gone.'

'You'll be lonely.'

'As to that, he hasn't been much with me for donkey's years. And these last weeks have been something terrible. Of course he's not a good son—he's not good in any way—but mothers can't lose the innocent things their son has done and the trusting things when he was too small to act for himself. Not that he ever was beautiful, even as a baby, and he liked to play tricks on visitors as soon as he could walk, but he'd always see the cat had her milk, and he wasn't more than six when he nearly killed another boy for throwing stones at a dog. I understand that in these days, sir, they say that all wickedness is due to something in the brain, or a gland.

'But that doesn't really excuse anything. Douglas has been bad all his life and he'll have to pay for it, but I'd share his punishment if I could, for I brought him into the world and some of it's my responsibility.' She added: 'You know that girl Violet that was here?'

'Of course.'

'She's run away to London with a married man. Jacob Tinnes at Caldicote Farm. His wife's broken-hearted. They've been together, happy, with children for twenty years. Of course there's wickedness in the world and always will be. Otherwise there'd be no fighting.'

I told her we'd be gone in another week. I hoped she wouldn't be lonely.

'I've plenty to do,' she said, quite sharply. 'I'm teaching Oliphant to embroider.'

'Oliphant!' I cried, amazed.

'Yes, he tells me there's nothing he wants to learn as much as embroider. But you're not to tell anybody, sir. He'd die of shame if anyone was to know. He was so disappointed when he found you weren't taking him, and we talked a bit, and at last, very shamefaced, he asked me whether I could embroider. So I showed him that chair in the corner there. Then it all came out. He thinks he has a gift, and I wouldn't wonder.'

In two days we shall be gone. Mrs. Mark came to say good-bye. I told her that of course she could come here whenever she wished. But she laughed and said she wouldn't dare.

'It's the funniest thing. You can't go back. For months I've been sentimental about this house, but I've begun a new life, and the two lives don't join. There isn't, in fact, any of the old life left. My mother was the most dominating woman who ever lived, I adored both my brother and sister. But I've found there isn't a fragment of them left. My sentiment about the rooms, the stairs, the garden—it's all nonsense. When I first came here, before I started a new life in this place, I fancied that I could recover it. But all you living people are too vital. You killed the ghosts, if there ever were any. I've got Dorothy Brennan to be fond of, and my cottage, and there's some rheumatism and a war coming. And you'll be back in three months. No, the present's the thing.'

But to me, although I didn't tell her so, she's herself something of a ghost. We are already passing over into a new country so long before we cross the border.

And at the top of the stairs in this house, I see her looking down, a charming girl, watching for her lover. Her real life now is in Dorothy, who herself will only realize that years and years later, when she looks back and understands what once she was given but didn't know it. . . .

The last night—the last evening. When, in half an hour's time, I close this book I leave it in its rather priggish honesty for three months' seclusion. I shan't take it with me.

Celia came in, a little frightened. She had nearly fallen into the old Italian chest in the hall, looking down into it for some handkerchiefs, nearly over-balanced and fallen in. 'And then the lid comes down on you and nobody can find you and you choke and die.'

She was frightened and I had to console her. Hadn't all our trouble been that I had never realized the child she was and is?

I have her now inside my heart to protect and guard.

Meanwhile I learn—can it be with a little shiver of apprehension?—that I in my turn am to be protected and guarded. The things that I am to be shown—by word of mouth!

All beautiful places—the little white ports, the purple seas, the islands scattered on the glittering waters like water-lilies, the sun rising, the sun setting! *She* will be my eyes!

But at least I have learned this lesson of our interdependence. The lesson that all mankind now must learn. The twin lessons of interdependence and charity. No one of us can move any more—can sigh or sneeze, cough or whisper—without disturbing the rest of us.

The Brennans, the old maids, Lizzie's dreadful Douglas, old Lamplough, my friend Mrs. Mark, Celia and I—unless we have fellowship together we have nothing. It seems to me that until we learn this fellowship—the fellowship, generous and understanding—of all living men on this earth, made so essential now by our close quarters, the impossibility of our escape from one another, there will be no peace.

I must not judge Douglas Gayner, and old Mrs. Lamplough must be throttled if she spreads her evil mind, and Dorothy and Gilbert and Simon must be trained, like plants, to grow straight into light and loveliness, and I must not lose myself in selfish attempts to save my own soul—and for why? Because we are all brothers together under God and are all of us, one with another, our brother's keeper.

And so I got Celia, as the final word in this house for a month or two, to get out my beloved-from-a-boy *The Dream of John Ball*, and I have written down on the opposite page of this Journal these famous words that I have so long known by heart. And when I lay the pen down Celia kneels by me and reads them. Then I catch her up in my arms, 'And so to bed——'

Forsooth, brothers, fellowship is heaven, and lack of fellowship is hell; fellowship is life, and lack of fellowship is death; and the deeds that ye do upon the earth, it is for fellowship's sake that ye do them, and the life that is in it, that shall live on for ever and ever, and each one of you part of it, while many a man's life upon the earth from the earth shall wane. Therefore, I bid you not dwell in hell but in heaven, or while ye must, upon earth, which is a part of heaven, and forsooth no foul part.

CHAPTER IX

By the Village Green—Three Figures—One Figure

SUNDAY MORNING, and the village of Garth in Roselands is as still and lifeless as the remotest crater of the farthest of the dead moons. The sea-mist has writhed its way across the fields, through the Sunday-morning houses, across the village green, where its watery web moistens the wings of the limping seagull, now the pampered, petted mascot of the village.

Three children stand just inside the Rectory gate waiting. On the other side of the green, poker-stiff in her neat manly jacket and skirt, the brass buttons of the waistcoat damped by the mist, the gaily-coloured fishing fly jaunty in her hat, a lady stands.

A motor-car appears. The children wave. It is gone.

Two of the children turn slowly into the house. But the smallest of them comes out of the gate and stares down the road.

The lady with the brass buttons on her waistcoat also stands there staring.